10|19

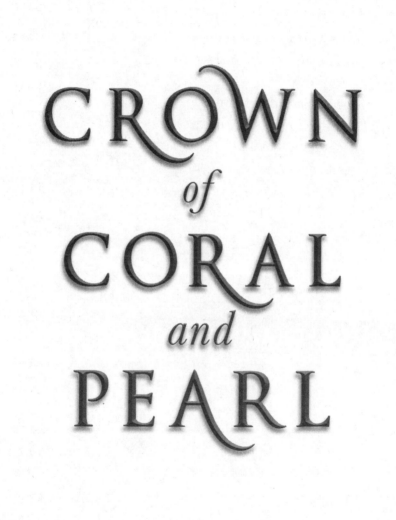

CROWN

of

CORAL

and

PEARL

MARA RUTHERFORD

CROWN
of
CORAL
and
PEARL

ink
yard
press

ISBN-13: 978-1-335-09044-7

Crown of Coral and Pearl

Copyright © 2019 by Mara Rutherford

InkyardPress.com

Printed in U.S.A.

To John, for giving me the world.
And to Sarah, for always guiding me home.

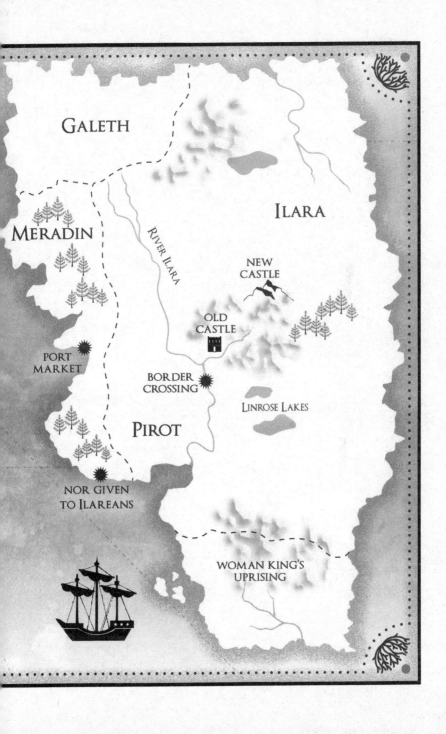

1

Sometimes I wonder if it was our names that determined our fates, or the other way around. Nor and Zadie: coral and pearl. Both precious to our people, both beautiful enough to adorn the necks of queens. But whereas a pearl is prized for its luster, its shape, its lack of imperfections, coral is different. It grows twisted. In its natural form, it can hardly be considered beautiful at all.

Still, Zadie and I were born as equals in beauty, grace, and wit. We were, the elders declared, the loveliest babies ever born in Varenia. Mother proudly rowed us around in our family's wooden boat, where Zadie and I would spend much of our childhood. She shaded our olive skin with wide-brimmed hats to prevent sunburn; she forced Father to sand down the sharp edges on our furniture; not a single dark hair on our heads was sacrificed to a pair of scissors. She inspected us every night for scratches or scrapes, then applied oils and salves while she scolded us to be more cautious.

After all, though Varenian women were blessed with hair as varied as the fish in our waters—from straight to ringlets, flaxen to ebony—and our skin was smooth and healthy in every shade from gold to burnished copper, beauty in our village was held to a higher standard. A girl's features must be symmetrical and well proportioned, her complexion clear, her gaze bright and curious, though never too direct. Her presentation should always be impeccable, no matter the time or place. To truly stand out, a girl could be nothing short of perfect.

Because in Varenia, being a beautiful girl wasn't just lucky. Once every generation, it determined which one of us would become a princess.

"Nor!" Zadie cried, pulling me back from the edge of the boat where I balanced on one foot. "What are you thinking? You can't risk an injury now."

I scratched at my scalp, tender from where Mother had plaited my hair extra tight as punishment for forgetting my hat yesterday. She was forever fretting that the sun would turn our silken hair brittle or—gods forbid—summon forth a freckle, but these days, the angry grumblings from my empty belly were loud enough to drown out Mother's shrill voice in my head. We'd been looking for oysters for hours, to no avail.

Zadie, ever the dutiful daughter, batted my hand away. "Please, for Mother's sake, behave. You know how nervous she is about the ceremony."

The ceremony. When hadn't Mother been nervous about

it? Every cloudless day spent in the shade of our stilt-legged wooden house, every missed pearl-diving opportunity because the sea was too rough… I owed them all to the ceremony and to our mother's obsession with it.

"Ours is a kingdom without borders," Father liked to say as he stood on the narrow balcony outside our house, shading his eyes with one hand as he scanned the horizon. Maybe that was true for him, but our life was a constant reminder that one day, the Crown Prince of Ilara would come of marrying age. And as it had been for hundreds of years, so would it be in three days—the elders would finally choose the most beautiful girl in Varenia to be his bride.

The last girl had left us twenty years ago, when the present king was still a prince and the shoals hadn't yet been plucked bare, but Mother assured us that she wasn't half as beautiful as Zadie and me. Before the incident, she teased the elders that they would have to send both of us to marry the prince and let him decide for himself, because we were as indistinguishable as two silver featherfish.

Now, of course, it was clear who would be sent. The small pink scar on my right cheekbone was all that stood between the crown and me. Anywhere else on my body, an imperfection smaller than a Varenian pearl might have been overlooked, but compared to Zadie's flawless skin, the jagged mark was impossible to ignore. Fortunately, I'd had the seven years since the incident to prepare for this, and seven years of relative freedom from our mother's constant fussing—at least compared to Zadie.

I flopped back onto the cushions in the bottom of our boat

and turned my face up to the cloud-dappled sky. "Are you ready for it?" I asked.

"For what?" Zadie feigned ignorance while she pulled her skirts over her exposed ankles.

"To leave Varenia. To leave Mother and Samiel." *To leave me.*

"You don't know they're going to choose me. You're just as beautiful as I am, and you never get sick. And I've heard rumors that Alys is being considered as well."

I arched a skeptical brow. "Mother says that even with my scar, I'm prettier than Alys will ever be. How did she put it? 'Alys has only to smile, and that snaggletooth will send the prince running for his nursemaid.'"

Zadie frowned. "Mother shouldn't say such things. Alys can't help it."

"Neither can Mother," I said with a wry look.

Zadie pulled on one of the lines hanging over the side of the boat, frowning at the tiny fish dangling from the end. Our waters had been overfished for years, though no one seemed to want to admit it. Zadie carefully laid the shimmering creature in the palm of her hand, removed the hook, and dropped it back into the sea. The fish was too small to eat, though we might have used it for bait, had there been anything larger to catch.

"I know Mother can be difficult, but she only wants what's best for us," Zadie said after a moment. "What she herself couldn't have."

Half a dozen snide comments popped into my head, but I held my tongue. "Perhaps you're right."

Though I'd never told her, I knew for a fact Zadie would

be the chosen one; the only one of us who would ever set foot on land—something I'd wished for since childhood. Because scar or no scar, Zadie was beautiful in a way I would never be. In Varenia, we were constantly searching for imperfections, whether in pearls or people, but Zadie only ever saw the good. Just last week, while I lamented the damage to our house from a passing storm, Zadie watched the sky, searching for rainbows.

So even when our mother was at her worst, Zadie could find something kind to say in return.

I would never be that good, that pure of heart. And that was a harder sort of pain to bear.

"I'm going swimming," I said, wishing I could shed my thoughts as easily as my skirts.

Zadie glanced around anxiously. As young women of marrying age, we should never be seen barelegged in public, but diving in a skirt wasn't just difficult—it was dangerous. Before, when oysters were plentiful, young men did most of the diving. But these days, girls and women helped out whenever possible. And in our family, with Father fishing every day and no brothers to share the burden, there was no other choice. Even Mother couldn't complain too much—she knew how badly we needed the extra money.

"Are you coming?" I asked.

"The salt will dry out our skin. Mother will know."

I placed my hands on my hips and grinned. "Last one to find an oyster has to make dinner tonight." The truth was, we couldn't afford to go home empty-handed. Not if we wanted to eat next week. But it was easier to pretend this was all a game, one in which the stakes weren't life or death. "Ready?"

She shook her head, but her fingers were already busy untying her skirt and tugging down her tunic to cover her thighs. "You're wicked," she said, then launched herself out of the boat into the clear water.

I dived in after her, letting the pressure build in my ears as I surged past Zadie toward the bottom, drowning out the little voice in my head that said, *I know.*

Several hours later, I was stirring a pot of watery fish stew over the fire when Samiel entered our house, his body still glistening with seawater from his swim over. Sami was our best friend, and the only boy in the village who had dared play with us as children. Not only was our mother strict beyond reason, our father was also the governor's best friend. Sami was exempt from Mother's scolding, however, seeing as his father *was* the governor.

"Don't tell me Zadie found an oyster before you did," he teased. Sami was as competitive as I was, but Zadie had gotten lucky today. The oyster lay on a small driftwood table nearby, already shucked and sadly lacking a pearl.

Our primary currency, the rare pink pearls that were only found in our waters, had also become scarce of late, as the Ilarean appetite for them continued to increase. The pearls were used to make jewelry for the nobility, but they could also be ground up and added to skin creams and cosmetics. Most Varenian families had a small jar of healing ointment made from the pearls, but that was to be saved for emergencies, since many of us were naturally healthy from spending so much time in the waters that were said to make the pearls special in the first place. After the incident, Mother had used the ointment daily on my scar in hopes of minimizing its appearance, but stopped once she realized it would never heal completely.

Sami dropped a tarnished brass button onto the table next to the empty oyster shell. "Look what I got for Zadie."

I *tsk*ed in disapproval. By law, Ilara was our sole trade partner for all the things the sea couldn't provide: clothing, fruits and vegetables, tools, books, barrels of fresh water. Even our firewood came from Ilara. But Sami was the exception to the rule. He often traded secretly—and illegally—with our cousins, the Galethians. Over a hundred years ago, a small population of Varenians had risked their lives to set foot on land, then quickly fled north on a herd of stolen Ilarean horses. Those horses became the foundation of the Galethian culture, just as the waves had formed ours.

"Wave children," the Ilareans called us. And that was exactly how they treated us: like children.

The Ilareans had access to resources we could only dream of—not just fresh water and food, but also sophisticated weapons and thousands of men. Occasionally a desperate Varenian would attempt to land on Ilarean soil, in search of an easier life away from the whims of the sea, but they were usually dealt with swiftly and decidedly by the soldiers who patrolled the shoreline. It was possible a few got away with it, but any violation of Ilarean law wouldn't just end in death for the defector in question—Ilara could eradicate our people swiftly and with little effort. They'd made that clear in all their dealings with us.

I poked at the button with feigned indifference, though in truth, anything from land fascinated me. "And what will

Zadie do with a button? Use it to fasten the trousers she doesn't wear?"

"I'm making her a cloak to take with her when she leaves. She'll be cold in Ilara."

Sami knew as well as I did that Zadie was going to be chosen at the ceremony. It was as hard for him as it was for me, in some ways, because he loved her, too. He always had. I suspected that Zadie returned his love, but they both knew she would leave to marry the prince someday, so their relationship could never be more than friendship.

"That's so thoughtful," I said. "But you shouldn't be trading with the Galethians. If you're caught, they'll hang you."

"Then I guess I can't get caught." He smiled, revealing teeth as white as shells against his tanned skin. Boys didn't carry the same burden as Varenian girls, at least not when it came to scars and sunburns. They had to provide for their families, however, and that was becoming harder and harder. Last year, two pearls had been enough to feed a family for a month. Now it took twice that many, yet somehow the quality of the goods they fetched was poorer. I had learned a long time ago not to ask questions about our trade relationship with Ilara—it was the elders' place to worry about such things, not mine. And according to Mother, I had far more important things to worry about, like the sheen of my hair or the length of my eyelashes.

But that had never stopped me from wondering about the world beyond Varenia.

"Any news from Galeth?" I asked.

"There's talk of an uprising in Southern Ilara."

"That's nothing new."

He shook his head. "It's getting worse. King Xyrus refuses to grant safe passage to the refugees heading north, even though the Galethians would welcome them with open arms."

"Anything to bolster their army."

"It's more than that. The Galethians were refugees once, too."

I turned the button over in my hand. It was engraved with a small, many-petaled flower. I'd heard of roses, though I'd never seen one before. I tried to imagine a world in which something as small as a button was deemed worthy of this level of craftsmanship.

"It's beautiful," I said before dropping the button into the empty oyster shell. "Just like Zadie."

Sami's hand closed around my shoulder, and I leaned my cheek against it. "What will we do without her?" I whispered.

There was a pause, then a cough. "I suppose we'll just have to marry each other."

I rapped his knuckles with the wooden spoon I held, and he pulled his hand away. "I wouldn't marry you if you were the last boy in Varenia."

He placed his hand on his chest, feigning offense. "And why not?"

"Because you're my best friend. And worse, you're the future governor."

"You're right. You'd make a terrible governor's wife, anyway." He snatched a dried date off the table and darted out of my reach.

"Do that again, and I swear I won't marry you. You'll be stuck with Alys."

He grimaced. "Imagine our little shark-toothed children. My mother would weep."

Zadie poked her head around the door and frowned. "You're *both* wicked, do you know that? Alys is kind and loyal. You'd be lucky to marry her."

"You're right," I said, chastened. I knew better than most what it was like to be judged by one's appearance.

Zadie twisted her wet hair at the side of her head, letting the fresh water from her bath drip into the bucket we used to rinse our dishes. Zadie never slept with seawater in her hair at Mother's behest, though fresh water from Ilara was expensive and meant to be saved for drinking and cooking.

"Would a wicked man bring you this?" Sami asked, proffering the brass button in its mother-of-pearl serving tray.

She gasped, then folded her arms across her chest. "I suppose he would, since an honest man could never have come by this."

He glanced at me over his shoulder, then moved closer to Zadie. "You like it, don't you? Please say you do. I wanted to make you a cloak to take with you to Ilara. It will be cold in the mountains."

"You don't know I'm going yet," she said, though her posture softened. "Besides, where would you get cloth for a cloak?"

"An honest man would never betray his source."

"An honest man wouldn't have a source to begin with."

I pretended to stir the stew—even watered down, it was barely enough for the four of us—while I watched them from beneath my lashes. I was grateful Zadie hadn't chided him for wasting money that could have gone toward food, but they should be distancing themselves from each other, if they knew what was good for them. If not for my scar, perhaps I would be the one going to Ilara. Then Sami and Zadie could marry as they pleased, and I would get to see more than an engraving of a rose on a silly brass button for another girl.

Maybe in another life, I thought bitterly. But not in this one.

"What's that wonderful smell?" Father asked as he entered the house behind Zadie, sending Sami stumbling away from her. Father had just come back from fishing in deeper waters, judging by the sea salt crust on his brow and his wind-chapped cheeks.

"The same thing we eat every night," I said. "Unless you caught something today?"

He gave a small, sad shake of his head, and my stomach grumbled in response. I tapped the spoon on the side of the pot to cover the sound. "That's all right, Father. The last time Zadie cooked fish, the house stank for a week."

Sami laughed, and Zadie pretended to be offended, gently pushing Sami aside. Even my father allowed himself a small smile at my attempt to lighten the mood.

My parents had noticed the way Sami and Zadie acted around each other—it was impossible not to—but Father was a little more tolerant than Mother, who wanted nothing to distract Zadie from fulfilling her ultimate purpose in life: becoming queen, since Mother herself had not. Twenty years ago, that honor had gone to another young woman, and Mother wasn't about to let history repeat itself. I was her safeguard, though in the past year or so, when it became more and more clear Zadie would make it to the ceremony unscathed, she'd focused the bulk of her attention on my poor sister.

Father cleared his throat and turned to Sami, who quickly hid the button behind his back. "I believe your father is looking for you. Something about you being missing earlier today, when you were supposed to be delivering firewood to your aunts?" He arched an eyebrow, but I could hear the amusement in his voice.

"Yes, sir. I was just leaving." Sami turned to give Zadie a kiss on the cheek, then me. "I'll see you tomorrow."

"Not tomorrow," Father reminded him. "The girls will be preparing for the ceremony, remember?"

He wasn't a particularly imposing man, at least not to me, but Sami flushed. "Of course. At the ceremony, then."

I wished Father would leave and give Sami a chance to say a proper goodbye. The next time he saw Zadie, she would be as good as betrothed to the Prince of Ilara.

"Goodbye," Zadie and I said in unison as Sami ducked out onto the balcony, where a rope ladder led down to the water. Our house, like all the houses in Varenia, was made from the wood of a sunken ship, but every few years we painted it an orangey-pink, a shade Mother favored that was also easy to see on the horizon, guiding us home during the daytime when a lantern would be of little use.

Father settled down onto a low stool carved from driftwood. "I see Nor is cooking tonight. Does that mean Zadie found the oyster?" He gestured to the shiny gray glob of flesh I'd laid in one of our cracked porcelain bowls. Some of our possessions were traded for, but others had been pulled up from shipwrecks. Mother never asked how I came by such items, particularly if I found her something that appealed to her vanity, like a hand mirror or a tortoiseshell comb.

Zadie and I shared a glance. To admit Zadie found the oyster meant admitting that she had been swimming today, against Mother's orders. She was counting on the impressive bride price the prince would send to the chosen girl's family once they married, but we had to eat in the meantime. And who knew how many oysters there would be tomorrow, or next week? Sami had overheard his father speaking to the elders at night in hushed whispers, so we knew things were worse than our parents let on.

"I found it," I said. "But I bet her there would be a pearl in it, and there wasn't."

"That's a shame. Well, as long as *I* get to eat the oyster, I suppose it doesn't matter who found it." Father winked at Zadie as she handed him the bowl. "You're good girls, both of you."

As he tipped back the bowl and let the oyster slide into his mouth, Zadie and I came to stand on either side of him. "I'll miss whichever one of you is taken from me," he said. "But I always knew this day would come. That's what I get for marrying the most beautiful girl in Varenia."

Mother stepped into the house from the balcony, twisting her own freshly washed hair into a braid. She had never dived deep enough to burst her eardrums—something many of the older villagers did to help with the pressure—and her hearing was some of the sharpest in the village. Only a few fine lines pulled at the corners of her eyes and lips, a testament to the benefits of wearing a sun hat (and of rarely smiling).

"Our beauty is a reflection of the favor Thalos has bestowed upon this family," she said, gazing out the window at the darkening waves, as if the ocean god himself were watching. A sudden burst of sea spray shot up through the cracks in our wooden floorboards, and Mother's eyes blazed with satisfaction.

"We will honor him with our sacrifice," Father added.

I squeezed Zadie's hand behind his back and wished the sun would never set. The ocean never gave gifts without expecting something in return, it was said, and Thalos was a hungry god.

2

The next two days were spent in the large yellow meetinghouse with the other girls of marriageable age. I personally thought it was silly to spend two full days preparing ourselves for the ceremony when some of us had been preparing our entire lives. Each elder had already made his or her decision, and for most of us, no amount of primping and preening could possibly make a difference. I would have rather spent the time alone with Zadie, knowing she'd be leaving me soon. But it was tradition, and in Varenia, tradition was as much a part of our world as the ocean.

The mood in the house was lively, almost giddy, like we were children preparing for a festival. The room buzzed with the sound of female voices, punctuated every few minutes by laughter. None of us were old enough to remember the last ceremony, but a few mothers, including mine, were there to supervise and tell stories while we fasted and bathed ourselves in fresh water that ought to have been saved for drinking. Zadie and I rubbed perfumed oil into each other's skin and braided our hair into intricate patterns, then unraveled them and started all over again to occupy the long hours.

I glanced around at the other girls, most of them friendly acquaintances. In a village as small and isolated as ours, there were no unfamiliar faces, though our overprotective mother had done her best to keep us away from the other girls our age. At night, she would often tell us stories of sabotage among young women old enough to participate in the ceremony: braids cut off in the middle of the night, stinging sea nettles rubbed on healthy skin, even hot oil burns.

Boys may be physically stronger, Mother always said, but girls could be twice as vicious. I had never seen any behavior to support her claim, but then, I hadn't spent enough time with the other girls to argue. With Zadie and Sami around, I was never lonely, but I would have liked the opportunity to make more friends.

As the sun extinguished itself on the horizon, anxiety and tension began to mount. The favorites, Zadie and Alys, sat surrounded by friends, who heaped praise on their girl while whispering insults about the opposition.

"Perhaps if Alys had never opened her mouth for the past seventeen years, this would be a fair match," a blond girl named Minika murmured. "But unfortunately for her, she's as gabby as a gull."

I cast an apologetic glance toward Alys, who in truth had only one slightly crooked tooth. Her mother had attempted to straighten it with fishing line made of horse hair, but the results had been minimal at best. Still, with her auburn hair and green eyes, Alys was undeniably beautiful. As was Ginia, with her bronze skin and tight black curls, and Lunella, whose large blue eyes and delicate features were the pride of her entire family. How the elders could possibly choose between them was beyond my comprehension, like trying to choose the most beautiful seashell.

Zadie gave Minika an admonishing look as she wove my hair into what I hoped was the final braid. My scalp itched and burned from her handiwork. "Enough, girls. Alys is a friend, and perfect just as she is. And if she is chosen to go to Ilara, I will pray for Thalos to carry her safely to shore, as will the rest of you."

"You are too kind," Lunella said. "As soft and pliant as a cuttlefish. The prince will have you for his supper if you don't watch out."

Zadie blushed and tucked a stray lock of hair behind her ear.

"What do you think the prince is like?" I asked no one in particular, hoping to divert some of the attention away from my sister. "We know so little about the Ilareans, though they seem to know everything about us."

"Like how beautiful our women are," Minika replied.

Mother sat in the center of the room on one of the colorful cushions that covered the floor from wall to wall. The house was barely large enough to contain thirty girls and women, not to mention all their cosmetics and clothing. "It's more than that," she said, "as you all know."

We all did know. Our history was woven into our childhoods like sea silk threads, so fine it was hard to tell where one stopped and another started. But we all settled in now, turning toward Mother as she began to tell the story. It seemed fitting to hear this tale, tonight of all nights, the night before my world would be changed forever.

"Many years ago, in a queendom whose name has been lost to time, there lived a wise and powerful queen. She gave birth to a daughter, whom she named Ilara, after the celestial goddess. Ilara's smile was as radiant as the moon, her hair as dark and shimmering as the night sky. It was said that her laughter made the stars shine brighter. Beloved by her people, she loved them all in return.

"One summer, when the princess was just sixteen, she journeyed to the shore with her family. She went to lavish parties and met many handsome young men, but none so handsome as Prince Laef, whose own land, Kuven, was far across the Alathian Sea. After weeks of secret meetings and stolen kisses, he asked her to marry him, and she happily accepted.

"But despite their mutual affection, Ilara's mother forbade the marriage. Kuven was a small and weak kingdom compared to the queen's, which at the time spanned the width and breadth of an entire continent, and Laef's father was a cruel ruler, who took much from the sea but gave nothing in return. Ilara's mother had planned a far more advantageous match with a prince from a powerful kingdom to the east, though that prince was said to be old and not particularly charming. As much as she loved her daughter, the queen could not afford to let her put the queendom in jeopardy."

Several girls groaned in disapproval.

Mother frowned. "I don't need to remind any of you of the importance of duty, do I?" She looked directly at Zadie as she said this, though no one understood the weight of her responsibility more than my sister. Zadie nodded solemnly while I barely managed to keep my eyes from rolling.

"Ilara and Laef returned to their homes, but the night before her wedding, they each gathered their most loyal servants and stole ships from their parents. He was an inexperienced sailor and she had never been at sea, but they loved each other too much to be parted. The next evening, their ships met in the middle of the Alathian Sea. For several days, they stayed on Laef's ship, there in the ocean, delighting in each other. They were married on the seventh day, with a plan to return to Kuven. Laef's father approved of the marriage, for he was certain Ilara's mother would have to agree to an alliance that would be greatly beneficial to his kingdom.

"As the sun rose on the day they were set to depart, Ilara's laugh danced over the waves like a skipping stone, and the prince took her in his arms to kiss her. The lovers had no idea that Thalos, the sea god, had been watching them. He saw that these two would bring happiness beyond measure to Laef's father, a happiness he did not deserve. As a punishment for never giving the sea what it was owed, Thalos vowed to take the one thing that meant the most to Laef—Ilara."

A shiver ran over my sore scalp, and I pressed closer to Zadie.

"Thalos summoned giant waves that tossed the ships about like driftwood. The lovers clung to each other, vowing to die together, if that was what it came to. But Thalos himself rode the crest of a wave taller than the ship's mast, and he tore the princess from Laef's arms, dragging her into the deep in his deadly embrace."

We all looked at the governor's house through a large bay

window, where the figurehead of Ilara's lost ship rose from the prow that formed Governor Kristos's roof. She was a maiden carved from wood, her paint long since worn away by the wind and sea, a single hand raised above her head as though she were reaching for her lover's grasp.

I didn't believe the story, at least not the part about Thalos, who I imagined was more of a spirit than a corporeal being. But the idea of a forbidden romance, of two young people risking everything to be together, had always resonated with me. To meet a stranger from a faraway land, to leave duty and responsibility behind for love… It was a fantasy I turned to when the thought of spending the rest of my long life in this one small village overwhelmed me.

There were murmurs among the girls. Even though we all knew the story, Mother had a way of telling it that made my skin feel prickly, like the hollow shell of a dead urchin.

"What became of Prince Laef?" a girl asked.

"When Ilara was pulled from his arms, he leaped into the water after her. He was never seen again. It is said the first blood coral grew there, from the hearts of the two lovers who had been separated in life, but were reunited in death." My mother looked at me now, and I fought against the tingling in my cheek. The blood coral had not only given me my name, but also my scar—and it had nearly cost me my life.

"And the servants?" another girl asked.

"Loyal till death. They had promised to look after their prince and princess and refused to leave the place where they died. This place, where Varenia now stands. They signed a decree, vowing that no Varenian would set foot on land until a new crown princess was born to replace the one they had lost."

"Why do we send them our women?" I asked, surprising even myself. It was a question that had haunted me for years, but which I'd never dared to ask before. Now seemed the perfect time to ask, since Mother couldn't ignore me here.

She narrowed her eyes at me. "As a penance for losing the princess, the servants sent gifts from the sea to Ilara's mother, who renamed her queendom in her daughter's honor. In the years that followed, a plague swept through the land. Thousands died, and many of the women who survived were left barren. The monarchy had always passed through queens until this time, but the queen had no other daughters, just a sickly son. And when he came of marrying age, there was a dearth of suitable brides.

"But Varenia, which as you know means fertile waters, was spared from the plague. When they sent a beautiful girl to deliver pearls and sea silk to the queen, the Ilarean prince fell in love with her, and thus began the tradition of the Varenian bride."

I watched Mother answer questions from the other girls, questions we all knew the answers to but asked anyway. It was part of the ritual. The air in the room had grown warm and pungent with perfume, and someone opened a hatch in the roof to let in the breeze along with the moonlight, which shone down on Mother's hair and face.

Our poor mother, who always believed she should have been chosen at the last ceremony but lost to another girl instead. Father still called her the most beautiful girl in Varenia and said he was grateful the elders were so foolish, because otherwise he would have lost her to the king. But Mother's resentment was too great to be appeased by the sweet words of our loving father, and nothing but Zadie's selection tomorrow would quell it. Sometimes I wondered if even that would be enough.

Late that night, Zadie and I tossed and turned next to each other on our cushions, along with every other girl in the house. It was too hot and stuffy, and there was too much riding on tomorrow to sleep. The repeated *slap-slap* of the waves against the pillars below us, a sound that normally lulled me to sleep, grated on my already raw nerves.

Zadie's breath was warm against my skin when she spoke. "Can I tell you something? Something I've never told anyone?"

I rolled toward her, my heart beating a little faster at the thought that Zadie had a secret. I told her everything. I always had. "Of course."

"I hope they pick Alys tomorrow."

I sucked in a breath. "What? Why? I thought this was what you wanted."

Zadie's features were obscured in the darkness, but I could imagine the worry dimples above her brow. "I want to stay here with you. I want to marry Sami. I love him, Nor."

Something cold stirred in my stomach, slick as an eel. Of course I wanted Zadie to stay, for her and Sami to be together. But I couldn't help wondering what role would be left for me in Zadie's life if her wish came true. "I know."

"Do you think they'll pick her? She *is* beautiful, and thoughtful and nurturing. Surely those things matter more than a crooked tooth, even in Varenia."

"It's possible," I said. "But don't you want to be a princess? Don't you want to see the world? Nothing can be worse than staying here forever."

"Varenia is my home. You and Samiel are my home. What more can the world possibly have to offer?"

Roses, I thought. And horses and castles and all manner of things I hadn't dared to imagine, surely. What *didn't* the world have to offer?

"Would you really want to go, if they chose you?" she asked.

"Yes," I said, without a moment's hesitation. But we both knew they wouldn't. "What are you going to do if they choose you tomorrow?"

When she blinked, her eyes were shiny in the moonlight. "I'll go. But it will be my body that leaves, and nothing more. Samiel has my heart, and you, dear sister, my soul."

The day of the ceremony dawned bright and clear, bringing with it both relief and dread. I needed to get out of that house, to breathe air that hadn't been shared with twenty-nine other women. But Zadie trembled beside me like a feather in the wind as we stepped onto the long dock that connected the meetinghouse to the governor's.

All the girls had left behind their sun-bleached tunics and salt-stained skirts for a proper gown, many of which had been passed down through the women in their families for generations. Zadie stood out in a brand-new silk gown as pink as the seven pearls my mother had traded to buy it, nearly two months' worth of food and supplies.

To his credit, Father had tried to reason with her. "Zadie is sure to be chosen even if she wears the burlap sack our grain comes in," he argued.

But Mother had ignored him and handed the gown to Zadie. "Pink for my pearl," she said, then turned to me and presented her old ceremony gown, which had once been white. "And red for you, Nor. The color of the coral for which you were named."

Blood. That was the word she hadn't said. The newly dyed cambric gown looked like it had been drenched in it.

The water surrounding the wooden dock was crowded with boats, entire families gathered in a single vessel for the ceremony. Some were dangerously low in the water, threatening to capsize if a toddler decided to switch positions, as toddlers were prone to do.

Sami stood next to his father, Governor Kristos, on the threshold of their house, painted a deep orange. The figurehead cast her long shadow over them, her blank eyes staring out to sea. Sami and I shared a momentary glance, his jaw clenching before his gaze returned to his feet.

"Good people of Varenia," Governor Kristos began. He was a tall man with broad shoulders and a thick brown beard streaked with silver. "From our humble beginnings, our village has been blessed by the sea. Not only does it feed and shelter us, but these waters have made us strong and virile. Our oldest villager has just celebrated her one hundred and fiftieth year, as you know."

Hundreds turned toward a boat near the dock, where Old Mother Agathe sat surrounded by her seven elderly children and countless grandchildren and great-grandchildren. We all bowed our heads in respect.

"Now the time has come to send one of our daughters to Ilara, where she will someday be queen. It is a loss for us all but also a great honor, and we do so not out of necessity but generosity."

I almost scoffed out loud but managed to hold it in. No, it wasn't *necessary*, as long as we didn't mind having our food and water supply permanently cut off. I didn't know when the Varenian tradition of handing over pearls and women had evolved from penance to retribution, when the vow to never set foot on land had become a law enforced under pain of death—but I knew I would have rowed to shore a long time ago if I'd had any choice in the matter.

The governor walked down the dock toward us girls, lined up like jewels on a chain. "The elders spoke long into the night as they considered this most important of decisions."

I glanced at the elders from the corner of my eye. They sat in chairs in front of the governor's house, a group of thirteen men and women who looked remarkably alert, given that not one was less than a hundred years old.

"Elder Nemea, would you like to make the announcement?" the governor asked a woman sitting in the center. Her braid, as white as sea foam, hung to her knees, and her faded skirts dragged behind her as she made her way slowly down the dock. Alys stood closest to the governor's house, and I felt the intake of breath all around me as the elder drew near her.

But she did not stop, and from somewhere behind me, I heard a gasp, followed by a muffled sob. That would be Alys's mother, a woman nearly as ambitious as our own. Once we passed from girlhood into young womanhood, our mother had forbidden us to socialize with Alys, something that had always saddened me. After all, if anyone in Varenia understood what our lives were like, it was Alys.

Zadie stood to my left, and Elder Nemea approached from my right. I kept my gaze lowered, as was customary in the presence of elders. Nemea's worn slippers came into view, and for one moment, I wondered if there was any chance she might stop in front of me. It was a silly—and fleeting—thought, for the next second she halted, directly in front of Zadie.

No one but a sister would have noticed, but I heard Zadie's breath quicken, just a fraction. I couldn't help myself: I looked up. Elder Nemea had raised one arm and placed her gnarled hand on Zadie's shoulder. I scanned the crowd for Mother and Father, whose boat was near the front of the crowd. Mother's eyes were locked on Zadie, and she made no effort to conceal the grin splitting her face.

"Zadie," Elder Nemea began. "In one week's time, you will leave for Ilara to marry Prince Ceren. You have brought honor to your family and all of Varenia."

Zadie bowed her head as Governor Kristos stepped forward to place a wreath of rare white seaflowers on her like a crown, a symbol of the real crown she would wear soon enough. He kissed her gently on each cheek. "My dear girl, we will miss you," he whispered so only Zadie and I could hear.

"And I you," she said.

He turned away from Zadie to face the people. "The elders have chosen!" he shouted. "And now, let us celebrate!"

A cheer rose up from the crowd, and I had to clench my hands into fists at my side to keep from reaching for my sister. When I glanced at Sami, I saw that his hands were balled as tightly as mine.

One week was all we had left. And then we'd never see Zadie again.

3

While the rest of the village broke open jugs of home-made wine and heaped our parents with praise, I retreated to our family's boat below the governor's house. I told myself my sorrow was purely for my sister, but a small part of me wept for my own loss. Not only would I spend the rest of my life in Varenia, I would do it without Zadie.

"Nor?"

I looked up to see Sami on the ladder leading down from his house. "Mind if I join you?" he asked. "I'm not really in the mood for celebrating."

I burst into a fresh bout of sobs as he dropped into the boat beside me.

"Oh, Nor. Please don't cry." He pulled me into his arms and held me while I tried to staunch the flow of my tears. There was an old legend that said pearls were the tears of the gods, but we mortals wept only saltwater, and we had more than enough of that around here.

Sami smoothed my hair back from my face. "This is what's best for Zadie, and for your family."

I glanced up, shocked. "What?"

"It's an honor, Nor. The highest honor."

"That's a lie, and you know it. If it's such an honor, why don't the Ilareans choose someone from their own kingdom? If we're so special, why aren't the rest of us allowed on land?"

"Nor—"

I pushed away from him and moved to the other bench. "She loves you, Sami. She told me last night. And now she has to leave us and marry some prince who will never make her happy."

Now it was his turn to look shocked. "She loves me?"

"Yes." I wiped the tears away with the back of my hand. "She said she doesn't want to go, that she wants to stay here and marry you."

Sami sat motionless for several minutes.

"Say something," I said finally. "What are you thinking?"

"She loves me."

"Is that really so hard to believe?"

"Yes!" He started to run his fingers through his brown hair before he remembered he was supposed to look dignified today. "I always *hoped* she loved me, and I sometimes thought that maybe she had feelings for me, but every time I tried to get closer, she pushed me away. I thought she wanted to go to Ilara. I thought every girl did."

"Trust me, so did I."

He shook his head and lowered his gaze. "Our fathers have been talking."

I fiddled with a loose thread on my bodice. "They always talk."

"No, this is different. My father told me tonight, that you and I are to be…"

I dropped my hands. "To be what?"

Sami dragged his eyes up to mine. "To be married."

The word hung in the air between us, as heavy as a storm cloud.

"Married," I repeated.

"As soon as we turn eighteen. Our fathers have always wanted this, I think, for our two families to be joined. They've always felt like brothers, and now they will be."

"But we can't marry," I blurted. "We don't love each other."

He sighed in exasperation. "Love isn't a requirement for marriage, Nor. Do you think Zadie will love Prince Ceren?" He spat the name out like a bitter pip.

"My parents married for love, and so did yours. If we talk to them, tell them what Zadie told me last night, maybe they'll change their minds."

But Sami already looked resigned. "The elders made this decision, not our parents. It just so happens it's what they wanted, too."

I was too stunned now to cry. I hadn't known what life without Zadie would look like, but I hadn't expected *this*.

The boat rocked back and forth as Sami came to sit next to me. "It could be worse," he said softly. "They could have arranged for me to marry Alys. And you could have been stuck with anyone. Would you have wanted that?"

I fisted my hands in my skirts. "No, of course not. It's just all too much right now. I can't make sense of it."

"At the very least, you'll be provided for. And when I'm the governor, I will stand up to the Ilareans, unlike my weak father."

I shot him a look out of the corner of my eyes. "Careful, Sami. Your father isn't too weak to stripe you like a sea snake if he hears you talk like that."

He wrapped an arm around my shoulders, and I knew then why we could never marry: because where he touched Zadie almost reverently, as if she were as fragile as a bird's egg, he touched me like a brother touches a sister. It was too comfortable, too self-assured. A man was supposed to envy every wave that touched his lover's body, not rest his arm on her shoulder like a cushion.

I shrugged out from under his arm. "I should find Zadie now. We haven't had a chance to speak."

I was relieved that he didn't try to stop me, but I wondered about his true feelings toward our betrothal. Was it just that I was the next best thing to Zadie, or did he really believe he could love me the way a husband loves a wife?

I tried to see him not just as a best friend, but as an eligible young man. He wore his finest tunic and trousers tonight, and his hair was neatly combed and oiled—or had been, before he'd ruffled it. But when I looked at his face, all I could see was the mischievous boy from my childhood, the one who had dropped anchor without securing the rope and told Father it was my fault, who had once stolen my tunic so that I had to return from diving wearing my skirts as a dress. When his eyes, rimmed with long dark lashes that were the envy of many a girl, met mine, I didn't feel anything but the same kind of love I felt for my family.

"I'll come by tomorrow afternoon," he said. "When your parents are out. Tell Zadie… Tell her the elders chose well."

I managed a small smile. "You should tell her yourself. Good night, Sami." I was reaching for the ladder to the dock when I felt his hand on mine.

"I didn't ask for this either, you know."

The coldness in his voice startled me, and I realized I had wounded his pride with my reaction to his news. Sami was kind and handsome, and he would make a good leader one day. Any girl would be lucky to marry him. But I needed him to understand how I felt.

"I am not my sister, Sami," I told him as gently as I could.

"I never said you were."

Our eyes locked for another moment before I climbed out of the boat, leaving Sami alone in the dark.

I was still grappling with Sami's news when I went in search of Zadie. I found her surrounded by the other girls from the choosing ceremony, and I was happy to see she was smiling, her golden-brown eyes beginning to glaze over as she took another swig of wine. We weren't normally permitted to drink, but it seemed like none of the rules applied tonight.

"You must envy your sister," a woman my mother's age said to me. "She gets to leave Varenia. She gets to marry a prince."

As if I wasn't aware. "Yes, ma'am, she is very blessed."

"And to think, if you hadn't saved her from that fishing net and cut your cheek all those years ago, it might have been you chosen tonight. It must be difficult not to blame her for your misfortune."

I glanced again at the woman and felt that same strange sensation in my belly, like a writhing eel. It was Alys's mother.

Contrary to what many Varenians thought, I had never once blamed Zadie for the scar on my cheek. It was a small price to pay for my sister's life. That didn't mean I had never envied my twin, or that I never wondered how things would be if the incident hadn't happened. But I often consoled myself with the fact that if I didn't have my scar, Zadie and I would have spent our lives competing with each other. The idea of viewing my sister as an obstacle, rather than my best friend, was unthinkable.

Alys's mother was like a flounder stirring up sand that had settled long ago, trying to bring painful memories to the surface. I buried them back down where they belonged. To hold on to the past was as useless as trying to find the same wave twice, Father always said.

"I'm happy for my sister," I said, then left to join Zadie.

We didn't return to our home until late into the night, after the entire village celebrated with enough homemade wine to hide the fact that there was no feast, as there should have been.

Mother was half-asleep by the time Father led her back to our house, but the triumphant smile on her face never faltered. She relished every single congratulatory word, drank in the jealous looks of other mothers, many of whom seemed to know that Mother would now have a princess *and* the governor's wife for daughters. Word traveled fast in Varenia, but it was clear no one had yet told Zadie about my betrothal, for while she was tipsy and exhausted, her mood was still riding the current of an entire village's elation.

I helped her undress and eased her onto our bed, then carefully folded up our gowns. I tried to imagine my sister in a whale-bone corset and high-heeled shoes—things I'd never seen but heard about from Sami, who had encountered all manner of people at the port where he did his illegal trading.

Only Ilarean men came to the floating market where we purchased our goods, and they never spoke to us about life in Ilara. They were polite but curt, keeping the conversation on business in their clipped cadence. (Though we spoke the same language, I'd always thought it sounded more musical on Varenian tongues.) But over the years, I'd gleaned small details about life on land from their clothing—never ornate, though fine—and mannerisms. And while Mother haggled, I often studied the intricate carvings on their boats: people and horses, trees and rivers, and dozens of creatures I couldn't name.

Perhaps, if I married Sami, I could sneak away with him and see those things for myself one day. Surely the governor's wife would have more freedom than a villager's daughter.

I pulled a blanket over my sister, my eyes filling with tears at the thought that we had so little time left. It was a crueler twist of fate than Alys's mother realized, that Zadie would leave Varenia and see the world, while I stayed behind and married the boy she loved. I scrubbed angrily at my tears, accidentally brushing the scar on my cheek. Without it, I might have been chosen, and Zadie could marry Sami. I didn't resent my sister in the slightest, but I muttered a curse to Thalos that would have made even Sami blush. None of this was fair.

I lay down on the straw-filled mattress next to my sister and carefully removed her seaflower crown, then began to release the braids in her hair. I'd thought she was asleep, but then I heard her breathe a sigh so weary, she sounded as old as Elder Nemea.

"What is it?" I whispered. Mother and Father were asleep in their own bed across the house, but we only had curtains to separate our rooms.

"It just all came back to me."

"What?"

"What tonight meant. For a little while, I allowed myself to forget. I was just a girl celebrating with her friends." She rolled over so I could work on the braids on the other side of her head. "I can't believe I have to leave in a week. I'll never see you again. It doesn't seem possible."

"Then let's pretend it's not," I said, fighting back fresh tears. "Let's spend this week doing all our favorite things. We won't mention anything beyond these seven days."

"It won't change anything."

"No. But neither will spending the next seven days crying. And I doubt the prince wants to find his new bride as swollen as a puffer fish."

She released her breath through her nose. I had finished with her hair and it was fanned all around her now, a mass of brown waves identical to my own. "Fine," she said. "What do you want to do tomorrow, then?"

"I want to watch the sunrise with you."

"That's in about two hours. Would you settle for the sunset tomorrow?"

"I suppose. Then I want to go out to the reef and swim

with the turtles. I want to find the fattest oyster we've ever found, one with four or five pearls inside, and have Sami trade it for fresh fruit. And then I want to—"

"I think that's enough for one day, Nor."

I yawned and pulled my hair out of the way before settling onto my side. We often slept like this, facing each other. We had since we were babies, Mother said. "Should we invite Sami?" I asked.

"Not tomorrow."

I smiled, relieved. I wanted a day alone with my sister. I didn't want to think about Ilara *or* about marrying Sami. Tomorrow would be about us.

Father agreed to let us take the boat for the day if we promised to bring back some pearls. There was never any guarantee we'd find even one, but I had a good feeling about today. As soon as we were out of sight of the house, I removed my hat and tied my skirts up between my legs. We were the only boat on the water—most people, like Mother, were sleeping off the festival and wine. Zadie looked a bit green herself, but I'd forced a ladle of fresh water and some porridge into her before dragging her into the boat.

She sat across from me now, her face shaded beneath the wide brim of her hat. Just because the ceremony was over didn't mean she could fall into her sister's slovenly ways, Mother had grumbled as we made our way out the door.

"You can remove your hat, Zadie. Mother can't see you out here."

She kept her gaze on the water. "I will, once we get to the reef. There's no point in taking risks now."

And when you get to Ilara? I wanted to ask. *Will you take risks then?* We had promised not to talk about Ilara this week, but our lives had revolved around the ceremony for as long as I could remember. Now that it was over, what else was there to talk about but Zadie leaving?

The sun was fierce today, without even the occasional cloud to provide relief. I leaned over backward, wetting my hair to cool off my head, and sighed as the water dripped down my neck. From now on, I would wear my hair loose and let my skin tan as much as a man's. We were all destined to look like Elder Nemea anyway, with her white hair and skin like a pelican's wattle. What was so wonderful about being beautiful, if all it meant was being sent away from the people you loved at best, and at worst, spending the rest of your life feeling inadequate?

I usually did the rowing, to spare Zadie's hands from becoming hard and callused, but we weren't in a hurry today, so I allowed my fingers to trail in the water and let the waves carry us toward the reef. Our oars were wrapped in fabric to prevent as much chafing as possible, but even when the occasional blister formed on my palms, it healed quickly. So quickly that I'd never earned another scar since the incident, despite my carelessness. The doctor believed my miraculous healing ability had something to do with the blood coral, but he couldn't explain it any further than that.

"So," Zadie said, "who would you consider marrying?"

A chill ran over my scalp despite the heat. "What?"

"I find Eyo to be quite handsome. And he always seems to find the pinkest pearls. His family is better fed than most."

Zadie had never asked me about marriage before. She knew

I wasn't interested in any of the village boys, that when I did daydream about the future, I always imagined a life on land, not here in Varenia. And I couldn't bring up Sami, knowing what I did. It would be better if Zadie went to Ilara without ever hearing of it. The truth would only hurt her.

I decided to play along. What harm could it do now? "Eyo is handsome, and he does find a lot of pearls. But have you ever gotten close enough to smell his breath?"

She laughed. "No. Why?"

"It smells like rotten fish. I couldn't marry a young man who smelled like that, not for all the pearls in the Alathian Sea."

"Tell me, then. Who is good enough for my dear sister? Iano?"

I shook my head. "Too short."

"Jovani, then. He's the tallest boy in the village and still growing."

I considered for a moment, fanning myself with my hat. Jovani was tall, and his breath didn't smell. He was fiercely protective of his little sister, who was the same age as Zadie and me. We didn't know each other well, but in the meetinghouse before the ceremony, I'd heard several girls talking about him. From what I'd gathered, he was very respectful of his parents and a hard worker.

Not that it mattered. I was destined to marry Sami. I remembered the way he'd slung his arm around me last night, and the eel twisted in my stomach once again. "I would consider Jovani," I said.

Zadie clapped her hands, pleased to have found me a suitable match. "You will have lovely children together," she said, before the smile vanished from her face. I knew exactly what she was thinking: that we would never get to see each other's children.

I couldn't let my thoughts sink so low today. I peered over the edge of the boat just as a turtle swam out of view. "We're here!"

"Already?"

"Look," I said, pointing to where the water changed color over the reef. My entire body was drenched in sweat, and I couldn't get out of my skirts fast enough. I scrambled over the side of the boat, then let myself sink a few feet below the surface and hung suspended, weightless, there in the place I'd always felt most free. The anchor dropped a moment later, and I waited for Zadie to join me.

She plunged in just inches away, sending bubbles into my face. I reached out and pinched her before she could get away, and then we took each other's hands and stayed there for a moment, smiling at each other, pretending we weren't trying to outlast the other. Even though I'd gone in first, I had the better lung capacity, and Zadie stuck her tongue out at me before shooting up toward the surface.

I bobbed up a moment later. "So, what will it be today? First one to find an oyster is off cooking duty tonight *and* tomorrow?"

"First one to find a *pearl*," Zadie suggested. "What good is an oyster without a pearl, other than as a snack for Father?"

I liked to think the oysters we found gave Father enough strength to travel to deeper waters to fish, but the truth was his ribs showed more than the rest of ours. He patted his flat stomach after dinner every night, pretending to be sated, but his portions had grown smaller as Zadie and I grew larger.

"Very well," I said to Zadie. "I accept." Then I took a deep breath and dived back down, eager to get to the oysters before my sister.

I spotted one almost immediately, and a nearby blood coral was a good sign, though I steered well clear of it. The relationship between the blood coral and the oysters was a mystery we accepted, even though the blood coral was highly toxic. All we knew was that it made the pearls in these waters pink, and a pink pearl was worth five of its paler cousins. But a blood coral cut was almost always fatal. The fact that I had survived mine was deemed a miracle by the doctor and elders alike.

There had been a shoal here once, but as the value of the pearls continued to drop, some of the villagers had grown greedy and stripped it bare. Our best bet was now the ocean floor, nearly fifty feet down. I pushed as hard as I could, reaching the oyster and barely believing my luck when I spotted another one just a few feet away. I grabbed both and pushed myself off the seafloor toward the surface. For dives of this depth, we didn't bother using rocks to weigh us down, or lines to pull us back up, or even oil in our ears and mouths to protect our eardrums. But for the men who dived as deep as one hundred feet or more, such precautions were necessary.

When I broke the surface, I looked around for Zadie, but there was no sign of her. I dropped my oysters into the boat and was getting ready to fill my lungs again to search for her when she popped up next to me.

"Did you find anything?" I asked, ignoring the way my

heart pounded in my chest. Seven years had passed since the incident, but I had never stopped worrying about my twin. The thought of her alone in Ilara without me to look out for her was almost unbearable.

She sighed and dropped a large clam into the boat. "Just this clam. Perhaps Mother can harvest some sea silk from the beard. But no oysters. You?"

"Two, not far from a nice, fat blood coral. I have high hopes."

She grunted in frustration. "I'm going to try down at the other end. Don't follow me."

"Fine, suit yourself. I'm going to try here again. Scream if you need me."

"What makes you think I'll need you?" she said, splashing me. Then she disappeared.

I took a few moments to slow my heart rate down as well as my breathing. Staying underwater for long periods of time required concentration and calm. The very worst thing you could do was panic, as Zadie and I knew all too well.

I filled my lungs with air and dived, this time a little farther to the left of the blood coral, which was surrounded by nothing but bones. Even the fish knew to stay away from it. I wondered which villager had been laid to rest here, their body wrapped in a shroud and weighted down with rocks. Was it someone I knew, or had the coral been here since long before I was born?

I remembered the coral I'd cut myself on vividly. It was one of the largest I'd ever seen, a red tangle of branches sprouting out of a rib cage that had split right down the middle. At ten we were deemed old enough to go out alone, though

Mother always sent Sami with us. He had stayed in the boat, fishing, while Zadie and I hunted for oysters amid the rocks on the seafloor.

Zadie and I had spotted the oyster at the same time. It was enormous, with a pink luster to its shell, probably due to its proximity to such a large coral. We knew to stay away from blood coral—it was a lesson every Varenian child learned before we were ever permitted to dive—but this oyster was too tempting.

We shared a look and immediately raced toward it, imagining a giant pink pearl that could feed our family for months. With our sights set on the oyster, neither of us noticed the fishing net caught on the rocks nearby. I reached the oyster first and turned back to grin at my sister, but Zadie was bolder back then. She came right at me, even though both of us were quickly running out of air. I propelled myself off the rocks and started toward the surface, when I felt her hand wrap around my ankle and pull.

I looked down at my sister, who had grabbed onto the fishing net as an anchor. I kicked at her hand with my free foot, confused and angry, but she refused to let go. With my lungs burning, I reached down to pry her hand away, and that was when I realized she wasn't holding on to the net, not on purpose. A large hook had caught itself in her tunic. She was clinging to me for help.

The look of fear on her face spurred me into action. I grabbed onto the net and pulled myself down, then began tearing at the fabric of her tunic. Zadie was starting to panic, which made it nearly impossible to stay calm myself. But I knew if I didn't, I'd run out of air, and we'd both drown. I managed to reach the shucking knife strapped to my ankle and slashed at the net, freeing Zadie. In her rush to escape, she pushed me backward. Directly into the blood coral.

I had never felt anything like it, not even when I touched the hot handle of a pan as a child and my palm had sizzled and blistered. The pain as my face made contact with the rough surface of the coral literally blinded me. What started out as a stabbing sensation in my cheek immediately radiated across my face, down my neck, and into my chest. I gasped without thinking, inhaling a lungful of seawater. I don't remember what happened after that, but Zadie told me later that she sent Sami down for me as soon as she reached the surface, knowing he could get to me far faster than she could.

I sputtered back into consciousness in the boat, after Sami had pumped the water from my chest. The scream that tore from my throat was so loud he nearly toppled over backward. Zadie was next to me, sobbing, apologizing, but I registered nothing except the throbbing pain spreading from my cheek throughout my entire body. I was unconscious again by the time we made it home and remained that way for two days.

Life was never the same after that incident so many years ago. Mother kept me inside for weeks after, until the wound had scabbed over and the pink skin underneath had emerged. She grew even more protective of us, and Zadie became subdued and cautious.

As for me, I both lost and gained something that day. At first, the scar was a source of shame. But I was coming to realize that beauty—at least as defined by my people—was more of a burden than a gift. To one of us, it offered the chance to leave Varenia, but was that really freedom if we didn't get to choose it for ourselves?

I knew what Zadie would say if anyone had bothered to ask her.

As the memory of the incident faded, I grabbed the oyster just a few inches from me and rose to the surface. That was when I heard the screaming.

4

"**N**or!"

I turned toward the sound of Zadie's voice. She was spinning in fast circles, her eyes darting in every direction.

"What is it?" I asked, already churning through the water toward her.

"It's a maiden's hair jelly! Thalos, it's everywhere!"

"Don't move," I called. "Just stay where you are."

Maiden's hair jellyfish were some of the most dangerous in the ocean, but they usually only came to the surface at night. They were easy to avoid then, thanks to the soft blue glow they emitted, but in the sun their bodies blended in with the water around them.

"Stop!" Zadie shrieked. "Look."

It was a small maiden's hair, at least. The bell was only about two feet in diameter, a near-translucent blob floating on the surface a few feet from Zadie. Long tentacles, as fine as the hair for which it was named, trailed around it. I couldn't imagine it coming to the surface unless it was dead, but even a dead jelly could still be dangerous. I ducked under the surface to see the extent of the tentacles. They were drifting in the current away from both of us.

I sighed in relief. "Swim backward," I told Zadie. "It will be okay."

Zadie did as I said, and I swam backward as well, until we were well clear of the jellyfish. By the time we made it back to the boat, we were both exhausted.

"Are you all right?" I asked, reaching for her hand.

"I'm fine. I know I overreacted. I just came up a few feet away from it, and it scared me. I thought…"

That you would be scarred. "It's all right. I did tell you to scream if you needed me," I teased.

We hauled ourselves over the side of the boat and flopped into the bottom, the rush of fear slowly draining from us. I kicked at the three oysters I'd collected with a limp foot. "Should we call it a day?"

"I didn't find anything."

"You found the clam. Mother can use the silk on the gloves she's making you." Weaving sea silk was one of the few manual tasks our mother performed. The strands of silk, harvested from the beards of a particular species of clam, were brown in the water, but when specially treated, they turned golden in the sunlight.

"So I found something that only benefits me? That's hardly a contribution to the family." Sami had offered to trade anything Mother made with sea silk at the port—its rarity made it even more valuable than the pearls in some circles—but

Mother refused. Unlike the blood coral and pearls, which existed because of Ilara and Prince Laef and all the Varenians who followed, sea silk was a gift from the sea, and therefore could only be gifted to another, not sold.

I handed Zadie the smallest oyster. "Here, this can be yours."

We tucked the oysters under the shade of the bench to keep them from spoiling, but as soon as we got home, I eagerly shucked the largest oyster I'd found near the blood coral. Zadie and I both gasped when we saw the row of five pearls inside the shell, all a vibrant pink.

"They're beautiful," Zadie said. "Some of the best I've seen in years." She reached for the shell and paused. "It must have been very close to the blood coral."

I shrugged. "I was careful."

"Nor." She touched her own cheek without realizing. I knew she still felt guilty for the incident, though I had spent months afterward assuring her that it wasn't her fault.

"It doesn't matter now, Zadie. You've been chosen. You're..." I cut myself off. I'd promised not to talk about Ilara. I forced a smile. "My beauty, or lack thereof, is no longer a concern—of mine or Mother's and certainly not yours. I can get as ugly as I like now."

"Jovani might feel differently," she said with a laugh.

"Yes, well, I'll have to make sure we have a speedy courtship, then, won't I?"

She smiled. "Mother would be thrilled to have both daughters engaged before their eighteenth birthdays."

Zadie had no idea how close to the truth she was. But perhaps my fate wasn't sealed yet. Maybe there was still a chance

Mother and Father would understand if I told them I didn't want to marry Sami.

I left the pearls in their shell and dropped the oyster meat into a bowl for Father. "And where do you suppose our loving mother is at this hour?"

"She told me before we left that she and Father had business with Governor Kristos this afternoon."

I nearly spilled the sack of grain I was struggling to lift. "Did she say what kind of business?"

"No. I assume it has to do with the preparations for my journey. The envoy from Ilara will be here in—"

"Six days. I know."

Zadie unbraided her hair and began running her fingers through the strands. "Sami said my cloak is nearly finished. He's supposed to give it to me tonight."

I studied her face for a moment. Did she know? Was she waiting for me to say something first? "I thought we said it would be just us today."

Her eyes dropped to her bare feet. I was just a little finger's breadth taller than her, but my feet were nearly a knuckle longer. There were other small differences between us as well, not just the scar, although that was the one everyone noticed first. Sami had been the one to point out my larger feet when we were twelve years old and still allowed to sleep together while our parents stayed up late, talking.

He'd leaped up and compared us, part by part, with only the moon to light his observations. "Nor's eyes are narrower than Zadie's," he'd said. "And Zadie's nostrils are rounder." He rubbed his chin and let his eyes travel down to our torsos. We weren't women yet, so he didn't linger long. "Nor has knobbier knees than Zadie," he added, and before he knew what had hit him, one of my too-long feet shot out and caught him right between the legs. He didn't make the mistake of mentioning my knees again.

It wasn't just that I didn't appreciate being scrutinized by my best friend; I got that enough from Mother. But being compared to my twin was always complicated. Sometimes when we were small, other children would whisper to me that I was the prettier twin, with a conspiratorial grin. The same thing had happened to Zadie. And while it was impossible not to feel a small flutter of pride in the moment—beauty was always on our minds, even then—I always felt defensive on Zadie's behalf. Because if I were prettier, it meant she was uglier, and a compliment at my sister's expense was no compliment at all. I didn't want to hear about my beauty in relation to Zadie's, or anyone else's for that matter. I wanted to be seen for *me*.

"It's fine," I said finally. "Sami is family. Of course he can come over tonight."

Her cheeks flushed when she raised her eyes to mine. "Have you noticed that he's grown lately? He used to be just a little taller than us. Now I have to crane my neck to look at him."

I pounded the grain into the mortar with a wooden pestle. The coarse flour would be used to make bread in our clay oven. The bread always turned out hard and flavorless, but it helped fill our bellies when we dipped it in stew, especially now that we had less fish to eat. "Yes, I suppose he has grown. We all have."

"And his voice. I know it's been deeper for a while, but now—"

"Don't do this." The words slipped out before I had time to call them back.

"Do what?"

I chewed my lip, treading mental water. Perhaps it was selfish, but I didn't want to be the one to tell her about my betrothal. "Don't allow yourself to think about him that way. You have to leave in six days. It will only make things harder for you."

She planted herself in front of me, forcing me to look at her. "*Nothing* could make this harder," she hissed. "I love him, and I have to leave him and marry some other young man I've never met, while he marries Alys or one of the other village girls, and it makes me want to *die!*"

I stared at her breathlessly, my sweet sister who had never uttered a harsh word against anyone. "Zadie."

"Don't tell me what to do or think or feel," she choked out, tears filling her eyes. "You get to stay here with Mother and Father and marry whomever you choose. You have no idea what I'm going through."

She spun away from me, but I was faster. I caught her slender wrist in my hand. We were the same size, but her smallness always surprised me. Would I feel this fragile in the arms of my future husband, whether he was Sami or someone else?

"Do you think this is easy for me?" I asked. "Do you think I want to stay behind while you go off and see the world? I don't *want* to stay here. And I certainly don't want to live here without you. I would give anything for you to be able to stay and marry Sami. If I could trade places with you, I'd do it in a heartbeat. But they didn't choose me, Zadie."

I'm the perfect seashell you pick up from the ocean floor, only to turn it over in your hand and see the crack. I'm the fabric with the tear in the seam that you give back to the trader and demand first quality. As far as everyone in Varenia is concerned, I'm you, only ruined. So don't tell me I have no idea what you're going through.

My blood pounded in my head so hard I had to sit down. I could never say any of those things to my sister. They were old insecurities, ideas I'd gotten from Mother and spent years overcoming. Zadie couldn't help the way things were any more than I could. I yearned to tell her about Sami, that I was being forced into a marriage just as much as she was. But I knew she wouldn't see it that way. It would just be another reason for her to be jealous, and I didn't want to fight with my sister now.

I pulled her into my arms, clutching her tight. She resisted for a moment, but her body finally went limp, and she sobbed against me until we heard the creak of the pillars below our house and the deep murmur of Father's voice mingled with the higher trill of Mother's. We took turns straightening each other's hair and wiping the tears from our cheeks.

Few people in Varenia owned a mirror, but we had never needed one.

"Well?" Father asked as he came up through the trapdoor in our floor. "Any luck today?"

"Just look what Zadie found," I said, pointing to the oyster with the five pearls. The other two had yielded three between them, but their color couldn't match the others.

Father's dark eyebrows rose. "Zadie found these?"

"Of course she did," Mother said, coming up behind us and resting a hand on Zadie's shoulder. She was in an unnervingly good mood. "She's our lucky pearl."

I could feel Zadie's eyes on me, but I didn't turn my head.

"We'll use them for Nor's dowry," Mother added.

Ah, yes, my dowry. Mother had been speaking of it for years, since shortly after the incident, the implication always clear that she'd never be able to marry me off without the promise of a good dowry.

"Calliope," Father chided her gently.

She ignored him and plucked the pearls from their shell. "Absolutely stunning. Where did you find the oyster?"

"Near the reef," Zadie answered.

"These must have been close to a blood coral to have such strong coloration. You didn't get close to it, did you, Zadie?"

"No, Mother. We are always careful."

"Good. Now hurry up and bathe. We're eating with the governor and his family tonight."

"Why?" I asked. It wasn't unusual for them to visit our home, but we never went to the governor's house for meals. That was an honor reserved only for family.

Family. Which I would soon be. "Oh," I breathed.

"What?" Zadie asked, her eyes darting from mine to Mother's. "Did something happen?"

"Governor Kristos has an announcement to make," Father said. "Wear the dresses you wore for the ceremony."

I tried to meet Mother's eye, to silently plead that this not happen now, but she ignored me and went to her room, humming as the curtain fell behind her. Zadie raised an eyebrow at me before heading out to the sunny side of the balcony, where the bucket of fresh water for bathing had been placed to warm.

"Father," I said in a low voice. "We can't do this to Zadie now. It will destroy her."

He glanced at me. "You know?"

"Samiel told me, after the ceremony."

"Zadie has a right to know before she leaves." He raised the bowl of oysters to his mouth and swallowed all three at once. "Besides, she should be happy that her sister is going to be the future governor's wife. It is a great honor for the entire family."

I placed a hand on his arm. "Father, she loves him."

He closed his eyes for a moment. "I know, Nor."

"Then let's wait to announce it. It's only six more days. There can be no harm in waiting."

"Your Mother doesn't want to wait," he said quietly.

So this was her idea. Zadie had given her everything she wanted. Why was she punishing her now? Was she trying to create some kind of wedge between us? I wouldn't put it past our mother to try to separate us, maybe even believing she was doing us some kind of a favor by severing Zadie's life in Varenia completely, giving her no reason to stay, but without ever asking anyone else how they felt about it.

Sami. Maybe if I talked to him, he could convince his parents to wait. I couldn't imagine he wanted this any more than I did. He loved Zadie. The last thing he'd want to do would be to see her hurt.

I was halfway through the trapdoor when Mother poked her head around the bedroom curtain.

"Where are you going?" she asked. "Dinner is soon."

"There's something I have to do. I'll be back in a few minutes."

"You'd better be. We need the boat." The communal buildings were connected to the governor's house with wooden docks, but many houses, like ours, were separated for privacy, something hard to come by in Varenia.

"I'll swim." I tied my skirts in a knot between my legs and dropped into the water with a splash. The sun was just setting, casting an orange glow over the water. I wouldn't get to watch it go down with Zadie tonight, but this was more important.

The governor's porch was lit with hanging lanterns, making it easy to find in the gloom of twilight. I hauled myself up the ladder and wrung out my skirts and hair before knocking lightly on the door. I wouldn't normally show up at the governor's house like this, but I knew if I stopped to consider my appearance too long, I'd lose my nerve.

The door swung open, revealing Sami's bewildered face. "Nor—"

"We need to talk," I said, walking past him into the house. I'd only been inside a few times, and its size, at least compared to our house, never failed to amaze me. It should be Zadie's future home, not mine. "It's about Zadie."

He pulled on my arm. "Now isn't the time."

"And you think tonight at dinner is? Ask your father to wait until after she leaves."

"He's not just my father, Nor. He's the governor."

I broke away from him. "Then I'll ask him myself."

"Are they here already?" Sami's mother, Elidi, called from the kitchen. Theirs was the only house in the village that had multiple rooms separated by permanent walls instead of curtains. Even Sami had his own room, though what a seventeen-year-old boy needed a private room for was a mystery to me.

Elidi and Governor Kristos appeared together, and for a moment they stared at me, bewildered by my presence. Or perhaps it was my clothes. I plucked at my skirts, which clung wetly to my legs, and suddenly wished I had taken the boat. But their gazes drifted past me toward the door.

Behind me, someone else cleared his throat.

I turned to find a stranger standing in the doorway. "Oh gods," I whispered to myself. He was a young man, a few years older than me at most, and as his gaze swept over my body, I became even more painfully aware of my sodden clothing. Our eyes met for one humiliating moment before I lowered mine to the puddle slowly forming at my feet.

"Nor, what are you doing?" Elidi hurried forward and ushered me back out the front door, past the stranger. "Where is your family?"

"They're preparing for dinner. I only came to speak to Sami."

"We have a visitor."

As if I hadn't noticed. "Who is he?"

"My husband will explain everything. Go home and clean yourself up. And please, when you return, come in the boat."

I nodded and scrambled back down the ladder, wishing I'd listened to Mother for once. As I swam back to our house, I tried to puzzle out who the young man could be. Judging by his strange dress and the even stranger behavior of Sami and his family, it was clear to me that he wasn't from our village, and I knew for a fact that no man in Varenia had ever looked at me before the way he had. I'd only had a moment to take in his appearance, but I blushed at the memory of his gaze, lingering in places Sami's never had.

"Where have you been?" Zadie asked when I popped back through the trapdoor.

"Nowhere."

"You'd better change quickly. Mother's almost ready."

Mother was arranging her hair in front of her mirror, still humming to herself. Did she know about the stranger, too? Was that what this was all about? I rinsed myself quickly with fresh water and slipped into my red gown while Zadie tried to fix my hair. Hers was perfectly plaited, as usual, and her skin glowed against the soft pink of her dress. I felt garish next to her, and I wondered if Mother had planned it that way on purpose.

"Come, girls," Father said, helping us all down into the boat. I dropped gracelessly onto the bench, my arms folded across my chest. I should have set the oars adrift on the current to delay the inevitable. As it was, Father's powerful arms brought us to the governor's house far too quickly. I volunteered to tie up the boat, fretting over the knot as long as possible. Perhaps I could slip away and skip this dinner altogether...

"Hurry up, Nor," Mother called as if she could read my wicked thoughts.

I scowled and climbed the ladder. Father and Governor Kristos shook hands while Elidi showed Mother, Zadie, and me into the communal room. A large wooden table—a proper one, not fashioned out of driftwood like ours—was set with more than half a dozen dishes: fresh grapes in glistening piles; cubes of melon and sliced figs; delicate white fish sautéed in broth; bowls of olives in black, green, and purple. It was more

food than I'd seen in years, and most of it from land. The
governor must have spent a fortune on this meal.

I watched Governor Kristos slap Father affectionately on the
back while Mother and Elidi embraced. "After all these years,
we're going to be brothers, Pax," Kristos said in his deep,
booming voice, one that seemed made for giving speeches.

I felt Zadie stiffen at my side. "What's he talking about?"
she whispered.

I was caught like a fish in a net, the sides closing in on
me no matter which way I turned. But before I could answer, the stranger appeared again, and everyone around me
dropped into a bow or curtsy, as if they were all in on a secret I'd been left out of.

"Who is it?" I hissed at Zadie as I dropped into an awkward curtsy next to her.

The governor answered for her. "My dear friends, this
gentleman is our esteemed guest for the evening, an emissary
from Ilara sent by the king himself."

The young man stepped toward Zadie and bowed again,
and now I recognized the Ilarean crest embroidered on his
black doublet: the profile of a young woman inside a heart,
with two daggers crossed behind it. He took Zadie's hand
and kissed it.

"My name is Talin," he said. "And you must be Zadie."

"Yes, my lord." I could hear the faint tremor in her voice.
"And this is my sister, N—"

"Nor," he said before she could finish. He glanced at me
with eyes the color of sea glass and smirked. "I believe we've
already met."

5

I could feel Mother's gaze burning into me along with the stranger's. *What did you do?* she demanded silently. But there was no time to explain. The governor gestured for us all to sit, and I found myself seated between Sami and Zadie, directly across from Talin. A million thoughts buzzed in my head. Did the Ilareans always send an emissary after the ceremony? Was he here to make sure Zadie really was the most beautiful girl in Varenia? And who exactly was he to the king, anyway?

I stole glances of him as discreetly as I could, though I should have kept my eyes demurely downcast, like Zadie. He was tall, his skin tanned to a shade similar to mine. His brown hair was threaded through with the kind of sun-gilded streaks Mother abhorred, but I doubted even she could find fault in his strong, even features and muscular build. His eyes were a startling blue-green, and while they should have been fixed on Governor Kristos, who sat to his left, or Father, who sat to his right, or at the very least on Zadie, more than once I found them studying *me*.

Mother and Elidi sat quietly through most of the meal, letting the men do the talking between courses. The food was fresh and delicious, but I was too anxious to eat. Mother couldn't still be planning to announce my engagement now, could she?

"Do the Ilareans always send someone to approve the elders' choice?" Father asked. I leaned forward a little too eagerly, and Zadie laid a warning finger on my leg.

Talin set his fork down and turned to my father. "I don't believe so, though this is obviously my first experience with the process. I can imagine it must be very strange for all of you, to have an Ilarean in your presence for the first time."

"No stranger than it is for you, I'm sure," Mother said, her lips curved in a gracious smile. This was as close as she'd ever come to royalty, and she was thoroughly enjoying herself. "And what do you think of our dear Zadie? Have the elders chosen wisely?"

She just couldn't resist the chance to show off. Talin smiled, but it didn't quite reach his eyes. Something told me he saw right through my mother, and I liked him for it.

"She is the most beautiful Varenian girl I have ever seen," he said.

Mother beamed, until she began to process his words. He'd only seen Zadie and me. Despite the implied slight to me, I almost giggled as her smile faltered.

"Prince Ceren is a lucky man," Talin added, and I felt Sami stiffen beside me. "I cannot imagine anyone more lovely."

But as he said it, his eyes drifted from Zadie to me. I

glanced away, my scar burning as the blood rushed to my face, but the conversation resumed as though no one else had noticed.

"You eat very well," Talin said. "This food is delicious."

I cast a sharp look at Sami, willing him to stay quiet, but if he saw me, it wasn't enough to stop him. "This is a very special occasion, my lord. I assure you that we don't eat like this every day. Particularly not the average villager."

Sami's father leveled him with a gaze that accomplished what mine could not. Despite Sami's feigned bravado, I couldn't imagine him ever standing up to his father.

Talin cleared his throat to break the tension. "What is the population of Varenia?" he asked.

"Roughly five hundred," Father answered. He helped keep track of our numbers for Governor Kristos. "We were nearly six hundred at one point, but the last few generations have seen our population shrinking."

Talin's brow furrowed. "Why is that?"

Father glanced at Kristos, as did Sami. They both knew the truth: that families were having fewer children because they couldn't afford to feed them.

The governor bared his teeth in a smile that looked more like a grimace. "Our guest does not wish to hear about such things tonight. We are here to celebrate." He reached for a pitcher of wine and filled the glasses, including Zadie's and mine, then lifted his own and gestured for the rest of us to do the same. "Not only is our lovely Zadie to join you in Ilara soon, but our families have another reason to rejoice."

The raised cup in my hand tipped dangerously as I realized what was happening.

Kristos turned to Sami and me. "To Nor and Samiel. Your coming union fills my heart with gladness. Now our two families will become one, as I've always dreamed. Thalos has blessed us all." He raised his cup to his lips and drank, as did Mother, Father, Elidi, and Sami. But Zadie had turned to look at me, and I found myself paralyzed under her gaze.

Sami elbowed me gently. "Drink."

"I—"

I gasped when Zadie's eyes rolled back in her head and she listed over like a sack of grain. Everyone else moved to help her, but I remained frozen with shock until Sami reached for my hand.

I wriggled free of his grasp. "Not now," I whispered.

Father helped Zadie onto her back, where she blinked up at the ceiling, her face drained of color.

"Is she all right?" Elidi asked as she looked around helplessly. "She's not upset, is she?"

"Just breathe," Father was saying to Zadie, who was taking in air like a fish out of water. "It's going to be fine."

Elidi turned to Mother. "Isn't she happy for her sister?"

But Mother didn't answer, just waved a paper fan over Zadie's face uselessly.

The governor grabbed his son by the arm and hauled him to his feet. "What's the matter with her?"

"There's nothing the matter with her. She's just surprised," Sami said.

"Was there something going on between you two?" the governor hissed.

"Of course not," Sami and Mother shouted at the same time.

I looked over at Talin, who had risen to his feet and stood silently watching us, momentarily forgotten by the others. When his eyes met mine, he lifted an eyebrow as if to say, *And what do you make of all this?*

I wondered how much he had overheard of my conversation with Sami. To me, his expression seemed to say, *Everything.*

"I'm fine," Zadie said, forcing herself to sit. "I took too much sun today and haven't had enough to drink. Can someone please bring me some water?"

Elidi rushed to the kitchen for a cup of water, sloshing it as she hurried back to Zadie. "There you are. It was awfully hot today, wasn't it, Calliope?"

My mother murmured something under her breath and moved everyone out of the way so she could help Zadie to her feet. "You're fine, aren't you, Zadie?"

She nodded, but her eyes remained downcast. I could tell from her clenched jaw that she was fighting back tears and failing.

As everyone returned to the table, Talin lifted his cup again.

"To Nor and Samiel," he said.

I drank this time, wincing as the liquid hit my tongue. It was much stronger than the watered-down wine from the celebration after the ceremony. Talin watched me over the rim of his cup, his eyes glittering with amusement. Next to me, Zadie lifted her cup to her lips and lowered it without sipping, without blinking or smiling. I wanted to tell her it wasn't my fault, or Sami's, that neither of us wanted this, but I couldn't here.

Finally, when all of the plates had been picked clean, the adults excused themselves to speak out on the balcony.

Talin lingered. He wasn't a man in the same way Father and Governor Kristos were, but he wasn't a boy like Sami, either. I was about to take Zadie aside to talk when he stepped in front of me. I swallowed and glanced up, taking in the damp curls at his neck and temples. He must have been roasting underneath all that heavy fabric. It served him right for smirking at me.

"Congratulations on your engagement," he said in a low voice. His accent didn't have the sharp edge to it that the Ilarean men we met in the floating market had.

Thanking him felt too much like I was a willing participant in the betrothal, so I bowed my head instead. He stood so close to me that the hem of my gown nearly brushed his black boots. Contrasted with such a dark color, the red suddenly didn't seem quite so gaudy.

"How are you enjoying your stay in Varenia?" I asked, my voice sounding small and childish to my ears. How unsophisticated must I seem to someone like Talin?

"I haven't been here long," he said. "Just a few hours. But the warmth and vibrancy of this place are like the break in a storm."

I glanced back up, startled by his choice of words.

He must have read the confusion in my face, because he opened his mouth to speak again before I had a chance to respond.

"Talin, please join us," Elidi called to him from the doorway.

He closed his mouth and bowed to me. "Please excuse me, my lady."

Talin followed Elidi to the door, but paused on the threshold, glancing back at me and smiling softly. I turned away, blushing.

Zadie looked so small and alone at the table. Ashamed for talking to Talin when I should be with my sister, I rushed to her side, but she refused to acknowledge me.

"Sister, please, look at me."

"You knew about this, and you didn't tell me," she said in a brittle voice.

"We just found out, and we were still hoping to talk them out of it. We had no idea they were planning on announcing it tonight."

She arched an eyebrow. "We? You're a 'we' now?"

I shot a look at Sami, who stood silently on Zadie's other side. He tried to take her hand, but she pulled it back into her lap without looking at him.

"This wasn't our choice, Zadie," Sami said. "You know I'd marry you if I could. But you're leaving."

"You say that as if I want to," she said, finally looking him in the eye. "Tell your father that you love me, that you want to marry me. He doesn't have to send me to Ilara. He can send Alys. Or Nor."

I flinched at her tone. "It wasn't the governor's choice. Besides, the emissary has seen you now. The elders can't just say they've changed their minds."

The tears finally spilled over her lashes and onto her cheeks. "Why not?"

"You're the most beautiful girl Varenia has ever known," Sami said. "They couldn't have chosen anyone else."

"And yet you don't want me."

He ran a finger up Zadie's cheek, catching her tears. I looked away, not wanting to bear witness to such an intimate gesture. "I've never wanted anything more than I want to marry you. We are all caught in the gods' plans, like fish in the current."

She clutched at his tunic. "Then swim against it. Change the plan. Don't let them take me from you."

He gathered her into him and rested his chin on the top of her head, and she sobbed against him, sadder than I'd ever seen her.

Anger and despair rose in me. This couldn't be the gods' plan for us. It all felt so wrong.

I went to the door at the back of the house and stepped onto the walkway, where I was immediately hit by a gust of hot wind. The red fabric of my dress whipped around my body, and my braids thrashed against my face. I placed my hands on the balustrade that had once belonged to Ilara's ship and leaned into the wind, calling out my prayer to Thalos. But if he heard me, he had nothing to say in return.

Later, after we'd said our goodbyes to the governor and his family and returned home, Zadie lowered herself onto our bed and rolled away from me before I could say a word. I'd seen her take Sami's hand earlier, when the grownups weren't looking. She'd forgiven him, and yet she had not forgiven me. With only five days left together, I wondered how many I would lose to her anger. My hand hovered over her shoulder, but she only pressed farther away from me, so I retreated to my side of the bed, feeling my own anger kindle in the dark.

None of this had been my choice. She had to see that. She knew I didn't love Sami, that I would have gone in her place if I could. Perhaps she just needed someone to blame—but I wished it didn't have to be me.

I slept fitfully that night, at times too hot and at others too cold, kicking off my blanket and then reaching for it again. When I woke in the morning, stiff and exhausted, Zadie's side of the bed was empty. I went to the balcony, expecting to find my twin, but she wasn't there, either.

The sea was calm today, a dark gray-blue that faded into the horizon, where the lazy sun slowly crept its way out of the water. I had always loved watching the sun rise and set, the raw beauty of nature. But now my stomach turned in a way that was becoming all too familiar. The thought of a hundred more years of this same view was maddening.

I was about to rise and go back inside when I heard a noise from below the house. I crept to the edge of the balcony and peered over.

Sami and Zadie were in our boat, whispering.

I had opened my mouth to call out, Zadie's name on the tip of my tongue, when Sami leaned forward. The next thing I knew, they were kissing.

For a moment, I just stared at the two of them. I'd seen people kiss before—mostly my parents, sometimes other young people at a festival or in a boat when they thought no one was looking. But this was my twin sister and Sami. And it wasn't just a short kiss. They were *still* kissing.

I pulled myself back onto the balcony and pretended to

watch the rest of the sunrise. If Zadie and Sami wanted to kiss, what difference did it make to me? I didn't love Sami that way. I didn't want to kiss him.

Then again, did I really want my sister kissing my future husband? I scowled and picked at a splinter in the wood. Mother would be horrified if she knew. Not that I would ever tell, but the fact remained. As much as I didn't want my sister to leave Varenia, a small part of me was grateful there were only a few days left until her departure. I couldn't go on like this.

Zadie must have come back up through the door, because a few minutes later, I heard her pad across the balcony behind me. A blanket settled over my shoulders as she dropped down next to me, resting her head in the crook of my neck, where she'd always fit perfectly. She smelled like wood smoke and sea salt and something distinctly Zadie. As our long legs dangled over the edge together, casting shadows on the water, I pushed away the thought that Sami might compare our scents one day, too.

Mother and Father were asleep and would remain that way for a while longer, judging by how much wine they'd had last night. My own head still felt fuzzy from the tiny bit I'd choked down.

"Nor."

"Mmm?"

Zadie lifted her head from my neck, and the sudden absence of heat felt like a greater loss than it should. "I'm sorry about last night."

"There's nothing for you to be sorry for."

"But there is. I was only thinking of myself, when you

didn't ask for this any more than I did. And if Sami has to marry someone else, I'm glad it's you."

I exhaled in relief. "Zadie."

"Yes?"

"I'm sorry, too."

"I know."

We reached for each other's hand at the same time, and I felt a warm tear slip out from my closed eyelids. How would I face all those sunrises and sunsets without her here? A part of me wished we could just take the boat and head north, toward Galeth. We could start a new life together there, where no one knew us, where our futures would be entirely our own. But I knew my sister would never run away from her duty, and I couldn't ask that of her.

Later that day, when we saw Sami, I had a hard time looking at him. I'd always loved him, in the way I imagined I would have loved a brother if we'd ever had one. Mother and Father never mentioned it, but I suspected she was never able to have more children after us. It was just as well. I couldn't imagine what she would have been like if she'd had more daughters.

As I watched Sami's gaze repeatedly slip to Zadie, the corners of his lips twitching in a grin, I thought about their kiss and what it meant. I had seen boys look at Zadie that way before, and I often wondered what it must feel like to be the object of such attention.

Until last night. Now I recognized the look on Talin's face—not a smirk, as I'd thought, but something more akin to admiration—and I had no idea what to make of it.

I imagined my appearance the first time he saw me, the way my wet tunic and skirts would have clung to the curves of my body. I wasn't a child anymore, and I should have known better than to go to the governor's house like that. Had my lack of modesty given him ideas? I flushed so hard at the thought that Zadie asked me if I was feeling unwell.

Maybe that was why he hadn't stared at my scar; he'd been too distracted by the rest of me. But he hadn't stared at it later, either, when I was appropriately clothed. His eyes hadn't snagged on it once, at least not that I'd seen. Perhaps scars were simply not as reviled in Ilara as they were in Varenia. Still, with Zadie in the room, I couldn't understand why his attention had continually strayed to me.

Could it be that, despite everything, Mother's training had rubbed off on me? She had always taught us both to be feminine, to sweep our gazes down and to the side when someone praised us, a faint smile on our lips, to keep our clothing tailored and flattering, though never too tight.

Just because you weren't born princesses, doesn't mean you can't act like them, she liked to say. *Behave like royalty, and that is how you will be treated.*

For all her faults, I had to give Mother credit. We *had* always been treated well by the other villagers, and of course by the governor's family. That came partly from Father's friendship with Kristos, starting when they were children themselves, but it was more than that. Mother presented us to the world as something as rare and beautiful as seaflowers, and that was what they saw.

I looked back at Sami and Zadie. He grinned like a fool as he watched her prepare our supper, his eyes following her every move. I'd seen Father risk his life searching shipwrecks for trinkets for Mother, just to watch her primp and preen in front of her mirror.

I wanted to believe that my value went beyond my beauty. I helped to feed our family; I cooked and repaired fishing nets; I made smart trades at the market. But it was Zadie who would bring in the bride price that would feed and clothe our family for years, all thanks to her beauty.

Beauty is power, Mother had told us time and time again, until the words rang as true as *the sky is blue* and *water is wet.* I didn't *want* to believe that a woman's worth was entirely de-fined by her appearance. But there was a small, nagging voice in my head that asked, *What if Mother is right?*

6

I didn't have time to think about Talin—who had disappeared as quietly as he'd arrived—in the days that followed. I had to do extra chores so Zadie could sit for an artist. He was painting her portrait, which would be sent to Ilara ahead of her. I imagined it hanging next to the portraits of all the other Varenian girls who had been chosen. Had they wanted to go, or had they also had reasons to stay?

In the evenings, Zadie went through the few items in the trunk Father had built for her. The castle was at the foot of a mountain range where the weather was much colder, but Mother had insisted she take our finest clothing (including both Zadie's pink dress and my red one), in addition to her tortoiseshell comb and a strand of white pearls Father had given Mother when they married. The trunk also contained the traveling cloak Sami had promised her, which he'd presented yesterday. It was made of plush green velvet, unadorned except for the brass button clasp at the neck.

"I've never felt anything so soft," I said, stroking it gently.

"Perhaps the back of a stingray."

"Yes, but that wouldn't make nearly as nice of a cloak."

Zadie's smile was strained. "No, I suppose not."

"What is it?" I asked. "I mean, I know what it is, but is there something in particular that's bothering you? Something I could possibly help with?"

She sighed. "I know it's foolish, but I keep thinking some kind of miracle will happen, that we'll come up with a way to change all of this. It's impossible, I know that. But I can't help dreaming of it."

"The only way they'd let you stay would be if you stopped being beautiful all of a sudden, and we both know that's never going to happen." If anything, Zadie had become even more beautiful these past few days.

Sorrow is good for the soul, Father had said after the incident, when I had recovered from the pain and sickness but had still not grown used to the feel of the torn flesh on my otherwise flawless skin. *Those who have never known pain or adversity are as shallow as the waves lapping on the shore.*

And what is wrong with being shallow? I'd asked him.

What lies beneath the surface of shallow waters? Nothing. It's only when you go deeper that the ocean comes alive. The deeper you go, the more mysteries and surprises await.

I had frowned and nestled closer to him, unconvinced. I'd never seen shallow waters, but I did know one thing about them: you could walk through them to the shore. And there could be no greater mystery or surprise than land. At least not to me.

Zadie folded the cloak and returned it to the trunk. "I just can't help feeling that the gods switched our fates somehow. That I was the one destined to stay…"

"And I was destined to go," I finished. I released my breath through my nose. "Well, we *are* identical twins. Even Father used to confuse us when we were babies. Maybe I'm really Zadie, and you're really Nor," I said with a laugh.

Before the incident, people often confused us, calling me Zadie so frequently that even now, I still responded to her name as readily as my own. There were times when I felt so close to my sister that I truly believed I was one half of a person, and she was the other. I couldn't live without her any more than a person could live with half a heart.

Zadie smiled, but when we lay down to sleep that night, she again presented her back to me, the way she had before. One of the greatest comforts in my life had been knowing that even if I couldn't make sense of my mother's actions, or predict what the future might hold, I at least knew Zadie's mind, maybe better than my own. She was predictable, reliable, honest, and good. She was responsible and even-tempered. She never surprised you by doing the unexpected. She was as straight as the horizon and as dependable as the sunrise. We had known this day was coming for as long as I could remember, and I'd always assumed Zadie had been preparing for it, just like I had.

I woke some time in the middle of the night to find Zadie missing. My concern only lasted a moment, until it occurred to me that she was probably off kissing Sami again. I told myself I wasn't jealous, but what if I was terrible at kissing? How did Zadie even know what she was doing?

For the past seventeen years, she had been as close to me as my own flesh. Now I was starting to wonder if I'd ever really known her at all.

She was beside me again when I woke in the morning. I looked down at her heart-shaped face, slack with sleep, and wondered if Sami would still have loved her if she'd been the one with the scar. I'd seen the way my mother's love for me changed after the incident. Even my father, whose love I'd never questioned, didn't treat me the same. He couldn't look at me without a touch of sadness or regret, as if he was seeing two versions of me: the one I'd been before the incident, and the one I was now.

I didn't mention Zadie's absence when she woke up, and neither did she. Father had left early with some of the other men to fish, and Mother was still asleep.

"What should we do?" Zadie asked as we readied ourselves for the day.

"I suppose we should look for oysters."

"We'll be leaving Mother without a boat. She would have to borrow a neighbor's. Or swim."

I grinned. "Even better."

We stayed out all morning, and for those fleeting hours, things felt the way they had been before the ceremony. We raced each other to the few oysters we saw, and I let Zadie beat me one time, like I often did. We even found an octopus hiding in the rocks and pried it free. At least there would be something other than stew for dinner.

When we returned to the house, Mother was home, as

we'd known she would be. She was lying on her bed, fanning herself, but she sat upright when we came up through the trapdoor.

"Where have you two been?" she moaned. "I've been stuck here all morning with no boat."

"We just wanted to spend some time together," Zadie said. "We only have two days left."

She frowned. "I know that. I thought perhaps the *three* of us could spend some time together for a change." She pulled us down onto the mattress next to her, tucking each one of us under an arm. "I can't believe in just a few short weeks, it will just be your father and me alone in this house."

I squirmed out from under her arm. "What do you mean?"

"The wedding. Elidi and I think we should do it on the night of the solstice. It's an auspicious time for beginning a new life together, and a family."

Zadie and I shared a horrified glance. A *family*? I wasn't even eighteen yet. I wasn't ready to marry, and I certainly wasn't ready to be a mother. "I don't understand the rush," I said. "Zadie will have just left. Can't we wait a bit?"

"We are lucky that Sami has agreed to marry you at all, Nor. I do not think it's wise to wait. Besides, with your sister gone, we will have one less person in the family working. Once you marry Sami, we will be provided for, you most of all. Don't you want your family to be secure?"

So this was about money, not me. I couldn't deny that we were struggling, but so was every other family in Varenia. At least we weren't eight or ten mouths to feed, like some. Our parents may not have been fortunate enough to have sons, who would have provided better over the years than Zadie and I could, but Mother had certainly managed to make the most of her daughters.

"Yes, Mother," I said. "I want my family to be secure."

"Good. We will make the official announcement of your engagement at Zadie's party in two nights. Then everyone in Varenia will know just how blessed our family is."

I woke that night to the sound of Zadie crying.

"What's wrong?" I asked, sitting upright and reaching for my sister. My fingers found only empty space where her body should be. "Where are you?"

"I'm here," she said. As my eyes adjusted to the dark, I saw her crouched at the foot of the bed. Tears glistened on her cheeks.

"What's the matter? Did something happen? Are you hurt?"

"No. I need—I need your help."

"Of course," I told her, but she remained where she was, twisting her hair over one shoulder. "Surely it can wait until morning."

Zadie rose without speaking and left our bedroom. Confused and still half-asleep, I followed her to the balcony.

"What is it?" I whispered. "What's wrong?"

"You'll hate me if I tell you. But that won't stop me. I can't go to Ilara. And I need your help."

She jumped off the balcony before I could stop her, and I dived in after her, terrified she was going to drown herself. Instead, she swam away from the house. I wanted to scream for her to stop, but I was afraid I'd wake half the village in the process, so I followed her.

When we'd been swimming for what felt like ages, we

reached our boat, anchored far from our house. "What are you doing?" I said between gasps for air. I hadn't known Zadie could swim that fast. I started to reach for the boat to haul myself in when Zadie thrust her hand out.

"Don't get too close, Nor."

"What? Why?" I followed her gaze to a rope going over the side of the boat. "What is that?"

She bit her lip. "I caught it, last night."

So she hadn't been with Sami after all. "Caught what?"

"A maiden's hair jelly."

I gasped and swam a few feet farther from the boat. "Zadie, no! Do you have any idea how dangerous that is? Did it sting you?"

"I used a large net. I haven't touched it. I haven't even looked at it since I caught it. I kept it out here all day, weighted down with an anchor. It's dead, for all I know."

I ducked down under the water, sure she was mistaken. Zadie couldn't catch a maiden's hair. She wouldn't even know how. But sure enough, the jelly was there, glowing faintly in the net.

I came back up and pushed my hair away from my face. "And just what exactly are you planning to do with it?"

"I'm going to scar myself with it. On my legs. Like Dido."

Dido was a girl we'd known since childhood. She'd been scarred horribly when she was only eight, when a dead maiden's hair had floated into the village. Varenians healed remarkably well, but her legs still bore the scars. She was one of the only girls our age who hadn't participated in the ceremony, the girl our mother held up as an example anytime we did something she considered risky or dangerous.

You wouldn't want to end up like poor Dido, would you?

"Why?" I breathed.

"If the only way to stay in Varenia is to stop being beautiful, then that's what I'll do."

I closed my eyes, remembering what I'd said to her the previous day, and inwardly cursed my own foolishness. "Is this all because of that stupid comment I made? This might get you out of leaving Varenia, but Sami would never be permitted to marry you. And you could die!" A sting from a maiden's hair jellyfish was rarely fatal, mostly because they were avoidable, and anytime someone was stung, they got away from it as quickly as possible. Dido had been small and a poor swimmer, and the jelly she'd encountered had been enormous, making it difficult to get away.

This jelly was smaller than the one we'd seen the other day, and juveniles were known to be less venomous than adults. But to expose yourself to a sting deliberately? Who knew what the consequences could be?

"If you can think of another way for me to stay in Varenia, I will happily listen to it. But if you can't, I don't want to hear anything other than whether or not you'll help me," Zadie said.

This isn't you! I wanted to scream. She sounded cold and unfeeling, like Mother. "I would do anything for you, Zadie. You know that. But I won't help you harm yourself." I started to swim away, but her hand gripped my arm fiercely.

She pulled me to her, until our foreheads were so close they nearly touched. After a moment, her face crumpled and she began to weep. "Please, Nor. I'm scared."

I stared at her for a few seconds, trying to imagine wanting something so badly I was willing to injure myself permanently for it. Zadie hadn't known pain like I had; she couldn't possibly understand what she was asking.

But she had seen me suffer. She knew what I'd been through. And just watching it had to have been excruciating for her, as I knew watching her suffer would be for me. If she was asking me to do this, she had to be desperate beyond measure.

My eyes burned with tears as I began to understand that Zadie was *already* in pain. Leaving Sami might not cause her physical injury, but I felt like I was being stabbed in the heart every time I imagined Zadie leaving Varenia. She would be feeling that about both me *and* Sami. I looked down at her hand gripping mine, at the unblemished skin of her arm. She had made it all these years without so much as a splinter, and she wanted me to help her undo all that in one instant?

"I can't!" I cried, the tears springing free of my eyes. "I won't do that to you, Zadie. I'm sorry."

I was already several lengths from her when she shouted after me.

"Then I'll do it myself!"

I turned to see her pull a knife from the boat and dive under the water.

"Zadie, no!" I plowed through the water toward her, reaching her just in time. I pulled on her shoulder, whirling her toward me, and for a moment we hung there in stillness, her face a mirror of the anguish I felt.

"Please, Nor," she cried the moment we surfaced. "If you won't do it for me, at least stay with me. I can't do it alone."

I hated myself for nodding. But I knew I would hate myself

more if I left and she seriously injured herself trying to do this by herself. "How were you planning to do it?" I asked shakily.

Some of the worry drained from her face, but I felt like I had absorbed all of it. "I'll cut off one of the tentacles and lay it on my legs. It will need to stay on my skin for a little while to ensure permanent scarring."

I stared at her in horror. "How do you know this?"

She started for the other side of the boat, away from the jellyfish. "Mother told me once. She said if a jellyfish ever stung me, the most important thing to do would be to remove the tentacles right away, and to use something flat and rigid to brush out the stingers. Otherwise I'd have permanent scars. It's a small maiden's hair. I don't think it has enough venom to kill me."

"You don't *think*?" I yelped.

"I'm sure it doesn't."

That was hardly reassuring. "And what will we tell Mother and Father? What will we tell the rest of the village?"

"That we went for a night swim and didn't see it. No one would believe I did this to myself."

She was right. I could scarcely believe it, and I was here with her. "What if Sami won't have you?"

"He loves me, Nor. I know that won't change."

I knew very well how love could be changed by a scar, but I didn't have the heart to tell her that. "His father is the governor. He might not allow it."

Zadie shook her head. "If Sami wants me, his parents will listen. And if not, we'll run away together."

I blinked in shock. I had wanted to run away with Zadie,

but I never believed it was something she would actually do. "Did you discuss this with him?"

"No, but I just know it. We kissed, Nor. And it was like a promise. That he loves me as much as I love him. That he would do anything for me. I can't tell you what that feels like, to know someone would do anything for you."

I inhaled sharply, her words a barbed hook in my heart. Hadn't she always known that I would do anything for her? "And yet you ask this of me? Why not ask *Sami*, if he loves you so much?"

She pulled me to her. "Because *you* are the twin of my soul. You know me better than anyone ever has or ever will. Because I trust you more than I trust Sami. And because you are the strongest person I have ever known. Only you can help me."

"It's not fair of you to ask me," I said, my voice breaking on a sob.

"You will protect me," she said through her own tears. "You always have, and you won't stop now."

I had to bite my lip to keep from crying out. A part of me was furious with my sister for even asking, for putting me in this position. I wanted to tell her no, to go back to my bed and sleep through the next two days, until all of this was over.

But she was right. There was nothing she could ask of me that I wouldn't do for her. And if this was truly what she wanted, then I couldn't let her face it alone.

"I will help you get the tentacle," I said finally. "But I am only doing this because I'm afraid you'll hurt yourself trying, not because I agree with it."

"I understand." She reached into the boat and handed me

Father's sharpest spear and a small net used to catch little fish. "Be careful."

I took the spear and net and ducked under the water. The jelly was mostly contained within the larger net Zadie had caught it in, but several tentacles had wriggled through the holes. As my tears mingled with the saltwater around me, I fought to still my shaking hands, and it took several attempts before I was able to lop off four or five of the thin tentacles. I reached out with the little net and caught them, still unsure if I was doing the right thing, then rose carefully to the surface, keeping the net at arm's length.

Zadie was holding a small piece of driftwood. "I thought it would be best to do this out here, so no one would hear me scream, but just in case, I'll bite into the wood. We should get into the boat now, in case I faint."

She had planned all of this, I realized. Maybe since the day we saw the dead jelly. "And then what?"

"And then we'll see."

I dropped the net and tentacles into the boat and hauled myself in after, landing in a heap next to Zadie.

We were both wearing only our tunics, and the seawater on Zadie's long legs glistened in the moonlight. She was still whole and perfect. It wasn't too late to go home and pretend all of this had never happened.

"Please stop this, Zadie," I begged. "What if we talked to Governor Kristos together? Perhaps he would agree to let me go in your place."

She shook her head. "Even if he allowed it, Mother never would. She is determined that this should be my fate."

And she doesn't believe I'm beautiful enough, I thought. She would never risk the elders choosing Alys to go in Zadie's place.

She sat down at one end of the boat and placed the driftwood between her teeth. "I'm ready," she said around the wood.

I picked up the small net, where the tentacles barely glowed at all. What time was it? How many hours did we have before our parents woke up and discovered what we'd done? What would Mother say when she found out? I knew everything was about to change forever, but I handed Zadie the net anyway. I thought of Dido's wounds, which I'd only seen once, when we went to visit her shortly after the accident. The flesh where the tentacles had touched her was raised and pink, as though a mass of worms was crawling over her leg.

I imagined Zadie with scars like that and began to cry, closing my eyes tight as she lowered the net toward her legs, bracing myself for her screams.

"I can't."

My eyes flew open, relief coursing through me. "Thank the gods."

She removed the wood from her mouth. "You have to do it, Nor."

"*What?*" I shook my head violently. "No. I said I would stay with you, but I can't be the one to do it."

Zadie set the net aside and dropped into the floor of the boat to kneel before me. "Please," she begged. "If I have to go to Ilara, I'll die of a broken heart. And you'll die, too, if you have to stay here without me. Maybe not for a long time, but this life will slowly kill you, too. I *know* you, Nor. You'll never be happy here."

"Don't do that," I said through my sobs. "Don't make it about what I want. I don't want any of this!"

She reached for the net again and thrust it toward me so forecefully that I flinched. "If you really love me, you'll help me."

I had never seen Zadie like this, her eyes so wide I could see the whites all around. She was wild with desperation, barely recognizable as my beloved sister. "Don't say that. Please."

She was frozen there, quivering with fear and anger and need. An honor, everyone called it. To be the chosen girl, to be beautiful, to marry advantageously. But this wasn't what honor was supposed to look like: a frightened girl on her knees, begging to be spared.

"I can't believe this is what you really want, Zadie. I can't."

"It is, Nor. More than anything else in the world."

It took all of my strength to take the handle of the net from her, but I felt her relief as if it were my own. She'd looked so taut I thought she might snap like a fishing line.

"I love you," I told her.

"You have been everything for me," she said, her voice thick with emotion. "My arms when I wasn't permitted to row, my legs when I wasn't permitted to dive. My lips when I couldn't defend myself from Mother. Now I need you to be my hands, Nor."

I bit my lip to stifle my cries. But if Zadie could not do this on her own, I would be the steady hand that she lacked.

I lowered the net until the first tentacle was hovering just above the bare skin of her thigh and hesitated once more. "Zadie, I…"

Before I could stop her, she reached out, took my hand,

and forced it down. Horrified, I wrenched myself out of her grasp and dropped the net, but the tentacles that had made contact were already adhering to her skin. Zadie winced as the tiny stingers grabbed hold of her leg, pulling themselves toward her.

Biting my lip was no longer enough. I bit my own hand to keep from screaming. The translucent blue lines clung to Zadie's leg, even as she began to tremble, even as she started to squirm away from the pain. Her skin reddened, then blistered. I watched in horror as the tentacles appeared to melt into her flesh.

"Get them off!" she wailed finally. "Please!"

"How?" I shrieked. I used my hands to scoop up seawater and tried to rinse away the tentacles, but the few that came off took strips of my sister's skin with them. In my frantic attempts to help her, a tentacle brushed against my arm. The pain was so excruciating I finally allowed myself to scream, knowing Zadie's suffering was a thousand times worse.

Desperate, I pulled her up beneath her arms and dropped her over the side of the boat, holding her afloat with one hand while I used the side of Father's spear to scrape off the remaining tentacles and as little of her flesh as possible.

By the time we were finished, Zadie was unconscious, and the water around us was dark with blood.

7

After I'd hauled her back into the boat, we lay there for a while as I tried to steady my breathing. I couldn't afford to pass out, not when Zadie's eyes remained closed, when she was so pale and motionless beside me. I needed to get us home as quickly as possible, but first I cut the rest of the jellyfish free of its net and slashed it to pieces with the spear.

Though the wound on my arm burned with every stroke of the oars, it was already healing. I could hardly bear to look at Zadie's leg as I rowed. Her right thigh had borne the brunt of the wounds, though a few stray pieces of tentacle had brushed against her left thigh and lower abdomen. Her face was pale in the moonlight, but the wounds were a harsh red even in the dark. The venom had entered her bloodstream almost immediately, and she was hot with fever. If I didn't get help soon, I was afraid she really could die.

But with Zadie unconscious, it was up to me to get our

parents, to explain what had happened, to help care for her. And I was afraid. Afraid that they would blame me, that Zadie's plan wouldn't work and they'd still send her, or send Alys instead, and then Mother would blame me for that, too. I was afraid for my sister, afraid that Sami wouldn't be able to look past these wounds. And worst of all, I was afraid of myself. Because I hadn't just allowed something like this to happen to the person I loved most in the world. I had helped, even if Zadie had forced my hand in the end.

I rowed harder as our house came into view, then quickly tied the boat to a pillar. I wiped the tears from my cheeks and scrambled up the ladder. "Mother! Father!" I yelled into the dark. "Help!"

I could hear them stirring on the other side of their curtain, but not fast enough. Father sat up as I threw the fabric aside. "What is it, child?" He used the word *child* when he couldn't tell which one of us was speaking.

"It's Zadie," I managed around the lump in my throat. I had never cried so much in my life, not even when I'd cut myself on the blood coral. "She's been stung by a maiden's hair."

Mother, who had been grumbling in her sleep, sat bolt upright. "What?" she cried, her voice shrill with fear.

My hands shook as I bent to help her up. "We were swimming, and we didn't see it until it was too late." The words were a lie, but the sorrow and terror were all too real. "She's unconscious in the boat. I didn't have the strength to bring her up."

"Thalos, no!" Mother screamed. My parents flew past me. I heard Father splash into the water, then Mother's shriek as she looked down through the door.

"My baby!" she cried. "What has happened to my beautiful baby?"

I was hit with a sudden memory of the day of the incident, when I was the one limp in the boat. *What has happened to my beautiful baby?* Mother had said the same thing about me. My knees were suddenly weak and watery, and I slumped onto the floor of our house, unnoticed.

Lanterns began to glow in other people's houses at the sound of my mother's screams. Father was shouting for help.

"Get Elder Nemea," he commanded, gently handing Zadie up to Mother through the door.

It took a moment to realize he was speaking to me. I forced myself to my feet, grateful for the chance to leave. I couldn't bear to look at my sister's legs, at the horrific results of what we had done.

Once I was back in the boat, some of my strength returned, and I rowed harder than I'd ever rowed before. I had to force myself to stop at Elder Nemea's house instead of continuing out of Varenia and away from Mother's screams.

The old woman was already coming out of her house when I arrived. "What is it, girl?"

"It's my sister," I called between breaths. "She's been stung by a maiden's hair. She's unconscious."

"Zadie? No, this can't be!" She disappeared back into the house and emerged a moment later with a heavy satchel. The village doctor would have been preferable, but he had died last year in a shark attack before he could fully train his apprentice daughter.

I took the satchel and helped her into the boat, then rowed home as quickly as I could. By then several people had gathered in boats around our house. Nemea and I hurried to the bedroom I shared with Zadie, following the sound of Mother's sobs.

"Move aside," Nemea said to my parents as she stepped past them, already removing salves and strips of cloth from the bag. Zadie lay on the bed, still unconscious, her brow beaded with sweat.

"How could you let this happen?" Mother screamed the moment she saw me. "How could you be so foolish as to take your sister night swimming at a time like this?"

I could have said it was Zadie's idea, that I hadn't wanted to go. I could have told Mother the truth, and part of me wanted to. But as my eyes fell on my sister's leg, on the missing flesh and pooling blood, I knew I could never betray her.

"I'm sorry, Mother," I told her tearfully. "We just didn't see it. I think it must have already been dead."

"Did you scrape away the stingers?" Nemea asked me.

"Yes, I think so. I tried my best."

"Good." She opened up a small whale-bone jar full of an iridescent pink ointment and began to slather it onto Zadie's leg. "The pearls will help heal her, but I'm afraid the wounds are too deep to ever disappear completely."

Mother sobbed harder at Nemea's words.

"But she'll live?" Father asked.

"She'll live, if we can get the fever down." Nemea asked me to wet some cloth with fresh water for Zadie's head and had me drip some into her bloody mouth, torn from the splinters when she'd bit down on the wood. The elder watched as I dabbed the blood away, but she didn't ask questions. Mother held Zadie's hands in a death grip, rocking back and forth on her knees and muttering prayers to Thalos and every other god she could name. Father paced while Nemea bound Zadie's leg in the cloth bandages.

I could see people through our window, crowding onto our balcony. "Look, Father," I said. Our house couldn't support the weight of so many. He went outside and told them to go, that there'd been an accident and they would hear more in the morning.

When I heard Governor Kristos outside, telling people politely but firmly to leave, I felt a wave of relief. He came into the house with Elidi and Sami and hurried to Zadie's side. With everyone crowded around her, Zadie was blocked from view, and Sami's eyes fell on me first.

"Nor, what happened?" he asked, crouching down next to me.

"We were swimming. She was stung by a dead maiden's hair. I got her home as quickly as I could."

He pulled me into his arms, and I let myself be comforted for a moment. Sami would take care of Zadie, no matter what happened.

Mother was weeping in the corner, with Sami's mother murmuring quiet words while Governor Kristos talked to Father. Elder Nemea had finished bandaging Zadie's wounds and was pouring water into a pot. I watched her put a handful of herbs and several globs of the pink ointment in and stir.

I rose with Sami's help and went to light the fire in our clay stove. "What are you doing?" I asked Nemea.

"The cream will help her injuries, but the broth will help with the fever."

When the mixture was steaming, she asked for a bowl and

ladled some of the broth into it. Father tried to prop Zadie up a bit so she could drink, but she was as limp as a sea cucumber. I thought I saw her eyelashes flutter, and she managed to swallow some of the broth, but she didn't wake up. It was probably better if she slept—the pain had to be terrible.

Nemea called my parents over. "This girl needs rest. She can't go to Ilara in this condition, assuming the prince will still have her at all. I will call an emergency session with the elders tomorrow and we will discuss what is to be done."

"She'll be fine," Mother said, straightening her spine. "She was born to be a princess, and she will go to Ilara in two days as planned. You chose her. You can't take that away."

The elder's gray eyes narrowed. "As I said, we will discuss it in the morning. For now, everyone should get some rest. When the girl regains consciousness, she will be in a great deal of pain. Continue to give her small amounts of the broth. If the pain is unbearable, she may drink some wine, but only a little."

"She'll be fine," Mother said again, but Elder Nemea didn't respond.

"Take me home," she said to Sami, who didn't balk at taking orders from an old woman half his size.

"I'll be back in the morning," he called up to me as he descended through the door. "Take care of her."

I nodded, wrapping my arms around myself. I was still wearing only my wet nightgown, but I knew that the cold seeping into me wouldn't go away, even after I was dry. "I will."

We were all awake by the time the sun rose, as red and angry-looking as Zadie's wounds. She hadn't spoken yet—she just sobbed as Mother rocked her and brushed her hair away from her face. Her fever hadn't broken, but the fact that she was conscious was a good sign. I was able to get her to take small sips of broth, but she wouldn't meet my eyes. Father continued to pace around the house.

"They can't change their decision now," he said. "Surely the king will understand a few scars on her leg."

I bit my tongue, though the scar on my cheek tingled when he spoke. It seemed so insignificant now, compared to Zadie's wounds. But I understood Zadie's logic—she'd needed to do something drastic to her appearance without altering her physical capabilities. A scarred woman could still provide for her family.

"Don't be foolish, Pax," Mother chided. "A few scars? The girl is *ruined*."

"Calliope," Father hissed. "Enough."

She turned away from him to me. "How could you let this happen?" she asked for the hundredth time. "Two days before she was supposed to leave? She's spent her entire life protecting her beauty, and one stupid decision has cost us everything."

I was too tired to hold my tongue any longer. "Not everything. I am still going to be the governor's daughter-in-law."

I'd expected her anger, but the slap caught me off guard.

My hand flew to my cheek. Mother had never hit us, which I always suspected had more to do with her fear of maiming us than out of love. Her eyes widened for a moment, as if she had shocked even herself, but she didn't back down.

"This is all your doing, isn't it?" she accused. "You've always been jealous of your sister. You've never been content to live here. You've always thought you were better than the rest of us, that Varenia was too small for you. But you are just one more insignificant, dull little fish floating in our waters. Do you really think they'll choose you over Alys?"

Father came to stand over us. "I said, *enough.*"

I had feared some people might suspect I did this to Zadie on purpose, but my own mother? Did she really believe me capable of such a thing? "I love Zadie more than life itself," I said, trying to mask my hurt from her and failing miserably. "I would never harm her so I could take her place! You must know that."

She turned away from me. "I don't know you at all."

Father took my hand and led me out to the balcony. "Tell me the truth, Nor," he said when he was sure the waves were loud enough to muffle his words, even for Mother's sharp hearing. "Was it an accident, or did Zadie do this to herself so she could stay and marry Sami? I know she loves him, and I've seen the way he looks at her. Did she ask you to help her?"

My stomach dropped like an anchor. Was it so obvious? "It was an accident."

Father's eyes were a darker brown than mine, almost black. His hair caught in the wind, revealing the slight receding hairline that made him look distinguished, wise. "The truth, Nor."

"It was an accident," I repeated slowly. Inside, the truth kicked and screamed at my throat, demanding to be released. I swallowed it down.

"Very well. Then we will see what the elders decide. Most likely Alys or one of the other girls will be sent in Zadie's place." Father sighed. "And I don't know if Sami will have her like this."

Gods help me, I was now being forced to defend every concern I'd raised with Zadie. "He will. He loves her."

"Regardless, his parents might not allow it." He cleared his throat. "Especially now that the entire village knows you will marry Sami on the solstice. We have your mother to thank for that."

My mouth dropped open. "What? No! I can't marry Sami now. That would kill Zadie."

He cleared his throat again, turning away just as I caught the glimmer of tears in his eyes. I'd never seen my father cry before.

I went to stand next to him at the railing, but I didn't look at him. I was afraid he would be ashamed, and that he would see the shame in my eyes, too. "If Sami doesn't marry Zadie, what will become of her?"

"I suppose it depends on the extent of her scarring."

A small whimper escaped me. "I'm scared, Father."

He pulled me close to him in an embrace, stroking my hair the way he had when I was a little girl, before the incident. "So am I, Nor. So am I."

The elders called Mother and Father to the meetinghouse a few hours later. I was left behind to care for Zadie, who was sleeping, though not unconscious at least. She still hadn't spoken to me, but she clutched my hand in her sleep. I was tempted to lift her bandages and look at how bad her wounds were, but I was afraid to disturb the healing process. Nemea had said she'd be by later in the evening to change the dressings and apply more salve. The little scratches on her abdomen already appeared to be healing, at least.

My sister *would* recover. She had to.

When Zadie blinked her eyes open, I immediately fetched her some fresh water to drink.

"How are you feeling?" I asked. "Are you able to speak now?"

She nodded. "Yes, I can speak."

I squeezed her hand. "You're not angry with me, are you? I can't bear it if you blame me for this."

She shook her head, her face paler than I'd ever seen it. "Nor, of course I don't blame you. This was my doing."

"Do you regret it?"

She tried to sit up straighter, then collapsed weakly onto the pillows. "I will only regret it if Sami chooses another bride."

I tensed, remembering what Father had said to me. If they tried to make me marry Sami now, I would refuse.

"Nor?" Sami pushed aside our curtain, as if I had summoned him with my thoughts.

Zadie immediately found the strength to sit up and rearrange her tunic. "What are you doing here?"

"I came to make sure you're all right, silly." He sat down on the other side of her and took her free hand. "How are you?"

"A little better. The pain is bad, but seeing you helps."

My eyes flicked down involuntarily. Somehow, in the past few months, I had gone from being the most important person in Zadie's life to second place.

He leaned over and kissed her lightly on the forehead. "We'll marry as soon as you have your strength back."

Zadie beamed. "Your parents agreed?"

"I haven't spoken to them yet." He swallowed, clearly nervous. "The elders are speaking with them right now."

"Then I'm definitely not going?"

"I don't know. I wasn't allowed in the room. But I heard Elder Nemea say you might not survive the journey, and it would be a…" He trailed off. I'd never seen him so uncomfortable.

"A what?" Zadie asked.

Sami sighed. "A disgrace to our people to send a girl with such terrible scars."

Her eyes filled with tears at his words, but she managed a smile. "None of that matters anymore, as long as I can be with you."

I may have fallen to second place in Zadie's eyes, but she had just gone from being the most beautiful girl in Varenia— her identity for seventeen years—to being called a disgrace. I sent a prayer to Thalos that Sami's parents would be kind and agree to their marriage. After all, her wounds had nothing to do with her ability to serve as his wife. As long as they didn't bother Sami, why should anyone else care?

Sami and I stood at the sound of Father's voice below. He climbed through the trapdoor and helped Mother up after. Her face was pinched, unreadable. A moment later, Elder Nemea's gnarled hand reached for Father's, and he pulled her up as though her bones were hollow as a bird's.

"What's happening?" I asked. Sami was still holding Zadie's hand.

Elder Nemea was the one to answer. "I'm sorry, but I'm afraid we have no choice. Zadie must go to Ilara, even if it kills her."

"No!" Zadie's scream rang out amid our stunned silence.

Sami's gaze met mine. A wordless conversation passed between us, and in his brown eyes I finally saw the truth: that he loved Zadie as much as she loved him. If she left, neither of them would ever recover.

Help us, he pleaded.

So I answered in the only way I could.

"No," I echoed, my voice sounding far steadier than I felt. "Send me instead."

8

Mother was the first to respond, with a cruel laugh. "You'd like that, wouldn't you?" She strode toward me and jammed a finger into my chest. "It's what you wanted all along. Even the elders know you did this."

I pushed her hand away and turned to Father. "What is she talking about?"

He let out a long, ragged sigh. "They believe this was your doing."

"What?" My voice was sharp with indignation, but inside I was riddled with guilt, like wormholes in coral. "That's ridiculous. Zadie was there—she'll tell them the truth!"

"I will," Zadie said behind me. "It was an accident, Father. A terrible accident, but nothing more. Nor would never even dream of hurting me!"

Mother stooped down beside Zadie. "You don't have to lie for her," she crooned. "You're still going to be a princess."

"Can't they send Alys?" Sami asked.

"They would, if they believed they had a choice," Father said.

I placed a hand on his arm. "What do you mean?"

There were dark circles under his eyes, and his skin was sallow, as if he'd aged ten years overnight. "Two generations ago, a chosen girl drowned a few days before she was supposed to leave for Ilara. The elders were forced to send a different girl in her place. When the prince discovered that he had received a girl of inferior quality, he punished our people by cutting off our water supply for a month. Dozens of Varenians died, mostly children." Father swallowed hard. "The elders are afraid that if we send Alys, the Ilareans will say we deliberately deceived them."

I had known the Ilareans were harsh, but this seemed extreme even for them. "What happened to the girl they sent?"

Father shook his head. "We don't know. The prince married an Ilarean girl instead."

"And what do you think they'll do with a girl who is severely injured?" I asked. "Sami heard Elder Nemea say that Zadie might not survive the journey."

"She may not survive, it's true," the elder said. "But the emissary has been here. He saw Zadie. If we send Alys now, he'll think it a deliberate deception. At least he knows that Zadie was healthy before. The prince will have to understand that this was just an unfortunate accident."

"And if he's still dissatisfied? What's to stop him from cutting off our water supply, our food, our firewood?" I turned to Nemea. "Let me go in her place. She's not strong enough."

"And what do you propose to do about your scar?" Mother asked, her voice full of derision. "The emissary saw it."

It. Not me. But she was right. Talin had studied me closely enough. I was sure he'd seen my scar.

Nemea scratched at a mole on her chin, considering. "I may be able to create something to disguise it. Some kind of a stain. I told the rest of the council that Zadie is in no condition to travel, but perhaps they need to see her for themselves. Scar or no scar, I have to believe the prince would prefer a living girl to a dead one."

My mother shook her head. "The prince isn't some fool buyer at the floating market. We can't just swap out one bolt of cloth for an inferior one when he isn't looking. If he discovers what we've done—"

"This isn't your decision," Sami growled.

I flinched, but it was at my mother's words, not Sami's. I'd long believed she saw me that way—as an imperfect version of Zadie—but she'd never said it out loud before.

"Give me some time to work on the stain," Nemea said. "And to try to convince the rest of the council. There were several who voted to banish Nor, and they might see this as the next best thing." She looked at me. "Do you really believe you can pretend to be your sister?"

I was too stunned at the mention of banishment to speak, but I managed a weak nod.

"Good. Come to my house tonight. This conversation doesn't leave here until we've decided."

She looked at Sami for a moment, as if she were about to ask him to take her home, but thought better of it. "I'll borrow your boat, Samiel. You can fetch it later."

When Elder Nemea was gone, Father lowered his voice so that only I could hear him. "Your sister has spent the past seventeen years preparing for this and only just realized she lacked the courage to see it through. You have two days to prepare. Are you sure you can do this?"

He knew. He knew it wasn't an accident, but he also knew it wasn't my fault. Had he argued on my behalf at the meeting? Had he at least tried to defend me to Mother? To the elders who wanted to *banish* me? In my lifetime, only two villagers had been banished—taken far out to sea in a small boat and abandoned with no oars—and their crimes had included attempted murder. Oh gods, did they think I'd tried to *kill* Zadie?

"Father," I said, hoping all of my questions could be conveyed in that one word.

But he only squeezed my arm and turned me back toward Zadie and Sami. "Your father has not yet decided what he will do with you, Sami. The elders believe you should marry Alys, now that Nor's honor is in question."

"I won't," Sami said as Zadie's hand flew up to cover her open mouth.

"Your mother agreed with them—" Father began.

"Traitor," Mother spat. "To think I called her sister."

Father went on, ignoring her. "But your father said we needed to deal with one crisis at a time. He wants to speak with you, Sami."

"And what about me?" Zadie asked.

Mother sniffed. "What *about* you?"

"Doesn't anyone care what I have to say? Don't the elders want to speak with me before they accuse my sister of being a liar or send me off to Ilara when I can't even stand? Are they really so quick to forget my existence?"

"Don't you see?" Mother said. "Without your beauty, you are *nothing*. That's all any of us are—bodies to cook food and bear children. You had everything, and you let your sister throw it all away. And now she will be a princess, and I will have to watch you wither into an old woman, spending the rest of your miserable life in *my* house. I thought I had made it clear how important this was. I thought you understood what was at stake. Now I can see you've learned nothing in the past seventeen years. And you shall pay dearly for it."

As Mother spoke, Zadie seemed to shrink in on herself, growing smaller with every word. I had always thought Mother's ambitions were about vanity, about righting a wrong against her twenty years ago, but it was clear this meant far more to her than that.

She had accused me of thinking I was too good for Varenia, but it was she who believed we had no value here beyond the symmetry of our faces or the curves of our bodies; that to be chosen to go to Ilara meant you were better than all that, better even than the men here. Was that why she despised me so much? Because she thought she saw something of herself in me?

The very idea stung me. I was nothing like my mother. "It is *you* who have learned nothing," I spat. "And you who has paid for it."

"Nor," Father said, trying to pull me back.

"You were never wronged, Mother. You think we are worthless if we're not chosen. Why? What is the value in being sent off to a king who keeps us poor and isolated, in marrying a prince who can't even be bothered to choose his own wife? All we talk about here is honor, but there is no honor in being beautiful, in having your fate decided because of a crooked tooth, or a bent nose, or a *scar*."

Zadie was sobbing loudly now. "Please don't fight," she said, but I ignored her. This had been building for years, and I couldn't stop myself now any more than I could stop the tides.

"You took two daughters who loved you and turned them into weapons to exact your revenge, never realizing that there was no enemy."

"Shut up," Mother screamed. "You ignorant, foolish—"

"Perhaps I *am* a weapon," I continued, despite Father's grip on my arm. "A blade honed on your bitterness. And perhaps I have come to stab you in the back."

She leaped at me, but Father flung me away just in time to catch her. I hit the floor hard but picked myself up quickly, ignoring the pain in my arms, yet unable to pretend my heart wasn't broken.

If Mother and the elders were so willing to believe this villainy of me, then let them. Zadie and Sami had each other now. I would go to Ilara, where none of the other villagers would have to see me again. And Father would forgive Mother, as he always did, for even he couldn't see past the power of her beauty.

The hours passed slowly after that. Sami retreated for a time to speak with his father. Nemea returned once to tend to Zadie's wounds, which she said were healing well under the circumstances, and Zadie slept for most of the afternoon. Mother, on the other hand, wailed and cursed me for hours, not caring who heard about her evil, traitorous daughter, while Father attempted to console her.

I lay in the boat beneath our house, trying to shut out her words and instead focus on the sound of the water lapping against the pillars, on the way the tiny fish that lived beneath our houses nibbled at my fingers as I dangled them over the edge. It was cool here in the shade, and I tried to imagine what it would be like in the mountains, so far away from everything I'd ever known.

Mother was devoted to the gods—not just Thalos, but Astrea, the goddess of beauty; Spiros, the god of weather; and others—but I believed in the spirits that lived in everything around me: the water, the birds, the air itself. It was all alive and beautiful and just as divine as any invisible god. There would undoubtedly be spirits in the mountains, too, but would they be the benevolent spirits I knew so well, like the fish and the birds? Or would they be fickle spirits, like the air and water, sustaining us while every now and then trying to kill us?

I rolled onto my stomach and pulled out the torn fishing net and the knife I had used to free the dead jellyfish. I could take these up there now and tell Mother that this had all been Zadie's doing, that she loved Sami and refused to go, and it was either help her or let her kill herself in the process. Perhaps Mother would have preferred that: a beautiful martyr rather than a victim who would die an old maid.

And what would have become of our family then? Without Zadie to speak for me, I would certainly have been banished for killing my sister, which was tantamount to death; one could only survive so long in an empty boat without food and water. Surely one spinster daughter and one princess were better than a dead daughter and a banished one.

For all we knew, Zadie might still be allowed to marry Sami after all, and Mother might yet have her governor's wife *and* her princess.

But Mother couldn't see past her own failed plans right now, and it was tearing her apart. She had spent her entire life focused on a crown she'd never seen, on a kingdom she would never enter. She was like a beautiful house built on stilts, only the stilts were lies, and accepting the truth meant destroying the foundation of her existence. Accepting this new outcome would mean admitting that life could, in fact, go on.

I heard her sobbing through the floorboards, Father murmuring comforting words. But what could he say to her now? Nothing could change what had already been done.

As the sun sank below the horizon, I took up the oars and rowed to Elder Nemea's house. I found her preparing a simple meal of dried fish and seaweed, with no fire to cook on. I looked around the one-room structure, expecting to see great-grandbabies playing in the corner, a granddaughter or two cleaning. Shouldn't someone be taking care of a woman who had lived one and a quarter centuries?

"Let me help you with that," I said, taking the knife from her hands.

"Thank you." She dropped onto a stool, her joints popping as she settled. "I know what you're thinking. 'Where are all her children and grandchildren to cook for her?' But I prefer to live alone. Maybe when I'm 150, I'll bring a great-grandchild or two in to help me."

"I didn't do it," I blurted. I hadn't come here to defend myself, but I suddenly realized it was important to me that at least one person outside my family believed me.

She ignored me and pointed to a bucket of water. "Bring me some, child."

I brought her the water and sat down on the stool next to her, forcing her to acknowledge me. "I didn't do it."

"Perhaps you did, perhaps you didn't. I won't waste what little time I have left on things that have already happened. It doesn't matter now."

"It matters to me that people know I didn't hurt my sister. I would do anything to protect her." Hadn't I proven that seven years ago? Varenian law said that every person had as much responsibility for a stranger as they did for family. To let someone die when you could save them would bring the worst kind of shame upon your family. This idea, this responsibility for each other, had been ingrained in me from birth, but it had nothing to do with my motivations for saving Zadie. I would always protect her, even if it meant tearing her from the steel clutches of Thalos himself.

"She loves Governor Kristos's boy, I'm told."

"Yes. And he loves her."

Nemea sighed and reached for a piece of dried fish. "If only love were as important as people believe it to be."

I hadn't slept or eaten since Zadie's injury, and I no longer had any patience left to offer. "What is that supposed to mean?"

"My husband died fifty years ago from diving too deeply, too quickly. I loved him very much. But romantic love doesn't last forever. Death will part us, if time or circumstance doesn't."

I shook my head. I hadn't come here for a philosophy lesson. "Will the elders allow me to go to Ilara or not?"

She leaned over and brought up a small narwhal horn jar in answer. "Here."

I opened the lid and looked down at the light brown ointment. It smelled foul, like bird guano. "What's in it?"

"It's made from brown algae and...other things." She dabbed a tiny amount of the stain onto her finger and touched it to my cheek. "There's a mirror on the far wall."

Skeptically, I walked over to a large fly-stained mirror that must have come from an illegal trade or a shipwreck. I wiped away a bit of salt and stared at my reflection. I had never seen myself in anything other than Mother's hand mirror.

It was like looking at Zadie, but not. I started at the top. Sami was right; my eyes were a bit narrower. My nose was straight and even, almost exactly the same as Zadie's, but perhaps her nostrils were a bit rounder. And my lips were full and pink, just like Zadie's, though I thought the bow in her upper lip might be more pronounced.

I gasped when I realized my eyes had drifted right past my scar.

Nemea laughed as my fingers flew to my cheek. The stain came away immediately. I turned back to her. "It doesn't stay?"

"It should last for the better part of a day, but it takes a few minutes to set. And it will come off after a quarter of an hour in water. It's the best I can do in such a short amount of time."

Tears pricked at the corners of my eyes. "Why didn't you give me this sooner?"

Her ancient face appeared next to mine in the mirror. "To what end, child? Hiding our scars doesn't mean they're not

there. Just as beauty cannot disguise who we really are beneath the surface."

Our eyes met in our shared reflection. Hers were cloud
gray, while Zadie and I shared our mother's golden-hued eyes.
Like honey, Sami once said, though neither of us had ever seen
it. He described it as "something insects make," and we had
both assumed it was an insult.

"Does this mean I'm going to Ilara?" I asked.

"Yes."

I whirled around to face her, but I was unable to form
words. She smiled and patted my shoulder. "Now, girl, you
should go home and prepare for your journey. Ilara is five
days by coach, and you will be sick for much of it."

I blinked at her. I'd never been sick since the incident, other
than from the blood coral poisoning itself. "Why?"

"You've never been on land before. Everything will be a
shock to your system, not least the food. Even the air is different, so they say. And you will be cold, though the guards
will bring proper clothing for you."

I thought of Sami's cloak. Would it be mine now? Would
all the beautiful fabrics in Zadie's trunk, the strand of pearls,
the comb, belong to me, as well? Or was I to have none of
the luxuries granted to my sister? And what would poor Alys
think of all this, when she learned that she had lost the crown
first to Zadie, and now to me?

"What if the king discovers what we've done?" I whispered
fearfully. "Will he punish everyone here?"

Nemea lifted one bony shoulder. "Yes. Although at this
rate, we'll all be dead of starvation in another five years any-

way. The question the king should ask himself is, without us, who will fetch his precious pearls?"

My breath caught. No adult had ever admitted how bad things were to me before or pointed out the king's dependence on us in such stark terms.

"Why doesn't Governor Kristos stand up to the Ilareans?" I asked. "Why don't the elders?"

"Revolution is for the young, child. Besides, what can any of us do from here? If we withhold the pearls, the king will withhold everything else. If we are caught trying to go ashore, we will be killed." She handed me the jar of stain. "Go on, then. Go home to your family. The other elders will have told them the news by now, and I imagine you'll want to spend as much time with your sister as possible."

As I walked toward the door, her words echoed in my head. What *could* anyone do from here?

"What about me?" I asked, turning back toward her.

Nemea eyed me curiously. "What about you, child?"

"I'll be there at the castle. I will have the king's ear. If I tell him how desperate we are, how without more food and water, there will be no one left to dive for the pearls... He'll have to do something. Won't he?"

She raised the same shoulder in a half shrug. "Perhaps he will, perhaps he won't," she said. But this time, she was smiling.

I didn't sleep that night. I doubted anyone in my family did, though aside from Zadie's whimpers, it was quiet. I held her hand through the long hours, telling her it would all be fine, that she and Sami would marry and bear lots of beautiful babies, though I don't know if she believed me.

While my mouth spoke of Zadie and her life here in Varenia, my mind was far away. I remembered my prayer to Thalos the night of the dinner at Governor Kristos's house, after I'd met Talin. I had asked him to send me in Zadie's place, to save her from the fate she didn't want.

But though I had made the prayer on Zadie's behalf, I couldn't deny that there had been a selfish undercurrent to my words. I didn't want to stay in Varenia and marry Sami any more than Zadie wanted to leave. I couldn't spend my life wondering if my husband was thinking of someone else every time he looked at me. I didn't want to stare at the same horizon, eat the same food, or see the same people for the next hundred years.

Had I caused this somehow? Was Thalos punishing me for being so wicked? Yes, I wanted to leave Varenia, but if I had known this would be the cost, I never would have asked for it.

I rose from our bed when I could see the blue of the water through the cracks in our floorboards. Today was my last full day in Varenia. Tomorrow morning Governor Kristos and Sami would row me to shore, where the captain of the king's guard would wade out to meet me himself.

Father was responsible for explaining all of this, as Mother still would not speak to me. "If the captain does not believe you are Zadie, I don't know what will become of you," he said.

A chill ran over my scalp, but I nodded. "I understand."

"You should go, enjoy your last day here."

"I don't think I can enjoy anything with Zadie so sick and Mother so angry," I said.

He let me lean against his chest. "Your sister will heal. Your mother will forgive you."

"Not before tomorrow."

"No, I suppose not. But all will be well again one day."

I would never see that day. I would never see any of them again.

"Go and find Sami," Father said. "See if he has convinced Kristos to let him marry Zadie. My friend is a good man, and I believe he will make the right decision."

I wiped the corners of my eyes with my tunic. "Yes, Father."

I checked on Zadie again before I left and found her being tended by Mother. Satisfied that she would be well looked after, I jumped off our balcony into the water. I could have taken the boat, but I preferred to swim today. It wasn't far to Sami's house, and who knew how long it would be until I saw the ocean again. Perhaps forever.

Sami was sitting on the dock outside his house when I arrived.

"Any word?" I called up to him.

A family rowed past in their boat, the mother glaring at me, no doubt cursing me for what everyone thought I'd done to Zadie. I lifted my chin and met her stare.

Sami splashed down into the water next to me, and the woman finally looked away. "Not yet," he said. "Are you all right? My parents told me what the elders decided."

I swallowed down my fear. "I'll be fine."

He looked older, as if the last of his boyhood had been

drained by the events of the last two days. "Did your father send you here?"

"Yes. He thinks your father will allow the marriage. What do you think?"

Sami swam into the shadows under his house and motioned for me to follow him. "I don't know. My mother is adamant I not marry Zadie."

"Why?"

"Because she thinks Thalos is punishing your family."

I flinched at the words. "For what?"

He lowered his gaze. "Your mother's pride."

"This has nothing to do with Thalos," I said, though I wasn't as sure as I pretended to be. "I can't deny my mother's pride, however."

Sami grabbed onto a pillar with one hand and pulled me to him with the other. His touch was rough, in a way I'd never felt before.

"You're hurting me," I said, ripping his hand away.

His voice was harsh as he asked, "She did this to herself, didn't she?"

I treaded water for a moment, my arm still sore from where he'd grabbed me. Zadie wouldn't want Sami to know the truth, but didn't he have a right to know? They couldn't build a life together with such a terrible secret between them.

"Yes," I said finally.

"Did you help her?"

I wanted to scream *no*. I hadn't wanted anything to do with it. I remembered the things Zadie had said to me, that I didn't love her if I didn't help her. That she would do it alone if I didn't stay.

I couldn't keep this secret for the rest of my life. I had to tell someone. "Yes."

Sami slapped the water with both hands, splashing us. "Thalos, Nor! Why?"

"I had no other choice!" I cried. "She got the jellyfish on her own and had it tied to the boat. I tried to leave, but she said she would do it without me if I left. I was afraid she'd kill herself. When the time came, I couldn't go through with it, but she forced my hand." I swiped away my tears. "I didn't do it, but I was there."

"Couldn't you have talked her out of it?" Sami asked, his own eyes damp with tears.

"Don't you think I tried?" I took a shaky breath and sent him a pleading glance. "She's my sister, Sami, and she begged me. She couldn't leave you. Don't you understand that? She would rather die than leave you."

Not me, I thought with no small amount of resentment. *Just you.*

"And what am I going to do if my father says I can't marry her? What then?"

I swallowed my tears. "You're just going to have to find a way."

"I'm the governor's son, Nor. I have responsibilities."

This time I grabbed his arm. I dug my nails into the familiar flesh until he winced. "And I have just agreed to pretend to be someone else for the rest of my life! You will not abandon my sister, do you understand?"

His jaw clenched. "I won't abandon her."

"Promise me."

He pulled my hand away gently and looked me square in the eyes. "I promise."

"Good." I believed Sami. I didn't know how he would fix all this, but I knew he would find a way. "There's something else we need to discuss."

"What?"

"You're always saying that when you're governor, you will improve our way of life. That you will stand up to Ilara."

"And I will," he said. For some reason, I believed him more now than I ever had before.

"What if there was a way for you to start now, before you become governor?" I asked him.

"What are you talking about?"

I pointed to his family's smaller boat. "Come with me."

9

"Where are we going?" Sami asked as I handed him the oars.

I gave him a wry smile. "The market. You're buying my family's grain and water this week." Mother hadn't asked me to buy anything, but she'd been too distracted by Zadie's injuries and her hatred of me to notice that we were low on nearly everything.

Sami's mouth dropped open for a moment, but he knew better than to argue with me. He shook his head. "I swear, you're as stubborn as a barnacle and as bossy as—"

I cut him off with a stern glare, and we both laughed. "We never would have made it as a married couple," I said. "You know that, right?"

"Oh, I don't know about that. We would have managed."

I covered my legs with my skirts, suddenly self-conscious, though Sami had seen far more of me. "I met with Elder

Nemea last night. She made a stain for my scar, but I'm afraid of what will happen if the king discovers our deception. Father said the last time the elders tried to send a second-rate girl, Ilara cut off our water supply. Dozens of children died."

He gripped the oars so hard I was afraid they'd splinter in his hands. "And no one did anything about it?"

I shook my head. "She also said Varenia will run out of food within five years if something doesn't change. We've overfished these waters, and without pearls, what will we trade?"

"Coral and sponges?" he said doubtfully.

"Anyone can find those a lot closer to shore. And the traders have giant ships that allow them to hunt whales and gather large quantities of fish at once. Varenian pearls are the only thing we have to offer."

Sami sighed. "I don't know what can be done, Nor. I've tried talking to my father, but he won't do anything. No one will."

He rowed in silence for a while, until finally the floating market appeared over the crest of the next wave. It was a string of covered boats selling essential goods along with the occasional pet no one could afford to feed. When we were girls, we'd begged Sami to buy us a pet monkey, and Zadie had cried when he told us no. He'd been right to refuse us, but I don't think he ever said no to her again after that.

"Maybe I can help," I said. "I'll be in Ilara, Sami. I'll be able to talk to the king. The prince will be my *husband*. Once I tell them how bad things are here, they'll have to do something."

He snorted. "Why? They don't care about us. They've made that perfectly clear. That emissary, Talin? He wasn't just here to check up on Zadie."

I felt my cheeks heat at the mere mention of his name. "What are you talking about?" I asked.

Sami dropped the anchor to keep us from drifting within earshot of the merchants. "After you left that night, he asked my father all kinds of questions. He wanted to see my mother's collection of pearls, which she assured him didn't exist. She had me sell off most of her jewelry at the market ages ago so she could help take care of the poorest families. He said the king insisted Talin visit an 'average citizen's house,' so he could see how everyone else lived."

"Thalos, why?"

He raised one eyebrow. "I don't know. He asked to see yours, but Father took him to one of my aunts' houses instead."

I felt a small pang of disappointment. I'd been so busy the past few days I hadn't thought about Talin much, though his sea glass eyes had showed up more than once in my dreams. I wondered if I would see him again, then chided myself for my foolishness. Talin was the one person who might see through my disguise, the one person I should pray to never see again.

"What do you think he wanted?" I asked Sami.

"I think the king sent him because he doesn't trust us. He believes we're keeping the pearls for ourselves, that we're lying when we say there aren't as many pearls as there were a decade ago. And I think that's why he keeps lowering the value."

"What are you talking about?" I asked, confused. "The market decides the value of the pearls. Not the king."

"I was trading a few weeks ago with a Galethian north of the port, and he told me that Ilarean smugglers are getting the same price for the pearls they always have."

I leaned closer. "So what are you saying? That the value of the pearls *hasn't* dropped, and we're getting paid less for them anyway?"

He nodded. "The king thinks if he pushes us hard enough, more pearls will suddenly appear. He doesn't believe that there are no more. Or at least, he doesn't *want* to believe it. Even if the emissary tells the king the truth of what he saw here, the king might not listen."

Was it possible that Talin had only come to spy on us? I thought of the way he'd looked at me, how his gaze made my belly flutter. Was I so naive that I had misread Talin's suspicion as curiosity or—even more humiliating—interest?

Sami continued, "Don't you see? We work harder than ever, and our economy never grows. We're worse off now than our great-great-grandparents ever were. And why? Why should we not be allowed to trade the pearls on the free market like everyone else?"

I sighed, exasperated. "Because of the lost princess."

"That was hundreds of years ago, if it ever happened at all. It has nothing to do with any of the Varenians who are alive today. They've deliberately kept us poor and powerless, Nor."

"I know, Sami."

He was speaking so fast I could hardly keep up. "And not only are we controlled by the Ilareans, but we send the most beautiful women to be their queens. If we're so beneath them, why do their princes want Varenian brides?"

"I don't know!" I shouted.

We sat in silence for a moment, the boat rocking gently from side to side. I'd been asking myself the same questions for years, and I was no closer to the answers now.

"What if I can find out?" I asked suddenly.

Sami glanced up. "What?"

"I'll be in the castle with the king and all his advisors. I'll be able to see what the Ilareans are doing with the pearls and why they need them so badly. I'll have the answers to all of our questions at my fingertips."

"You want to *spy* on the king?"

I shrugged. "Is it spying if I live there? If I happen to over-hear people talking?"

He started to shake his head. "No, Nor. That's not what I meant."

"So, what? We wait until you're governor? What makes you think you'll be able to stand up to the king when your father can't?"

Sami's clenched his jaw. "And you think *you* can? You've spent your whole life worrying about being beautiful, not learning how to govern."

I felt my anger start to rise, but fear tamped it back down. My mother's words echoed in my head. *Beauty is power.* Maybe that was true here in Varenia, but who knew how things worked in Ilara? "I don't know if the king will listen," I ad-mitted. "But I have to at least try."

"It's too dangerous, Nor. And if you were found out...it could have terrible consequences for all of us here."

I reached for his hands. "I know it's risky to spy on the king. I know I could take the easy way, abandon our customs and adopt the Ilarean ways. And I could pretend that every-thing is fine here in Varenia, that my family has enough to eat, that Zadie can heal instead of being forced to dive. But I will know the truth. That with every sunrise, Varenia comes closer to the day when there isn't a single oyster left. And what will you do then? When the King of Ilara refuses to give you water and firewood, when there are no more fish to catch? It's not enough to *try* anymore. If we don't *do* something, now, you're all going to die."

Sami pretended to look up at the clouds, but I saw the tears he was trying to keep from falling. "All right," he said. "Find out what you can." Then he frowned. "But how will you get information to me even if you do manage it? No Varenian bride has ever returned to our village."

"You'll have to come to me."

"Nor—" He followed my gaze to the floating market.

Every face in Varenia was familiar to me, but from here, with everyone milling about, they all looked the same. If Sami could get somewhere he could blend in, perhaps...

"The port," we said simultaneously.

He took a deep breath. "It could work. Their next market isn't for more than three weeks. That may be enough time for you to arrange things."

"But how would I find you? You told me the port market is enormous."

"There's a man who sells kites. He's easy to find because he ties several of his kites to the stand. We could meet there, at midday."

I settled back into the boat, exhilarated and overwhelmed. "I might not make it the first time."

"I know."

"But keep coming, every month. I'll do everything in my power to get there."

"So will I."

We bought what we needed at the floating market quickly, neither one of us wanting to waste any more of the time I had left. As Sami began to row us home, a family passed us, their faces grim. If they recognized me as the village outcast, they didn't say anything.

Then I noticed the dark cloth in the bottom of their boat, covering a lumpy object about five feet long.

A body.

The family was going to bury their dead. Sami and I dropped our heads at the same time, touching our hearts in a gesture of sympathy. The father nodded at us when we lifted our heads again, and they continued on in silence.

Varenian funerals were private, solemn rituals. Only the immediate family attended. That way no one else needed to feel as though they had to avoid certain places out of respect for the dead. I had attended one funeral as a child, that of my father's father. He'd been killed by a windwhale, a predatory white whale with a giant dorsal fin that acted like a sail, making it one of the fastest creatures in the ocean. My grandmother had been left a widow. Fortunately, most of her children were grown then, and she went to live with one of my aunts.

I didn't remember the words my father spoke, only the way the cloth had clung to the body as it hit the water, briefly revealing my grandfather's features. He was weighted down with rocks and sank quickly, though we'd all known it wouldn't be long before the sharks gathered.

Why don't we burn the bodies? I'd asked my father, thinking anything would be better than being eaten, even if you were already dead.

Because, child, as we take from the sea, so must we give. Through Thalos, the ocean provides us with our food, with the pearls we harvest. It makes us strong and healthy. And when we die, we must return to the ocean, so that it, too, can have nourishment. So that the blood coral may grow from our hearts, and begin the cycle anew.

I touched my scar as the memory faded. "Everyone thinks I tried to hurt her, Sami—maybe even kill her." I looked down, my eyes burning with unshed tears. "I think my own mother started the rumor."

"Maybe, but it's Alys's mother who spread it. She's furious that you were chosen in Alys's place."

"Not because I'm more beautiful than her. Only because they had no choice."

He reached over and squeezed my hand. "Listen to me, Nor. You're not a second-rate girl. You never have been."

I chuckled wryly, but he didn't join me.

"I mean it. I can't think of any other girl who would be willing to spy on the king, not even Zadie. Your mother taught you to believe your scar made you ugly, but it has made you brave."

"Brave?" I kicked at the sack of grain. "I'm terrified, Sami."

He laughed, a deeper version of the laugh I'd always loved as a girl.

"What's so funny?"

"You're not afraid of anything, Nor. You never have been."

He was wrong. I was afraid of leaving Zadie and Father, of leaving the only home I'd ever known. I was afraid of being alone among strangers, of having to pretend to be someone else. I was afraid of marrying a young man I'd never seen, knowing I had no more choice in the matter now than when I'd been betrothed to Sami.

And worse than that, I was frightened of the person I was becoming: a woman who lied to everyone, who disrespected her parents, who helped her sister injure herself. A woman who would spy on a king.

A woman who would steal a crown.

There was no celebration that night. The big send-off that had been planned for Zadie, as well as the announcement of my engagement to Sami, had been called off after the accident, and the village was as quiet as it was on a typical evening.

It was just as well. I couldn't have taken the whispers and stares.

I would see Sami one last time in the morning, when he took me to shore. Other than him, the only two people who wanted anything to do with me were here in our house, so home was the only place I wanted to be tonight.

Even if my mother still wouldn't look at me.

"Do you have everything?" Zadie asked. She was able to sit up now, and a bit of her color had returned, though I could see she was still in a good deal of pain.

"Yes," I said, patting the trunk of belongings that should have been hers. Father had insisted I take it, despite Mother's protests. "Please, you don't have to worry about me."

"No, it's always been your job to worry about me." She squeezed my hand. It wasn't an accusation. She was acknowledging my sacrifices, not just now, but every day for the past seven years: rowing to spare her hands, taking the blame for every misadventure, staying behind with her when Sami wanted to go exploring, and she was too worried about the cost to her beauty. How ironic, now, that it had all been for nothing. That here I was, with my rougher hands and sun-kissed skin, going in her place.

I had cooked my final supper here in Varenia, as Mother refused to and Zadie couldn't (and Father, well... Father couldn't prepare porridge if he was starving). All we had was bread made with the grain Sami had bought for us, and some dried fish. If he didn't marry Zadie, I was afraid they'd run out of food even sooner than Elder Nemea foretold, even with the bride price, assuming the prince accepted me and actually sent it. I found most of the pearls we traded at market, and even if she hadn't been injured, Zadie wouldn't be able to dive enough to make up for my absence.

She made a valiant attempt to lighten the mood at dinner. "Just think, you'll get to see a horse tomorrow, Nor. A real horse, up close. You may even be able to ride one."

"Do you think so?"

She nodded, and we shared an excited squeal. For the first time in days, it felt like the old us again.

"Imagine how much you'll see on a five-day journey on land. Far more than you'd see in five days at sea, I'm sure."

It was strange, how the conversation had turned. These were the kinds of things I used to say to Zadie. Was she trying to boost my spirits by reminding me, or was she regretting her decision?

"Remember your manners when you go," Father said, the most he'd spoken since this morning. "You still represent this family, no matter how far away we may be."

"She does *not* represent this family," Mother snapped. "She is as good as dead to us."

Zadie placed a hand on her arm. "How can you say such a thing? Our Nor is going away forever, and these are the words you'd have her remember you by?"

"I would hope she would remember me by all the sacrifices I made to ensure that she have the best possible marriage prospect, despite her...flaws. But she chose to throw all that away, so she can remember me however she likes." Mother stood up and disappeared behind her bedroom curtain, leaving her bread and fish untouched.

"Don't listen to her," Zadie said weakly.

I realized that no one had eaten, not even Father. Maybe Mother was right. Maybe I *had* acted ungratefully. She could have arranged a marriage between me and someone else in the village, but she had chosen Sami. I may not have been beautiful enough to marry the prince, but she'd still considered me worthy of the governor's son.

If I could bring myself to believe that any of her actions had been done from a place of selflessness, perhaps I could have understood my mother. But as things stood, I didn't think I'd ever be able to.

"Come, let's get you to bed," I said to Zadie, helping her back to our bedroom. She couldn't bear any weight on her injured leg, but she had enough strength to stand now, and that was promising. Perhaps she'd be able to see me off properly tomorrow, at least from the balcony.

I unwove the braids in her hair and helped her wash with a cloth and fresh water. Even weak and sickly, she was beautiful, her gold eyes radiating love and compassion, a sad smile on her soft pink lips. When she laid a hand on my cheek, I set the cloth down and covered her hand with my own.

"What is it?" I asked.

"I can't believe I'm never going to see you again."

"Oh, Zadie." I knew it was true, but if I let myself think like that, I'd never be able to get through this.

"I was terrified to leave Varenia, but I never considered how frightened you would have been to watch me go. I was so focused on being forced to leave that I never thought about what it would feel like to stay."

That was the difference between Zadie and me. Though I had always imagined the day she would leave Varenia from my perspective, I had also dreamed it a million times from hers. And I'd always felt staying was the worse option.

"You'll be all right," I said. "You have Mother and Father. And Sami."

She squeezed my hand. "But I'll never have the one person I love best of all. He may have my heart, but you, my dear, beautiful Nor, are the twin of my soul."

I wept then. We both did. For all the years we had both sacrificed for Mother's foolish dream, for the things we had borne for each other—me, the knowledge that I was not and never would be enough in the eyes of our mother; Zadie, the weight of having to be more than enough, of having to achieve perfection. Here and now, as raw and vulnerable as the wounds on my sister's legs, we were beautiful in a way our mother would never understand.

In that moment, I realized how foolish it was to be jealous of my sister's love for Sami. I knew now that I couldn't possibly love any man more than I loved my sister. We had spent almost every moment together for seventeen years. What could possibly touch that? What could break it? Not Mother and her dreams. Not even Thalos himself.

I should have prepared myself for the morning, should have carefully washed and plaited my hair as Zadie would have done, and laid out my best outfit and slathered my skin in oil and perfume. But instead I fell asleep in my sister's arms, still wearing the tunic I'd worn all day, my cheeks stained with the salt of our tears, and my heart beating in time with hers.

Mother had given us one gift, at least, that no amount of time or distance could erase: each other.

10

I woke to the touch of Zadie's fingers on my temple in the gray light of predawn. "What is it?" I asked, rubbing the sleep from my eyes.

"It's our last sunrise together. I didn't want you to miss it."

She laughed when I sat up.

"What?"

"Your hair. It would make a fine nest for a wayward bird."

"Zadie!" I gasped as I touched my head. "An entire family could roost in here!"

"I'll fix it later. Now hurry!"

We sat on the balcony outside our room, our legs dangling over the edge like always. I prayed for a spectacular final sunrise, and the sun did not disappoint. The horizon glowed bright orange just above the water, then slowly made room for the bright yellow orb that pushed the orange up and away, spreading the light into the fading darkness and out over the water.

Zadie rested her head on my shoulder, and I pressed my cheek to her hair. I tried not to think about this being our final sunrise together, the final time I would hear her voice or see her face. I couldn't. It wasn't fathomable. Surely tomorrow I would rise from the same bed and return to this same porch, the only home I'd ever known. How could I imagine anything different when I'd never even left Varenia?

"Girls," Father called. "Sami will be here soon. Nor needs to prepare."

"Yes, Father," we chimed in unison.

True to her word, Zadie undid the damage from last night, first telling me to wet my hair with fresh water so she could comb and plait it. I asked her to keep the braids loose; I had no idea when I'd be able to remove them.

"What should I wear?" I asked, flipping through my small stack of clothing.

"A simple tunic and skirts. There will be clothes for you in the carriage. And leather-soled shoes, or so I was told."

I stared down at my bare toes. Mother sometimes forced me to wear slippers for special occasions, but I preferred to go barefoot. "I have to wear *shoes?*"

Zadie's head fell back as she laughed, and I realized she didn't appear to be in pain for the first time in days. The worry lines on her brow were gone, and she no longer winced every time she moved.

"Are you feeling better?"

"I am, actually." She unwound the bandages on her thigh, and I was pleased to see that the wounds, though still pink and raw, showed no sign of infection. An image came to my mind of Sami someday tracing those winding scars with his finger, and I felt a moment of peace. As long as they had each other, I wouldn't worry for my sister. She loved it here. She always had.

I changed into my best white tunic and pale blue skirts. Zadie helped me apply the stain from Elder Nemea to my cheek, and we both marveled at how well it worked. If I waited just a little while, it didn't come off even when I rubbed at it. After, I ate a small bowl of porridge with dried figs. I was afraid I'd be ill if my stomach was too full, and I didn't have much of an appetite anyway.

"Nerves," Father said. "I expect it's normal to be anxious on a day like this."

"Yes, Father."

We turned at the sound of Sami calling from outside the house.

"It's time," Father said.

I looked around for Mother. "Where is she?" Even she wouldn't miss saying goodbye to me, I thought, though doubt nibbled the corners of my mind like a hungry fish.

"She said she had something she needed to do."

"But surely she'll be back to see me off?"

He shook his head. "She didn't say."

I clenched my jaw to keep it from trembling and picked up the trunk. "Help Zadie out, would you? She's doing better today, but she could still use a hand."

I went to where Sami and Governor Kristos sat in their boat, both looking dignified in their finest clothing. I'd always thought Sami looked more like his mother, but today I saw some of his father in him.

He reached up to help me with my trunk. "Are you ready?"

I nodded, though the eel in my belly writhed violently. "I think so."

"Where's your mother?"

I shrugged, trying to mask my hurt. "She's not here."

Even the governor frowned at my words.

"It's fine," I lied. "Let me just say goodbye." I turned to my father, who held my sister in his arms like a child. He set her down gently so he could remove something from his tunic. It was a long silk pouch, red with pale pink embroidery.

"What is it?" I asked as he placed it in my hand. The object inside was hard and thin.

"It's a knife, made from the blood coral that nearly killed you."

I nearly dropped the pouch. "What?"

He smiled. "Don't worry. It's sheathed."

I slid the opening of the silk pouch down an inch, revealing an ivory handle carved with seaflowers. "Why do you have this?"

"While you were sick, when we thought we were going to lose you, I found the blood coral and smashed it to pieces with a mallet."

"What were you thinking?" I asked. "You could have been killed!"

"I was careful. Well, careful enough."

I removed the knife from the pouch. The sheath covering the blade was made of stingray leather. I pulled gently on the handle, just enough to glimpse a sliver of the coral blade.

"The coral itself can't hurt you," he explained. "Not when it's dead. But if it breaks the skin, the cut will be lethal."

I searched his eyes. "Why are you giving this to me?"

"Turn it over."

I obeyed him and gasped. Even Kristos's eyes widened at the sight of the massive red pearl set into the hilt, the size of my thumbnail and perfectly round. But it was the color that shocked us all: a bright, radiant red, as red as any blood coral I'd ever seen. I hadn't even known red pearls existed. It had to be worth as much as twenty pink pearls.

"Where did you get it?" I asked, stroking the pearl reverently.

He tucked a stray hair behind my ear. "From the oyster you and Zadie found that day."

"Why didn't you sell it?" I asked, thinking of all the food and supplies we could have purchased with it.

"It belongs to you. It always has."

I tucked the knife back into the pouch and wrapped my arms around my father, squeezing him tightly. "Thank you, Father, for understanding me so well. I will miss you."

"I will miss you, too." He didn't try to stop the tears welling in his eyes. "Thalos blessed this family when he brought you to us. Both of you."

"Take care of Mother," I said, my voice breaking on the words. "She doesn't know it yet, but she will miss me."

"Of course she will."

I turned to Zadie and cried harder.

"Don't cry, darling," she said, though she was weeping as hard as I was. "I love you so much."

"I love you, too."

She managed a smile. "Now who's the one who will be as swollen as a puffer fish?"

"I don't care," I said.

She dried my tears with her sleeve anyway. "You've sacrificed everything for me, and I will never forget it as long as I live."

"You would have done the same for me."

"But you didn't ask it."

I held her as hard as I dared, once again surprised at how small she felt in my arms after embracing Father. A wave of fear washed over me. "I'm not sure I can do this," I whispered into her ear.

She leaned back to look me in the eyes. "Mother always told us that beauty is power. She believed that our value was something that could be weighed and measured like a pearl at market. But for the last seven years, since I scarred your cheek, I have watched you become independent and strong. Your curiosity leads you to ask questions other girls never even think of. You've always been beautiful, Nor. That scar on your cheek? Most people in the village don't even notice it. That's not what made the elders choose me over you. They chose me because they believed I would go along with their plans, that I would make the prince a docile and subservient wife."

"Zadie—"

She placed her hands on my shoulders. "Mother was *wrong*, Nor. You have the power to do anything and everything you dream of, more than any person I've ever known. And that power, that inner strength, *that* is what makes you the most beautiful girl in Varenia."

I shook my head. I didn't feel powerful at all in that moment. I felt sad and scared and very small. "I love you" was all I could manage.

"I will see you again, in this life or another. Now go, meet your destiny." Zadie pressed a kiss to my forehead and stepped back as Father helped lower me down to the boat.

Sami put his arms around me, not like a brother or a lover, but like a friend, and I was more grateful for him than I'd ever been. The governor himself took up the oars to row us to shore.

I told myself not to look back. I kept my back straight so that Zadie's last image of me would be one of the power and strength she was so sure I possessed. What she couldn't see were the tears, the way I dug my nails into my palms and bit down on my lower lip, so I had a different kind of pain to focus on.

As Zadie's cries were lost to the wind, I recited her final words in my head, attempting to draw strength from them. I was not abandoning the people I loved; I was meeting my destiny, just like we had talked about.

Realization slammed into me like a wave. I may not have asked her to sacrifice for me, but she had done it anyway. She hadn't told me about her plan because she knew that I would never risk her life if I believed I was going to profit from it in some way. But somehow she had wrested our destinies from the hands of the elders, from Mother, from Thalos himself, and put them to rights.

Bittersweet tears slid down my cheeks. How could I have ever doubted her?

I turned abruptly, hoping I wasn't too late. All the houses of Varenia, painted in their pinks and yellows, reds and oranges, stretched out across the horizon like a glorious sunset. In front of our rapidly shrinking house, I could barely make out Zadie's tiny figure in the distance. I raised a hand to show that I understood, and the sob I'd been holding in burst out of me as she raised hers in return.

Sami held me tighter, and I cried until I was finally out of tears.

I eventually fell asleep on his shoulder and woke hours later to the sun beating down on me. Sami and his father took turns rowing for the rest of the day. They were both strong men, but despite leaving not long after sunrise, the sun was sinking rapidly toward the horizon now. Even with my hat, my head was aching from being out in the sun for so long, and my good shirt and skirts were nearly soaked through with sweat. Both men wore thin linen tunics and trousers, a luxury I wasn't allowed. Fortunately, they'd brought food and water with us, but I couldn't imagine how they would find the strength to make the journey back tonight.

Finally, the horizon began to change. We were coming ashore southeast of Varenia, and here, at last, was the land I'd dreamed of my whole life: a long stretch of sand in both directions, then farther back, the blurry green haze of the forest.

More details began to come into focus as the waves picked up and started driving us faster toward shore. A line of ten or fifteen men stood facing the sea, their expressions unreadable from here. Their torsos were covered in something hard and stiff, like a turtle's shell, and their horses stood in a row behind them, massive beasts that seemed to loom larger the closer we got.

Sami set the oars down for a moment, letting the waves do the work. "Nor?"

My eyes met his. "Yes?"

"Are you ready?"

I almost laughed. Of course I wasn't ready. I would never be ready. The idea of Sami and his father abandoning me here with a dozen strange men was absurd. How would I ever find the strength to leave this boat?

But I bit back my fear. I had to be strong now, so that when Zadie asked Sami if I'd been afraid, he could tell her that I went bravely. "I'm ready."

He nodded. "I'll drop anchor a little ways out from shore, just fifteen feet or so, and the captain will come for you, with another guard for your trunk. The captain will probably present a gift to my father, say a few words, and then we'll leave."

"I understand. Thank you."

He ignored his father's stern gaze and took my hands. "I promise I will take care of Zadie. Please try not to worry."

"I know." I leaned forward and kissed him lightly on the cheek, saying goodbye to the boy who had been our best friend and trusted accomplice for as long as I could remember. "We would have managed," I whispered as I pulled away, referring to the marriage that would never be. "But you will make Zadie the happiest woman in Varenia."

"I'll spend my life trying," he whispered back. "Remember, keep your eyes and ears open."

"I will."

Governor Kristos leaned forward and took my chin in his large hands, examining my cheek closely. "The stain is holding. Good."

I tried to hold back my tears as he released me. "I know things didn't end well between our families, but—"

"It's all right, Nor." He pulled me into a fierce embrace. "You have always been like a niece to me. Be careful in Ilara. I have never met the prince, but I have heard he can be…difficult. He may not take as kindly to your impetuous nature as the emissary did."

I wondered what he meant by *difficult*. "Yes, sir."

"I'll look after your family, I promise."

"Thank you." I kissed him on the cheek as Sami dropped the anchor over the side of the boat.

I scanned the group of men to see who was coming for me and blinked when two stepped out from behind the other guards. They were clad only in loose white tunics and tight trousers, their feet bare. I covered my mouth with one hand to suppress a giggle. The older man had blond hair and a trimmed beard; the other was as smooth-cheeked as Sami. They looked small and weak without their shells, and I told myself to be calm. These men weren't hungry sharks circling bloodied waters. They were more like the small fishes clinging to a shark's underbelly; nothing to fear at all.

But as they entered the water and came closer into view, I saw that they were not so small. In fact, both men were taller than any man I'd seen in Varenia, including Jovani. Their shoulders were as broad as Governor Kristos's, and their mouths were set in grim lines.

I dropped my hand, the smile vanishing from my face, and felt a bubble of panic rising in my throat. Two strange men were coming for me. I'd never met a stranger, at least not until Talin, and these men had no laughter dancing in their eyes.

"I can't go with them," I whispered to the governor. But he only stared ahead at the men, his expression as grave as theirs.

"Greetings," Kristos said as the men approached the side of the boat, chest-deep in the water.

"Good day, Governor Kristos," the bearded man answered. Beneath the facial hair, his skin was tanned but unlined. "I am Captain Osius of King Xyrus's guard." His eyes flicked briefly to mine, but his gaze didn't linger long. Instead, he scanned my entire body. Perhaps Talin had described Zadie to him, and he was confirming that I was the girl the prince had been promised.

"Milady," he said finally, reaching his hand out to me. "It is an honor to meet you."

I let him take my hand. He brought it to his mouth, his whiskers tickling my skin as he kissed it, and I had to force myself not to look away at the awkwardness of the gesture. "Thank you," I managed.

"My second in command, Grig, will help get your belongings to shore. I'm afraid protocol dictates that you may not set foot on solid ground until we are within Ilarean borders, so I will carry you to the carriage."

I yanked my hand back. "Carry me?"

"Yes, milady. I promise I am up to the task." His eyes crinkled in the corners, and I felt myself relax a little. Despite his size and serious expression, I suddenly felt that he was someone I could trust, this captain who had the word *sea* in his name.

He turned to Kristos. "We would like to present the lady's family with these gifts," he said, gesturing to a sack Grig was struggling to keep out of the water. "The rest of the bride price will be sent after Prince Ceren agrees to the marriage."

Kristos grunted in acceptance, and Grig laid the bag in the bottom of the boat. I wondered what was in it; something useful, I hoped, like food or clothing.

Sami helped Grig lift my trunk out of the boat, while the captain held out a hand to me. "Now then, milady. May I help you down?"

I placed one hand in Captain Osius's, hoping he wouldn't notice how badly it trembled. I rose on numb legs and was grateful when Sami took my other arm, steadying me. I glanced back at him once, forced a smile, and stepped into the waiting arms of the captain. Grig, carrying the trunk on his head, turned toward shore, and Osius followed.

I watched over his shoulder as Sami raised his hand in one final farewell, before picking up the oars and disappearing over the crest of a wave.

11

This was it. Quite probably the last time I would ever see anyone I knew again. A cold pit formed in my stomach, as if the slippery eel had just turned to stone. I let my chin fall against the captain's damp tunic; he didn't falter in his stride toward land.

When I began to feel the ocean falling away and my wet skirts growing heavier as they dragged in the water, I raised my head again. The captain's footfalls left soft impressions in the sand, something I'd never seen—the only sand I'd ever touched had been underwater. I longed to bury my own feet in it, but the captain had said I couldn't walk here. The sand made a crunching noise as he walked farther inland, and then a softer sound, like grain spilling out of a sack.

I had thought so much about how different things would look on land, but I'd forgotten all about how they'd sound.

And *smell*. As we got closer to the row of guards, a sharp

scent like chopped onions filled my nostrils, the odor of a dozen men dressed in heavy leather after a day spent in the blazing sun. And beyond that, something stronger, but warm and almost sweet: what I would later recognize as the smell of horses.

Captain Osius walked past the other guards and their horses into the tree line, and I stared up in wonder. The trees were immense, bigger than any plant I'd ever seen, but the leaves that rustled in their branches were small and delicate. I reached out and plucked one off a branch as we walked past, rubbing it between my fingers. It felt smooth and slippery. When I brought it to my nose and sniffed, I felt Captain Osius's chest heave up and down. He was laughing at me.

I dropped the leaf and stiffened in his arms, realizing how ridiculous I must seem to someone like him, someone who'd seen so much more than I had. It wouldn't matter that it was his king who had kept me an ignorant "wave child" in the first place.

From now on, I would keep my curiosity to myself.

"Here we are, milady."

The carriage was a large wooden structure with doors and windows, like a house on wheels, with four brown horses harnessed to the front. It was nearly dark now, but there were lanterns hanging from the sides of the carriage, illuminating the intricate carvings in the wood.

"Milady," a young woman said, stepping out of the carriage and dropping into a curtsy. For a moment, I forgot myself and stared. Her white-blond hair was pulled back in two long fishtail braids that framed a sallow face as pale as a sun-bleached sand dollar. When her sky blue eyes flicked up to mine, I noticed purplish smudges below them, giving her a tired and almost sickly appearance.

Her dress was made of a heavy, dark gray fabric, pulled tight across her torso to accentuate a flat chest and the tiniest waist I'd ever seen. I glanced down at my own sodden tunic and skirts, feeling like the drowned rat that had once come in on a sack of grain from the floating market and sent Zadie and me screaming out of the house. I could imagine what this woman was thinking: *this is what the most beautiful girl in Varenia looks like?*

"Good evening," I said, nodding in what I hoped was the appropriate manner.

She smiled. "I'm Ebb. I'll be your lady's maid in Ilara. And on the journey, of course. You must be… Well, I can't even imagine what you must be feeling right now. But getting you out of those wet clothes is the least we can do."

"We should depart within the hour, Ebb," Captain Osius said as he handed me into the carriage. "Be sure she gets some hot tea into her before we go."

The interior was more spacious than it seemed from the outside. There was a bench on either end covered in deep crimson velvet. White cloth was hung over the windows, and heavier red drapes were pulled to either side. Ebb closed them now.

"For privacy," she explained. "It's a bit dark, but we'll do our best."

There was a lantern in here, but only one candle, and I was grateful for the dim lighting. I was crouched over, unable to stand up straight in the carriage, and a puddle was starting to form around me on the floor. My feet squelched on the damp fabric. Was nothing left bare in Ilara?

I flinched when I felt Ebb's hand on my back.

"It's all right, milady. I'll just help you out of these wet clothes and get you dried off a bit."

The next several minutes passed in awkward silence. No one had ever seen me without clothes on, outside of my family. It was summer, but tiny bumps sprang up on my bare skin, and I couldn't keep myself from shivering. Ebb threw a thick blanket over me and urged me to rub myself dry. I watched in horror as she cracked open the carriage door and kicked my sodden clothing out into the dirt.

"Why would you do such a thing?" I blurted. "Those are perfectly good clothes."

When she smiled, I could see the bones of her face shift. "Don't worry, milady. There are dozens of gowns waiting for you in the castle. Here." She lifted up one of the seat cushions and brought out a gown made of the same stiff, heavy fabric as hers, in an even darker shade of gray. "This is just a traveling gown, mind you," she added when she saw my face fall, but it wasn't the quality that troubled me. We never wore such somber colors in Varenia.

"Do you wear more colorful clothing in Ilara?" I asked hopefully.

"Not at court. We wear mourning colors, for the lost princess," she said, but there was no emotion in her voice, as if this were as obvious as the fact that the sun rose in the morning and set at night. "We just need to get you into your undergarments first."

I cocked my head, and she laughed a little, covering her

mouth with her fingertips. She had a kind laugh, and I realized that even though I probably seemed childlike to her and Captain Osius, they weren't making fun of me. They just didn't know what to do with me.

"I'll help you," she said. She produced a short-sleeved shift and slipped it over my head. The white fabric was so thin it was nearly transparent, far finer than anything I'd ever owned, and fell just below my knees. Afterward, she helped me into a pair of long silk stockings, followed by a pleated petticoat, and finally the dress, which fastened up the back with tiny hooks that Ebb clasped with remarkable speed. The neckline was square and severe, and the bodice was so tight that I found myself taking short, rapid breaths as my rib cage was prevented from expanding fully by the fabric. The entire process seemed to take ages, and we were both sweating by the time she was finished. I sat back on the bench, hardly able to believe I would have to go through this process every day.

"That will do for now," she breathed. "It's stuffy in this carriage."

"For *now*?"

She smiled again. "Try not to worry. You'll get used to all of it in time."

I wasn't convinced, but I nodded weakly. "Can I please get some air?"

"You're not allowed to leave the carriage, but we can open the windows."

I pushed past Ebb as she parted the curtains and opened the windows, desperate for fresh air. The cool breeze that hit me was welcome now. I couldn't imagine I'd ever be cold again in all this clothing. I was still sucking in breath when Captain Osius appeared from the front of the carriage.

"Milady," he said, bowing. "The gown suits you. Are you ready to leave?"

I glanced down at the gown, which suited me about as well as a lobster shell fit a crab, then back at Ebb. "I—I believe so."

"Very good." He nodded and disappeared again.

"Best sit down, milady. The ride can be a bit bumpy at times."

Before I could take a seat, the driver yelled something to the horses, and the carriage lurched forward, sending me sprawling against the velvet cushions. I looked up at Ebb, who gave another of her kind laughs and helped me sit up. "You'll get used to it, milady. I promise."

A few minutes later, my senses bombarded by too many sights, sounds, and smells at once, I ran to the window, threw back the curtains, and emptied the contents of my stomach all over the carriage door.

Just as Elder Nemea had predicted, the rest of the journey was long and painful, as I suffered through what Captain Osius called "land sickness." And sick I was, even worse than the time Zadie and I had inadvertently purchased bad meat from a trader. Ebb cared for me like a child, helping me to change in and out of my dresses, bringing me cups of a tea made from ginger, valerian root, and bugbane to help with my sickness. The ingredients were as foreign as everything else, but they did settle my stomach enough that I was able to eat a bit on the third day.

I didn't see anyone except for Ebb, with the occasional

glimpse of Grig or the captain outside the window of the carriage. Ebb and I slept inside, and at night, the deep laughter of the men around the fire, coupled with the thick tang of wood smoke, made me ache for home. The carriage began to feel like a net around me, and I fought against a sensation I'd never experienced, like something inside of me was clawing to be free. When I wasn't sick, I napped, but try as I might to pretend the carriage was a boat and the rough road beneath us a choppy sea, my mind and body would not be fooled.

On the morning of the fifth day, Captain Osius came to check on me before we started moving. "We'll be on Ilarean soil in a few hours," he assured me. "You'll finally be able to leave the carriage and stretch a bit."

When Elder Nemea had told me the journey would be long, I hadn't understood that I wouldn't be able to leave the carriage for days. Ilara had once stretched across the entire continent, but in the past few generations, uprisings had become more common, and we were traveling through two other territories on our journey. The first, Meradin, was mostly thick forest, with small villages here and there along the road. It had been easy to take from the king, apparently, because it was close to the shore, and the king never ventured far from the mountains.

But the land we traveled through now, Pirot, was more disputed. Every week, the rebels claimed more land. A large river was the last physical border protecting Ilara from invaders, Ebb explained.

"When will we reach the castle?" I asked Captain Osius, trying not to sound too desperate. But I didn't know how much longer I could last without fresh air and sunlight.

"Not until sunset, I'm afraid. But don't worry. Soon the road will be nothing but a distant memory." He smiled, but even he looked like he was ready to be home. His beard was becoming unruly, and there were dark circles under his eyes.

We rattled to a stop a few hours after breakfast, and I flew to the window, ignoring Ebb's pleas that I remain in my seat. We were stopped at the foot of a large wooden bridge that spanned a shimmering mass of water so vast, I at first mistook it for the ocean.

"The River Ilara," Ebb explained, joining me at the window.

"Does that mean...?"

"Yes, milady. Just across the river is your new home."

I peered farther out of the window. *Home.* The word would always evoke Varenia for me, even if I spent the next hundred years in Ilara. Captain Osius was speaking to a man standing at the foot of the bridge. He was dressed similarly to the captain—Ebb had explained that the thick leather plates the men wore were called armor, designed to protect them in battle—but the crest painted on his chest was a white tree framed by a black-and-silver shield.

"Who governs Pirot?" I asked.

"King Xyrus would argue he is still the ruler here. But these soldiers wear the crest of Lord Clifton." She lowered her voice. "He's actually just a commoner who made himself a lord. These are his soldiers."

Sami had mentioned talk of war in the South, but this wasn't the South. Did he know the disputes reached this far north?

The chatter outside grew louder and more animated, and Ebb tugged on my sleeve. "Best to wait inside."

"I'm hardly outside," I started to say, when a man's face appeared next to the window.

He was the same man Osius had been speaking with. He was shorter than the Ilarean guards, with a body the shape and size of a water barrel, and his breath stank of alcohol.

"So, this is to be your new queen?" he asked Osius. He examined me so fully I felt the scar on my cheek burn. I'd been careful to keep it covered, reapplying the stain whenever Ebb left the carriage, but I wasn't sure I'd ever stop being conscious of it. "The most beautiful girl in all of Varenia." He licked his lips. "I bet your commander wishes he were the firstborn instead, eh?"

The captain strode over, looking furious. "To prevent us from crossing is an act of war, Riv."

"Steady on, Os." The man leered at me before returning to the front of the carriage. "Let 'em cross!" he called to someone I couldn't see.

"Are you all right, milady?" Osius asked me.

I took my seat. "I'm fine."

"Don't worry about him," Ebb said. "He's an ignorant mercenary. Most of Clifton's soldiers came from the South to escape the woman king."

I raised my eyebrows. "'Woman king'? Don't you mean queen?"

"She calls herself a king, and they say she's amassing an army. These men fled to escape conscription, preferring to work as sellswords instead. But they don't belong here. King Xyrus will drive them back as soon as he's well."

"Is the king ill?" I asked.

She caught her lip in her teeth and glanced at me sideways. "I misspoke, milady. He caught a chill recently, but he's on the mend. As healthy as any man of forty."

Forty. My father was forty-two, and he was even more fit than Sami. Fifty was considered a Varenian male's prime. But since we lived longer than the Ilareans, perhaps forty was considered a bit older here. Still, how unhealthy could a man be at that age? A *king*, no less.

The wheels bumped over the wooden planks of the bridge, but my eyes were on the water beneath it. I'd never seen a river before. The water, so clear I could see the rocks and stones on the riverbed, rushed toward us faster than a wave. I scrambled past Ebb to the other side of the carriage and threw back the sash. Farther downriver, the water became white and frothy as it swirled over larger rocks, tumbling toward some unseen destination.

"Where does it go?" I asked Ebb, but her eyes were closed and her normally hollow cheeks were puffed out, as if she were holding her breath. "Are you all right?"

She didn't respond until we finished crossing and were back on the road. Her eyes fluttered open, and she exhaled noisily.

I eyed her curiously. "What were you doing?"

Ebb looked a little sheepish when she answered. "Keeping out the water spirits, milady."

"The what?"

"It's nothing. You should rest up."

"We have water spirits, too," I said, thinking of the ocean around Varenia, how sometimes I'd speak to the spirits through the cracks in our floorboards, asking them to guide me to the best oysters the following day. "But we don't try to keep them out."

I fell asleep for several hours and awoke to sunlight on my face. Ebb had insisted on keeping the curtains shut for most of the journey due to the dust on the road, but she'd pulled them back now to reveal the captain riding alongside us.

"Is everything all right?" she asked him. She'd been worried about "robbers and vandals" before we'd reached Ilara's borders, but she seemed more relaxed today.

"Yes, all fine. We're just—"

"The castle!" I yelled, startling Ebb. I pointed past her to the large stone edifice in the distance. It was massive, the size of one hundred houses at least. Crimson and gold Ilarean flags waved from towers that stretched up toward the clouds. It was surrounded on all sides by gently rolling hills covered in purple and yellow wildflowers, and a small river shimmered in the valley between them. It was even more beautiful than I'd imagined, and for a moment, all my discomfort faded.

"I'm sorry, milady," Osius said. "But that is the *old* castle. We haven't reached New Castle yet."

My smile broadened. If this was the old castle, the new one must be even more magnificent. "Are we stopping? Say yes, please. I have to see it."

"I'm afraid we can only stop for a bit. We still have a few hours' journey ahead of us."

Ebb dropped the sash and urged me back onto the bench.

"It's beautiful," I said. "Why would anyone ever want to leave?"

"New Castle is much safer. Only the king's guard lives here now."

Safer than a giant stone building? What would she think of my little wooden house back in Varenia? "So this is where the captain and his men live?"

"Yes. And the prince."

"The prince?" I was going to meet my future husband *now*, in a dress the color of soot, and stale from five days trapped in a cage? My hands flew to my hair, which felt just as ratty and tangled as I feared. "I can't meet him now!"

Before Ebb could respond, Grig opened the door. "We're going to change out the horses and leave a few of the guards here, as we're in safe territory now, milady. The captain said you wanted to get out and stretch your legs for a bit?"

At the sight of the open door and the blue skies beyond, I forgot about my hair and dress. "Yes," I breathed, already rising to my feet.

"Your shoes, milady," Ebb said, tugging at my skirts.

I sat back down, and Ebb presented a pair of black silk slippers topped with neat little bows. They looked far too delicate and small for my feet, but somehow they slid right on. Captain Osius stepped forward and held his hand out to me, and I took it eagerly. I was so fascinated by the sights around me that I forgot to look down, and my foot landed in a muddy rut in the road with a squelch. I squeaked at the sight of brown mud all over my new slippers. My very first step on land, and I'd made a complete mess of it.

The captain patted my hand reassuringly and led me across the road onto the grass. It was softer than I had imagined, like stepping onto a sponge. In a way, I felt like I was back in the ocean, but instead of being surrounded by blue, everything was green, from the grass to the trees that arched overhead.

I started to smile over my shoulder, excited to see Zadie's reaction to all this. We had imagined the castle when we were small, but never had we dreamed up anything like this. She must be as stunned as I was.

My smile fell as my eyes landed on Ebb instead of Zadie. Somehow, in my excitement, I'd forgotten. I was so used to sharing everything with my sister. Now, every time my gaze landed on the empty space where my twin should be, I felt an ache in my heart at the realization that we would never share anything again.

"Don't worry, milady," Ebb said, taking my other arm. "No one will harm you." She had mistaken my sorrow for trepidation. A small party of guards was riding out to meet us, and two men on foot led four black horses so large they dwarfed their handlers.

As the riders came closer, I noticed that the young man in front was wearing metal armor, which glimmered in the fading sunlight. One hand held the reins while the other rested on the hilt of his sword. His horse was a silvery gray with a white mane that flowed down to its muscled chest. When the young man stopped and dismounted, the guards bowed, and Ebb dropped into a deep curtsy.

I lowered myself shakily next to her, my eyes downcast in respect. But to whom were we bowing? Surely not the prince. I couldn't imagine Ebb would allow me to meet him in such a state.

My heart hammered in my chest as the young man reached for my hand. I didn't even know what to call him. Prince? His Royal Highness? Though we'd been traveling together for five days, Ebb hadn't prepared me at all for this first meeting.

But when I glanced up, the turquoise eyes that met mine did not belong to a stranger, and the lips that brushed the back of my hand were all too familiar, though his mouth was set in a grim line very unlike the amused smile I'd seen in Varenia.

Talin's gaze held mine for ten heartbeats that felt both like an eternity and not nearly long enough. "Welcome to Ilara, my lady. I believe we've already met."

12

For a moment, I wondered if I would faint like Zadie had when Governor Kristos toasted my engagement. Talin had told us he was an emissary—why was everyone bowing to him? And for the love of Thalos, did he know who I really was?

"Talin," I said, and the people around me gasped. "I'm sorry. Sir Talin?"

"This is *Prince* Talin," Ebb murmured next to me, and I glanced over at her with wide eyes.

Oh gods, was *Talin* my fiancé? Had he come disguised as an emissary, just so he could see his future bride for himself? Did Governor Kristos know? Did Mother? No, that was impossible. She would have had some kind of fit if she'd believed she was in the presence of royalty.

Then I remembered the circumstances of our first meeting and flushed so hard, I was sure he would be able to read my thoughts.

"I'm King Xyrus's second son," he clarified. "Prince Ceren, my older brother, awaits you at New Castle."

I should have felt relief, but a strange sense of disappointment washed over me instead. I realized I was staring at him and dropped my gaze again. If he knew who I was, he showed no sign of it, but that didn't mean he wouldn't come to realize it eventually. Talin was supposed to be an emissary I never saw again, not my future husband's *brother*.

I didn't notice he'd kept hold of my hand until he dropped it and the warmth of his touch disappeared. He turned to Osius. "Please, get our future queen to the castle. She's clearly overwhelmed and exhausted from her journey."

I curtsied again, not daring to look at him, and followed Ebb back to the coach. "I don't understand," I murmured as I sat down.

"I'm sorry," Ebb said. "I ought to have explained everything. This is all my fault."

"It's all right, Ebb. But please, could you explain it to me now?"

"Prince Talin is Prince Ceren's half brother and the commander of the king's guard. He lives here, at Old Castle. His mother was sent here from Varenia, like you."

The last Varenian bride was Talin's mother? "And the crown prince?"

"Was born to an Ilarean queen, milady. Prince Ceren will explain everything when we arrive. I promise."

I leaned back against the cushions, my mind racing with unanswered questions. What had happened to Ceren's mother that Talin was born to another woman? Was Talin's mother the king's mistress? The thought was horrifying. All this time, we'd been sending our women to Ilara, with no idea of what was really happening to them. What were our elders thinking?

For the past few days, I'd been so overwhelmed by exhaustion and sickness that I hadn't had much room left to spare for nerves or even grief. But now I wished more than anything that I was back in our house with Zadie, singing songs with made-up words that drove our mother out of the house, muttering in annoyance. I could face anything with my sister and would do anything for her, but I didn't feel brave now. I felt sick and tired and very, very frightened.

We finally came to a halt when the waxing moon was already high in the sky. I climbed out of the carriage facing west, toward home. Then I turned around.

I found myself staring at a wall of darkness, far blacker than the sky itself, which was studded with stars. I looked up, and up, and up, until my neck was craned so far my head was nearly touching my spine. Finally, I saw sky again. What in Thalos's name was I looking at?

Ebb took my arm and led me forward. "Welcome to New Castle."

I staggered back a step. "What?" I asked, my voice barely more than a whisper.

Captain Osius appeared on my other side and took my free arm. "We leave the horses here, milady. I'm afraid it's a bit of a climb to the top of Mount Ayris. If you're too tired, we can wait until sunrise. There's an inn at the bottom of the castle. I could send word to the king."

"No," I said, not wanting to put this off any longer. "I'll climb. It will be nice to stretch my legs after the long journey."

Several men in Ilarean livery appeared from somewhere in

the base of the mountain and took the horses. Others handed torches to the guards, who surrounded me. Now that I could see better, it started to make sense. The mountain was the castle. Or the castle was the mountain. Sami had once described mountains as giant waves made of stone, but I saw nothing here that reminded me of the ocean. As my mind adjusted to what I was seeing, I noticed narrow slits in the sheer face of the mountain. Windows. Faint lights glowed behind some of them.

There were stairs carved into the very stone, which we began to climb in a line, one by one. Someone had fastened a rope to the cliff's face with giant metal spikes, and I used the rope to haul myself up when my leg muscles started to burn. I'd always considered myself strong, but I could barely breathe, my chest heaving against the bodice of my gown as I struggled to fill my lungs. I wanted to tear the dress open and kick my worthless slippers over the side of the mountain, but I didn't have the energy. Ebb was breathing hard as well, but she didn't complain.

"How much farther is it?" I wheezed when it felt like we'd been climbing for hours. The stone stairs were jagged and uneven in height, forcing me to pay attention to every step. The wind blew my already faint words away so fast I was afraid Ebb wouldn't hear.

"Halfway," she called over her shoulder.

My knees buckled at the reply, and I would have fallen backward if not for Grig's hand in the small of my back. "Easy does it, milady. We can call a halt if you need to rest."

I shook my head. "I'm fine. Just a bit dizzy."

"We all have a hard time at the beginning. You'll get better at it."

Twice more I faltered, and Grig's hand was there to steady me. When I was queen, I would see to it that Grig got some sort of promotion.

Finally, when my muscles were shaky with fatigue, the stairs leveled off and I found myself on a wide platform. "Who built this?" I asked Grig. He at least had the decency to appear winded.

"The entrance to the castle is the mouth of a cavern. Princess Ilara's brother, King Maldon, built the walls."

An iron door as tall as five men standing on top of one another loomed above us. A guard called out, and a smaller door swung in, admitting the guards one by one.

The cavern inside was massive. The ceilings soared so high above us, I half expected to see clouds. But someone had polished the stone ceiling until it was as smooth as the inside of a seashell, then painted it with elaborate scenes in reds and blues, cream and gold. There were multiple fireplaces along the sides of the hall and lanterns hanging from the ceiling high above.

Beneath my feet, the floor was made from the same dark gray stone as the mountain, and its polished surface helped reflect the glow of light from above. At the far end of the room—if one could even call it such—sat a throne carved from the dark stone. It was tall and wide enough for two men, the stone cut and polished in a way that made the facets shine like black jewels. I had imagined a throne before, but it was nothing like this thing jutting from the floor, as dark and imposing as the mountain itself.

It was also empty.

I turned to Ebb. "Where is the king?"

"We'll meet him in his chambers, once you've had a bath and a chance to change."

I'd never been so excited about the prospect of bathing in my life. I followed Ebb across the room to one of the many corridors that split off from it, taking care with my steps, as the floor was slippery and my shoes provided hardly any traction.

As soon as we entered the corridor, I realized how dark it was in the castle. Yes, it was nighttime, but I hadn't spotted a single window yet. The ones I'd seen from outside must be for lookouts. Here, the only light came from a few flameless torches, the ends wrapped in what appeared to be some kind of algae. It glowed pale blue, like a maiden's hair jellyfish.

"What is it?" I asked, pausing to get a closer look. The light was as bright as blue flame, but there was no heat.

"Lunar moss, from the forest," Ebb said. "It glows when the moon is up. It works best on a night like tonight, when the moon is almost full. Servants harvest it once a month for the torches."

"And when there is no moon?" I asked.

"We use a fungus called foxfire, but it doesn't give off quite as much light as the lunar moss."

I shuddered at the thought of even less light. "What about the daytime? Aren't there windows?"

"In the places with adequate ventilation, like the great hall, there are fires. No windows, I'm afraid. It does tend to get a bit darker as you go farther into the mountain, but your eyes will adjust."

Without fire, it wasn't just dark; it was cold. The heat of

my exertion during the climb had left me, so I wrapped my arms around myself and followed Ebb.

"Ah, here we are." She paused in front of a door where a guard stood watch. He opened it silently at our approach and stepped aside to let us enter.

Inside was another smaller corridor with several doors leading off from it. She turned down another hall. "Here are your chambers."

Ebb led me into the large room, its ceiling polished and painted like the one in the great hall. Tapestries and rugs covered the stone surfaces, adding a small amount of warmth. An enormous bed sat in the center, piled high with blankets and fur throws.

The only other furniture was a large wooden wardrobe, with doors carved into strange swirling shapes. For a room that was roughly the size of the governor's house, it was surprisingly bare. Then again, this wasn't someone's house; it was merely a place to sleep.

A bath had been prepared in a stone tub carved out of the wall. A folding screen of painted silk stood next to it.

"Now then, shall we get you bathed and changed?" Ebb asked. "I'll have a light supper brought, so that you can eat while I fix your hair. It's very late, and the king will want to get his rest."

I felt the same way. My eyelids were heavy, and my muscles ached from the climb. "What about the prince? Will I meet him tonight?"

"I don't believe so. But I'm sure he'll be here tomorrow."

That was a relief, at least. I undressed behind the screen and climbed into the stone tub before the cold air had a chance to seep in. This was my first hot bath ever, and after so many days without washing, it felt wonderful. My aching muscles immediately began to relax. Ebb undid my braids and washed my hair with some kind of perfumed soap that lathered and foamed, then rinsed it all out with more warm water. I began to worry the water might rinse the stain from my cheek, but Ebb didn't seem to notice anything amiss.

I could have stayed in the bath forever, but Ebb's clipped movements reminded me we were in a hurry. I climbed out and immediately regretted it when the cold air hit my bare skin.

Ebb handed me a towel, then walked to the wardrobe and opened the doors. "Now, milady, you'll need to choose your gown quickly. I believe this one is appropriate for the occasion, but there's also—"

"You choose," I said, sensing her urgency. "I trust you."

As promised, a light repast sat on a small table to the side of a stool, where I perched so Ebb could get to work on my hair. I nibbled on some kind of dark bread and a creamy cheese with figs, but I was too anxious to eat more than a few bites. Ebb began to coil my hair, twisting and pinning with a deftness I hadn't expected. Despite her efficiency, she was much gentler than Zadie, and she left half of my hair down, which was a nice rest for my scalp.

After, she helped me into a dark blue gown embroidered with threads of gold. I had grown used to the subdued clothing, though I still didn't like it, but I admired the way the metallic threads shimmered in the light from the lunar moss set into small lamps in the wall.

When Ebb left to change as well, I opened my trunk from

home, which a servant had delivered while I was dressing. I pulled out the little jar of stain for my scar and approached the large standing mirror slowly. I'd seen my reflection in the hand mirror in the carriage, but I hadn't seen all of me at once. Not in my entire life, now that I thought about it. I wasn't sure I was ready for this.

But before I could stop myself, there I was. Or at least a version of me, unlike anything I'd ever imagined. Who was this girl with the stilt-straight posture and neatly styled hair? The fabric of the gown was richer than all the others I'd worn, and I ran my hands across the flat plane of my stomach and the curves of my hips, accentuated by the corset.

Even my face was that of a stranger. My cheekbones appeared more pronounced, though that could just be the shadows in the dark room playing tricks on me, and the way Ebb had pinned up my hair made my neck seem long and graceful. I looked a little like my mother, I realized, with her golden eyes and proud mouth.

The scar was still covered by the stain, but I reapplied it anyway. Without the mark on my cheek, I could almost pretend I really *was* Zadie.

"What do I do?" I asked my reflection, as though my sister were there with me.

Square your shoulders, I imagined her saying. *Chin up. The elders wouldn't have chosen us if they didn't believe we could do this.*

I heard the door open behind me. I turned to Ebb, my heart suddenly beating faster. This was it. I was going to meet the king.

"You look lovely, milady," she said, handing me a short

capelet made of the softest black fur. "It's cold in the corridors, milady. This will help keep you warm. Are you ready?"

I nodded and strode past her down the corridor, as though I'd been born to do this. In my mind, Zadie walked just behind me, assuring me I had.

Our company grew as we walked to the king's chambers, far from the great hall. I noticed Grig and the captain fall into line behind us, and multiple servants seemed to appear out of nowhere, wearing dark, nondescript clothing under shawls and gloves woven from some kind of animal fiber. We came to a stop at a pair of tall stone doors painstakingly carved with horned beasts and roses, reminding me of the little button Sami had traded for. Zadie and Sami had insisted I take the traveling cloak with me, since Zadie wouldn't need it in Varenia, but I'd never taken it out of the trunk during our journey. Now that I'd seen Ebb toss aside entire outfits like they were refuse, I realized how little value a single brass button would have to these people. I wondered how many pearls Sami had sacrificed for it.

The moment the doors opened, I was hit with the sickly sweet smell of illness, like a bin of rotting fruit at the floating market. Someone had gone through a good deal of trouble to try to hide the odor with perfumed incense, and the combination of smells was nearly overpowering. Several ladies stood near the king's bed with little sachets pressed to their noses.

I'd thought my bed was large, but King Xyrus's bed was twice the size of it, made larger by the skeletal man who sat propped up against a stack of pillows. He was so pale he nearly faded into the white linens surrounding him. His gray beard was long and straggly, matching the few tufts of hair left on his liver-spotted head. He looked ancient, older than the oldest Varenian elder. This man couldn't possibly be the same age as my father.

I was led forward by Captain Osius, who stopped to kneel before the king. I imitated the ladies around me, wishing I'd practiced more back home, but curtsying as deeply as I dared without falling over.

The king's watery eyes blinked open at the sound of the captain's voice. "Your Grace, pardon the late hour. We have brought a special visitor from Varenia."

With the help of a nobleman, the king sat up a bit straighter, smacking his lips like a child who'd just woken from a long nap. "Ah yes, Zadie. Welcome to Ilara, my dear."

I blinked at the sound of my sister's name on an Ilarean tongue, the *z* sounding almost like an *s*. No one here had called me anything but *milady* thus far, and it was a good reminder that I was supposed to be my sister.

I stepped forward and took the king's outstretched hand, doing my best to breathe through my mouth. I nearly jumped when he started to cough suddenly and violently, his entire withered frame shaking from the effort, and released his bony hand as gently as possible. How could this be the man controlling the Varenians? If the governor knew about the king's condition, why didn't he stand up to him? And if he didn't know, I would make sure Sami passed along the information, if I ever made it to the port market.

I waited patiently for the king to sip his wine, sloshing some of the dark red liquid onto the white bedclothes. I expected him to speak again when he finished, but he settled back down among his pillows and closed his eyes.

The nobleman assisting him stepped forward and kissed my hand before lowering himself in an exaggerated bow. After that, one by one, the other lords and ladies stepped forward, each offering their services and welcoming me to Ilara. The ladies, dressed in gowns made of various shadowy fabrics adorned with beads and bows, fussed over me and noted how well I looked after such an arduous journey. The lords were dressed similarly to Talin when he'd visited Ilara, but none had his air of warmth and vitality.

Prince Talin, I reminded myself. My future husband's *brother.*

Some of the lords and ladies were pale, like Ebb, probably from spending so much time in this dark mountain. But even those who weren't naturally fair-skinned looked wan and tired. I noticed a few people had used some sort of white powder to make their hair lighter. I'd never felt so alone in my life as I did there in that chamber, surrounded by all these otherworldly strangers.

Finally, when I was sure I would faint from exhaustion, Ebb found me and whispered in my ear that we should retire for the evening. Back in my chamber, she helped me undress for the night and prepare for my first real rest in days. The bed was so tall, a small footstool had been provided to help me climb in. Once among the blankets and throws, I felt ridiculous. Why would one person need so much space to sleep?

Ebb went to the door and curtsied. "I'll leave you now, milady."

I glanced around the massive room, only now realizing there was no other place to sleep. "You're not staying?"

She seemed surprised for a moment, then smiled. "It's not proper for a servant to sleep in this part of the castle, milady. There's a bell on your nightstand. If you need anything, just ring, and one of the guards will alert me."

I should have known a servant wouldn't sleep with a future princess, but I'd never slept alone before. I was coming to think of Ebb as a friend, when I needed to remember that this was her job, nothing more. Still, I couldn't deny how grateful I was to have her here. "Thank you, Ebb. For everything."

She blushed and curtsied before slipping out the door. There was no fireplace here, presumably because there was nowhere for the smoke to escape, which explained all the blankets. The only light in the room came from the lunar moss. I burrowed down in my covers, feeling like an eel poking its head out of a grotto.

I must have fallen asleep without realizing it, because I woke up some time later thinking I was drowning, flailing in the sheets as though they were a fishing net. I kicked the blankets away from me until they lay piled on the floor. Now it was just me in a nightdress on top of the giant feather mattress. And I was freezing.

I pulled one of the fur throws off the floor and wrapped myself in it, feeling even more pitiful than I had in the carriage. The room was somehow cold and stuffy at the same time, the bed was far too soft, and it was too quiet without the soft breathing of my sister and the faint snoring from my father across the house.

My little trunk had been placed at the foot of my bed, and I scooted over to it, still wrapped in the blanket. As I lifted the lid, I was hit with the briny scent of the ocean, and the throb of homesickness was so intense my eyes filled with tears. I tucked my few pieces of clothing inside the wardrobe. The coral knife and pearl necklace went in my nightstand.

Sensing Ebb's exhaustion earlier, I'd let her go without undoing my hair, but I wasn't used to sleeping with pins in it. I went to the full-length mirror and sat down cross-legged before it, feeling ridiculous in my nightgown with the voluminous sleeves and lace-edged neckline. I set to work unpinning my hair, then massaged my scalp with my fingers the way Zadie would have done had she been here.

With my hair in wild waves around me and the soft blue light of the lunar moss reflecting off my skin, I looked like the sea witch from the stories Sami used to tell us. According to Varenian legend, she lived deep in the ocean, causing storms that sank ships and drowned sailors, whom the witch took as her lovers. The stories were violent and inappropriate for children, which made us delight in them all the more. Mother would have been appalled if she'd ever caught us; she believed only the gods had the power to cause storms and sink ships.

I gathered my hair around me and crawled back to the pile of discarded blankets on the floor, which felt a little closer to my straw mattress from home. I pulled a wayward throw up to my chin and cried myself to sleep.

13

I was woken by a shriek, followed by the sounds of the door being flung open and an armed guard forcing himself into the room.

"Milady, are you hurt?" the guard asked.

I sat up, blinking in the gloom, and rubbed my eyes. Ebb stood in front of me, a freshly laundered pile of linens in a heap at her feet, her hands covering her mouth. The guard stood behind her, one hand on the hilt of his sword, his mouth slightly agape.

"What is it?"

"I'm sorry, milady. It frightened me to see you in such a state."

I turned around and caught sight of myself in the mirror. It was worse than I'd feared. My nearly waist-length hair was everywhere, and I was tangled up in my nightgown. Noticing my bare legs for the first time, I hastily pulled the fabric down and did my best to subdue my hair.

"You may go," Ebb said to the guard, who was still frozen in place. He snapped his mouth shut and made a hasty retreat.

"I'm sorry, Ebb," I said, my cheeks burning. "The mattress was too soft, and there were too many blankets, and the pins in my hair were pinching my scalp. I couldn't sleep like that."

She regained her composure quickly, at least. "I understand. I'll knock first next time."

"That would probably be better for everyone."

As Ebb stooped to gather up the linens, I realized that the moss lanterns had gone dim. It wasn't until I looked up that I understood where the light came from. There were dozens of holes cut into the ceiling high above me, and a small amount of light filtered down through the glass in each one.

She followed my gaze. "The most important chambers have these skylights."

As charming as the term *skylights* was, their existence didn't make me feel important. Was I really going to spend my days in perpetual semidarkness? I was a creature of the sun and air, not some pale worm who'd spent her entire existence under a rock at the bottom of the ocean. The walls around me suddenly seemed unbearably heavy.

"I need air," I said.

"Milady?"

"*Fresh* air. I can't live like this." My heart had begun to pound in my chest, and I was finding it hard to breathe. My skin prickled and itched with sweat. "Please, Ebb!"

"What can I do?" she asked gently, though I could see my panic was beginning to unnerve her. "Even if I was allowed to let you leave, you can't go out dressed like that. Try to take some deep breaths."

"I can't," I said, clawing at my chest. "That's the problem."
My eyes darted around the room. I needed something of Varenia to cling to, something that could bring me back to myself. My eyes landed on the bath, which hadn't been emptied
last night due to the late hour. Ebb had promised someone
would take care of it this morning.

Without thinking, I stripped off my nightgown and plunged
into the tub, forcing my head under the surface. The water
was freezing, but that actually seemed to help. For a moment,
I just sat there, my hair fanning out around me, my heart rate
instantly slowing. I counted out the beats. One. Two. Three.
Four. All the way to one hundred.

I had started counting from one again when I heard muffled shouts from above and opened my eyes. It was Ebb. I
lifted my head from the water and pushed the dripping hair
off my face.

"What's the matter?" I asked, barely out of breath.

"You were down there for ages! I was afraid you were
drowning."

Now that my senses had come back to me, I realized just
how cold it was in the water. "Can you bring me a towel?"

She brought over several and helped me out of the tub.
"How did you do that, milady?"

I smiled as I wrung my hair out over the tub. "It's easy
for me. We do that from the time we're little in Varenia. I'm
sorry for worrying you. I just needed to calm down, and I
couldn't think of another way."

"I understand. At least, I think I can imagine how I'd feel
if I was taken from Ilara to live in your home. All that open

water... From now on, I'll make sure you have a warm bath prepared every morning *and* evening, if you'd like."

I couldn't imagine having access to so much fresh water, but the bath had helped immensely. "That would be nice, Ebb. At least until I'm settled."

She helped me dress in a silky black gown that flowed behind me as I walked. Ebb said that everyone here was in mourning for Princess Ilara. Did that mean no one had worn anything but mourning colors for hundreds of years? I thought of my red dress, of how I must have looked to Talin in such a bold color. That alone must have been shocking.

Ebb pinned up my hair in the same half-up style, which I quite liked. It wasn't as messy as wearing it all down, but it meant my neck wasn't bared to the chill.

"Everyone is talking about you this morning, how lovely your complexion is. One of the cooks said it's all the sunlight that makes you Varenians so healthy. We don't get much sun here in the castle."

"So I'm learning." I felt guilty for thinking Ebb looked ill when I first met her. I appreciated the loveliness of her white-gold hair now, her fair skin. She would have burned to a crisp in Varenia, but it suited this place somehow. It wasn't her fault she had no access to light and fresh air.

My stomach growled loud enough for both of us to hear it. It was impossible to keep track of time here in the mountain.

"What time is it?" I asked as Ebb fastened a long gold chain around my neck. A heavy black jewel hung between my breasts. It was cold and uncomfortable, but I didn't want to seem ungrateful. I'd never worn jewelry before.

"Nearly midday. I'm afraid you slept through breakfast, but I figured you needed your rest after the journey you've had."

I gasped and nearly knocked over my stool as I rose. "Midday! Is the royal family expecting me?"

"Not to worry. The king was a little overwhelmed by the commotion last night and has decided to keep to his bed today. I'll take you down for luncheon, and then you'll have a tour of the castle."

"And the prince?" I asked, checking to make sure that the stain was still covering my scar completely as I passed the mirror.

"I'm not sure, milady."

As Ebb led me back through the corridors, I tried to memorize our route. I noticed channels cut into the stone, with trickles of water running through them, and looked questioningly at Ebb.

"Rainwater from above," she explained. "It collects in the channels and gathers in wells throughout the castle."

Clever, I thought as we walked past the great hall and down a flight of stairs to a smaller hall with a long table stretching nearly half its length.

"This is the dining hall," Ebb said. "You may take meals in your room if you prefer, unless the king or prince requests your presence, of course."

She gestured for me to sit next to the chair at the foot of the table, presumably where the prince sat, though I had the room to myself at the moment. Servants brought me six different courses. Some, like the olives and grapes we'd had in Varenia, were familiar and delicious, but others, like the cubes of bloody red meat on a silver platter, made my stomach turn.

There was enough food for several families here, and I hated wasting it, but I couldn't eat this much food in a week.

"Ebb," I whispered when the server had left. She hurried toward me.

"Is everything all right?"

"This afternoon we need to go over a few things. Like how to address people, and what the three different sizes of forks are used for. And what are those little round white things that jiggled when the man set them down?"

"Quail eggs, milady."

"Yes, well, I need to know how to eat them. If they're any good."

She smiled. "We will begin your lessons this afternoon."

"Oh, and I was wondering when I'll be able to meet the queen. I would love to speak with her."

The door at the far end of the hall slammed closed with a *bang*, and Ebb and I looked up to see a young man in black walking toward us. Ebb dropped into a curtsy before I'd even had a chance to stand.

"You must be Zadie," the man said. His skin was the whitest I'd ever seen, even paler than Ebb's, and his straight blond hair, which was pulled back into a ponytail at his nape, had more of a silver cast to it than Ebb's did. His eyes were a steely gray under elegantly arched brows. I couldn't stop myself from staring.

Ebb cleared her throat lightly.

"Y-yes," I stammered. "And you are?"

I thought I heard Ebb groan a bit next to me.

"I am Prince Ceren," he said with a chuckle. "Your future

husband. And I'm afraid it will be impossible for you to meet the queen, my dear."

This was the prince? I could have imagined the exact opposite of Talin and still wouldn't have come close. "Why is that?" I asked, my voice trembling like the little white quail eggs.

"Because, my lady," he said, his eyes never leaving mine. "The queen is dead."

A nervous laugh slipped out of me, and I turned to Ebb, sure that the prince was joking. But Ebb only gave an apologetic shake of her head. I faced the prince again. "I'm sorry for my confusion. I was told everything would be explained to me once I arrived. Is your mother the queen?"

"She was. She died in childbirth." His voice betrayed no hint of emotion.

"Oh, I'm so sorry." Why hadn't Ebb explained all of this to me? I didn't even know if Talin's mother had been married to King Xyrus. "And the last Varenian girl sent here?" I asked, hoping that sounded diplomatic enough.

"My father's second wife is also dead. It doesn't go too well for queens around here, I'm sorry to say."

I wanted Ebb to tell me he was making some kind of sick joke, but she seemed as cowed by this man's presence as I felt. I forced myself to stand and dropped into a curtsy. "Your Highness."

I almost recoiled when he reached for my hand. His fingers were long and as white as a ray's belly. He wore a dark metal ring on his right hand, set with a small red stone. I shivered as he brushed his lips across the back of my hand. There was something unnatural about him. His features were handsome, like his brother's: a straight nose, a strong jaw, and a sensuous mouth. But his smile was cold, and his pale eyes revealed no feelings at all.

I pulled my hand away and tried to smile at him. He helped lower me back into my seat and settled into the chair next to me. "How did you sleep, my lady? Was the room to your liking? Was the bed large enough?"

My cheeks colored when I realized how foolish I'd been to wonder why *one* person needed a bed so big. "Yes, thank you."

"Good. I thought I might show you around the castle today, seeing as my dear father won't be making it out of bed himself."

My eyes darted to his. "You must have better things to do than give a tour of the castle," I said softly.

"Nonsense. It's the least I can do after you've come so far to be my bride."

I couldn't help squirming in my seat. I suspected he knew he was making me uncomfortable, and he was enjoying it.

"How old are you?" he asked.

"Seventeen."

"Ah yes, precisely the age of Queen Talia when she came twenty years ago. I was only a babe at the time, so I have no recollection of it. But she is a part of many of my childhood memories. As is my brother, Talin. He was born just a year after they were married. Father didn't waste any time." His smirk held none of the amused charm of his brother's. Beneath my gown, my skin crawled.

"When did Queen Talia die? No one in Varenia has heard this news." Or if they had, they hadn't bothered to tell me.

"It was four years ago now, I believe. When Talin was just

fifteen. He was made commander of the guard not long after. At my request."

Something about the lack of emotion in his voice told me Ceren hadn't done this because it would be best for his brother, though perhaps it was. I couldn't imagine Talin in this place. "Can I ask how she died?"

"Murder."

I gasped and clapped a hand to my mouth. He'd said the word so casually, as if it meant nothing, the death of a woman who must have been like a mother to him in some way.

"It was a servant," Ceren continued. "The queen's blood was found all over her room. The carpets were drenched with it, though Talia's body was never found. We suspect it was hidden away in one of the many abandoned chambers in the castle. The servant was beheaded the next day."

My meal began to climb its way up my throat. Everything I'd learned since coming here had been far worse than I'd imagined, but to discover that the last Varenian woman sent to Ilara had been murdered frightened me in a way I couldn't describe. As children, Zadie and I had spent hours pretending to be the queen of Ilara, making crowns out of seaflowers and draping ourselves in Mother's dresses, a game she'd actually encouraged. She would lift our chins with her fingertips and help us practice our curtsies. They'd been lessons, I realized now, not games. I should have paid better attention.

I swallowed when Ceren brought his hand up and placed two fingers under my chin, just like Mother had. I was suddenly conscious of my scar, knowing if he looked close enough, he'd be able to see the raised skin under the stain. He slid his fingers down my throat and rested them in the hollow at the base of it. It was the strangest gesture, but I forced myself to meet his gaze. His enlarged pupils were as black as the mountain that surrounded us.

His fingers trailed farther down, until they rested just above my heart, near the black jewel. I heard Ebb's sharp intake of breath behind me.

"Oh, don't sound so scandalized," the prince said to Ebb over his shoulder. "She's going to be my wife soon enough." His eyes flicked back to mine. "Your heartbeat is strong and steady. That's good."

I swallowed the bile in my throat.

"How does it feel, knowing you'll be queen of all of this soon?" His voice was soft enough that only I could hear it, his fingers still resting above my heart. Could he feel how fast it was beating now? "I've never seen your home, but I can't imagine it can compare to the beauty and splendor of Ilara."

I should have sunk my teeth into the flesh of my tongue to stop myself from speaking, but I didn't. "On the contrary, Your Highness."

Something flashed in his eyes, but he smiled. "I see. You'll have plenty of time to tell me about it over the next… Well, I suppose how long you're with us remains to be seen."

Terror coursed through me as he ran his fingers back up to my throat. He was so much bigger than I was—he could probably snap my neck with his bare hands if he wanted to.

Finally, Ceren lowered his hand and stood, wiping his lips on a napkin even though he hadn't eaten anything. "I'll be at your room in an hour to take you on your tour. Perhaps you'll find something here to your liking after all."

14

Back in my room, I paced over the scattered carpets, my mind racing. Ceren was cold and cruel. How could I marry someone who spoke so lightly of murder, who seemed to relish other people's discomfort?

A small part of me wondered if the truth about my identity would get me sent home to Varenia. But I knew deep down that he would likely kill me, and worst of all, punish my people. I couldn't risk that. The only silver lining I could find in any of this was that at least I was here instead of Zadie. The thought of that man touching my sister made me want to destroy something. I settled for pummeling one of my eighteen pillows.

"Milady," Ebb said quietly, placing a light hand on my shoulder when I'd finished my tantrum. "The prince will be here soon."

I looked up. "I can't marry him, Ebb."

Her eyes were soft and sympathetic. "Be careful," she whispered, glancing around the room as though someone might hear us. "Sound carries strangely in this mountain." She placed a finger on the wall next to a small hole carved into the stone. No doubt it led through to another chamber, where someone could listen if they chose.

Let them hear me, I thought. What was the worst they could do? Stick me in a cave and force me to marry the most disagreeable man in history? Oh wait, they'd already done that.

I smacked another pillow for good measure.

"How could you not tell me the queen was dead?" I asked, resuming my pacing. "Didn't you think I had a right to know? She was one of my people, Ebb. The only person here who might have understood me."

"I am sorry, milady. But I was expressly forbidden to speak of the late queen."

"By whom? The prince?"

"By the king himself."

I folded my arms across my chest, remembering the way Ceren had touched me there as though it were nothing, and sat down on the bed. "He probably knew I'd never come if I found out the previous queen had been murdered. How did she die?"

"They believe she was stabbed, because of all the blood. That's what I heard, anyway. I was still living in the village then."

I patted the bed next to me, inviting her to sit. Ebb bit her lip, hesitating, and then perched at the edge of the mattress. Perhaps this was not an appropriate way for a lady and her maid to interact, but I was used to confiding everything in someone else. Right now, I didn't need a servant; I needed a friend.

"We could send word to the prince that you're too tired for the tour, put it off for later."

"What good would putting it off do? I'm supposed to marry the man, remember?" I shuddered at the thought of his cold hands on my bare skin. "Do you know when the wedding is planned for?"

"They'll want to have it before the king passes, I imagine."

I raised my eyebrows. "That could be tomorrow."

"He's been in a similar condition for six months, at least."

I turned to her fully, forcing her to meet my gaze. "When will I be allowed to leave the castle?"

"I—"

We heard footsteps just before a heavy knock on the door. My stomach plummeted like a stone.

"Will you come with me?" I asked Ebb. "Please?"

The door flew open before she could respond, and we both jumped to our feet. Ceren stepped forward, but he had the decency to pause on the threshold at least. "Are you ready, my lady?"

I nodded and glanced behind me at Ebb.

"Your maid can wait here. I'm sure she has plenty of work to keep her busy."

My mouth opened and closed like a fish, but Ebb only bobbed a quick curtsy and handed me my wrap. "Very well," I said, pulling the black fur capelet around my shoulders. "Lead the way."

"After you. I insist."

I hated the idea of having my back to Ceren, but I didn't

see much of a choice. I began to walk down the hallway when a guard stepped up beside me.

"Milady."

I turned and smiled at the familiar, boyish face. "Grig, you're here."

"I hope that's all right."

"It's wonderful." He offered me his arm, but I was too conscious of Ceren's presence behind me to accept.

"You're one of my brother's men, aren't you?" the prince asked.

Grig turned to bow. "Yes, Your Highness."

"Don't you have work to be doing? We have plenty of guards here at New Castle."

"Prince Talin asked that one of us remain here with the lady."

Ceren raised his eyebrows. "I'm surprised he could spare you. He says there aren't enough men at Old Castle these days, that we're 'vulnerable' to attack."

I thought of the guard at the bridge, of the woman king to the south. Was an attack on Ilara really so out of the question?

"Shall I leave, Your Highness?" Grig asked.

Ceren waved a hand at him. "No, no. You're here, you may as well stay. Wouldn't want to anger dear Prince Talin, would we?"

Prince Talin. At the sound of his name, my mind went back to yesterday, to when he'd dismounted his horse and taken my hand. I blushed at the memory of his gaze holding mine. I couldn't imagine Talin taking sick pleasure in tormenting me the way Ceren did.

Of course, Talin was also the only person in Ilara who

might be able to guess my secret. I should be grateful he lived far away and that our chances for interaction were limited.

I should be. But I wasn't.

"Ah, I know that look," Ceren said, taking my arm and prodding Grig on ahead of us. Gods, was it that obvious? "My brother is blessed with both a handsome face and a charming disposition. He's a favorite here at court."

There was a bitterness to his tone that hinted at jealousy. But Ceren was not unattractive, and my mother was living proof that charm could be an illusion.

"Did he make an appearance at Old Castle yesterday?" Ceren asked.

"Yes. And we met in Varenia, as I'm sure you recall." The words were deliberately pointed. I wanted to know why Ceren had sent his brother as his errand boy.

"Oh yes, I'd forgotten. He said you were perfect. 'As pure and unblemished as a Varenian pearl.' I hate it when he's right."

The night we'd had dinner at the governor's house, Talin had said he couldn't imagine anyone more lovely. He had been looking at me when he said it, but if he truly believed that lack of imperfection equaled beauty, then I must have been mistaken. My scar tingled as my cheeks heated with embarrassment.

"'Beware the lionfish, my dear,'" Ceren said in a low voice.

"What?"

"Isn't that how the Varenian song goes? I remember Queen Talia singing it to Talin when he was little. You wave children love your lullabies."

The line was part of a Varenian cradle song we all grew

up with. It warned children to stay away from dangerous sea creatures, but each line had a hidden meaning. For example, lionfish are curiously beautiful, a spectacle of a fish that begs to be touched, despite their venomous spines. But we weren't just to beware of lionfish; we were to steer clear of anyone too flashy, too proud. I was surprised Ceren knew this, and that he would use it to describe his own brother.

"'Beware the lionfish, my dear,'" I murmured. "'Beware the fish that's made of stone.'"

"Hmm?"

"That's the next line of the song." The stonefish was even more dangerous than the lionfish, in part because it had stronger venom, but also because it was hard to see. A stonefish could blend in to the rocks around it so well you wouldn't know it was there until it was too late and you'd placed a hand or foot directly on top of it. The message there was clear: be careful and cautious with your heart, for things are not always what they seem. At least the lionfish made its presence known.

"I haven't heard it in years, so you'll forgive me for forgetting."

I inclined my head.

"Your name means pearl, does it not?"

"Yes," I said, my thoughts immediately turning to my sister. I had always been the coral, never the pearl. Now I was supposed to be the thing everyone wanted, the object a future king desired above all else.

I had slowed my pace to match the prince's, and Grig was now almost out of sight at the end of the corridor. Ceren moved his hand from my arm to the small of my back.

"There's something in here I'd like to show you," he said, reaching for a door I hadn't noticed in the dim corridor.

I wanted to call out to Grig, but Ceren ushered me through the door before I could say anything. We were in a chamber roughly the size of my bedroom, and for a moment I feared this was Ceren's personal chamber. He went to the far side and lit a match from a small lantern, then touched it to a pile of logs in the fireplace. As the wood caught fire, more of the room came into view.

It appeared to be a workroom, not a bedroom. There were three tables of varying sizes, all covered in glass bottles and bowls, as well as various objects I had no words for. On the floor in the corner lay what looked like an empty sack. A long hose was coiled next to it.

"This is my study," the prince said. "I love to learn, about anything and everything." He picked up a small bowl that was filled with pink pearls of all shapes and sizes. "One of the things that most fascinates me is the Varenian pearl. I'm sure you know people here use them in creams and ointments for all manner of ailment. I burned my hand on the fire last week." He held his hand up, palm out. "Not a trace of the blister. No scar. Miraculous."

I looked at the bowl of pearls and felt my anger rise. There were enough there to feed my family for a year. We were harvesting the pearls to extinction, and for what? To spare one man from a blister?

"Your people know far more about the pearls than I do, no doubt," he continued. The words coming out of his mouth were perfectly harmless. He'd said nothing sinister or frightening in the past few minutes, and yet my heart hammered in my chest. He clearly harbored some sort of animosity toward Queen Talia and Prince Talin, maybe toward all Varenians. I wiped my sweating palms on my skirts. My body was telling me I was in danger, even if my mind didn't want to accept it.

Ceren walked over to the empty sack and held up a corner of it to show me. "This will be my greatest invention yet. It's an underwater breathing apparatus. With this device, a man can stay underwater for ten minutes, maybe more. But it's not ready, unfortunately. The test we conducted yesterday had rather disastrous results, I'm sorry to say. We lost a servant in the process."

He watched me for a reaction as I struggled to conceal my horror. How could anyone dismiss death so casually?

"Such a shame, really. He was just a year younger than you. By the time—"

"Milady?"

I spun around at the sound of Grig's voice. "Grig!"

"I'm terribly sorry. I didn't realize you'd stopped until I was halfway down the next corridor. Is everything all right?"

"Why wouldn't it be?" Ceren snapped. "She's been with me the entire time. What could be safer than that?"

I could think of a thousand things safer than this man—a hammerhead shark, perhaps. Or even a riptide.

I took hold of Grig's arm. "I'm sorry, Your Highness, but I'm afraid I'm not feeling well. Still adjusting to land, I think. I'll return to my chamber for a bath, if it's all right with you."

"Ah yes, your baths. I heard you've ordered two a day. You must feel like a fish out of water here, hmm?"

Had he found out about my baths from a servant, or from one of the tunnels through the stone? And if someone was listening to me, did that mean they could also see me if they wanted to?

I cleared my throat. "Yes, that is precisely how I feel. Thank you for showing me your…room."

"We can resume the tour later, when you're feeling better."

I was almost through the doorway when Ceren called after us. "Oh, and Grig? Feel free to return to Old Castle. Your services here are no longer required."

I lay in my bath until the water had turned cold and my skin began to pucker. Since leaving Varenia, I hadn't washed my face unless I was sure I was alone, and even then I immediately reapplied the stain. I was getting so used to seeing myself without my scar that on the one occasion the stain wore off in my sleep during the journey, the sight of it had startled me.

Ebb wrapped a towel around me as I stepped out of the tub onto the cold floor. Far worse than the oppressive weight of the stone around me was the darkness. It had only been one day without sun, and already I ached for it so deeply I could feel it in my bones. I looked up at the pathetic skylights and scowled. The amount of light that filtered through was barely enough to illuminate the room during the day. How had Talia survived here as long as she did?

The king was planning to attend dinner that evening, so Ebb dressed me in another dark gown, this one with a diamond-patterned skirt, the rows of diamonds made of different fabrics to highlight the contrasts. The collar was up to my throat, but a diamond had been cut out of the bodice to reveal the bare skin beneath, right where Ceren had touched me. I had never worn anything that exposed my chest like this in Varenia.

"Why must everything be so dull and colorless?" I muttered as I smoothed out the wide skirts with my palms.

Her eyes met mine in the mirror. "It's as I told you, milady—we're in mourning for Princess Ilara. She died at sea when she was kidnapped by a prince from Kuven."

"I thought Prince Laef and Princess Ilara ran away to be together," I said, confused. "That's what we were told in Varenia."

Ebb frowned. "You must have misunderstood."

I shook my head. No doubt in Kuven, people claimed that Ilara was responsible for Prince Laef's death. "But how can an entire kingdom still be in mourning for a princess who died hundreds of years ago?"

"When Ilara died, her younger brother Maldon became the crown prince, as she had no other sisters," she explained. "He was only ten at the time, and Ilara's death hit him extremely hard. He developed a debilitating fear of water. That's why the castle was moved here to Mount Ayris, away from the ocean and rivers, and even lakes. He also ordered a decree that everyone wear mourning clothes under penalty of death. The decree has never been lifted."

"But why not?"

"I'm not quite sure, milady." She began to pile my hair onto my head, fastening it with jet pins that glittered amid the coils. "I believe it's because we've been waiting for a new princess all this time. A princess who will restore the queendom to what it once was, who will quell the uprisings and unite the territories under the Ilarean flag. But our kings only ever have sons."

I twisted my mouth to the side. I still didn't see why we had to wear such joyless clothing.

"Shall I powder your hair, milady?" Ebb asked as she adjusted the final pin.

I turned to look at her. "Whatever for?"

"Some of the lords and ladies do it to curry favor with Prince Ceren."

I shook my head, and she continued to fix my hair. I tried to imagine myself doing this, day in and day out, for a century. The thought brought tears to my eyes.

I wiped them away and took a deep breath. I had only left Varenia a week ago. I still had two weeks to learn something valuable to tell Sami at the market, aside from the fact that the Varenian queen was dead and her husband might soon follow in her wake.

Be brave, I told myself. *For Zadie. For Varenia.*

15

The dining hall was filled with lords and ladies and dozens of servants, all witnesses to what I was sure would
be many missteps on my part. Ebb and I had gone over the
cutlery and various forms of address, but I hadn't fully memorized everything yet.

Unfortunately, she couldn't stay with me through the meal.

I closed my eyes and thought of Zadie again, of what she'd
say to me if she were here. I searched for the inner strength
she said I possessed, but I felt empty, hollow, like a shell of
the girl who believed she was meant for a world bigger than
the one she knew. I wished I'd taken something of Zadie's
with me to hold on to; that I had something more tangible
than memories.

A servant showed me to my seat, which, as I'd feared, was
the same place where I'd eaten lunch. Ceren would be at my
side for who knew how long. Lords and ladies followed my
example and came to the table, nodding at me solemnly.

Ceren entered a few minutes after I did. His hair was loose around his shoulders, falling in ribbons to the middle of his chest. Though I found his paleness peculiar, it also fascinated me. It was as if he'd been carved from a block of white stone. And there was something in his expression, the awareness in his eyes and tension in his posture, that hinted at his intelligence.

Everyone, including me, dropped into a bow or curtsy, but I watched him from under my lashes. He looked bored, like he'd rather be back in his room fiddling with whatever it was he was working on.

Then his eyes fell on me, and that glimmer returned to his eye, a sharp look I didn't like. He strode toward me and took my hand, bringing it to his lips once again. They were firm and dry against my skin.

"You look lovely, my lady."

I was saved from responding by the sudden shift in the air that signaled someone else approaching. The king, surrounded by lords and ladies, slowly shuffled into the room, looking pitifully small under his giant fur robes. It was a wonder he could walk at all. He carried a golden staff that was probably meant to be ornamental, but I could tell he was using it to prop himself up. The walk from the door to his seat was short, fortunately, and he collapsed into his chair just as someone else entered the room.

It was Prince Talin. Dread washed over me even while I found myself craning my neck for a better look. It wasn't just that he was handsome; he stood out here, as vibrant as a parrotfish in a school of gray mullets. He wore a midnight blue doublet, his brown hair curling just above the high collar.

I slipped my hand free from Ceren's, who still hadn't let it go, and I felt him stiffen beside me.

"Lionfish," he whispered in my ear.

Stonefish, I thought back.

I straightened as Talin approached our end of the table. I had no idea where the second son of a king sat, when there could only be one foot and one head at a table. Most of the chairs had lords and ladies behind them, but the one to my left was empty—a fortunate arrangement, since my scar was on my right cheek.

He bowed when he reached me, and I curtsied back, finally feeling a bit steadier in the process. The brothers greeted each other coolly. Everyone else took their seats when the princes sat, and I realized that my chair was much closer to Talin's than Ceren's. The king and his heir had the ends of the table to themselves, while the chairs along the sides were pressed together to accommodate so many guests.

"How have you enjoyed your time in Ilara so far?" Talin asked in a low voice.

I glanced at him sideways and tried to imagine how Zadie would behave in this situation. "New Castle is an interesting place," I said, because my sister would never insult a man's home. "I can see I have a lot to learn about your people and their ways."

I could feel Ceren straining to hear us, but there was too much chatter in the room.

"They are your people now," Talin said.

They were no more my people than the Varenians were Ceren's, but I nodded anyway. I wanted to ask him about his trip to Ilara, why he hadn't told us he was a prince. I wanted to know if he recognized me. I wanted to know if he'd thought of me after he left Varenia, or if I'd merely been an insignificant detail in his report to Ceren about Varenia.

And, ridiculous as it was, I found myself wanting to brush away the hair that had fallen in front of his eyes.

But I couldn't. He had to believe I was Zadie, and I was destined to marry his brother either way.

I shivered, wishing I'd worn a warmer gown.

"You look beautiful," he said, his voice so soft I wondered if I'd imagined it.

Though the compliment pleased me, I couldn't meet his eyes, knowing that Ceren was watching us. "Thank you."

"How is your family?" he asked, sitting back a bit while a servant filled his cup with wine.

"I'm not sure," I said. What was happening between Sami and Zadie? Had Mother forgiven her yet? Had she forgiven me? Were they hungry, or was Father managing to catch enough fish to feed them?

"But they were well when you left?"

I shrugged. "As well as can be expected."

"Nor must have been very sad to see you go."

My eyes flew to his involuntarily. There was no flicker of doubt there. Surely if he knew I was Nor, he would say something. "She was heartbroken."

"I'm sorry. I can only imagine what a loss it must be."

I closed my eyes to keep them from filling with tears. It was the first time someone here had acknowledged that coming to Ilara was a sacrifice. "I was deeply saddened to learn of your mother's passing. I would have liked to have known her."

"She would have treated you like a daughter." His voice

was thick with empathy, something I never would have expected here. He couldn't know how much his words both pleased and saddened me.

"I would have liked that very much," I managed.

There was a commotion at the end of the table as the king rose with the help of a strapping lord, raising his cup in a toast. As he spoke of "our beautiful future queen," a hundred eyes fell on me.

I rose and raised my glass, murmuring a barely audible thank-you. As I sat back down in my chair, my sweaty palm slipped on the wooden armrest, and I listed to the side. Talin reached out and caught my arm in his hand, propping me back upright in my chair.

"I'd blame the wine, but you haven't tasted yours yet," he said.

"I'm just nervous." I glanced at his hand, still lingering on my arm. "All of this is so new to me."

He leaned closer to be heard above the conversation, and I inhaled as quietly as possible. He *smelled* like sunlight, like fresh air and living things. "My mother used to feel out of place at these dinners, as well. She didn't speak much about Varenia, but I could always tell when she was thinking of home."

Home. The word was too small for everything it meant: the ocean, our house, my parents, Zadie. Why had I wanted to leave?

"Did she ever feel at home here?" I asked, searching his eyes. "Did she ever belong?"

He frowned. "I don't know the answer to that, I'm afraid." He lowered his voice further and slowly loosened his grip.

His trailing fingers left heat in their wake, unlike the chill I'd felt at Ceren's touch. "You would be wise to spend less of your time talking to me and more with my brother. He isn't pleasant when he's jealous."

"Is he ever pleasant?" The words were out of my mouth before I could stop them. "I'm sorry, I didn't mean that."

Talin's eyes crinkled as his lips curled in the tiniest smile. "This should be interesting," he said, before straightening in his chair and turning to the lady on his other side.

I spent most of the meal listening to the conversations that bubbled around me. Unable to join the chatter because of where he sat, Ceren sipped his wine and tasted his food, but it was clear he took no joy in any of it. His cold eyes drifted around the room, and I dreaded the moments they landed on me.

I had lost count of the courses when two servants appeared with a platter that they placed directly in front of me. In the center was a large pie, as fat as a giant sea turtle. Everyone turned to stare as Ceren rose and came to stand behind me.

"I had this baked especially for you," he said in my ear. "Do you like it?"

His right cheek brushed against my left, blocking my view of Talin. His skin was cool and smooth against my flushed skin. "Yes," I said. "Thank you."

Ceren took up the filigree serving fork and knife and cut carefully into the pastry on either side of me, the way you would for a child. He continued to cut in a wedge, and then he carefully pulled away the layer of crust. Something stirred in the dark recess, and everyone at the table leaned forward just a bit. I found myself wanting to press back, but I couldn't with Ceren standing behind me.

"Patience," he said.

A black, winged creature burst through the pastry with a shrill cry and flapped madly toward the ceiling.

"They're birds!" someone shouted to a smattering of applause.

But I'd seen birds many times in my life, and they didn't fly the way this creature did, erratic and unpredictable. A moment later, another one emerged, using the little claws at the tops of its leathery wings to work its way out.

"No, they're bats!" a nobleman exclaimed, and there was a gasp of surprise from the crowd. A few women squeaked in horror.

After the second bat flew away, an entire swarm of them— at least twenty—clambered out of the pie, all flapping to be free. Several were covered in treacle, making it harder for them to fly. The wretched creatures rolled onto the table covered in the sticky golden syrup, sending howls of laughter up among the nobles. Most of the ladies screamed and ran from the table, and suddenly wineglasses were tumbling left and right.

Ceren stayed perfectly still, his arms on either side of me, trapping me in my chair.

The king had somehow managed to sleep through the commotion. The servants did their best to clear plates and spilled glasses while dodging and dipping to avoid the bats. A maid appeared behind us and whispered something inaudible in Ceren's ear.

"I must attend to something. I'll return as soon as possible," he said. "I hope you enjoy your dessert."

I slumped back in my chair the moment he left the room, finally releasing some of the tension I'd been feeling all evening.

"Are you all right?" Talin asked, gently flicking a sticky bat away from his wine.

I sighed. "I think so. What was that all about? Is bat pie a traditional Ilarean food?"

He snickered. "No. We may seem strange to you, but I assure you, we're not *that* strange. I imagine my brother was trying to get a reaction from you."

"Why?"

"He likes to push people, to test their loyalty."

I stared at the collapsed crust of the pie. "My loyalty? I don't exactly have a choice in the matter. I belong to him now."

Talin drained his wine, but I didn't get the sense it was because he relished the taste. "Yes, well. My advice is that the next time he shows you something vile or repulsive, you pretend to be impressed. That's the fastest way to win his affection."

I had no interest in Ceren's affection, but I couldn't tell Talin that. Still, it was probably safer to avoid making my betrothed into an enemy.

At the far end of the room, a man began to play a stringed instrument that made a sound I could only compare to whale song. Talin leaned toward me, and I had to resist the urge to move closer to him. "It's called a viol," he explained. "It was my mother's favorite instrument."

"We have some stringed instruments back home, but they sound very different."

I noticed that his eyes lit up whenever I mentioned Varenia. "It's nice to hear more about where my mother came from," he said. "I miss her stories about Varenia. They made me feel connected to it, even though I'd never been there."

"I enjoy talking about it. It makes everything feel more real, like this isn't just a dream." *Or a nightmare*, I added silently.

The music from the viol was faster now, and many of the lords and ladies joined together to dance. Talin smiled at me. "I'd ask you to dance, but I'm afraid you wouldn't feel comfortable."

"Thank you," I said, both pleased that he wanted to dance with me and grateful he understood why I couldn't. "I think I'll just watch for a few minutes."

Talin took my arm, and we walked to the end of the hall closer to the musician. A few of the ladies watched me and whispered behind their fans, no doubt gossiping. Spending time with Talin was dangerous in more ways than one, apparently.

"He uses a bow to strum the viol," Talin said. "Of course, if I tried it would sound like a dying cat, but a skilled musician can make the most beautiful music you've ever heard."

The dancers had picked up their pace in time with the music. They moved in a circle, hands clasped. We'd had dances in the meetinghouse in Varenia sometimes, though Zadie and I hadn't been allowed to dance with the boys since we were children.

Talin glanced down at me. "Would you like to try, now that you have a better sense of the steps?"

I caught the eye of a woman standing across the room. There was something about her that was both familiar and foreign at the same time. Despite her rich clothing and intricate hairstyle, she seemed as out of place here as I felt. She observed me for a moment, then let her eyes rest on Talin's arm, still entwined with mine, and gave the tiniest shake of her head.

"I'm not sure it's appropriate," I said finally.

"For some reason you don't strike me as the kind of girl who worries about propriety."

My stomach twisted. Now I was sure he'd heard Sami and me that night in the governor's house; that he recognized me despite my fancy clothes and rehearsed manners. But he was right. I wanted to dance with him.

Without waiting for my answer, Talin led me to the center of the room. Another noble took my free hand, and as the viol continued to play, we moved in a slow circle to the right. I tried to copy what the other dancers did, but I couldn't seem to catch the rhythm. Fortunately, the men supported my weight so that it hardly mattered what my feet did.

As the beat quickened, we began to move faster and faster. The bats looped down from wherever they'd roosted, illuminated by the massive chandelier filled with lunar moss. Tonight would be the full moon, I realized. That explained why everything was so bright.

The wine I'd consumed with dinner was beginning to take hold. I looked over at Talin. He was watching me with a smile on his face, the kind of smile that could make a girl forget about being ladylike. I felt warm all over, my heart pounding beneath the diamond cutout in my bodice.

Perhaps this was why Mother hadn't wanted us to dance.

The music was playing faster than ever now, and somehow my feet seemed to know the steps on their own. I tipped my head back and laughed, so dizzy that I was sure the room would keep spinning long after I stopped. We whirled and whirled until suddenly, the music stopped, and I found myself clinging to Talin's doublet to keep from falling.

"I'm sorry," I said as his face came into focus.

"Don't be."

The muscles of his chest strained under my palms as he caught his breath, and I became very aware of his hands at my waist as I struggled for air against the stays of my bodice. He felt so solid and safe that I momentarily forgot my surroundings. Slowly, I leaned closer to him, like a tide pulled by the moon.

"See, my lady? This isn't just a dream."

My cheeks flamed under his gaze. "Isn't it?"

Ceren's voice over my shoulder cleared my head instantly. "There you are, my pearl."

I whirled around and dropped into a curtsy. "Your Highness."

His smile was strained. "It's late, and I believe you've had a bit too much wine." He held out his arm for me expectantly.

I nodded and bobbed a quick curtsy to Talin. "Good night."

He bowed, his hair falling in damp waves that reminded me of the night we'd met. "Good night, my lady. I'm sorry you can't stay longer."

So am I. For an instant, I wished he would tell his brother the truth about who I was, so that Ceren couldn't marry me. But Ceren's pull on my arm was firm and insistent, and as I walked away, I realized the part of me that wanted to stay was the part I would never be able to listen to again.

16

Ceren's grip tightened as he pulled me down the hall toward my chambers. "What were you thinking?" he demanded when we reached my door. "Dancing with my brother in front of everyone, before you've even danced with me?"

"I'm sorry," I stammered. "I didn't know. He told me—"

"I don't care what he told you. Has all that seawater pickled your brain? Surely you could see the way people were watching you."

My head was beginning to pound from the wine, and my arm ached from where Ceren's hand still grasped it. He saw me wincing and released my arm. I took a step backward. I wanted to hurt him the way he'd hurt me, but I needed to imagine I was Zadie now, to behave the way Mother would expect me to. Otherwise I'd get myself killed before I did anything useful.

I bowed my head. "Please, forgive me."

He released a deep breath through his nose. "I suppose it's not your fault. Though I did warn you about my brother."

I nodded. "You did. I understand what you meant now. I'll be more cautious in the future."

He took my hands in his. "Are you cold? Your fingers are like ice."

I blinked at the change in his tone. It was fear, not cold, that so froze my hands, but I didn't want him to think I was weak. "I left my wrap in the ballroom. I'll ask Ebb to bring it for me later."

"Very well. I'll leave you now. Good night, my lady."

"Good night."

I hurried into my room, where Ebb was laying out my nightgown on the bed.

"Are you all right, milady?" she asked when she saw my face. "Did something happen?"

"I did something foolish and paid the price for it. I'll know better next time." I took a seat on the stool in front of the vanity, and she began to unpin my hair. As she massaged my scalp, I felt some of my fear begin to drain away. Ceren hadn't actually done anything to me, and I could imagine it *had* looked rather bad, me dancing with his brother while he was away.

"Why don't the princes get along?" I asked. "Did something happen between them?"

Ebb glanced at the small hole in the wall nervously.

I found a handkerchief and stuffed it into the opening. "Better?"

She sighed and waved me back down onto the stool. "From what I've heard, Prince Ceren was always a difficult child. His mother, Queen Serena, may she rest in peace, was a beautiful Ilarean lady who King Xyrus had loved from an early age. But Serena was frail and fragile, and Xyrus's father, King Lazar, urged Xyrus to choose a Varenian bride, despite not marrying one himself."

King Lazar would have been the king who refused to marry the replacement girl from Varenia—the man who'd cut off our water supply. I raised an eyebrow at her in the mirror. "What became of the Varenian girl sent to marry Lazar?"

She glanced down. "It's not my place to say."

My stomach soured. Ceren had said it didn't go well for queens at New Castle. I couldn't imagine a rejected princess had fared any better.

"Anyway," Ebb continued, "King Xyrus defied his parents' wishes and married Serena, who died while giving birth to Ceren. A year later, he married Queen Talia, who'd been living as a lady in the castle."

"But why was Talia sent here in the first place, if Xyrus was already in love with Serena?" I asked.

"To tempt Xyrus away from her, I believe. Lazar's fear—that Serena wouldn't survive childbirth—had been well-founded. But everything seemed better after King Xyrus married Queen Talia and she gave birth to Prince Talin. Even the king's health seemed to improve. She was a kind and generous queen, often visiting the poorest villagers and offering them food and blankets."

"So she was allowed to leave New Castle?" I asked, surprised.

"Of course, milady. The king loved her so much he would have let her go anywhere."

"And Varenia? Would he have allowed her to go there?"

Ebb shook her head as she dropped the hairpins into a little porcelain dish. "Oh, no. The king is very superstitious about Varenia. All the nobility are. Except Prince Talin."

That must have been why Talin was the one who traveled to Varenia for Ceren. "Why?"

"Because of Princess Ilara."

"But that's ridiculous. She died hundreds of years ago." I remembered the way Ebb had held her breath over the bridge. "Is that why you're afraid of water? Because Ilara drowned?"

"I'm not afraid of water," she said, bristling. "Not small amounts of it, anyway. But large bodies of water are best avoided. Everyone in Ilara knows that. I had a little cousin who died chasing a ball that rolled into a lake."

"And you think the water spirits took her?"

"Of course, milady. What else?"

Most likely the child had drowned because she didn't know how to swim. In Varenia, we were literally born in the water. Fearing the ocean would be akin to fearing the air we breathed. But the story of Princess Ilara was deeply enmeshed in Varenian culture, even now. I supposed it was only natural that would be the same here, in Ilara itself.

"Who raised Ceren after his mother died?"

"It was his nursemaids, mostly, though the queen did spend time with him. She wouldn't let anyone else take care of Talin, though. She was with him all throughout his childhood. I've never seen a son more loved by his mother."

That explained Ceren's jealousy. He had grown up without a mother, while his brother had Talia. I felt a twinge of sympathy for Ceren. "Thank you for telling me this, Ebb."

"Of course, milady." She finished helping me into my

nightgown and tied my hair into a loose braid. "Is there anything else I can do for you?"

"There was a woman in the dining hall tonight. She looked familiar." I could tell from the fear in Ebb's eyes that I had stumbled back upon the subject she wished to avoid. "She was the rejected Varenian girl, wasn't she?"

Ebb sighed, looking at the hole in the wall again. "Yes. Her name is Lady Melina."

So *Melina* was the replacement girl, the one who'd caused the Varenians to be punished two generations ago, when all those children died of thirst. Ceren's grandfather, King Lazar, had not married her, and yet she was still here, forty years later.

"I would like to speak with her," I said carefully. "Can you arrange for us to meet?"

Ebb looked doubtful. "I can try, but I should warn you— Prince Ceren has never liked Lady Melina."

"Why not?"

"He finds her presence at court...distasteful."

My face grew hot with anger. "Why? Because she's Varenian?"

Ebb shook her head and came to kneel before me. "No, milady." She lowered her voice to a whisper. "Because she was King Lazar's mistress."

My anger soured to disgust. Melina han't been good enough to be queen, but she'd been good enough to warm the king's bed? "That's hardly a reflection on her. I want to meet her. As soon as possible."

Ebb chewed on her thin lower lip. "I can try, but it won't

be easy. She keeps to the shadows. Sometimes she'll appear when you had no idea she was even in the room."

If Lady Melina kept to the shadows, then perhaps that was where I'd have to meet her. "We'll meet somewhere inconspicuous, when the prince is busy. I promise I'll be careful."

"I'm glad to hear it. I only want what's best for you."

I leaned down so she would have to look me in the eye. "And you think Prince Ceren is what's best for me?"

Ebb flushed. "I think not angering him is what's best, milady."

I couldn't argue with that.

After Ebb left, I lowered the tiny curtains that hung over the alcoves where the lunar moss was placed in glass lanterns. It was too bright in here for sleep, and the light illuminated the strange creatures woven into the tapestries and carved into the wood.

I picked up one of the lanterns and held it up to the tapestry closest to my bed. What I'd thought was an amorphous blob was actually a lake, embroidered with tiny blue stitches. A young woman perched on a rock near the water, combing her hair. Something dark and serpentine lingered below the surface of the water. It had a human's head, but its mouth was filled with sharp teeth.

A loud knock on the door nearly caused me to drop the lantern. I laughed at myself for being so jumpy and set the lantern back down in its alcove. I was still smiling when I opened the door, assuming Ebb had forgotten something. But it was Ceren who waited on my threshold, his face as pale as candlewax against the darkness of the corridor.

"Your Highness," I said, dropping into a curtsy. "What are you doing here?"

He walked past me into the room, closing the door behind him. "Your wrap." He handed me the fur capelet I'd left in the dining hall.

"Thank you," I said, pressing it to my chest to cover the thin fabric of my nightdress.

Ceren pulled back one of the curtains I had lowered, illuminating the room in the eerie blue light. "It's a full moon," he said absently. "They say strange things happen during the full moon."

I stayed where I was near the door. "Do they?"

He strode toward me, crossing the room quickly. I was pressed all the way against the door when he took my hands in his, causing me to drop the wrap. "I'm sorry I mistreated you earlier. But you must understand that there are people watching us at all times. The lords and ladies... They like to talk, to gossip. If I'm going to be their king someday, they must respect me." His silver eyes glowed pale blue in the light of the lanterns.

"Of course," I said. "I understand."

He held on a moment longer before dropping my hands and stepping back. My breath left me in a rush. I stepped hastily away from the door and retreated toward my bed.

Ceren turned to leave, then whirled back around to face me, his long hair fanning around him. "The pie."

"The—the pie?"

"You never told me if you liked it."

Talin had told me to act impressed, if I wanted to earn Ceren's affection. I had no more desire for his affection than for another bat pie, but I did want him to leave. "Oh, yes!" I said as cheerfully as I could muster. "It was very…unique."

He nodded, seemingly pleased. "Good. It wasn't easy getting all those bats together. As it was, we lost several during the baking."

I covered my grimace with the back of my hand. I wasn't squeamish, but harming innocent creatures for entertainment was not something I could condone. "Perhaps next time, you could put something less…alive in it." I smiled as sweetly as I could. "The other ladies got a bit hysterical."

"But not you. You're made of stronger stuff than they are, aren't you?" Ceren sent me an admiring glance, then kissed my hand and slipped out the door, leaving me bewildered and more than a little unnerved.

To my relief, Ceren was gone the next day. A servant told Ebb he'd left New Castle to collect more supplies for his experiment. I asked her to set up my meeting with Lady Melina immediately. As much as I wanted to hide in my room and avoid the stares of the court, I only had a little while to gather information for Sami. And anything that might take my mind off the fact that I was going to marry Ceren—possibly very soon—was welcome.

Ebb was hesitant, but eventually I convinced her that there was no danger, since the king was still in his chambers and Ceren was absent. At the end of the day, she agreed to take me to the library for a meeting.

The library was an unfinished cavern Ebb said was rarely used, but I found it beautiful. The ceilings had been left in their raw, natural state, with pillars of stone for support. There were spiral staircases on either side of the finished part of the chamber, but there was really no need for them, since most of the upper shelves were empty. In order to keep the books safe from the damp, the room had more skylights than any other chamber I'd been in. I waited for Melina under one of the lights, soaking up as much sun as I could.

Lady Melina came alone. She had to be close to sixty, but aside from a few strands of gray hair among the black, she could have been my mother's age. Her complexion was sallow from so many years inside New Castle, but she was still unquestionably beautiful.

"Hello, child," she said as we took a seat on a cushioned bench.

No one had called me "child" since leaving Varenia. I was surprised to find that I'd missed it. I bowed my head. "Lady Melina."

"How are you adjusting to life here in the mountain?"

I kept my eyes downcast, staring at the lace edging of my sleeves. She wasn't old enough to be an elder, but she was nevertheless worthy of my respect. "Very well, thank you."

"And how do you like your future husband?"

She was feeling me out, testing me. I didn't know if I could trust Lady Melina, but right now, she was the closest thing I had to a potential ally. "He's very…unusual," I said carefully. "I don't know what to make of him yet."

"I suppose you'll have plenty of time to decide, once you're married."

My lip curled involuntarily at the word, but I quickly rearranged my features. "Of course."

"But if you ask me, that boy is rotten to the core," she murmured.

I looked up finally. "Prince Ceren?" I whispered, surprised by her candor. She must have seen my reaction.

Her eyes were a deep blue-violet that stood out against her dark hair and clothing. "He is violent, unpredictable. These little lords and ladies here, they think there is safety in numbers. They believe they're like fish in a school, in no danger from the shark circling around them. But one moment, the shark will snap, devouring a fish before the others even know what has happened. I've seen it many times. A lord says something that displeases the prince, or a lady offends him in some way, and the next day the person is gone, never to be seen again. It's all so clean and quiet…until you're the one being eaten."

Her words stunned me. I was grateful for her honesty, but this was so much worse than I'd imagined. "Surely they're just sent back to their families?"

"Perhaps. That's what the others choose to believe. But people are dispensable to that boy."

That boy. She despised him, clearly. "What happened to you, after the king realized you weren't the chosen girl?"

Her violet eyes widened. "Someone told you?"

I wanted to tell her my own story—it seemed only fair, considering I was asking for hers. But we'd just met. It would be stupid to assume I could trust her. "Just that the king discovered the truth, and our people were punished."

Lady Melina rose and began to pace over the woven rug. I noticed her bare toes peeking out from beneath her hem, and my heart clenched at the reminder of home, though I wasn't sure how she could tolerate the cold bite of the stone floors here. "When Lazar saw I was not the girl from the portrait, he was furious, even though I explained countless times what had happened," she told me, her tone full of bitterness. "He said he could not marry someone so unworthy. So instead he married an Ilarean lady, cut off Varenia's water supply, and made me his mistress."

I felt myself growing sick at her words. "But why not send you back to Varenia?"

She shook her head. "I believe he wanted to maintain Ilara's relationship with Varenia. And while his pride wouldn't allow him to marry me, I think he still desired me for himself."

"I'm so sorry."

"Don't feel sorry for me, child. Lazar was never cruel to me personally, and Prince Ceren is far worse than his grandfather ever was. He'll be the death of all the Varenians, mark my words."

"What are you talking about?"

She arched an eyebrow. "Has he taken you to his study yet?"

"Yes," I said. "So?"

"He didn't spend a year working on his little device so he could make friends with the fishes. He thinks that whatever is wrong with him can be fixed with the Varenian pearls, if only he had enough. And he knows he can only push our people so far before they starve to death, or worse, revolt."

"But Ceren seems perfectly healthy," I said, confused.

"It's this mountain," she said, looking up at the raw ceiling above us. "Something about it kills the Ilarean royals while they're still young."

"I imagine it's the lack of sunlight and fresh air."

She sighed impatiently. "You've seen the king, child. He's two decades younger than me and looks a thousand years old. It's more than that."

"So Ceren is afraid he'll end up like his father?" I asked. Lady Melina nodded. "And he thinks he can harvest the pearls himself with a sack and a hose?"

She laughed at the incredulous look on my face. "If you don't believe me, go see for yourself. He tests it at night. But be careful. He has spies everywhere." She started toward the door. "Which is why you and I shouldn't meet again."

I rose, hurrying to catch up. "But you're the only person here I can really talk to. Can't we meet in your chambers?"

Lady Melina continued her swift pace. "To invite you to my rooms would be like swimming directly into the shark's jaws."

"In my chambers, then. Or at meals."

"Prince Ceren prefers to see as little of me as possible, and I'm happy to say the feeling is mutual. But you need to stay on his good side, or at least try. And you won't do that by meeting with me, child. Make some other allies here at court. You'll need them."

"Just tell me one thing," I begged, unable to keep the desperation out of my voice. "Will I ever be permitted to leave New Castle? Please say there's some hope."

She turned her piercing eyes on mine. "There is no hope for any of us, child. We are all trapped in this mountain like lobsters in a cage, waiting for our turn to die."

17

I spent the next day in bed, alternating between drowning in self-pity and plotting my escape. If I could somehow get to the market, Sami could take me back to Varenia and we could tell Governor Kristos everything. The fact that Lady Melina had been made a mistress instead of queen should be reason enough for us to put an end to the ridiculous pact we had with Ilara.

But then I remembered how difficult the journey here had been, in a plush coach with a personal servant, and I knew there was no way I'd be able to make it to the port market on my own. Lady Melina was right. I needed allies. And I wouldn't make any by wallowing in my room.

No one seemed to know when Ceren would be returning, so I decided to make the most of whatever time I had to myself. At breakfast the next day, I struck up a conversation with one of the ladies sitting nearest to me. Lady Hyacinth was around twenty, though her powdered hair and high-necked taffeta gown made her look much older. Ebb had assured me that this lady was well worth knowing—she was part of the king's military council and had an extensive knowledge of the uprisings sprouting up around the kingdom, particularly in the South.

After we exchanged pleasantries at breakfast, she invited me to her chambers for tea with several other lords and ladies.

"Aren't you lovely!" one of the women commented, inviting me to sit next to her on an overstuffed brocade couch. "I passed Varenia once, on my way here from Kuven. We didn't get close enough to see any people, though. Our loss, clearly."

I blushed, and Lady Hyacinth exchanged a knowing smile with her friends. "I told you she was darling. Much better than that awful Lady Melina."

"Let's not even talk about her," a lord said with an exaggerated shudder. "That woman frightens me."

I spoke only when spoken to, trying to glean any useful information I could, but Hyacinth was much more interested in talking about court politics than anything outside the castle. Several of the other ladies were busy knitting. It was so cold in the mountain that when the women weren't at meals displaying their fine gowns, they bundled themselves in knitted cowls and shawls, warming their hands in gloves. Knitting these garments, I discovered quickly, was about as fun as repairing fishing nets.

When Ceren returned the following day, I decided that I would somehow find a way to broach the subject of leaving New Castle. Even if I didn't make it to the market this month, I couldn't spend the rest of my life drinking tea with

Lady Hyacinth and her friends, knitting fingerless gloves. I'd go mad in a matter of weeks.

Before dinner, I asked Ebb to dress me in something she thought Ceren would like. She eyed me strangely, but didn't question my request. She chose a heavy plum-colored satin sleeveless gown with an attached cape that drifted behind me like the wings of a manta ray when I walked. The bodice was fitted, but not low cut, and it didn't leave me feeling vulnerable like some of the gauzier gowns in my wardrobe.

Ceren came to my chambers and offered to escort me to dinner. I noticed that his cheeks had just a hint of pink in them, as though the time away from the mountain had done him some good.

"You're looking well this evening," he said as we walked to the dining hall arm in arm.

I smiled. "I was just thinking the same about you."

But he did not return the smile, and I got the sense that the compliment displeased him somehow. Perhaps he didn't trust it.

By the time we reached the lull between dinner and dessert that night, Ceren had consumed several cups of strong Ilarean wine, more than I'd ever seen him drink before. I'd learned to avoid wine since the night I'd danced with Talin by asking the servants to fill my glass with water before they brought it to the table.

"Your Highness," I said, trying to keep my voice steady, though my hands trembled in my lap. "I was wondering if I might be permitted to go to one of the villages. I saw so little on my journey here, and I imagine there is far more to Ilara than New Castle."

He swirled his wine in his glass, pretending to be very interested in the contents, but I knew there was more going on behind his granite eyes. Everything was a calculation for him, a tallying of sums and differences.

"No," he said finally. "I don't think that's a very good idea."

I was disappointed but not surprised. "Oh. Can I ask why not?"

He tilted his head back and drained his cup. "The villages aren't the best representation of Ilarean culture. Perhaps one day I'll take you to one of the estates, but everything worth seeing is already here in New Castle."

I bit my lip to hide my scowl. If I couldn't go to a village a few miles from the castle, how was I ever going to get to the market? It would take days to get there, and the trip would undoubtedly require an escort. It seemed impossible now. I imagined Sami searching for me, risking his life just by being there. I couldn't even warn him that I wouldn't make it.

My anger flared hot and bright. I remembered the way I'd envied the other chosen girls' freedom, but now I saw the truth: they were far more trapped in Ilara than I'd ever been in Varenia. I had prayed for the wrong thing that night at the governor's house, and now it was too late.

I wanted to remind Ceren that the former queen had been allowed to visit the villages, according to Ebb, but mentioning Queen Talia was a risk. If the king was here, he might persuade Ceren on my behalf, but he was "resting" again tonight. He seemed to spend the majority of his time resting, which made me wonder how he was able to do any kind of ruling.

"There may be an opportunity for you to leave the castle

soon, however," Ceren continued. "If everything goes well with my experiments. I'll know more after tonight."

My pulse quickened, though I kept my expression neutral. "What's happening tonight?"

He pushed his chair back with a screech. "Nothing to concern you, my dear. Enjoy the rest of your meal."

If Ceren believed he was close to success with his device, it concerned me more than anyone else in New Castle. I finished eating and left the hall, determined to find out what he was up to.

I was nearly back to my chambers when someone called my name. I turned to see Lady Hyacinth trailing after me.

"There you are," she said, as though we'd bumped into each other by accident. "I was hoping you'd like to join us again." She clasped her hands in front of her to display her fingerless gloves and glanced pointedly at my bare hands.

"I'm afraid I'm quite tired this evening," I lied. Spending time with the nobles only served to show how out of place I was here, and I had more important things to worry about than knitwear.

Hyacinth steepled the points of her long fingernails together. Ebb said it was a sign of rank; the longer your nails were, the less manual labor you did. I kept mine neat and short, as I always had. You never knew when you would need to use your hands.

"What a shame," she said. "We do so want to get to know you better."

It had only taken one afternoon with them to discover that the majority of "teatime" was spent gossiping, and when it came to me, they had very little to work with so far. I planned to keep it that way. "Next time," I told her with a forced smile, hurrying down the hall before she could protest.

Lady Melina had told me to see the device for myself, and that was exactly what I planned to do. I asked Ebb to help me bathe and dress for bed early, claiming exhaustion.

"It's the mountain," she said as she brushed out my hair. "People come here healthy, and within weeks they're sick and run-down. That's why the king is in such a dreadful state."

So Lady Melina wasn't the only one who thought the mountain was causing the king's illness. Ceren wasn't sick like his father, but he was lean and lanky compared to Talin. Many of the other people at court also appeared weak and tired, even early in the day. "Then why do the nobles come here?"

"Some are hoping for more land, loftier positions. The young ladies are sent by their fathers to try wooing Prince Talin."

"Not Ceren?"

Ebb lowered her voice. "Ceren has always been determined to marry a Varenian."

That seemed odd, considering how he felt about Queen Talia. But my thoughts had snagged on Ebb's remark about someone else. "And Talin?" I asked, trying to sound mildly disinterested. "Does he favor a particular lady?"

"Not that I'm aware of," she said, glancing at me from the corner of her eye.

Ebb was a bit too shrewd sometimes. "Do you have any siblings?" I asked to change the subject.

I caught her smile in the mirror. "An older brother, milady."

"Where does he live?"

The smile evaporated, and I knew I'd asked the wrong question. "He's here, in the castle." Ebb set down the brush. "Can I get you anything else?"

I excused her, but the nagging feeling that something was wrong followed me later when I covered myself in a thick wool wrap and headed out into the corridor. I'd only done a little exploring on my own, but I had some sense of my way around now.

The halls were cold and deserted at this time of night. I passed the occasional servant, and they politely acknowledged me with a nod of the head and a quick bow or curtsy, but aside from the guards scattered along the corridors, I was mostly alone. The lunar moss torches glowed very faintly, bathing everything in their eerie blue glow. I felt like some sort of strange deep-sea creature sensing my way through the dark; someone could be standing right next to me, and I wouldn't know it.

I was starting to lose my nerve when I saw a pale light ahead in the gloom. It whisked past the corridor I was in and down a narrower one. I hurried to follow it, thinking it was another lord or lady who could direct me back to my chambers, but quickly saw that it was Ceren, carrying a lantern emitting a soft green glow. His white-blond hair trailed behind him as he rounded another corner.

I only hesitated for a moment. If he caught me, I'd tell him I was on my way to visit Lady Hyacinth and had gotten lost. Fortunately, my slippers were soft-soled and made no sound on the stone floors, and my nightgown hardly rustled when I moved. Ceren took another turn, and I hung back long enough to peer around the corner before following him. His long black robes scraped the floor as he walked, like nails scritching at a door.

We were deeper in the mountain than I'd ever been before, the floors sloping down more steeply as we went. The corridors were smaller here—I could touch both sides if I stretched my arms out, and the ceilings barely cleared Ceren's head. I hadn't seen a guard for a while now.

I gasped when something fluttered in my hair: a moth, tangled in the strands. Ceren turned and raised his foxfire lantern, and I pressed myself flat against the wall, praying he couldn't see me in the shadows. I had no logical excuse for being this deep in the mountain other than following him, and the realization that I had put myself in a very dangerous situation struck me. Ceren could do anything to me down here, and no one would hear. I may as well have been a dozen miles away from civilization. My heart rate quickened as I felt the weight of all the stone surrounding us press in on me.

I could die in this tunnel, and my body might never be found.

When Ceren turned back around and continued on, I slid down against the wall, taking deep breaths to steady myself. I couldn't linger long—Ceren had taken the only light with him, and I was completely blind without it. I rose shakily to my feet and felt for the next corner, but I was too late. He was gone.

I blinked into the blackness. He couldn't have disappeared. It was just dark, I told myself, and there was probably another corner up ahead. I continued to feel my way along the wall, hardly daring to breathe. Suddenly the wall fell away, and the air around me was cooler, less oppressive. Ahead of me, I could see something shimmering on the ground.

And then I heard it. Water.

As my eyes adjusted to the darkness, I saw the green light of Ceren's lantern bobbing in the distance. I took a cautious step forward. I was in a giant cavern, with a vast underground lake spread out before me. Farther ahead, I could make out more faint green lights and shadows passing in front of them. Ebb had made it seem like no one in the castle would willingly go near a large body of water, including Ceren, but there were other people here. *Why?*

I kept my hand against the wall of the cave, which was only a foot or two from the water's edge. Several times I could feel the coldness seep into my slippers as the water lapped gently against the stone shore. The green lights were closer now, but I still couldn't make out the voices of the shadowy figures. I crept as close as I dared, until I could just make out the people's silhouettes in the dim light, and crouched behind a column formed by a massive stalagmite.

"How long were you under?" I heard Ceren ask.

"Seven, maybe eight minutes, Your Highness." The voice was that of a child, thin and high-pitched and frightened. "Please don't make me go again. It's dark down there, and so cold."

I couldn't make out Ceren's next words, but they were gruff and angry.

The child spoke again. "Ten minutes? But my brother—"

Another man's voice cut the child off. "How long do you need, Your Highness? We can buy more time with a larger air bladder."

I crept out cautiously from behind the stalagmite to get a better look. I could just make out the sack and hose I'd seen in Ceren's workshop, but now the bag was filled with air.

"I won't be able to gather enough oysters in seven minutes. Of course, that's assuming there are any to be had. The Varenians claim they're impossible to find, and evidently only one in a dozen will have a pearl. I need more time."

"We'll keep working on it, Your Highness."

"Of course you will. I've already told Talin about the test. You have a week to get it right."

"Yes, Your Highness," the two voices said.

So Melina was right. With a device that allowed Ceren to breathe underwater for ten minutes, he could dive far more efficiently than any Varenian. True, some of our men had been known to hold their breath for that long, but not while hunting. The longest I had ever stayed down was five minutes, perhaps six during the incident. And if Ceren was able to create more devices, he could easily use his own men to harvest the pearls. He would not only render the Varenians obsolete, he would cut us off from our only source of income.

Ceren would be the death of us all, just like Melina said.

I shifted back into my crouch behind the stalagmite just as Ceren's robes resumed their swishing. He was only a few feet away when something stirred in the water.

Ceren froze. He was so close I could hear him breathing, remarkably slow and steady. Whatever was happening, he wasn't frightened. But I had to bite my lip to keep from screaming when something pale and slimy dragged itself out of the water. Ceren pounced on it so suddenly I jumped.

"Quick!" he called to one of his servants. "Bring me a knife. This one's fat enough to serve for dinner."

The creature wriggled in his grip. It was nearly half Ceren's size, with a long tail and tiny eyes.

"What is it?" the boy asked as the other man handed Ceren his knife.

"Have you never seen an Ilarean cave salamander, boy?" Ceren asked. "They're considered a delicacy. Sadly, most of the giant ones have been killed off by now. But it's entirely possible they've been swimming just inches from you, and you never even knew it. Lucky for you, they're blind."

He took the knife and sawed off the salamander's head without bothering to kill it first. I'd killed and gutted more than my share of fish, but there was something about the way Ceren hacked away at the body, with no skill or regard to providing a clean, quick death, that made my stomach roil.

When he'd finished, Ceren dropped the knife and told the servants to deal with the body. He crouched down at the water's edge not three feet from where I stood behind the stalagmite. I was holding my breath, but with my heart racing and fear coursing through me, I wouldn't last more than a couple of minutes. Ceren calmly rinsed his hands in the light of the lantern. There was an obscene amount of blood, and he was taking his time.

Finally, when I thought my lungs would burst, I exhaled as quietly as I could. Slowly, Ceren's head began to turn. I ducked farther back into the shadows, cursing myself for following him down here. *You're going to die in this stupid cave! The salamanders will have your bones for breakfast!*

My eyes were shut tight as I waited to be discovered. But

several moments later, I heard the *scritch-scritch* of Ceren's robes again. When I opened my eyes, he was moving away from me, back toward the entrance of the cave. I was about to collapse with relief when he began to sing in a quiet, surprisingly lovely voice.

"Beware the lionfish, my dear. Beware the fish that's made of stone. Beware sweet nothings in your ear…" His voice trailed off as he left the cave.

When enough time had passed, I fumbled my way back through the dark. What a fool I'd been to think I could come to Ilara and spy on anyone. Ceren was too intelligent, and I was far too naive. He'd probably seen me when the moth flew into my hair and let me follow just to toy with me. I wondered if killing the salamander had also been for my benefit. The memory of the blood on his white skin and the fear of being caught overwhelmed me, and I stopped to vomit up the remains of my dinner in an alcove.

It was brighter here, at least, and I breathed a sigh of relief when I passed a guard. I wasn't alone anymore. I finally reached a familiar hallway and hurried back to my bedroom, where I found Ebb asleep on the little settee in the corner.

I roused her gently. "I'm sorry, Ebb. I got lost," I said as she blinked and sat up.

"Milady!" she gasped, her expression filled with relief. "I came back to check on you, and you were gone. I was so worried. Are you all right?"

I wanted to shake my head and collapse into her arms, but I forced a smile. "I'm fine. The mountain can be very confusing in the dark."

"I understand. I'll draw you a map later. I don't like walking alone down below, and I've been living here for years. I know the rumors about Mount Ayris are just fairy stories, but sometimes they get in my head and I scare myself silly."

"What rumors?" I asked as she helped me into bed.

She glanced at me from the corner of her eye, her mouth twisted in a grin. "It's silly, milady. But they say that thousands of years ago, there were giants, great big men and women who shook the ground when they walked. The god Theale was angry that the giants were destroying his creations, so one night, when they lay down to sleep, he turned them all to stone. They say the giants' blood froze in their veins and became the bloodstones that used to be mined from the mountain."

"Bloodstones?" I asked. Now that the adrenaline had drained out of me, I realized how exhausted I was. My eyelids were growing heavy under the soothing tones of Ebb's voice.

"Beautiful red jewels with magical properties. They were said to make the wearer so powerful, she could command armies to certain death if she chose. But over the years, people grew greedy and stripped the mines bare. Countless wars were fought over the remaining jewels. Here, in Mount Ayris, the mines were flooded by the Bloody Queen Ebbeela to end the fighting once and for all. I'm named after her, you know. Well, I'm named after Saint Ebbeela, as she came to be known after her death."

"The Bloody Queen?" I asked incredulously. "How could she possibly earn a sainthood?"

"She was actually a very wise, fair ruler. After the mines were destroyed, she paid off the kingdom's debts and Ilara prospered during her reign. She earned the 'bloody' part of her title after she had her son killed. But history hasn't been kind to him—they say he was unwell in the head, milady, and she didn't trust him to rule."

Her words sounded far away, like I was halfway in a dream already. "Where are all the bloodstones now?"

"Gone, milady. Scattered to the edges of the world. They say there was once power in the blood of men, but we abused that power, and the gods took it back."

In my semiconscious state, the words *bloodstone* and *blood coral* began to muddle. The idea that they were in some way the same was the last thought that struck me before I fell asleep.

18

I was sure Ceren had seen me in the cave, and I waited for him to acknowledge it at dinner the following night, but he greeted me with the same cursory bow as usual. He wore a loose burgundy tunic, unbuttoned at the throat to reveal several inches of his pale, smooth chest, and a black leather belt at his waist with a knife tucked into it.

"I believe I mentioned a possible excursion outside the mountain," he said as he forked a wobbly bite of reddish-brown meat into his mouth. "Beef liver," he said, noticing my expression. "It's said to improve one's health."

I'd never much cared for meat, but the way it was served raw and bloody here in New Castle had put me off it completely. Particularly now that I'd seen Ceren's butchering skills. For all I knew, he was eating salamander liver. "Are you unwell?" I asked.

His gray eyes flashed to mine. "Do I look unwell to you?"

"No, of course not. Just a little pale perhaps."

"I have my mother's coloring. She was fair, like me. Talin was fortunate to inherit his mother's looks and constitution." His tone was begrudging, despite the compliment.

I hadn't seen Talin in days. I was about to ask how he was faring when Ceren stabbed another chunk of meat and waved it at me.

"I'm happy to say everything went well last night, and we are ready for the next phase of my experiment."

I kept my eyes on my plate. "Congratulations."

"Since you seem so curious about my work, I thought you might like to join me next week when I test it out."

A chill ran up my bare neck into my hairline. "Join you?"

"Come now. You should be excited. It involves your favorite thing."

I kept my face blank. "And what would that be, Your Highness?"

He laughed. "Water, of course."

I wouldn't go back down to that lake for all the pearls in the Alathian Sea. I smiled, hoping I looked more coy than terrified. "You're mistaken. Water is not my favorite thing."

He leaned closer. "No? Then please, enlighten me."

"Sunlight is my favorite thing, or at least the thing I miss most about Varenia."

"Not your family?"

"I don't consider them *things*."

Ceren scratched at his chin for a moment. "Well then, you're still in luck, my dear. My experiment also involves sunlight. Assuming the weather cooperates."

I turned toward him, my mouth dropping open in surprise. "Do you mean…?"

"Yes, we'll be going outside. Of course, only if you want to."

I had to force myself not to bounce in my chair. "When?"

"Tuesday," he said with a chuckle. "If that suits your busy schedule."

It didn't seem possible, but I'd been away from Varenia for nearly two weeks. Tuesday was three days before the market—enough time for someone to deliver a message for me, if I couldn't make it there myself. "That should be fine."

"Then it's settled. Come, there's something I want to show you."

He led me down several corridors until we came to a hall I'd never seen before. Torches lined the walls, each illuminating a painting. As we walked, I realized what I was looking at: the portraits of every Varenian woman who'd come before me. And oh, how beautiful they were, each as fresh and vibrant as a seaflower. Now that I'd been away from my home and spent some time among the Ilareans, it was easy to recognize what made the Varenian queens special. Even rendered in paint, they seemed *alive* in a way no one here did.

As we approached the end of the hallway, I slowed further. The third portrait from the end was the girl who should have come instead of Melina. The engraved plaque on the frame bore the words *The Lost Princess Zita*. Next was Talia's portrait. She had olive skin like mine, curly golden-brown hair, and eyes shaped like Talin's, though more green than his. And there was a softness to her gaze that made her appear gentle and kind. If it was a true likeness, the elders' decision had been fair, I thought. And Mother would never have any idea how lucky she'd been.

Ceren took a step toward the next portrait. He'd been observing me the whole time. "I thought perhaps you'd like to see how your own portrait looked."

I joined him in front of the painting, but before I could study it he turned me around to face him, so that the portrait and I were side by side.

"The likeness is very good," he said. He placed one long, pale finger against my jaw and tilted it to the right. "Yes. I was quite pleased when I saw whom your elders had chosen as my future wife. You looked strong and healthy. Though I must say, he got the eyes wrong. There's a fire in them that the artist didn't capture."

Fear coursed through me as his finger traveled up my cheekbone to the outer edge of my eye. When I blinked, a tear seeped out.

He wiped it away and examined his fingertip for a moment. "Did you know that tears have approximately the same salt concentration in them as blood?" He put his finger to his lips absently and turned me around to face the painting. "What do you think, my lady? Did the artist do you justice? Or should I have him beheaded and use another artist the next time?"

His words had faded into the background by now, the rush of blood in my head drowning them out. Because for the first time since leaving Varenia, I was staring at my beautiful sister. I was looking at Zadie.

"You seem upset, my pearl," Ceren said. "Is everything all right?"

I forced myself to breathe deeply, though I was constrained

by the dress Ebb had chosen for me: a tight black corset covered in iridescent feathers that fanned across my chest, leaving my neck and shoulders bare. I looked like a silly little bird, one who had willingly hopped into a gilded cage, only to find her wings had been clipped when she tried to fly away.

"I'm fine. Just homesick, I suppose."

"And that is completely understandable. Come, I have one more portrait I'd like to show you." He led me down another hallway into a large chamber. He stopped in front of a portrait of a pale woman with hair almost as fair as his own, framed in gold-leafed rosettes and scrollwork. Her gown was a luminous white, trimmed with lace and pearls. The only color in the painting was the pink of her lips and cheeks. I had to admire the artist who was able to paint that much detail in shades of ivory, eggshell, and bone.

"My mother," he said, confirming my suspicions. "She was beautiful, wouldn't you agree?"

I nodded. "I can't help but notice she's wearing white."

"This was her marriage portrait. Even Ilarean royals don't wear mourning clothes to weddings." He glanced at me. "Father knew he should marry a Varenian woman. But he'd already fallen in love with my mother, whose family had been at court for generations. It's a rather romantic notion, to marry for love, don't you think?"

"I suppose so."

"Of course," he continued, "it didn't work out so well for them. Mother died in childbirth, and Father ended up marrying Lady Talia anyway. But I suppose I should be grateful he chose love first. Otherwise I would never have been born."

How lucky for me. I took in the room, pretending to be fascinated by its contents while I sifted through possible topics of conversation. As I scanned the oil paintings and tapestries, my eyes landed on a small glass dish piled with pink pearls. Varenian pearls. They were what would be considered inferior in quality, unevenly shaped or too small. We got very little for them at market.

"Ah yes, my pearls," Ceren said. "I take one every day for my health. Such powerful little things, aren't they?"

My mouth fell open. "You swallow them whole?"

"Sometimes. I prefer to grind them up into powder and drink them. I feel the effects much more rapidly that way. Surely you understand."

I nearly laughed. "No, Your Highness. We don't eat the pearls." I remembered the broth Nemea had made for Zadie, but I knew that was a rare occurrence. I'd never seen it before in my seventeen years of life.

He pursed his lips. "Please, my dear, be honest. It's all right to confess. I won't punish your people for it."

"Punish us for what?"

"For eating some of the pearls yourself."

I blinked, incredulous. "I assure you, no one in Varenia can afford to keep the pearls for themselves, and certainly not to *eat.*"

"Is that so? Then how do you explain why the Varenians live for over a century, whereas my father is dying at forty?" There was a sharp edge to his voice, the kind that meant I was treading in dangerous territory.

"I'm afraid I can't explain it. Perhaps it's the lack of sunlight that causes it. The mountain—"

"The mountain is none of your concern."

I recoiled at the growl in his voice. "Of course not. I'm sorry."

He had turned away from me, back toward the portrait of his mother.

"Queen Talia was the one who introduced me to the pearls, you know," he mused. "She told me about their healing powers. She said the village doctor sometimes used them in creams when people were gravely injured."

It was hard to say how much of Zadie's fast healing had been due to the fact that all Varenians healed quickly and how much was the result of Nemea's ointment.

"Yes, I've heard of that being done," I told him, trying to sound nonchalant.

Ceren continued to gaze up at the portrait.

"Queen Talia was always trying to help people. She often took me into the sun because it was supposed to be good for me. All it did was burn my skin."

It had likely been an innocent mistake. Exposure to sunlight *did* make people healthier, I was sure of it. But for someone as pale as Ceren, I imagined direct sunlight could bring on a nasty burn quickly. "That must have been painful."

He took a seat on a settee and gestured for me to join him. "It was. But I couldn't deny that the pearls made me feel stronger. And when I am injured or unwell, I take several pearls and feel better almost instantly."

"Does the king use them, as well?"

His eyes darted to mine. "No. I'm sorry to say they didn't have any effect on him."

Had the king even tried them, or was Ceren keeping all the

pearls to himself? Clearly it wasn't the king who was lowering the value of the pearls. It was Ceren, and he was doing it to make himself stronger. If he ate one every day…that was nearly four hundred pearls a year, roughly eight times what my family had gathered last year, when the oysters had been particularly scarce. And those were just the ones he was consuming. I thought of the bowlful in his lab, of the creams and ointments he'd probably made, not to mention the rest of the market's demand. Once he started using his devices, the pearls would be gone within months.

Things here were so much worse than Sami and I could have ever imagined. And it might already be too late to turn back the tide that Ceren had set in motion.

"I heard you spoke with Lady Melina," he said, tearing my thoughts away from the pearls.

He has spies everywhere. "I did, briefly, in the library."

He clucked his tongue. "A future queen shouldn't associate with her kind. If it were up to me, I'd have been rid of her years ago."

"Rid of her?" I asked in disbelief. "She's a *person.* You can't just toss her out like a pair of worn slippers."

He flashed a brief, wolfish grin. "Thank you for putting that so eloquently, my dear. That's exactly what she is. Damaged. Used. *Worn.*"

Heat flamed in my cheeks. "If you despise Varenian women so much, why did you bring me here? Why not marry an Ilarean woman, like your father and grandfather? It's obviously worked out very well for them." I immediately knew I'd gone too far, and the way his features slowly hardened frightened me. I rose and stepped backward, but he quickly closed the space between us.

"Do you think I want you? Do you think I find you beautiful? I could have any woman in Ilara if I wanted." He took my chin in his hands, squeezing it between his thumb and forefinger. "My father was a fool to marry for love. My mother was beautiful, perhaps, but she was also frail. Her family had spent too many years at New Castle, just like my father's. Their love, and this cursed mountain, have put our kingdom in jeopardy. As far as I'm concerned, you're a vessel for the future king, and nothing more."

I tried to struggle free, but his grip was like iron. Finally, the truth was out. I had been brought here to bolster the royal bloodlines. My beauty had never mattered to Ceren at all. He only wanted a Varenian bride for her strength.

"How terrible it must be for you," I said through gritted teeth, "to marry someone you despise."

His hand dropped to my throat before I could scream, the hate in his eyes unmistakable. How could I have ever thought he was emotionless? I clawed at his chest, my feet scrabbling against the stone as he lifted me off the floor. I could feel my strength starting to go, and with all my remaining effort I lashed out with my right foot, sweeping one of his legs out from under him.

He fell to the ground in a heap, and I dropped back to my feet, leaping out of his reach. I gasped for air, my hands on my knees, my throat raw and searing. I moved toward the doorway, wanting to run, but afraid to take my eyes off him.

Ceren climbed slowly to his feet. "If you ever do something like that again, I'll have you thrown off this mountain."

"I would rather die than marry you," I spat, and gave in
to my urge to run.

The marks Ceren's hands left on my neck faded quickly,
but I still felt their crushing weight on my flesh. I went to
Melina's chambers late that night, despite Ebb's protests and
Ceren's threats. I needed to find a way to delay his progress,
at least long enough to warn Sami.

Melina's room was far down in the mountain, where it
was even colder than the main floor. I pulled the hood of my
cloak over my head as I passed a guard and eventually came
to the room Ebb had described. A maid answered the door,
her knit cap pulled low over her ears.

"Lady Melina is sleeping, milady. I can't disturb her at this
hour."

"It's urgent," I said, sliding past her into the small ante-
chamber. "Please wake her."

The maid wasn't lying. When Melina finally emerged from
her bedchamber, her long braid was half unraveled and her
cheeks were puffy from sleep. "What is it, child? It must be
close to midnight."

"May we speak in private?" I said, indicating her maid, but
Melina waved off my concern.

"My maids can be trusted. I pay them well to be sure of it."

"Is that how you know so much of what goes on within
the castle?"

A faint smile lifted the corners of her lips. "Ceren isn't the
only one with spies."

I sat down on a settee and motioned Melina closer. "I followed Ceren yesterday to the lake. I saw the device. I believe you now."

She nodded, as if she'd expected this.

"Ceren also threatened to kill me, and he made it clear he harbors no love for you."

"I told you he was dangerous."

"He's going to test the device on Tuesday, outside the castle. He's invited me to go with him. I believe he means to conduct the test himself."

She shifted her weight, impatient. "And how does this concern me?"

I lowered my voice further. "If I can tamper with the device somehow, ensure that his test fails, perhaps it will delay his plans."

She arched a brow. "And possibly kill the prince in the process?"

While a part of me knew the easiest way to put a stop to all this would be to rid the kingdom of Ceren himself, I shook my head. "I'm not a murderer." Most likely he would run out of air and swim to the surface. I couldn't imagine any of the lakes here were that deep. And as much as I would have liked to destroy the device, doing so would mean I never had a chance to leave the castle in the first place.

"Is there a way to get a message to someone in the port market on Friday?" I asked.

Melina eyed me shrewdly. "What are you up to, child?"

"The Varenians need to know of Ceren's plans. I intend to warn them, even if I can't stop him."

"If you can get to one of the villages, you can pay someone to get a message to the market. But I have no idea where Ceren is conducting his test, and I highly doubt he'll take you to a village."

"I have to try."

"The prince does not make idle threats, Zadie. You need to be prepared to face the consequences of your actions."

I swallowed the lump in my throat. "I am."

"Then I will help you in whatever way I can."

19

In order to sabotage the device, I needed a better sense of how it worked, which meant I needed Ceren to show it to me. But after our last encounter, I wasn't sure if he would even speak to me.

To my surprise, he greeted me with a "Good morning, my lady," as he sat down at breakfast. His eyes didn't meet mine.

"Good morning, Your Highness."

"Sleep well, did you?"

So he was going to pretend last night hadn't happened? Fine. I almost ignored him, but Mother's voice came to me then, reciting one of her lessons about men. Like most of her advice, it was rooted firmly in manipulation. *The key to a man's heart is his pride, followed closely by his appetite. Flatter a man, and he is yours for the taking.*

Ceren claimed he didn't find me beautiful, but I could see I'd managed to wound his pride nevertheless. I picked at a piece of honeyed fruit. "I was wondering if you might show me your device again," I suggested tentatively. "I'm so curious to see how it works. You've said only that it's an underwater breathing apparatus, but I don't understand how such a thing is possible. It sounds miraculous."

He spared me a brief glance from under his pale brows. "You'll see it for yourself on Tuesday."

I sipped my water to hide my annoyance. If flattery wouldn't work, perhaps another insult would. "I've heard that the Ilareans are afraid of water. I gather you'll test it in a shallow pond?"

He raised his chin. "My device can be used at far greater depths, I assure you."

"But how is that possible? A snorkel only works a foot or two below the surface."

Ceren set his fork down and leaned on one arm. "You really do have an interest, don't you?"

I ignored the patronizing tone in his voice. "Yes."

"If you're so curious, I'll show it to you now. Come with me."

I didn't like the idea of being alone with Ceren again, but I had to take any opportunities that were presented to me. I followed him to his study, where he unlocked the door with a heavy iron key kept somewhere in his tunic. I had no idea if there was another one, but I'd need it to get back into the study later.

"Here we are," he said, indicating the device. "It's relatively simple. This bag is filled with air, supplied by a double bellows. The hose is connected to the bag, and the diver breathes through the end of the hose."

While Ceren went into more detail, I inspected the hose itself. It was nothing more than a hollow, flexible tube. A hole or kink would cut off the diver's air supply. It seemed that everything depended on the integrity of the hose. Of course, at a depth of only ten or fifteen feet, it wouldn't be a problem to go back up to the surface for air. But at fifty feet or more, where we found many of our oysters? An inexperienced diver could easily run into trouble.

I had no idea how often Ceren inspected his device, but if I returned Monday night and cut just a small hole in the tube, perhaps that would be enough. At the very least he'd have to find more supplies, and maybe that would buy me the time I needed to warn Sami of Ceren's plans. Whether or not Governor Kristos would act on the information was out of my hands.

On Monday evening, I received an invitation from Lady Hyacinth to have tea in her room after dinner. I hadn't yet managed to get a copy of the key to Ceren's study, and I wasn't in the mood for gossip and knitting, but Ebb insisted I go.

"Tea is a euphemism for wine," Ebb explained. "And other beverages. It might help you sleep. Besides, you need to get out of your rooms more," she said as she retied my corset with more force than seemed possible for such a delicate woman.

"Why?" I asked between breaths. "My odds of running into Ceren are a lot lower if I stay here."

"Ah, but so are your odds of running into other people." She tied the laces firmly and turned me around to face her.

"Other people? Like who?"

She smoothed the front of my dress and smiled. "You'll see."

Confused and a little annoyed, I made my way to Lady Hyacinth's room. I didn't have time for knitting. I had to find a way to get into Ceren's study.

An idea struck me as I walked, and I made a quick detour down another hallway. I hummed quietly to myself, pretending to look distracted as I fished a pin out of my hair. If I couldn't get the key itself, perhaps I could pick the lock.

I cut through the hall of Varenian portraits and paused before Zadie's just long enough to say a little prayer for her and Sami. I felt the eyes of every woman as I passed, and I reminded myself that I was doing this for them, and for every young girl in Varenia who would spend her life wondering if she was beautiful enough. The story of Princess Ilara was just a convenient excuse to prop up a dying royal dynasty, and all of our hard work was merely a means to supply one man with pearls that would never cure a corrupt heart.

I was rounding the corner to Ceren's study when I saw someone emerge from the door. I ducked back, but it was too late.

"Who's there?" a male voice asked.

I turned to run and nearly screamed when a hand clamped down on my shoulder.

"Zadie?"

I looked up to find Talin's blue-green eyes peering down at me. "Prince Talin!"

His grip loosened, but his hand remained on my shoulder, and I could feel the warmth of his touch even through my knit shawl. "What are you doing out here alone at this hour?" he asked.

"I'm on my way to meet Lady Hyacinth. For tea."

"Tea? Shouldn't you be in bed?"

I dropped my gaze, and his hand slid away, leaving a burning trail as it went. "My maid thinks I need to socialize more. I've been spending too much time alone."

"Come now," he said. "Surely my brother has kept you occupied."

"Your brother and I had a little fight." I didn't expect sympathy from Talin—Ceren was his brother, after all, and I was a girl he hardly knew. But I also didn't want him to think that Ceren and I were in any way friendly.

"I thought I told you to be careful," he said, but there was concern in his voice. "What happened?"

"It's nothing," I murmured, but my eyes flicked involuntarily to the door of Ceren's study.

He glanced behind him. "You shouldn't be here, my lady. Ceren doesn't appreciate interruptions when he's working."

My breath caught. Ceren was in there *now*? What would have happened if I'd picked the lock with Ceren inside? "Were you helping him?" I asked.

"No, no. Ceren doesn't like help with his inventions. I only came to tell him that our father wishes to see him. And that I'll be accompanying him to test the device at one of the Linrose Lakes tomorrow, on the king's orders. He may be my brother, but he's also the crown prince."

"And are you an inventor like your brother?"

"Nothing like Ceren. He's been tinkering since he was a small boy. He claims this is his greatest invention yet." He smiled conspiratorially. "Though I must say, my favorite was a tube he filled with mirrors and colored glass. He gave it to me for my tenth birthday because I loved color and light, something we are in short supply of in New Castle."

I couldn't help returning his smile. "So there is kindness in your brother after all."

The smile faded. "Of course, my lady."

"I'm sorry. I didn't mean… I should get to Lady Hyacinth's room. She'll be expecting me." I tried to edge around him. "I'll see you tomorrow, at the lake."

He frowned and placed his hand on my lower arm. "I know what it's like to lose the person you love most in the world," he said suddenly. "I understand what it's like to be forced from your home. But please, for your own sake, keep your head down."

His tone and expression were so earnest I didn't know how to respond. "That's never really been my strong suit," I said, then smiled apologetically. "But I'll try."

I waited for him to smile back, but instead, he ever so gently circled my wrist with his fingers and brought my hand up to his face, laying my palm against his cheek. After a moment, he turned his head and pressed a kiss to my palm, before bowing and disappearing into the dark.

For several minutes, I stood with my back against the wall, trying to catch my breath. What was that? What did it mean? I still didn't know if Talin recognized me, though the idea that he'd have done such a thing if he believed I was Zadie didn't feel possible. I stared at the door to Ceren's study, wishing I could just barge in and rip the hose apart, no matter the consequences. But if Ceren killed me now, sabotaging the device would be for nothing. It wouldn't do my people any good if I couldn't warn them of Ceren's plans.

I decided Lady Hyacinth could wait, and instead made my

way to Lady Melina's chambers. If Ceren was in his study, he was busy, and while his spies might report my whereabouts, it was a risk I'd just have to take.

Melina answered the door herself in a long violet robe.

"What are you wearing?" I asked, admiring the garment. It seemed like it had been ages since I'd seen another person wearing anything bright or colorful.

"What the king doesn't know won't kill him," she said, ushering me inside. "What are you doing here?"

"I can't get into Ceren's office."

"No, I imagine you can't."

I let out an exasperated sigh. "If I can't get in, I can't tamper with his device. This was a stupid plan. I don't know why I ever thought I could be a spy. Sami was right. I spent my entire life trying to be beautiful, not learning anything useful."

Lady Melina pointed to a couch. "Sit down. I'll get you something to drink." She went to a side table and poured amber liquid into a glass. "Here. It burns going down, but it will help. Now tell me what happened."

It did burn, and I nearly spat out the foul liquid. But as I explained what had taken place with Talin, the tension in my limbs began to release. "I don't know how to stop Ceren," I said, easing back onto the pillows. "And I don't want to marry him."

She sat down next to me. "Of course you don't, child. But that's not why you're here, is it?"

"What do you mean?" I asked, feeling loose and languid, like I was underwater.

"You didn't come here just to marry the prince. I remember what I was like when I was chosen, how honored I felt.

I would have gladly married King Lazar, arrogant as he was, if he would have had me. I didn't even mind being his mistress at first. I thought I could change his mind about me, if I just did everything he asked." She shook her head. "By the time Talia arrived, I had no more illusions about my life here. She was so young and beautiful and just as desirous to please as I had been. I didn't have the heart to tell her what it was really like here, so I let her find out for herself. Sometimes I regret that choice."

I laid my head on Melina's soft shoulder, the silk of her robe slippery beneath my skin. "But I'm not like that?"

She brought one hand up to my hair. "No, child. You aren't like that. You are curious and wary and shrewd. Even when I told you all the horrible things waiting for you here, you didn't consider giving up for one moment. Did you?"

"Maybe for a moment," I said, yawning.

Her shoulder shook a little with laughter. "We should get you to bed, child. Sabotage or no sabotage, you're leaving the castle tomorrow. And I want to hear all about it when you get back."

20

Somehow I made it back to my room that night. I was angry with myself for failing at my task, but I had been lucky. If Talin hadn't stopped me, I would have been caught breaking into the study by Ceren himself. Fortunately, there was still a chance I could get a note to Sami. I scribbled the quickest explanation I could on a scrap of paper and folded it up in a silk handkerchief before tumbling into bed.

It felt as if only a few moments had passed when Ebb entered my room to wake me the next morning. "I can't believe the prince is letting you leave the mountain," she said as she pulled back my blankets.

I sat up and rubbed my eyes. "Have you been to the Linrose Lakes before?" I asked.

She shuddered slightly. "I've heard of them, but I've never been myself. You won't go in the water, will you, milady?"

"No. But not because of the water spirits. Anyway, you'll be there to keep an eye on me, won't you?"

She shook her head. "I'm afraid not."

"I realize I'm still new to Ilarean customs, but it seems odd that I wouldn't be allowed to take my lady's maid with me."

Ebb leaned down to my ear as she helped me out of the bed. "It *is* odd. But the head maid said something about the need for discretion. Prince Ceren is only taking one servant—the younger brother of the page who died recently."

"I see." Could that be the boy I'd heard in the cave? No wonder he'd been so frightened, if his own brother had died during the experiments.

"Don't worry, milady. Just think of how good all that fresh sunshine will feel after days trapped in here." Her eyes flicked to mine. "Prince Talin will also be there today, I'm told."

"You knew he was here last night, didn't you?" I asked. "Is that why you encouraged me to go to Lady Hyacinth's rooms?"

She grinned slyly and walked to my wardrobe. "I was told he'd be attending the gathering."

"Well, he did not." At least, I didn't think he'd gone there after I saw him. "And anyway, I don't know why you'd assume I'd want to see Prince Talin when I'm betrothed to his brother."

Ebb didn't even try to look chastened as she changed the subject. "What would you like to wear? It may be warm if it's a sunny day."

I let her choose a deep green silk dress instead of one of the heavier satin or velvet gowns. Though it was cold in the mountain, Ebb insisted summer days in the rest of Ilara were long and warm.

"When I was little, I would run through the fields on my

father's lands with my brother all summer long," she said with a faraway look in her pale eyes.

"What does your father do?" I asked as she helped me into the dress.

"He was one of the king's closest advisors, until the king fell ill and Ceren replaced those nobles with his own favorites. My father lost most of his land after that. I send what little money I make home to him."

"Are you able to see your brother, at least?"

She paused for a moment. "Do you have any siblings, milady?"

Talking about Zadie was a risk, but I couldn't expect Ebb to confide in me if I wasn't willing to do the same. "One. A sister."

"Then perhaps you'll understand if I don't speak about my brother, milady. I would do anything to protect him."

I nodded. I couldn't imagine what danger Ebb needed to shield her brother from, but I knew a thing or two about protecting a beloved sibling.

When I arrived in the dining hall, Ceren was standing behind his chair, waiting for me. Talin's place was empty. I glimpsed Lady Melina at the far end of the table, speaking with an Ilarean lord. She didn't make eye contact with me until a servant presented Ceren with a tray of pastries.

"Sleep well?" she mouthed with a smile.

I smirked, only a little embarrassed. I *had* slept well after the drink she gave me, probably the best I had since coming to Ilara.

When we'd finished eating, Ceren took my arm and led me toward the massive iron doors. "Are you ready, my dear?"

My heart fluttered in anticipation. "Yes."

The guards pulled open the smaller door set into the larger doors, creating a bright rectangle of light against the darkness of the hall. Ceren urged me forward, and I stepped through, my eyes half-closed against what I expected would be blinding light after so much time in the dark. But it was like I'd stepped directly into a cloud, all gray swirling mist. Still much brighter than inside the mountain, but not the sunshine I'd been craving.

Ceren laughed at my expression. "Don't worry, my lady. Once we descend, you'll see your beloved sun again. Follow me, please."

I had forgotten that leaving the mountain would mean having to climb back up tonight, but I was so happy to be outside, breathing fresh air, that I didn't care. The descent was much faster than the ascent, and as promised, we broke free of the clouds after just a few minutes. I paused on a stair to look out at the valley before us.

Soft hills of green and gold, like the rolling waves of the ocean, were spread out below. Here and there I could see the glint of a lake or stream. The sky above us was a clear blue dotted with light, fluffy clouds. But as dazzled as I was to see it all, I also felt something dark and ominous at the edge of my consciousness: the knowledge that this was just for today, and that in a few hours, I would have to return to the darkness behind me.

"Don't look so sad," Ceren said, turning to gaze up at me. He wore a dark hat with a brim so large it shaded his entire face, and I noticed that his hands were gloved, despite the heat. "You should enjoy this moment. Who knows when you'll see it all again."

I had a fleeting desire to nudge him over the edge of the wall, just to see his reaction when he realized someone had stood up to him.

"Come along," he said, disrupting my traitorous thoughts.

When we reached the bottom, a carriage was waiting for us, smaller than the one that had brought me here. The guards mounted their horses as Ceren helped me in. Unlike the last carriage I'd ridden in, there was only one bench. It would just be the two of us inside, and I prayed that the trip was short.

My skirts were thin enough that I could feel the warmth of his thigh against mine. I kept my hands clasped neatly in my lap so he wouldn't be tempted to take one of them, but when the carriage went over a large bump, I threw out a hand to steady myself, grabbing the nearest thing available: his forearm.

I released it immediately, but I could feel Ceren smiling next to me. How he loved to see me squirm, like a worm on a hook.

"I'm impressed with how quickly you've adjusted," he said. "They say it took Queen Talia nearly six months of sickness before she finally got used to living here. But you're different than she was. She was so self-aware, and her actions were always calculated, like she was performing in a play all the time. It was as if she'd spent her entire life worrying about how her behavior looked to other people."

"She did," I said, the words tumbling from my lips before I could stop myself. "That's exactly how she spent her life. You have no idea the amount of pressure there is on Varenian women to be beautiful, all so we can be the one chosen to come here."

"You say that like it's a bad thing."

I glared at him from the corner of my eye. "It's all such a waste. You wouldn't care what I looked like, as long as I can provide you with healthy heirs."

He chuckled, a low rumble in his chest. "My, aren't we feisty this morning. Of course your beauty matters to me. If I must marry a wave child, I far prefer a pretty one. But you're right, it does seem foolish to waste so much time on vanity. My mother was beautiful, too, but what good did it do her?" He shook his head sadly, then added, "At any rate, you're nothing like Talia."

I arched an eyebrow in question.

"You speak your mind, for one thing. I never heard Talia say anything sharp or angry to my father. She was always the perfect lady, as delicate as a flower."

Not so delicate, I thought. A flower could not have survived the journey to Ilara, let alone a life in that horrible mountain.

"No, you strike me as someone who's more careless with her beauty," he continued. "For example, most women with your bone structure would wear their hair pulled back, to show off their cheekbones. But you've worn yours down today. Don't worry, your hair still looks lovely, but it's not as flattering. I can hardly see that delicate neck of yours."

I bit back a growl at the memory of his hands on my throat, but he was right. I never thought about whether or not a particular hairstyle was flattering. Zadie would have.

"And while I know you're desperate for color, the green gown was a poor choice. You should have chosen the feathered gown, or the one with the diamond cutout. You have so few chances to display your flesh for my brother, after all."

I hated the way he made everything vulgar and ugly. "In Varenia, I wore whatever we could afford. Our pearls don't buy what they used to," I told him.

"See, just one of the many ways you are lucky to have been rescued from poverty. I would wager you have fifty gowns in your wardrobe right now, and I'd order fifty more if you asked for them."

I looked out the window, grateful that the curtains had been pulled back today, so I could see out as we rode. "I have no need for one hundred dresses, nor even fifty."

"So you don't like them?"

I turned back to him. "It's hard to think about dresses when I know my family could very well be hungry tonight, especially without me there to dive for pearls." I almost mentioned my injured sister but stopped myself just in time. I had to control my emotions around Ceren, no matter how much he rankled me.

Before he could answer, the carriage rattled to a stop. I felt it rock as the driver leaped down and came to open our door.

"We're here," Ceren said, handing me out of the carriage. "Lake Elwin, the largest of the Linrose Lakes."

Talin and his guards stood off in the distance, some mounted, others holding on to their horses' leads as they waited for our arrival. Talin was still on his dapple gray stallion, looking as majestic as the day I'd seen him at Old Castle. There was a part of me that wondered if he'd help me if he knew what Ceren had planned for the Varenians. I wanted to believe that he'd helped me last night.

But he'd also convinced me to dance with him at the ball when he must have known how his brother would react. I couldn't help thinking that Ceren was right. Talin was a lionfish, beautiful but dangerous, drawing me in even though I knew he could cost me everything.

When he spotted me crossing the field, he dismounted and walked forward to meet us. He bowed in front of me, his brown hair falling over his brow. "My lady."

"Your Highness." I curtsied, letting my own hair shadow my face, always conscious of my scar around him. I looked away quickly, pretending to take in the landscape. "I didn't get to fully appreciate Ilara's beauty during my journey here."

I could feel his gaze on me. "I always believed Ilara was the most beautiful thing in the world, until I visited your home."

I had promised myself I would avoid eye contact with him today, but my glance betrayed me at his words. Was he referring to Varenia, or Zadie? Or was it somehow possible he meant *me*?

Ceren's hand landed heavily on my shoulder, staking his claim. "Thank you for meeting us, Talin. I know your men are busy, but I think what you're about to see will impress even you."

"Are you so difficult to impress, Prince Talin?" I asked.

He smirked in response, and something caught in my chest.

"Only when it comes to me," Ceren said. "Isn't that right, brother?"

Talin ignored him and took my arm. My pulse quickened at the contact. "I am very impressed with your bride-to-be," he said over his shoulder.

I could feel the tension rolling off Ceren as he walked on

my other side. Along the bank of the river, Ceren's guards and the young page were inflating the air bag with a pair of large bellows.

Talin scratched at his hair. "I must say you've outdone yourself this time, Ceren. I have absolutely no idea what I'm looking at."

Ceren continued on toward the device. "Not to worry. You will soon enough." He unclasped his coat and handed it to the boy. "I'm afraid I need to undress for this presentation. My lady, please avert your gaze. I wouldn't want to spoil our wedding night."

I scowled and turned away gladly. A few moments later I heard a splash, followed by Ceren gasping at the cold. I turned around to see his head and bare shoulders floating above the water, his hair fanned out around him on the surface.

"Is it really necessary for you to do this yourself?" Talin asked. "It seems dangerous, and none of my men can remove their armor fast enough to help you should you need it."

"I wouldn't go in there if my life depended on it," one of the guards muttered.

"At least let me take my armor off before you go in," Talin said, but Ceren brushed off his concern.

"I won't need help. Boy, hand me the hose and goggles."

The waters around Varenia were crystal clear, and we were used to opening our eyes underwater, but this lake was murky and dark. The little page tossed the goggles to Ceren. He looked terrified, but it was hard to say if it was the water, Ceren, or the contraption that was scaring him. Probably all three.

Ceren placed the end of the hose in his mouth and took

a few breaths to test it. Then he removed the hose for a moment and told Talin to time him before diving under the surface of the water.

One of the guards began to count off the seconds as we watched from the edge of the lake.

"How deep is it?" I asked Talin.

"I have no idea. Ten feet at the most, I'd think. You didn't see it, but he weighted his feet against the buoyancy." He thought for a moment. "You knew about this, didn't you?"

"Your brother showed it to me, yes."

"Where? In his study?"

I bit my lip. Did he suspect my real motives for lurking near there last night? "Yes," I admitted.

He searched my face. "You've been to the flooded bloodstone mine, haven't you?"

His eyes reminded me so much of home, it made my heart ache. "If you mean the lake in the bottom of the mountain, then yes." I was only vaguely aware of the guard reaching two hundred.

"He took you all the way down there?"

I hesitated again. I didn't like to lie, but I couldn't admit out loud that I'd spied on the Crown Prince of Ilara, especially not to his brother. I gave a curt nod.

"Do you know why my brother created this device?" Talin demanded.

"Yes—to harvest the Varenian pearls for himself."

I could tell by his reaction that he had already realized this. "I'm surprised my brother would show this to you. He knows it means the end for your people."

"*Our* people," I said, fiercer than I'd meant to. "And yes, he knows. I think he enjoys causing me pain."

"Sadly, I'm afraid you might be right."

I knew Ceren's guards were watching us, but I took a step closer to him, taking in his scent of sunshine, sweat, and horses. "Doesn't it pain you to think of what will become of them? You've seen Varenia now, eaten at our governor's table. You know my family. You can't just pretend we don't exist anymore."

I watched his profile for a response, but his expression didn't change. Just when I had almost given up hope, he found my littlest finger in the folds of my skirt and wrapped his own finger around it. It was only a fraction of a moment, but it was a far more intimate response than I'd expected.

Lionfish! my subconscious shouted, and I twitched my hand away from his, but my heart pounded with something other than fear.

"That's ten minutes," the guard said. I looked over at the page, who knew that we'd reached the end of the test as well as I did.

"He should surface any moment now," I said.

Behind me, the guard resumed counting.

A sense of dread washed over me, raising gooseflesh on my bare forearms. "You don't understand. He hasn't tested the device for more than ten minutes. He should have surfaced already."

"He's probably just showing off," said the same guard who had vowed not to enter the water.

I looked at the page again, to where his foot rested just inches from the hose, and realized what he'd done.

Talin had begun to remove his leather armor, but I could see immediately that he'd meant what he said earlier—the process would take several minutes, and right now every second counted. I was frozen in place, unsure of what to do. Ceren's death would be the end to all of Varenia's problems. If he died, Talin would inherit the throne, and while I may not trust him entirely, I did not believe he would cause further harm to his own mother's people.

And if Ceren lived, he could be affected for life. Who knew how long he'd been without oxygen? I thought of the poor page. He couldn't be more than twelve years old. Ceren would be so furious and humiliated by all of this… It wouldn't go well for anyone.

But in Varenia, if someone was in danger, you helped them, unless the risk to yourself was too great. Banishment was the only exception, and that was different. Dangerous criminals couldn't be permitted to stay in Varenia, and at least they had a chance of survival. But how could I live with myself if I stood by and watched a person drown? Even if that person wouldn't have done the same for me.

"Damn it!" Talin swore as he tore at one of the dozen buckles on his armor. "Someone do something!"

"Unbutton my gown!" I screamed, presenting my back to Talin. If he wanted his brother alive, there was no time for propriety. "Now!"

21

After a moment's hesitation, Talin unfastened the buttons as fast as he could, and I yanked off the sleeves and stepped out of the dress in my undergarments. Kicking off my slippers, I raced past the stunned guards and dived into the water, reminding myself not to inhale when I broke the surface.

It was the coldest water I'd ever been in, and my entire body screamed in protest. The lake was dark and silty, but my eyes adjusted quickly. I followed the hose down, passing ten feet and realizing that the lake was much deeper than they'd thought. Then I saw Ceren's hair, waving in the current like a sea fan.

His eyes had rolled back in his head. He was unconscious, but I had no way of knowing if he'd been out for many minutes or one. One of his feet was untied from its weight, but the knot on his other foot was stuck. He must have realized he was running out of air and been unable to free himself.

I pulled on his foot with all my strength until it tore free of the weight, then yanked the hose from his mouth and started to haul him upward. My feet were already numb, and for a minute I wasn't sure I had the strength to get us both back to the surface.

I could let go of Ceren now and easily return to shore. I owed him nothing. He was cruel and selfish. He'd admitted I was nothing to him but a body, just like Mother said. But the truth was that I'd been under less than two minutes. There was no danger for me, not yet. And I had been raised to believe that letting someone die was tantamount to killing him myself.

I broke the surface and gulped in air, Ceren bobbing up next to me a moment later. I hooked one arm around his chest and began to push toward shore with the other. Talin and several guards had waded into the shallows, and while the guards took over and hauled Ceren onto dry land, Talin scooped me out of the water, sodden as I was, and carried me to the soft grass on the bank.

"Are you all right?" he asked, pushing my wet hair out of my face. "You were under for so long."

"I'm fine," I panted. "I need to help your brother."

"Help him?" Talin echoed incredulously. "He's gone. He was under for nearly fourteen minutes."

I crawled over to where Ceren was, cursing my wet clothing, and bent above him to listen for breathing. I didn't hear anything, and his chest wasn't moving, so I pressed my fingers to his neck. Once more, it crossed my mind that I could do nothing. If he wasn't dead already, he would be soon.

I glanced over at the page, watching me with wide hazel

eyes. He gave the smallest shake of his head, and I knew then for certain he had stepped on the hose, cutting off Ceren's air. Had Lady Melina put him up to this, or was this revenge for his older brother? Perhaps it was both.

And then I felt it. A tiny stutter of a heartbeat, and that was all it took. I pinched his nose, ignoring the gray cast to his skin and blue lips, and began to blow air into his mouth. Several of the guards gasped. They had never seen anyone resuscitated this way before. I'd never had to perform the procedure myself, but all Varenian children were trained in how to do it. I'd seen it several times, when fishermen got the cramps in their joints that could signal death, and once when a baby had fallen off a dock in Varenia and nearly drowned. I continued to blow into his mouth every five seconds, watching his chest carefully. After a minute had passed, I began to lose hope.

Suddenly, Ceren's muscles tensed and his eyes flew open. I moved away just before he vomited. A combination of water and whatever he'd eaten for breakfast bubbled up through his lips, and I quickly rolled him onto his side to help clear his airway. I wiped at his mouth with the hem of my undergarment and rolled him back when he'd finished. A hint of color was already returning to his lips and cheeks.

I couldn't help myself. I smiled. Whatever happened next, a man was alive because of me. "Get Prince Ceren a blanket!" I yelled at whoever would listen.

Ceren looked up at me, his eyes lit by the sun so that they were no longer gray, but closer to the iridescent scales of a silver moonfish. He tried to sit up, but I pressed him down gently. "You need to rest."

He glanced down at his body, and for the first time I became aware of his naked torso, his long limbs and the blue map of veins beneath his pale skin. He was muscular, but so thin I could count every rib as he heaved for air.

I looked back into his eyes just as Grig threw one of the fur throws from the carriage over Ceren's body, and I was surprised by what I saw there: shame, humiliation, but also surprise. Talin had said Ceren pushed people away to test their loyalty. Perhaps I had proven mine today.

"Thank you," he said, taking my hand in his. "I owe you my life."

Captain Osius helped Ceren, who was only semiconscious, into the carriage while the other guards mounted their horses.

"We'll escort you back to the castle," Talin said to me as he handed me another throw. "But we should get you changed first." He made a valiant effort not to look below my neck as he pulled the blanket tight around my shoulders.

"I'm fine. I should be with Prince Ceren."

"Osius will stay with him. There's only room for two people in the carriage, and you've done more than your share for my brother today."

"Then how will I get back?" I asked.

"You'll ride with me."

I raised my eyebrows. "Do you think that's a good idea?"

"Don't worry, my lady. My men are discreet. Right now I'm far more concerned that you'll catch cold in those wet clothes."

"Why, do you have a spare gown lying around?" I said with a smirk.

"Perhaps if you remove your… Your gown is still dry, my lady."

I was too delighted by his discomfort to be ashamed when he offered to hold the blanket up for me so I could change. When I'd finished, I pulled my hair over my shoulder and presented my back to him.

"Can you help me with the buttons?"

There was no response. I glanced over my shoulder to find Talin blushing as pink as a cooked shrimp.

"I wasn't permitted to bring my lady's maid," I said, suppressing a giggle. "I could ask one of your men to help me, if you prefer."

He released his breath, and the warm air on my bare skin sent a shiver down my spine. "You're cold," he said, as if that gave him the permission he needed.

His fingers fumbled against the small of my back as he struggled with the tiny loops on the gown, and I felt a sudden wave of gratitude for all those stupid buttons. After a few failed attempts, he seemed to get the hang of it, stepping closer to me as his fingers climbed up my back to my shoulder blades. Without my undergarments, there was nothing between his hands and my flesh, and I felt every brush of skin on skin like a flame licking from my back down to my core.

"Thank you," he said softly as he finished the last button, his fingers still lingering on my nape. It took all my willpower not to press back into him, but I tilted my head, exposing more of my neck to his warm breath, relishing the way the small hairs there stood on end. I didn't ask him what he was thanking me for. I didn't want to hear Ceren's name. I wanted this moment to last forever.

"We should go," he said finally, though there was longing in his voice. And regret. He led me over to his stallion, who stood patiently waiting while the other horses stomped and snorted, ready to go home.

"I've never ridden a horse," I said, staring up at the massive creature.

"All you have to do is hold on to me," he said with a crooked grin. "Surely you can manage that."

Grig helped lift me up onto the horse behind Talin, where I sat sideways, thanks to my skirts. My hair was still wet, and the cold of the lake hadn't left my skin, but the heat of the horse and Talin himself began to warm me. He clucked to his horse, and I gripped him a little tighter. The trot was more uncomfortable than I'd imagined, each stride causing me to bounce painfully against Talin's leather armor.

"It will be smoother if I canter," he said over his shoulder. "But we'll be going fast. Are you afraid?"

"A little."

He laughed softly. "There's nothing to be afraid of." He clucked again and the horse broke into a canter. Immediately the stallion's gait smoothed out into something tolerable, and if I closed my eyes I could almost imagine I was back in our family's boat, riding the waves instead of an animal.

"Better?" he asked.

"Much. Thank you."

"There is one problem with this," he said, sounding very serious.

"And what's that?"

"We're going to be back at the castle far more quickly."

I couldn't help laughing. Perhaps it was the sense of power

I'd felt saving Ceren's life, but I wasn't afraid now, even though I knew I should be. I pressed myself against Talin's back and let the rising and falling sensation of the horse's gait lull me to a sense of inner calm I wasn't sure I'd ever feel again when I left Varenia.

As we neared New Castle, Talin slowed the horse to a walk. Reluctantly, I released my grip on him a bit, since I no longer had the excuse of speed. I glanced down at the wrinkled silk of my gown, my long hair wavy and loose over my shoulders. How was I going to explain my appearance to Ebb?

After a few minutes, Talin turned his head toward me. "Why did you do it?" he asked.

"What?"

"Save my brother. You could have let him die out there today, and you didn't. You risked your own life for his."

I toyed with one of the buckles on his armor. "Yes."

"Why?"

It was only one word, but it held all the feelings that had passed through my mind while I rescued Ceren. *You could have been free*, it said.

"It's Varenian custom," I explained. "If the god Thalos wants the life, he must fight for it, too. And you asked for help, so I gave it."

"Thalos," Talin murmured. "I heard my mother speak of him when she told me the story of how the Varenians came to be."

"It must seem very silly to you."

He shook his head. "The only thing that ever seemed silly to me is that the Varenians should suffer because a pair of foolish young lovers died in a shipwreck."

I smiled to myself. I'd never heard anyone put it quite so bluntly before. "I used to think so, too. But now I can see that it has very little to do with a legend and far more to do with power and control. And money."

"You mean the pearls. Ceren believes they make him stronger."

"Maybe they do."

Talin's voice sounded far away when he answered. "If they did, my father wouldn't be dying at the age of forty."

Ceren had said his father wasn't helped by the pearls, but he himself hoarded them like treasure, obsessed with the idea that they could prevent whatever illness was killing the king. Surely he wouldn't be killing off servants to harvest the pearls if they didn't work. "Were you close with your father as a child?" I asked.

"Yes, very. It must be difficult for you to imagine him as anything other than the bedridden man you've seen, but he was young once. Never healthy, I suppose, but healthier. He would often go into the villages with my mother and me."

"Where was Ceren when you went into the villages?"

Talin kept his eyes on the road. "Ceren stayed behind with his nursemaids. He didn't like to leave the mountain."

"I pity him sometimes," I admitted. "It must have been a very lonely childhood."

He nodded. "I loved my mother with all my heart, but I never agreed with her treatment of Ceren. I think she resented him, knowing that the crown would pass to him someday and not me."

"But he was just a child."

"I know, but I can imagine how she must have felt, leaving

everything in Varenia behind only to be my father's second wife. I think she believed that if I became king someday, she could put a stop to what's happened—what's still happening—to your people."

When his eyes met mine, I felt a surge of hope. Did that mean Talin disagreed with his brother's plans? "If only Ceren felt the same way," I ventured.

We were almost at the castle, and the carriage was rat-tling up behind us. "Ceren is afraid. He sees my father dying young and worries he will share the same fate. And despite his many shortcomings, my brother loves his kingdom. He doesn't want to see it fall into our enemies' hands."

"Which enemies?" I asked.

Talin glanced at me over his shoulder. "It's hard to say. We have many at the moment. Not just Lord Clifton, but the Galethians to the north and the uprising to the south, as well."

"And you think he should continue to exploit the Varenians for the sake of Ilara?"

His jaw tightened. "No. I shared my mother's views on that even before I visited your home." The carriage passed us, and Talin brought his horse into line with the captain's. For a moment, I dared to hope that this accident could change things. I'd seen something in Ceren's eyes, some shred of humanity that he kept hidden behind his pale mask. He was still the child who'd lost his mother and never felt as loved as he should have been.

Ceren had said he owed me his life. Perhaps in return, he would give the Varenians theirs.

Talin dismounted at the base of the mountain and turned to help me, reaching up to my waist and lifting me as if I weighed no more than a child. I could feel the heat of his hands through the thin silk, with not even a shift or petticoat between us. And, gods help me, I wanted his hands to move higher, lower, everywhere. I wanted to kiss him the way Zadie had kissed Sami, long and slow and secret.

As my feet touched the ground, I looked up at him, unsure of what I'd find. We hardly knew each other, but Talin felt like a stepping stone between this life and the one I'd left behind. And for a moment, I hoped I might not have to face that distance alone.

But then his eyes skidded away from mine to my right cheekbone, and my stomach clenched like a fist.

My scar. I hadn't been in the water very long, but I'd rested my right cheek against Talin's back while we were riding. I resisted the urge to touch my face, but Talin's eyes hardened all the same as he stepped back from me and bowed.

"Have a care, my lady," he said. And then he was gone.

22

When I finally made it back to my room and stepped in front of my full-length mirror, I shouldn't have been surprised to see the small patch of exposed pink skin on my cheek, not after the way Talin had looked at me. But even though I had long ago accepted my scar as a part of who I was, I had gotten used to seeing myself without it.

My eyes filled with tears as I took in the torn, mud-splattered hem of my gown and the snarls in my hair. I smelled like lake water, which, out of context, was not exactly pleasant. But the worst part wasn't that Talin had discovered the truth—it was that he had looked at me the way Mother looked at me after the incident. Like I was a stranger.

Ebb gasped in horror when she came in behind me. "Milady, what has happened to you?"

I turned around, feeling weary down to my bones. "I'll explain everything. Just please have my bath prepared."

She nodded, her blue eyes round with surprise, and darted

off down the hallway to fetch a maid. When the bath was ready and we were alone again, I told her about Ceren.

She sat unblinking, her mouth slowly falling open, as I recounted his near drowning.

"For Thalos's sake, Ebb, would you stop looking at me like that?" I said when I finally finished and her expression hadn't changed.

"I'm sorry. I've just never heard anything like it. You saved him from the water spirits. You brought him back from the dead!"

I rolled my eyes and motioned for her to help with the buttons on my dress. As her fingers deftly unfastened them, I thought of Talin, my stomach twisting with a mix of desire and hurt. "Of course I didn't. If he'd been dead, I wouldn't have been able to save him." I could already see how this story would go with the servants. Rumors that I'd resurrected a dead man would be flying by dinner. "You can't tell anyone, Ebb. Prince Ceren will share the story when he's ready."

"Yes, milady."

"I mean it. If I hear a word of gossip about this because of you, I'll start making you empty the chamber pots every day."

She stifled a giggle. "I understand. Let's get you out of these wet clothes and into your bath."

I stayed in the tub for a long time, scrubbing away the smell of lake water with lavender-scented soap and combing out my waist-length hair. Ebb had suggested cutting it to make it more manageable, but I wouldn't allow more than a trim. I knew that Zadie would never cut her hair, and I didn't want to look different from my sister. My reflection in the mirror would be the only way I had to watch her grow old.

When the water started to get cold, Ebb helped me out of the tub. She handed me my towel and held up the little bone jar.

"Shall we cover up your scar, milady?" she asked. "The stain must have come off in the water."

Shame washed over me as I realized that she'd likely known about my scar and the stain all along. Why had I thought I could fool everyone? And *to what end?* Zadie had said people in Varenia hardly noticed my scar, and Ebb didn't seem at all disgusted or concerned. But I remembered the way Talin had looked at me just hours ago and felt my eyes well with tears.

"Would you mind leaving me for a moment, Ebb?"

"Of course," she said gently. "Just ring if you need me."

When she left the room, I let the towel fall and went to stand before the mirror. Without the fancy gowns and hairstyles, I looked so much like my sister I didn't know if our own parents would be able to tell us apart. Except for the scar.

My mother had never even thanked me for saving Zadie. She'd made me believe the scar was a source of shame, an imperfection that would define the rest of my life. I'd always thought it was a small price to pay in the grand scheme of things. Without it, I wouldn't have been permitted to dive as much as I had, to become a strong enough swimmer to save a grown man. Zadie wouldn't have been able to do what I'd done today. And yet I knew that my mother would be more upset that I had exposed my scar than proud of me for saving Ceren.

I ran my finger over the slightly raised skin on my cheek, then down to the crook of my neck, remembering the feel of Talin's hands—how delicate they'd been against my back, how strong and sure they'd felt on my waist. He may have guessed before, but I was sure Talin knew who I really was now. Would he feel compelled to tell his brother? Ceren had made his concerns clear, and they revolved around my ability to produce a healthy heir, not my beauty. But after today, it was clear Talin felt more loyalty to his brother than I'd originally believed. My only hope was that Ceren's gratitude was greater than his anger would be if he ever learned the truth.

I dabbed the stain on my cheek and said nothing when Ebb returned to dress me in another beautiful gown. As she arranged my hair, I remembered the handkerchief with the note for Sami inside. In all the commotion, I had lost the handkerchief and completely forgotten my mission. Some spy I'd turned out to be.

I was late for the evening meal by the time I reached the dining hall, and every eye in the room turned on me as I entered. I feared the rumors might have already circulated without Ebb's help, and sure enough, there were murmurs of "she saved his life" and "some kind of magic."

I wanted to shout at them that it had nothing to do with magic, that I'd merely breathed air into his lungs, but I went quietly to my place. Talin and Ceren were nowhere to be seen. I ate as slowly and methodically as I could, unwilling to allow the other lords and ladies to see me ruffled.

When dinner was finished, Lady Hyacinth approached. "You've created quite the stir," she said as she took my arm. "Everyone is talking about the accident."

I glanced at her out of the corner of my eye. Whatever I said now would quickly make its way through the castle. "Are they?" I asked.

She grinned and patted my hand. "Discretion. I can appreciate that. Will the prince be all right?"

"Yes, I think so. What exactly did you hear?"

She guided me to a bench in an alcove where we could speak more privately. "We heard he was swimming in the lake and a water spirit disguised as a giant snake pulled him under. But you dived in and killed it with your bare hands."

I laughed. "Please don't tell me you believe that."

"No, of course not," she said. "But you did save him, didn't you?"

If everyone knew that I'd saved Ceren, perhaps he'd feel more pressure to be kind to me, even if Talin told him the truth about who I was. "I did. He was drowning, and I pulled him out of the water and breathed air into his lungs because he didn't have any."

"Where did you learn to do it? No one has ever heard of such a thing."

"I spent my entire life in and on the sea. My people risk their lives every day diving for the pearls your people seem so obsessed with." I gestured to the pink pearl pendant hanging from her neck, unable to keep the edge from my voice. The Ilareans treated me like a child, but they were as ignorant as I was when it came to anything outside their own experience. They probably had no idea where the pearls even came from.

"I heard another rumor," she said, lifting her fan to cover her entire face except for her eyes, which sparkled with what could either be mirth or mischief. It was hard to read her expression with her mouth covered.

When I didn't respond, she went on, undeterred. "I heard

you rode on the same horse as Prince Talin, in nothing but your undergarments."

I rolled my eyes. Who started these rumors, I wondered. One of the guards? "Your crown prince almost died. He needed a guard in the carriage with him, and there was only room for two people. So yes, I rode on Talin's horse. I was also soaking wet and smelling of lake water. And I was clothed, for what it's worth."

She laughed lightly. "You're very brave, you know. It must have been so frightening for everyone."

"It was." I knew no one else would understand how close Ilara had come to losing Prince Ceren today. Had I done the right thing by saving him? Not just for me, but for the kingdom? Would he rule fairly and wisely, or had I done nothing but spare a tyrant's life to the peril of many others?

When Talin entered the room, the murmurs started again. He strode toward me, ignoring the looks of the lords and ladies, and I felt Hyacinth straighten up beside me.

Talin's bow was short and perfunctory as he quietly asked, "Can I see you for a moment?"

He hadn't even addressed me properly. I rose and curtsied. "Of course, Your Highness."

He didn't take my arm or slow his stride to wait for me, and I did my best to keep up with him down the corridors leading to Ceren's rooms. His features were tight; I'd never seen him so agitated. Had something happened to Ceren since we returned? Would I be blamed for it?

The guards opened the door to let us in, and Talin marched over to Ceren's bed. He was still pallid, his lips tinged blue, but he was very much alive.

"What is it?" I asked, not understanding the concern on Talin's face. "Is everything all right?"

"He won't talk to anyone but you," Talin explained. "He insisted on having his 'bride' here."

Talin had not yet spoken with his brother about my true identity, it seemed. Ceren stretched out his hand to me, and I felt compelled to take it.

"My dear Zadie. Thank you for coming."

I curtsied. "I'm glad to see you're feeling better."

He smiled at me, then turned to Talin. "The rest of you may leave. I need to speak to her alone."

Talin clenched his jaw but ordered the men out. He glanced at me over his shoulder once before slipping through the door, as well.

"Is everything all right?" I asked, trying not to sound nervous.

"I need to ask you what happened, without you feeling threatened by Talin and his guards."

I cocked my head. "Why would I feel threatened?"

"I know now that you are the only one I can trust. You were the only person who tried to save me, even though you could have easily let me drown. I need to know—who was it?"

"I don't understand. Who was what?"

He pulled so hard on my arm that I was now inches from his face. "Who was it who tried to kill me?" he hissed.

Dread washed over me. Thalos, he knew. "No one tried to kill you. It was a terrible accident, perhaps a kink in the hose that limited your air supply. The water was much colder than we could have anticipated, and you're not used to it."

"I was breathing perfectly well for the first seven minutes

or so. This was no mistake. Who else touched the device while I was down there?"

"No one. I swear it."

"You were watching the whole time?"

I lowered my eyes, remembering the moment I'd shared with Talin, his finger brushing against mine. "Almost the whole time. The only person near the device was your page."

He dropped my hand and fixed his gaze on the ceiling. "I knew it."

"But he didn't touch it," I said, realizing what a horrible mistake I'd made. "We all would have seen if he'd tried to tamper with it. He was several feet away from it at all times."

"You can't say that for sure if you were only watching 'most' of the time. That boy blames me for his brother's death, so he tried to take his revenge."

"He's just a child. It couldn't have been him."

Ceren sat up, still holding me in place so that his face was just inches from mine. "Why did you save me?"

I blinked. "What?"

"Why didn't you just let me drown? Everyone else would have been pleased, I'm sure. Talin would have been king. You could have married him if you'd wanted to. I doubt even my own father would have cared. So why did you save me?"

I could have tried to explain about the customs of my people, but I was tired and frustrated. I let out a long sigh. "Because *I* cared. Because I couldn't just stand there and let you die." I could never forgive Ceren for what he was doing to the Varenians, but his life wasn't mine to take.

He closed his eyes, and for a moment I thought he'd gone

to sleep. "I'm sorry I haven't treated you better. What is it you wish from me?"

"I don't understand," I said, my brow furrowed in confusion.

"What do you want? What will it take to make you happy here?"

My heart stuttered in my chest. I had failed to get my message to Sami, but now Ceren was offering me another chance. "My freedom."

His eyes flashed open. "I can't let you leave Ilara."

"I know. I don't expect you to let me go. But I would like to be able to leave the castle. Not every day, but every now and again. I need fresh air and sunlight to survive, Ceren."

I had forgotten to use his proper title, but he didn't seem to notice. Instead, he reached up and brushed a strand of hair from my face. "Just like a flower," he said. "Very well. You may leave the castle once a week. My guards will escort you."

It was such a small thing, and I shouldn't have had to ask, but I smiled in relief. "Thank you."

"And where do you wish to go?"

I thought of Zadie at fourteen, pretending that she couldn't reach an oyster she wanted but was too lazy to dive for. It had only taken a few flutters of her lashes, a single caress of his arm, to convince Sami to get it for her. I'd sat in awe of my sister that day, as she returned home with a nice fat pearl she hadn't even dived for. Sami, however, had slid down a notch in my esteem.

"When I was a girl, I saw the port market from my family's boat once," I said, fabricating a memory from Sami's stories. "I couldn't make out many details, but the Ilarean ladies in their fine gowns and the handsome Ilarean soldiers in their leather armor fascinated me. I vowed that I would see them in real life one day." I placed a tentative hand on his arm. "I would do anything to go, if you'll take me."

I held my breath while Ceren considered. After a moment, his lips twisted in a grin. "Your false flattery is wasted on me."

I flushed, embarrassed that he'd seen through my act so easily, but at least I didn't have to pretend to enjoy his company.

"But I will take you to the market next month, if you wish."

I tried not to look too disappointed. "Isn't the market this Friday?"

"I'm hardly in the best shape to travel at the moment," he said. "You've waited this long. I'm sure another month won't hurt."

It wasn't what I'd been hoping for, but it was a lot more than I had dared to dream of this afternoon. "Thank you," I said gratefully. "That means more to me than you know."

His lips curled in what was perhaps the first genuine smile I'd seen from him. "You're welcome. Now go, before I change my mind."

23

I was foolish to think that just because he'd been kind to me, Ceren would let the accident go. He kept to his rooms for two days—"recovering" was the official word—but Ebb told me that his device had been brought to his chambers, and I had no doubt he would examine it until he found someone to blame.

I tried to keep to my room, too, feigning exhaustion, but Lady Hyacinth insisted I join her for tea. I was surprised to find it was only Hyacinth and myself when I arrived. As we waited for a maid to deliver the tea service, she asked a few more questions about the accident, but I could tell her mind wasn't on gossip.

The maid finally appeared and filled our cups with tea before scurrying away, and Lady Hyacinth turned to me. For the first time, she wore her hair natural, the auburn curls cascading down her back. I couldn't imagine covering up such lovely hair. Without the powder and makeup, she looked more like the twenty-year-old she really was.

"I'm so glad we finally have a chance to speak alone," she said, adding sugar to my tea without asking. "Tell me, what's it really like in Varenia?"

I was startled by the change in her demeanor. She was usually tipsy and jovial, laughing and gossiping like the other ladies she entertained. "I beg your pardon?"

"Are the people there going hungry, like Prince Talin says? He came back from his trip to your village with surprising reports about a lack of pearls and a very modest existence, which angered his brother to no end. But you don't look hungry. You look strong and vital."

I had no idea how to answer. I had never trusted Lady Hyacinth, per se, but she had always seemed relatively harmless. I should have known that a woman who sat on the king's war council didn't spend all her time drinking and playing card games with her friends.

"We are healthy, for the most part," I said. "But our waters have been overfished, and we don't get as much for the pearls as we used to."

She sipped her tea and leaned back against the silk cushions. "So why not consume the pearls yourselves? Or come to shore and make a life for yourselves on land? All these years, and aside from the Galethian escape, your people have never ventured a coup. As a strategist, I find it mystifying."

She had a point. They were questions I'd asked myself, but life in Varenia was relatively peaceful. People rarely talked about Ilara, aside from in the context of the ceremony. And the situation with the pearls had come on so slowly and insidiously. It wasn't like people were feasting one day and starving the next. We'd all just learned to make do with less as time passed.

"I suppose it's because it's all we've ever known," I said. "To be honest, I was hoping to understand it all a little better when I came here, but I still can't explain it. I know there is a fear that if we come to land, we will be captured and executed."

"But surely if you came a few at a time, you'd be able to make your way north unnoticed. There are so many refugees on the roads these days, you'd hardly be conspicuous."

"Our news is controlled by what we hear at the floating market. We didn't know about the uprisings."

She tapped her lips with a long-nailed finger. "So ignorance is a large part of it. I see."

I didn't like the way she was discussing Varenian oppression like it was something to be studied. But maybe we *were* willfully ignorant. Yes, searching for pearls occupied most of our men's time, but the women? I thought of Mother, how obsessed she was with the ceremony. The Ilareans had given us something else to focus on with the choosing of a Varenian princess, had even made it seem like an honor. But had the Ilareans done that, or had we? It was impossible to tell what had come first. All I knew was that in my seventeen years, the only people I'd ever heard question it were Sami and me.

"Why are you so curious about all this?" I asked finally.

Lady Hyacinth picked up a ball of unraveled yarn from a basket and began to slowly wind it around her hands. "Come now, Zadie. You must know the first rule of warfare."

I shook my head, a voice inside of me screaming that I didn't want to hear the answer.

She smiled, her dark green eyes glittering. "Know your enemy."

My meeting with Lady Hyacinth haunted me. She had called Varenia an enemy, which seemed both ominous and illogical. We were firmly held under Ilarean rule and far too few in number to fight for independence. I wanted to talk to Lady Melina, to see if things had been different in Varenia during her time, but she didn't respond to any of the notes I sent her.

On the third day, Ceren summoned me to a meeting in the great hall. I'd never seen him sit on the throne before; I'd never seen anyone sit on it, in fact. But with a dark metal crown circling his loose hair, and a cloak of black velvet over his shoulders, he looked the part of the king he would one day become.

I glanced around at the other people who'd been called to the meeting and knew immediately that something was wrong. Talin was there, with Grig and Captain Osius, along with the page, several of Ceren's guards, and a smattering of lords and ladies. But it was the presence of Lady Melina that troubled me the most.

"Thank you all for coming," Ceren said once we'd all gathered. "I've spent the past few days examining my breathing apparatus, and it has become evident that someone deliberately tampered with it. An attempt on the crown prince's life is a heinous crime that cannot go unpunished, though thanks to my future bride, that attempt was unsuccessful." He smiled at me, but there was no warmth in his eyes, and I felt my stomach churn as his gaze traveled to the little page.

"This boy," Ceren said, pointing with one long finger at the child, "was the only one close enough to the device to have tampered with it, according to witnesses."

My heart pounded in my chest as I realized what Ceren was preparing to do.

"Indeed, I found a telltale kink in the hose that is all the evidence I need to condemn this traitor to death."

A few of the ladies gasped, and I could feel Talin's posture go rigid next to me.

"Unless, of course, there is someone else who will take responsibility for this crime? I sincerely doubt that a boy of eleven plotted to kill his future king all on his own."

My gaze slid to Lady Melina, and I suddenly understood why she was here. Ceren would never have invited her if he didn't suspect she was involved somehow. And maybe she was. I had told her I couldn't get the key the night before we went to the lake, and it was entirely possible she'd put the page up to this. Worst of all, tampering with the device had been my idea, and Ceren didn't suspect me because I'd saved him.

"Well?" Ceren said. "No one will spare this child's life? Very well. I've decided that since he didn't quite manage to kill me, I won't throw him from the mountain as I normally would. No, in my generosity, I'll give him a chance to fight for his life. Guards, prepare to take him below."

I turned to Talin. "What does he mean, fight? Where is he taking the boy?"

"There is…" He swallowed before continuing. "There is a creature below the mountain. It lives in a different lake from the one you went to. Occasionally, Ceren will feed it a prisoner, rather than having them thrown off the mountain."

My eyes went round with horror. "A *creature*? That eats *people*?"

He took my arm as we fell in line behind Ceren and his guards. Lady Melina was behind us, talking to one of the ladies. "I've never seen it," he whispered. "No one but Ceren and his guards have. He calls it Salandrin."

"We can't let him do this," I said, unable to keep the hysteria from my voice. "He can't feed that poor child to a monster!" Oh Thalos, I should have let Ceren die in that lake, no matter what Varenian ethics dictated. I had spared him just so he could take the life of a child.

The tunnels leading to the bottom of the mountain became too narrow for us to walk side by side, and I crept along behind Talin, his back the only thing I could see in the darkness. The boy was weeping softly up ahead, despite the guards' orders that he keep quiet. Every now and then I heard a grunt or a cry, and I knew they were beating him into silence.

The closeness and the lack of air here were making me light-headed. I reached out to brace myself on one of the walls and was surprised to find it rough and muddy, not at all like the finished corridors elsewhere in the mountain. And then I realized this was not a manmade tunnel at all. Whatever lived down here *traveled* through these holes.

I was starting to think I might faint when we finally reached our destination—a cave bathed in eerie blue light. I looked up expecting to see lunar moss torches and gasped when I saw what was creating the effect. There were thousands of tiny lights above us, shining like pale blue stars.

"What is that?" I asked Talin.

"They're glowworms. They hang from the ceiling of the cave."

Their beauty was shattered by the screams of the page. Two of the guards walked to a rocky outcrop ten feet above the water, dragging the boy with them. The lake was dark in places, but in the areas where the light from the glowworms reflected on the surface, I could see that the water was deep. Something white and massive swam past before disappearing again into the shadows.

I let out a startled cry and ran to Ceren, grabbing hold of his cloak without thinking. I heard the lords and ladies behind me murmur in disapproval.

"Please, don't do this," I pleaded. "He's just a boy. Show him some mercy."

"If not for you, I myself would be dead," Ceren said sternly. "Don't you think the punishment should fit the crime?"

In Varenia, we had a fairly simple system of justice. If you committed a crime, you were either forced to right the wrong—returning a stolen item, nursing a person you'd injured, disqualified from the ceremony if you harmed another girl's chances—or, if the crime was severe enough, you were banished. We never killed anyone for their crimes, even though we all knew banishment was tantamount to death. A man had been banished a year earlier after trying to poison his brother with puffer fish meat. Fortunately, the poisoned man had lived. His brother was never seen again.

"I think considering the boy's age, and that his brother died during one of your experiments, you should be more lenient than you might otherwise be," I suggested. "The people here

are terrified of water. To make those boys go into the dark
lake below the mountain was cruel. Even the guards were
afraid at Lake Elwin."

He narrowed his eyes at me, and I realized I'd just admitted to following him to the other underground lake. "I gave
everyone the opportunity to speak on the boy's behalf," he
said, looking past me to Lady Melina, who stood among the
other lords and ladies, her face blank. She was not going to
sacrifice herself for the page, that much was clear.

My mouth went dry and my pulse raced, as if my body
knew before I did what I was about to say. "I'll go," I blurted.
I was terrified of whatever was in that water, but I knew in
my heart it was the right thing to do. Stopping Ceren had
been my idea, and I'd promised Lady Melina I was willing
to pay for the consequences of my actions.

Ceren's brows knitted together. "What do you mean, you'll
go?"

"In the lake, with the monster. You said you'd give the
boy a chance to fight for his life. Let me fight on his behalf."

He stared at me in disbelief. "Don't be ridiculous. That boy
doesn't stand a chance against Salandrin, even with a weapon."

"So you'll give me a weapon?"

"I'm not letting you go at all." He grabbed me by the arm
and pulled me farther away from the others. "Why are you
covering up for Lady Melina? I know she was behind this."

"How do you know that?" I asked. "How do you know it
wasn't an accident?"

"That woman has always despised me, and I checked the
device right before we left New Castle. There's no way the
hose got kinked all on its own."

"So you have no proof, and yet you're willing to kill a child?" I cried. "You're *alive*, Ceren. That's what matters. Send the boy back to his family. They've already lost one son."

Ceren was quiet for a moment, and a spark of hope lit in my chest. But then he shook his head. "I can't let him go now. I've accused him publicly."

I shook my arm free of his. "Then I'm going in his place. I couldn't stand by and watch you die, and I won't let the boy die, either."

His eyes darted back and forth, searching mine. "You'd really risk everything for some servant boy? His life is worth nothing compared to yours."

"*My* life is worth nothing if I ever believe that."

He shook his head. "You're a brave girl, I won't deny that. But I need you alive. I'm sorry." He turned away.

"I'm the one who planned it!" I yelled, loud enough that all the lords and ladies could hear. "I put the page up to it. I'm the one who should be punished."

Ceren whirled back to me. "Stop it!" he snarled. "You saved my life. No one is going to believe you did this."

"I had a change of heart," I said, folding my arms across my chest. "And now that I've admitted it in front of witnesses, you can't hold the boy accountable."

The other members of the court rushed forward. "I always knew she couldn't be trusted," one of them said.

"We should have an Ilarean queen," a lord muttered.

"She must pay for what she's done," another said.

I could feel Melina's eyes on me, but she kept her silence. Apparently she wasn't willing to sacrifice herself for me, either.

Ceren stalked up to Talin, who hadn't said a word through any of this, though his eyes flitted between his brother's and mine. "Tell her to stop this, Talin."

"What makes you think she'll listen to me?" Talin hissed.

Ceren scowled. "Oh, please. I'm not a fool. I've seen the way she looks at you."

I couldn't bear to see Talin's reaction, not after what had happened at the lake. I kept my eyes on the page, who was crying quietly. He was all that mattered now.

I heard Talin release a heavy breath, and then his hand was on my shoulder, drawing me aside. He leaned so close his lips almost brushed my ear. "You don't have to do this," he said. He swallowed thickly. "I know you want—"

"It's not about what I *want*," I said. "I can't let that child die. I'm a strong swimmer. At least I have a chance."

I could tell as our eyes met that he saw me—*me*—for who I really was: stubborn as a barnacle, maybe, but someone who fought for what she believed in.

For a moment, I thought he might insist on going himself. But he must have seen the resolve in my gaze, bcause instead of protesting, he nodded and drew a knife from the sheath at his waist. "Go for the eyes," he said as he handed me the blade. "I'll help in any way I can."

His grip on my shoulder remained fierce, despite his words, and I let my hair fall forward, obscuring us as I brought my hand up to his, half expecting him to jerk away at the contact. But though he inhaled sharply against my ear, sending shivers down my spine, he made no attempt to move, and I knew he felt the same spark that I did.

"I'm sorry if I've been cold," he murmured. "You did nothing to deserve it."

"Thank you." A moment later, I gently removed his hand, but kept my eyes locked on his. Ceren might suspect my attraction to his brother, but if I was about to die, I needed to make sure *Talin* knew it was more than that. "Your kindness has been like the break in a storm," I said, understanding now what he'd meant in Varenia. Life here was dark and cold and unforgiving, but Talin had made it a little more bearable.

He held my arm for a moment longer, his jaw clenched tight. "I wish things were different—" he began, but I stopped him.

"So do I."

He released me slowly, and I could see him wrestling with what to do. I shook my head a little, telling him silently not to dive in after me, no matter what happened.

The guards were waiting for orders from Ceren, but I climbed up beside them and took the boy from their hands. "Go now," I whispered to the page. "Leave the castle and go home to your family before anyone realizes you're missing."

His eyes widened, but he nodded and scrambled off the rocks. I set down the knife and pulled off my gown to more gasps. My shift only fell to my knees, but I needed to move freely. I studied the lake for a moment, ignoring the murmurs of the crowd. The water would be cold, but at least I'd be able to see with the light from the glowworms. I'd need to stay away from the shadows. As I peered over the edge, the finned back of the creature sailed past again. It had to be twenty feet long, bigger than the great man-eating sharks that lived farther out to sea.

Ceren looked horrified, but Talin held him back. Fear coursed through my veins like it had the day of the incident, when I'd thought I might lose Zadie. But fear could be useful. It could be turned into strength. I grabbed the knife, nodded at Talin once, took the largest breath my lungs could hold, and jumped.

As the frigid water closed over my head, I opened my eyes to take in my surroundings. Here, the lake was about twenty feet deep. From what I'd seen of the beast, it looked more fish than lizard, but if it had created the tunnels down here, it had to be able to breathe on land as well as in the water. I kept my back pressed against the rock and the knife in front of me as I searched for the creature.

When I broke the surface several minutes later to take another breath, I felt something brush against my feet. "Look out," Talin shouted, and I dived back down to see the creature's white tail disappearing into a crevice on the other side of the lake.

The head appeared a moment later from another crevice. So that was Salandrin's lair. My first impression of the beast was that it was similar to the giant cave salamander, with thick white flesh and short legs ending in clawed feet. But the head was longer and more tapered, like a moray eel, and when it opened its mouth, I saw dozens of razor-sharp, cone-shaped teeth. It swam past me, back into the shadows. I counted three sets of legs, though the hind legs were small, probably vestigial.

I'd also noticed that it had tiny red eyes, like the salamander. If I had to guess, the creature was blind.

But it knew I was here. It had sensed me when I went to the surface for air. It could likely feel the vibrations in the water. I moved away from the wall, just a few feet, and the creature came rushing out of the shadows, its mouth wide-open. The water around me began to surge forward, as though I was caught in a tide. Salandrin was sucking me into its maw.

I reached back for the rocks and grabbed hold, wedging my fingers as far into a crack as I could, but the force of the suction was incredibly strong. My head was inches from the surface and I was running out of air, but if I let go, I'd be sucked right in.

Instead, I put the sheath of the knife in between my teeth and turned to grab the rock with my other arm, rising just long enough to fill my lungs. When I went back under, the creature was swimming past. I grabbed the knife and slashed at the last stumpy leg, slicing it clean off. Salandrin writhed in agony, and dark blood filled the water instantly, blinding me.

When it cleared, the monster was gone.

Most likely it had gone back to its lair. I didn't want to play its cat-and-mouse game; waiting was just making me colder, and I was risking hypothermia the longer I stayed in the water. If I was going to die, far better to get it over with quickly. So I took another breath, propelled myself off the rocks, and swam directly toward the crevice.

The head emerged when I was still only halfway across the lake. I dived toward the bottom, where a crop of stalagmites thrust up into the water like an underground forest. I pulled myself down between them just as the monster swam past, using its strong forelegs to reach for me. The claws met stone and Salandrin shot forward, circling back around for another pass.

Now my choices were greatly diminished. I had only three or four minutes of air with my adrenaline pumping this much, and the moment I went to the surface, the beast would come. In open water, I was as good as dead.

Go for the eyes, Talin had said. He was right. It didn't matter that the creature wasn't using its eyes to hunt me. The eyes were the gateway to the brain, and if I stabbed deep enough, the monster would die.

As it passed overhead again, I reached up and took hold of one of the clawed feet on the second pair of legs. The talons dug into my flesh, but I held on with all my strength as the creature writhed in the water. It turned to snap at me, but I was too far back for it to reach me. I stabbed the knife into the thick flesh of its side and let go of the talon, my own blood mingling with the monster's. Wedging my fingers into the soft flesh, I withdrew the knife and stabbed again. Hand over hand, I made my way toward its head.

Salandrin thrashed harder, and I nearly lost my grip on the knife. There was blood everywhere from the multiple stab wounds, and my air supply was getting too low. I fought the pain in my lungs as I made my slow progress along the creature's back. When it stopped wriggling, I briefly wondered if I'd managed to draw enough blood to kill it, but then it shot forward so suddenly I would have been ripped off had I not grabbed hold of its spiny dorsal fin just in time.

I looked up and realized it was heading back toward its lair. I didn't want to end up in the crevice with the beast, where I would be blind in the dark. It could be much deeper than it looked, and if I got myself trapped in there, I'd drown.

I was almost at the neck—I had to make my move now. With all my strength, I surged forward and drove the knife deep into the soft spot where the neck met the head. The pain disoriented the creature for a moment, and it slammed into the wall next to the crevice, pinning me against the rock. The monster's body tensed and I involuntarily screamed as its ribs burst through its flesh, narrowly missing me. It was a horrifying defense mechanism, but it was undeniably effective.

I was out of air. I was trapped between two of Salandrin's ribs, which were as sharp as daggers and three times as long. And I'd dropped the knife.

The ribs retracted suddenly, and before I could think, the monster shot into its lair. I didn't know how long I had, so I pushed up toward the surface, gasping for breath to fill my burning lungs.

My frantic eyes found Talin's, just a few feet away. He reached out for me. Then searing pain shot through my leg as Salandrin grabbed me and pulled me back below the surface. I was caught in the monster's jaws, its teeth clamped tight around my right leg. I expected it to open its mouth and suck me in right there, but instead it circled the lake until I was again out of air and faint from blood loss.

It came close enough to the surface once that I was able to take a breath before it went back down. It was toying with me, torturing me—killing me slowly instead of eating me right away.

As it passed in front of the crowd gathered on the shore, I lifted myself up enough for what I was sure was my last breath. And then I saw Talin's hand, reaching out for me once again. I reached for him, too, but instead of flesh, my hand met metal, and as the creature dived, I realized I had a knife in my hand.

Without thinking, I twisted around until my torso was lined up with the beast's eye, and then I plunged the knife into the eyeball with all my strength, elbow-deep in blood and mush, too numb to even feel what I was doing. The jaws released instantly, and my hands slipped free of the knife. I kicked toward the surface with my uninjured leg and felt a strong arm gripping mine before my terror exploded into blackness.

24

I woke in my chambers. I had no idea how much time had passed or who had tended to me, but my injured hand and leg were bound in soft white bandages. There was no pain, and I suspected I had probably healed already.

I sat up and reached for the pitcher of water on my night-stand. Ceren was asleep in a chair that must have been brought in while I was unconscious, but when I set the pitcher back down, his gray eyes flashed open, immediately finding me.

"You're awake." He rose and came to the edge of my bed.

I recoiled when he reached for my hand, hurrying to cover myself with the blankets. "What are you doing here, my lord? Where's Ebb?"

"Your maid was exhausted from keeping watch over you all night and day. I told her to go get some rest."

I knew my injuries were extensive, but I hadn't realized the damage was that serious. "I've been unconscious an entire day?"

"A little more. I'll send for the doctor to change your bandages."

I shook my head and tried to keep the panic out of my voice. "Please, don't."

His brows knitted together. "Why not?"

Because I don't want you to see that I'm already healed. "I just want to know what happened."

He settled farther onto my bed. "Talin pulled you out of the water. Your leg wasn't torn as badly as we'd feared. The royal physician dressed your wounds. I fed you some broth with ground-up pearls. I believe that's why you have so little pain."

I didn't correct his mistake. Let him think it was the pearls that had healed me. "Where is Prince Talin now?"

The worry on his face evaporated. "He's back at Old Castle. Where he belongs."

"Of course. I only wanted to thank him. Without the knife—both knives—I would have died."

"I'm sure you'll see him soon enough." He was quiet for a moment, and then he huffed out a soft laugh. "It's funny—you escaped the rumors that you'd saved me from a water spirit at Lake Elwin, only to then face one yourself here in Mount Ayris. The nobles are calling you a witch."

I twisted my mouth to the side. "Is that a good thing or a bad thing?"

"It's nothing to concern yourself with," he said, waving his hand dismissively. "Once you're their queen, they won't dare speak ill of you."

"And what about the monster in the mountain? Salandrin? What do the nobles have to say about that? They probably believe it's one of their so-called water spirits. You'll never get them to dive for pearls for you now, no matter how many of your devices you make."

Another moment of silence followed. When his eyes finally met mine, the truth I hadn't wanted to see was written on his face.

"You were never planning on making the Ilareans dive for the pearls, were you?" All this time, I'd been worried that my people would go hungry. I had never once considered they might be forced to work directly for the prince. "What will you do? Make the Varenians dive even more than they already are? It won't get you what you want. If anything, you'll simply run out of pearls faster. The shoals are gone. You're lucky we scrape together as many pearls as we do every month."

He barked a mirthless laugh. "Lucky, am I? Lucky to have a father who is dying at forty because of too many years spent in this mountain? Lucky that I will likely share the same fate?"

"Then leave!" I shouted, no longer worried about what Zadie would say. "No one is forcing you to stay."

Ceren leaned down over me, his long hair surrounding me like a curtain. "Look at me! Do you think I can spend my life outside this mountain? I'm as incapable of surviving out there as a cave salamander. My vision is poor from a lifetime spent in darkness. My skin burns after just a few minutes in the sunlight." Slowly, he composed his features and leaned back. "I am many things, my lady, but *lucky* is not one of them."

I felt a fleeting stab of sympathy for him. But he was just one man with one life. Did he truly believe his was worth the freedom of an entire people?

He looked at me as if he could read my thoughts. "This isn't only about me, Zadie."

"What do you mean?"

"My father is dying, and if something should happen to me before I'm able to produce a healthy heir, this kingdom will be without a ruler," Ceren explained. "Our land has weakened along with my father. We use resources we don't have to keep a large army. My brother has entire regiments posted along our borders, and those soldiers have to be fed. And when the villagers aren't able to pay their taxes because their crops have failed, who do you think they blame? Not the weather, I can assure you. So I realize my existence may seem of very little consequence to *you*, but thousands of people rely on me on a daily basis. Including the Varenians. Or perhaps you'd like to live under the rule of this so-called woman king to the south? I hear she captures women and children and uses them as soldiers."

I had nothing to say in response. Ceren was right. I hadn't thought about the larger consequences of a kingdom without a strong ruler. "But what about your brother?"

"What about my brother?"

"If something should happen to you, wouldn't he be next in line for the throne?"

He cocked his head at me, the silvery strands of his hair sliding off his shoulders. "Is that what you would like to see happen?"

I shook my head, suddenly realizing what I'd said, how it must have sounded. "No, of course not. That's not what I meant."

"Why not? I don't doubt there are many others who feel the same way. Certainly it was my stepmother's hope. Unfortunately for her, that's not how Ilarean succession works."

I raised my eyebrows in question.

Ceren sighed. "This land was once a queendom. There hasn't been a princess born since Ilara died, but our laws still state that if an Ilarean king dies without an heir, or before the heir comes of age, the crown passes to the queen."

"Are you saying that if you died before we had children...?"

"Yes, you would be the ruler of Ilara." His lips twitched at the corners. "Of course, we need to get married before that can happen."

This was what Ceren did. He pushed people, making them as uncomfortable as he could, to see how they would react, to see if they would reject him the way his own stepmother had. I wouldn't give him the satisfaction of my discomfort. "How old does the heir have to be before he can rule?"

"Twenty-one. My birthday is in five months. Let's hope my father can make it that long."

Ilara was in peril, I realized, but not just from foreign enemies. I knew pressing Ceren further was likely ill-advised, but I had to ask. "And if he doesn't? Who would take the crown?"

He rose to his feet. "It would mean civil war. Now if you'll excuse me, my lady. I'm sure all this talk of rulers and succession is exceedingly dull for you. I'm glad you're feeling better. As soon as you're well enough, you may take your day of freedom."

I sat up a little straighter. "I can?"

"You're surprised I would honor my words after your arrogant and nearly disastrous actions?"

My eyes rolled involuntarily. "That's not exactly how I would put it, but yes."

"Whether or not you had something to do with what

happened at Lake Elwin, you still saved my life. And some-how you managed to survive Salandrin. I can't very well kill you now. But I also can't let you get away with that kind of reckless behavior. It wouldn't do for the nobility to see you go unpunished for the crimes you so stubbornly admitted to."

The spark of hope I'd felt when he mentioned freedom im-mediately died. "What are you talking about? The page—"

"The boy is gone. I suspect I have you to thank for that, as well. No, it's clear to me that your own life means far less than that of the people you love."

It felt like the cold water was closing over my head again, but I was on dry land. "What have you done?" I whispered.

Ceren raised his chin. "Your family has had their drink-ing water cut off for one week. No one at the floating mar-ket will trade with them."

I lunged toward him, filled with rage, but he held me down easily with one hand. "How *could* you? They're innocent in all this!" My eyes burned with tears at the thought of Zadie and my parents without water. Would Sami help them? Had the other villagers taken pity on my family, or did they still think I was a liar who had plotted against my own sister?

"I've been generous," Ceren said, still pinning me against the bed. "They'll survive, this time. But if you ever try some-thing like that again, the entire village will see what hap-pens when one of you tries to take advantage of me. Do you understand?"

I nodded reluctantly, my cheeks streaked with tears, and waited until he'd left the room before I screamed into my pillow.

★ ★ ★

When Ebb returned, she told me more of what had happened after I'd killed the monster. Talin had carried me to my chambers, where Ebb had applied the stain to my scar before Ceren had a chance to see it.

"Did Talin say anything?" I asked her.

"No, milady. He was too concerned over your wounded leg. How is it feeling now?"

"It hurts, but I can bear it."

"Good. I gave you some of the poppy tea the king often drinks. I can fetch more if you like."

I shook my head and turned away from her, unable to stop imagining my family's suffering. They couldn't sleep through it like I could. And they wouldn't, even if it was a choice. We struggled on a daily basis in Varenia, but we didn't drink tea to numb the pain. We prayed to the gods for help, but we still got in our boats every day and exhausted ourselves to keep our families fed. We relied on each other.

"We are few, but we are strong," I murmured.

"Milady?"

I turned back to Ebb, realizing I'd spoken out loud. "It's nothing. I'd like to rest now, please."

"Of course, milady. I'll be right down the hall if you need me."

I hardly left my room for the rest of the week. There was no one in New Castle I wished to see, least of all Ceren. He came once more, but I refused to speak to him, and he didn't try again. But each night, when the rest of the castle was abed, I made my way to the portrait hall, where I had imaginary conversations with Zadie. Mostly I apologized for letting her down, for letting everyone down. The only thing stronger than my desire to return to my family was my fear for my people. If it weren't for that, I would have escaped, or died trying.

At least my wounds were fully healed, though I kept them bandaged to avoid suspicion. I had realized something after Ceren told me he'd cut off my family's water supply: if he ever discovered that the coral had something to do with my healing abilities, he would become as obsessed with that as he was with the pearls. And once he learned that the blood coral only grew from the bodies of the Varenians, my people might not just become slaves. They could be slaughtered.

Tonight, I kissed my fingers and pressed them to Zadie's painted lips before turning toward the end of the hall. I gasped at the sight of a cloaked figure approaching me. Instinctively, my hand reached for my skirts. I kept the coral blade my father had given me strapped to my leg now, just in case.

"Calm yourself, child. It's only me."

I exhaled through my nose. "Lady Melina, what are you doing here?"

She pulled me into a shallow alcove in the wall. "I've been forbidden from speaking with you. But there's something you need to know, so that in case you have another opportunity to put an end to the prince, you don't squander it like you did the last time."

"I'm so sorry, Melina. None of this has turned out like I planned."

"Never mind that now. What's done is done. But you need to know that it was Ceren who killed Queen Talia, and there is no doubt in my mind he'll do whatever it takes to become king."

A cold chill crept over my scalp. "A servant murdered the queen," I whispered. "Ceren told me."

"He's full of lies. You must see that by now."

"But surely if that were true, someone would have done something." It wasn't that I didn't think Ceren capable of murder, but Talia had been his stepmother; his brother's mother and his father's wife.

"He covered his tracks well. The servant he blamed for the crime was a sweet young girl who wouldn't hurt a flea, but she had no money or power to defend herself. No one believed she did it, not even the king. But what could anyone do? The queen's body was gone, and there was blood in her chambers. It was clear Talia had been murdered, but without a body for evidence, no one could accuse the real killer. Certainly not someone like me."

"They never found Talia's body," I said, remembering what Ebb told me.

"No. Just the smears of blood on her walls and carpets. They found blood in the servant's quarters as well, and on her gown. But it was the middle of the night when Ceren found her, asleep in her room, and she was completely oblivious to the queen's death."

That did seem a bit odd. "How do you know she wasn't just pretending?" I asked.

"First of all, only a fool would kill a queen and return to her bed without washing the blood off herself. Second, as I said, she had no motive. And third, how did Ceren even know where to look? The girl wasn't a lady's maid. She was a lowly chambermaid, the kind who empties chamber pots and draws baths if she's lucky. She couldn't have been older than thirteen. She never would have been allowed to be alone in the queen's presence, and frankly I don't think she was strong enough to overpower Talia. Nor was she in any way capable of making a body disappear."

Lady Melina was right. It didn't make sense for a servant to do something like that, not unless she had a very strong motive. And Ceren? What was his motive to kill the queen?

The answer came to me immediately. The crown. If the king died before Ceren's twenty-first birthday, Talia would be next in line to rule, not Ceren. "If the crown had passed to Talia, what would have become of Ceren?"

"It's hard to say," Melina admitted. "It's only happened once that I know of, a thousand years ago, when a queen refused to relinquish the crown to her son once he turned twenty-one. He tried to have her deposed, and she had him executed."

The Bloody Queen. I remembered Ebb's story of the wise queen who had risen to power. She must have been the start of the queendom that ended with Princess Ilara's death. "And you think Ceren was afraid the same thing would happen to him?"

"I believe that boy would do anything for the crown, including kill his own stepmother."

I thought back to his words earlier. Everything he told me had made sense: the kingdom needed a strong ruler, and without the pearls, Ceren believed he would die young. But if he was capable of feeding a child to a monster, he was more than capable of killing a woman who stood in his way.

I had been a fool to trust a single word from Ceren's lips.

"Is this why you stayed at New Castle?" I asked. "To try to stop Ceren from ascending the throne?"

She nodded. "I don't know when I'll see you again, child. But promise me something."

"Of course," I said.

"If you have another opportunity to end this, don't let it pass you by."

25

Ceren might be a liar, but he kept his word to me: I was allowed to leave the castle for one day each week. He surprised me further by agreeing to let me take riding lessons. I knew now that it wasn't enough to warn Sami about Ceren's devices or even his plans to enslave the Varenians. Lady Hyacinth had called my people the enemy, and Ceren had to be stopped before he could become king. And if I ever had the opportunity to leave New Castle, my only hope of escape would be by horseback. Ceren had made no further mention of our market trip, but I would get there this time, with or without him.

My riding lessons were at Old Castle, an hour's ride from New Castle. There were stables in the base of the mountain, but Old Castle was where the horses were bred and trained. Grig was my instructor, and by my third lesson, I could canter independently. I had trousers made so I could ride astride my horse, which felt far more secure than sidesaddle, even though Ebb found the entire thing inappropriate.

I had another secret motive for going to Old Castle once a week, though I barely admitted it to myself. Talin hadn't been at the castle since I killed Salandrin, and I still hadn't had a chance to thank him for saving my life. But he was never there when I came for lessons, or if he was, he didn't come to see me.

I understood it to some extent. Ceren was obviously aware of the connection between us, and rubbing it in his face wouldn't make things better for either Talin or myself. But even though the sun on my skin and the freedom I felt on horseback made me so happy I nearly wept with joy every time I stepped out of the castle, I yearned for something beyond fresh air.

I dreamed of Talin often, only to wake up with a hollow feeling in my chest. I remembered how he had looked at me before he handed me the knife, how I'd felt seen for who I really was.

I wanted that feeling again.

After a successful fourth lesson, I rode back to the barn with Grig, both of us laughing at how I'd nearly fallen off after my horse decided to let out a joyful buck for no apparent reason.

"Milady!" a voice shouted from across the fields. I turned to see a young squire galloping toward us. Grig and I shared a worried glance and rode to meet him.

The squire pulled his horse to a skidding stop in front of

me. "It's the king, milady. He's very ill. The prince needs you to come at once. And I'm to fetch Prince Talin, as well."

"He's not here," I said, but Grig was already digging his heels into his horse's flanks.

"I'll tell him," he called over his shoulder. "Go!"

Ceren's guards, who accompanied me on every outing, guided their horses to stand on either side of me. "We'll ride back, milady," one of them said. "It's faster than the carriage."

"Is that necessary?" I asked the squire.

He nodded. "The prince seemed very concerned. The doctor said the king may not make it through the night."

I gaped at him over my shoulder as my mare took off with the guards' horses. "What?"

"That's right," he called. "Prince Ceren told me to tell you. The king is dying!"

The king had been dying for years, I told myself as we galloped toward the castle. This didn't mean anything. It couldn't.

It crossed my mind that now might be my chance for escape. The guards had already outpaced my small bay mare, and with so much concern for the king, it might be a while before anyone even noticed I was gone. I was already on a horse. How far could I get before they caught me?

As if to answer my question, Talin came thundering up beside me on his gray stallion, and I knew I wouldn't make it ten feet if I tried to run. I looked up at him, wondering how far away he could possibly have been to catch up with us this quickly. Not far at all, I surmised, which meant he *was* deliberately avoiding me. I wanted to ask him why, but how could I now, when his father was dying?

It was like the gods were toying with us, bringing us together only to pull us apart again, like Laef and Ilara. They had fought against the fates so hard, only to lose each other in the end. Perhaps it would have been better to simply let go.

We arrived at the base of the mountain in half the time it normally took by carriage. Climbing up the mountain was easier every time I did it, but today I was already winded from the ride. Two-thirds of the way up, I knew if I didn't stop to catch my breath, I'd never make it the rest of the way. I was about to sit down on the steps when I felt a strong arm wrap around my waist.

"I've got you," Talin said, hauling me back onto my feet. He didn't look at me as he took my hand and began to pull me up the stairs, but the feeling of having my hand wrapped in his made it harder to catch my breath, not easier.

When we reached the platform leading to the main entrance, I tried to stop for a moment to compose myself. I had hoped to go back to my room and change before dinner. I was sweaty from the climb, my hair had unraveled partially during the ride, and I had no idea what the other lords and ladies would make of my attire. But if they saw me fretting over my wardrobe before going to see my future husband and his dying father, I'd only send more rumors into circulation.

Before I could even brush the dirt off my breeches, Talin pulled on my hand and marched us past the guards into the great hall. Lords and ladies stood in clusters, their murmurs punctuated by the occasional sob of an elder as she pressed a handkerchief to her eyes. If the people had been alerted, things had to be even worse than I feared. My thoughts darted to and fro like startled fish, but I focused on the warmth of

Talin's hand on mine and how easy it felt to be led by someone else for a change.

Ebb came scurrying out from a corner and rushed to my side. "There you are, milady. I was starting to worry. Is everything all right?"

"I'm fine. How is the king?" I lowered my voice. "Is he really dying?"

"That's what they're saying. Prince Ceren came looking for you several hours ago. I think he was so distraught he'd forgotten you left."

I had seen Ceren in many moods, but distraught wasn't a word that came to mind when I thought of him. We strode down the corridors to the king's chambers, passing more worried nobles on the way. When we reached the king's room, a guard opened the door for us without speaking. The royal physician was bent over the king in his bed. Ceren paced the length of the room, rubbing his chin with his thumb.

Talin dropped my hand the moment we entered the chamber, and I was immediately reminded how cold it was inside New Castle. I clasped my hands in front of me and took a cautious step forward.

"Your Highness," I said quietly, afraid to disturb anyone. "I apologize it's taken us so long to get here. We only just heard the news."

Ceren looked up at the sound of my voice. "You're here," he said, striding toward me and gathering me up in his arms. I tensed immediately. We hadn't interacted much since he told me what he'd done to my family, and now he was turning to me for comfort?

"How is Father?" Talin asked.

Ceren released me and led us over to the king's bed. "Not well, I'm afraid. He was fine this morning, and then something happened, an attack of some kind. The doctor has been bleeding him off and on all day, but nothing is helping."

I glanced at the bowl of blood near the king's bed and shuddered. We didn't bleed people in Varenia. Blood was acknowledged as our life force, the thing that kept us strong, so to deliberately drain ourselves of it would make no sense. I didn't understand how anyone could think taking blood from an already weak man was beneficial, but who was I to question an Ilarean doctor?

"They don't think he'll make it through the night," Ceren continued. "I've given him several pink pearls to swallow, but he hasn't been able to get them down, not even ground up into powder. That's how weak he is."

I glanced at Talin, who looked sad but stoic. Ceren, meanwhile, was practically wringing his hands. "Is there anything I can do?" I asked Ceren, though my words were meant for his brother.

Ceren took my hand and kissed the back of it. "I'm afraid there's nothing—"

"Would you sing to him?" Talin asked suddenly.

I slipped my hand free of Ceren's. "Me? Sing, to the king?"

He nodded. "He loved my mother's singing. It soothed him even after the most difficult day. I think it would help him now."

"I—of course." I moved to the head of the king's bed and sat down on a small stool. The king was barely able to turn his head toward me, though I knew he sensed my presence.

He was so thin and frail that when I took his hand, it felt as light as the hand of a child.

"What should I sing for him?" I asked Talin.

"The lullaby, the one about the lionfish," Ceren said, coming to stand behind me. "I believe you know it well." Before, when he'd mentioned wave children and our lullabies, there had been derision in his voice, but his tone held a hint of something else now, though no less disturbing.

I cleared my throat lightly. I didn't have the finest singing voice in Varenia, but it was passable.

> *Beware the lionfish, my dear,*
> *Beware the fish that's made of stone.*
> *Beware sweet nothings in your ear,*
> *And the heart as hollow as a bone.*
> *Beware the shark and ray, my dear,*
> *Beware the jellyfish of blue,*
> *Beware tongues sharper than the spear,*
> *And a lover's heart that isn't true.*
> *Lull yourself with the blue whale's song,*
> *Cradle yourself in Thalos's arms,*
> *But don't stay under for too long,*
> *Steel yourself against false charms.*
> *Love is greater than the ocean,*
> *Time is longer than you know,*
> *But once your fate is set in motion,*
> *There's no telling when you'll go.*

Singing the song now, as an adult, I realized how morbid it was, hardly the appropriate thing to sing to a dying man.

But the king's eyes had fluttered closed, a small smile on his lips, and I prayed he would find some rest.

Ceren rested a hand on my shoulder. "That was beautiful. Thank you."

I turned to look up at him and found his ivory cheeks glistening with tears, though his face was impassive. Every time I convinced myself he was incapable of emotion or empathy, he surprised me. How could a young man who wept for his father kill his own stepmother?

"You're welcome," I said. "Is there anything else I can do for you now?"

He shook his head. "Go and change. We'll have a quick supper in the hall and then I'll return for the night."

"Are you sure you wouldn't like me to stay with the king? I don't mind."

"No. You should rest. Who knows what the coming days will bring?"

"Yes, Your Highness." I stood and turned to go. Talin lingered near the door, watching me. Our eyes met briefly as I passed him, and I saw gratitude there but also something else. I had left off the final verse of the song. Had he noticed? I wanted to ask him, but I merely bowed my head and left.

Ebb spotted me as I emerged from the king's rooms and bustled ahead of me down the hall to my chambers, where a dress had already been laid out for me. It was suitably simple and unrevealing, with just enough silver embroidery along the hem and collar to keep it from being plain. I didn't want to wear anything too cheerful, but too somber would be like admitting there was no hope for the king's recovery.

Ebb untied my braids, brushed my hair quickly, and coiled it back up into several buns at the back of my head.

"This will have to do for now," she said. "I expect the prince is too upset to notice, though you really should have bathed."

I'd never seen her so rattled. "Is everything all right, Ebb?"

"I'm sorry, milady. It's just that everyone is in a terrible tizzy about the king."

She straightened my brush on the vanity several times, and I placed a steady hand on her trembling arm. "Don't worry. Everything will be fine."

"It's just, if the king dies..."

"Ceren will become king on his twenty-first birthday. He's been practically ruling in the king's stead for months anyway."

She shook her head. "It's not just that."

"Then what is it? Please, you can trust me."

Her sky blue eyes met mine reluctantly, glistening with unshed tears. "It's just...you'll have to marry the prince. Within the week." She burst into sobs, and I was so caught off guard by her emotion I hardly had a chance to process the meaning of her words.

I pulled her into my arms and let her cry, utterly perplexed by the conversation. Why was she so worried about me marrying Prince Ceren? That had been the plan all along, hadn't it?

After a moment, she managed to regain her composure and fetched one of my handkerchiefs. "May I?"

I nodded, and she dabbed at her eyes.

"I'm so sorry, milady. I don't know what's come over me."

"Ebb, you don't need to worry about me. I've known all

along I would have to marry Ceren." Of course, I'd never imagined it would be within the next week. The reality of that fact was hitting me suddenly, and now I was the one who needed to sit.

"And you're not afraid of marrying him?" she asked.

"I can't say it would be my first choice, but no, I'm not afraid of him," I lied. "Why are all the nobles so upset?"

"They're worried about what will happen to the crown."

"But he's been ruling in his father's place for months. Why can't things just continue as they are?"

"It's not that simple. If King Xyrus dies without passing on the crown, Prince Talin will have the right to challenge his brother."

Was that why Ceren was upset? Because he was afraid he'd lose the crown to Talin? I knew I couldn't believe anything he said or did was real—why did I continue to let him fool me? "And how will they determine who gets it?"

"They duel for it. To the death, unless one of them agrees to yield."

Talin was stronger than Ceren. If there was a duel, he would likely win. That fact would not have escaped Ceren. "Would the people be unhappy if Talin took the throne?"

"No, milady. But there have been rumors that the woman king has her eyes on the Ilarean throne. The people are afraid any kind of dispute here could leave us vulnerable to attack."

My head spun with all the information. Wars and succession, thrones and crowns. I hadn't known about any of this before I came here. I'd assumed I could spy on the king, report back to Sami, and save Varenia. But our people weren't even a consideration to anyone but Ceren, and even then, it was only so he could get the pearls. The king was dying, the kingdom was being threatened from within and without, and right now, my people had no idea that their fate hung in the balance as much as Ilara's.

26

Talin may have been the stronger brother, but Ceren was cunning, and it was this thought that worried me as I sat between them at dinner. They hardly spoke to each other, no doubt lost in their own thoughts about what would happen if it came to a fight for the crown. But I finally felt like I had all the pieces to a puzzle I hadn't known I was trying to put together. The motivations behind Ceren's actions—punishing my people, killing the queen, being willing to marry a woman he clearly despised—were now painfully obvious.

As the servants cleared our plates for the dessert course—even a "quick meal" required five courses, it seemed—Ceren tossed his hair over his shoulder and turned to me. "Perhaps you've forgotten amid all the turmoil, my lady, but we are only five days from market day at the port."

I frowned in confusion. "The king is ill. I would hardly expect you to leave his side at a time like this."

"No, unfortunately. I cannot leave now. Which is why I've decided my brother will take you."

Talin's head snapped up. "What?"

"It's a five-day journey by carriage each way. I don't want my bride gone so long. But you can make the trip in two and a half if you go by horse. You'll be gone less than a week."

Talin's fork clattered to his plate. "I can't leave now, Ceren. You heard the doctor. Father could die at any time. I have to be here, in New Castle."

"You have another meeting with Lord Clifton, if I'm not mistaken. With the woman king gathering strength, we need his official pledge to the crown, and his guarantee that his mercenaries will stand with us as well, should it come to that. You can meet with them on your way to the market. I promised Zadie she could go, and I have no intention of going back on my word."

I glanced at Talin, who looked about ready to leap across the table for his brother's throat. He knew exactly what Ceren was doing: sending him away while the king lay dying, in hopes that if he took a turn for the worse, Ceren could seize the crown uncontested.

"The trip really isn't necessary right now," I protested weakly, but one look at Ceren's face told me this had nothing to do with me and my desire to visit a market.

"I won't go," Talin said finally.

"While father is incapacitated, I am prince regent," Ceren said coldly. "Which means that my word is law. You'll go, or I'll have you thrown in the dungeon for treason."

My eyes darted back and forth between the brothers, as different as sun and moon, wave and mountain. Talin's rage was unmistakable, while Ceren sat as impassive as always, cutting delicately at a piece of fruit. He hardly faltered when Talin slammed his fist on the table and stalked out of the dining hall.

"There now," Ceren said to me. "I promised you a trip to the market, and a trip you shall have."

"Thank you," I said, my eyes trailing Talin as he left. I would finally have the chance to warn Sami of how dire things were, yes. But by going to the market, I could be keeping Talin from the crown. And Talin might be the only person capable of stopping Ceren. I could only pray the king would last the week.

Our traveling party consisted of Talin, Grig, Ebb, two of Ceren's guards, and me. Captain Osius was left in charge of the king's guard, and the entire army, should it come to that. I was surprised that Ceren would risk Ilara's safety by sending his brother away at a time like this, but he obviously thought Talin was a greater threat than the woman king.

Without a coach or wagon at our disposal, we were forced to pack light. Grig attached my small bundle of clothing to my mare's saddle while the other men filled their saddlebags with food and water. We would be staying in inns along the way, and I would have a few hours on Friday at the market.

Grig hoisted me onto my mare's back before helping Ebb into her saddle. She had grudgingly agreed to wear breeches and claimed to have some riding experience from her childhood, but she didn't seem particularly excited about the journey. No one did.

"We'll meet with Lord Clifton this afternoon," Talin said as we started down the road. One guard rode in front, the

other at the back, while Talin and I rode side by side with
Grig and Ebb behind us. We weren't alone, exactly, but it was
the first time we'd been anything close to it since our frantic
ride back to New Castle.

"It shouldn't take long," he added, "but we'll have to ride
late this evening to make up for lost time. I hope you're prepared for it. Five days on the road isn't easy for even a seasoned
rider, and the inns we'll be staying at are humble at best."

"You forget who you're speaking to," I said, trying to keep
my tone light. "I spent seventeen years in a house smaller than
my bedroom at New Castle."

His eyes flicked to mine. "I have not forgotten."

We rode in strained silence for most of the day, but I
couldn't help glancing at him every few minutes, willing
him to look back. At times the road narrowed, and our horses
were forced so close together our legs touched, but all he did
was apologize. *Look at me!* I wanted to scream. And occasionally he did, but he never smiled, and he rarely spoke. Even
then, it was just to ask if I needed to rest.

We stopped briefly for lunch and didn't stop again until
the late afternoon, when we were well past the River Ilara
and deeper into Lord Clifton's territory, Pirot.

"Why are you meeting with Lord Clifton?" I asked, my
curiosity finally getting the better of me. "I thought he was
trying to steal land from your father."

Talin glanced down at me. "He is. Pirot is still part of Ilara,
at least for now. But Father has been ill, and my brother's concerns have been elsewhere."

"The woman king in the South?"

"You know about that?" he asked, holding eye contact longer than he had all day.

"A little. Lady Hyacinth invites me for tea frequently."

He smiled wryly. "Lucky you. And to answer your question, yes, Ceren is concerned about the woman king, though perhaps not as much as he should be. His experiments take up more time than anything else lately." He reined his horse closer to mine. "Lord Clifton is an opportunist, but he has no military experience. His men are a bunch of mercenaries who only care about money and land. The woman king is more organized, and I think Clifton is scared."

I raised my eyebrows. "Are you?"

"Of the woman king? No." He shook his head, then gestured ahead of us. "We're here."

Talin asked Grig and one of Ceren's soldiers to wait outside the encampment with Ebb and me, and I was grateful, remembering my uncomfortable encounter with the mercenary at the border. I sat in the shade of an apple tree with Ebb, enjoying the crisp fruit and the chance to stretch my legs.

"I saw you talking with Prince Talin," Ebb said, tossing an apple core lazily to the side.

"And?" I didn't bother with pretense anymore. Ebb knew most of my secrets now.

"I'm glad to see you two speaking again. That's all."

"Mmm-hmm."

Talin emerged from the tent, and Ebb leaped to her feet, pulling me up with her. "Apologies," he said as he mounted his stallion. "That took longer than I expected."

"How did it go?" I asked him as Grig helped me back onto my mare.

"Clifton will lend us his men if it comes to war," Talin said quietly. "Of course, we're to concede a large parcel of borderland to him in exchange for the men, but the land is hardly any good to us if Ilara is attacked. We'll also have to allow more refugees across the border." His face was serious, but I could tell from his tone that he was pleased with the outcome.

"I'm glad it went well," I said. "And I'm sorry that Ceren made you come with me. I know you'd much rather be with your father right now."

"It's not your fault. I should be grateful Ceren sent me here and not to end another skirmish." His expression turned wistful. "And I'm afraid I'm not much use to my father now. His fate is in the hands of the gods."

By the time we arrived at the inn that night, I was more exhausted than I cared to admit to Talin. He hadn't been lying—the rooms were modest, with two narrow beds and a cracked porcelain ewer and bowl for bathing. I shared a room with Ebb and only saw Talin briefly that evening at dinner.

The inn wasn't full, but there was a constant stream of people through the dining room, and I found myself staring at the other customers. They were dressed simply in tunics and shifts, but not a single one of them wore mourning clothes. One of the advantages of living in Pirot, I supposed. They were all tanned from laboring in the sun, their faces creased from hard work and from smiling. There was more joy in this one inn than I'd seen in all of New Castle.

Was this what Ceren hadn't wanted me to see? That life outside of New Castle was far better than inside it?

My sleep that night was the best I'd had since coming to Ilara. I could look outside the window and see the moon and stars. Our lantern was lit by flame instead of moss. And in two days, I would finally get to see Sami. How I would evade Talin and the guards I didn't know, but I hadn't come this far to give up now.

We left early the next morning, Talin once again falling in line next to me. It was midmorning by the time he finally spoke.

"You're a natural, you know."

I glanced up at him. "What?"

"On a horse. Who knew life on the ocean would prepare you to be a horsewoman?"

I blushed at the unexpected compliment. "I've spent many hours balancing on the edge of our family's boat, much to my mother's dismay. And our cousins the Galethians are famous for their abilities on horseback."

"I've seen them at the port. It's incredible how their horses obey them. They don't even tie them up. Anyone who attempts to steal a Galethian horse will receive a swift kick in the unmentionables. They say the horse can only be ridden by its rider, and that a Galethian horse will protect its master in battle until death."

"I believe the Galethians don't consider themselves to be masters of their horses, but rather partners," I countered.

"And how do you know so much about them? I thought the Varenians had no contact with Galeth."

"We don't. But we pick up bits and pieces from the Ilarean traders." It was a lie, but a small one. Everything I knew about Galeth I'd learned from Sami. "Did your mother ever learn to ride?" I asked.

"No, unfortunately. She was always afraid of horses. She

said anything that large belonged in the ocean, not on the land."

I laughed. "So what did she do for fun? I can't imagine she loved knitting any more than I do."

"No, she didn't. She liked walking, though. She'd walk for miles when she was allowed. For all his faults, my father did love her and granted her a relatively large amount of freedom."

"Then she was luckier than I am."

He looked back at Grig and Ebb, who seemed to be getting along just fine together. "Do you think you can manage a little trotting?" he called back to them. "We should try to make up some time. I believe it's going to rain soon."

When they both nodded, Talin spurred his horse forward, and the little brown mare followed. I found the trot less difficult to sit now than I had the first time, but it was still my least favorite gait.

"Are you all right?" he asked, sensing my discomfort.

"Something feels off." I peered over the mare's shoulder. "Could she be lame?"

"She does look a little sore. She's newly shod, and she's not used to such long distances."

I patted her on the neck and murmured an apology. "What can I do for her?"

"She needs rest, but we still have some distance to cover. I suppose you could join me on Xander, get some weight off her."

"Your brother wouldn't like that," I said, hating that even when I was away from him, Ceren shadowed my thoughts.

Talin smirked, reminding me of that first night we met. "What my brother doesn't know can't hurt him."

The last time I had agreed to something against my better judgment—dancing with Talin—I had incurred Ceren's wrath. But he was right. Ceren wasn't here. And the thought of being close to Talin again was too tempting to resist.

I glanced back at the guards. "What will we tell them?"

"The truth." He motioned for Grig to join us. "The mare is sore. Zadie will ride with me for the rest of the afternoon."

"Yes, Captain." Grig tied the mare's reins to his saddle and helped me dismount. When Talin reached down to help me up, I swallowed back my trepidation and took his hand.

"Would you like to sit in front this time?" he asked.

I felt confident on my mare, but Xander was a huge animal with a completely different demeanor. Still, Talin was looking down at me with such confidence that I nodded and let him pull me up.

Once I was seated before him, our torsos touched from seat to shoulders, and I could feel the warmth of him even through his leather armor. As I took up the reins, he wrapped his arms around my waist, and I wondered if I was really as small in his arms as I felt.

"Where are you going, Your Highness?" one of the guards called from behind. "Prince Ceren told us Lady Zadie wasn't to leave our sight."

"Then it's a good thing you aren't Zadie," Talin murmured in my ear. My body flushed hot, then cold, at his confirmation that he knew who I was. How long had he known? And was he happy I was Nor, or was he about to punish me in some way?

"We'll wait for you up ahead," he shouted to the guards. Then he clicked his tongue and dug his spurs into the stallion's sides, and we were off. I fell back despite what I thought had been preparation, but Talin's solid torso was there to support me. Once I got over the initial shock, I managed to sit up straighter and focus on the task at hand.

I felt like I was back in a boat again, riding the rolling waves, and I was so caught up in the sensations—of the horse beneath me, the wind against my face, the pull of the stallion's head against the reins as he fought to go faster, the solid feel of Talin's body behind me—that I forgot to be afraid.

"Excellent," Talin said over my shoulder. "You can give him his head, if you're ready."

I nodded and let the reins out a bit through my fingers, and the stallion surged forward again. We were still on the road, but there was something about the sight of the green hills far ahead, the wide blue sky all around us, that gave me the same sense of freedom the horse must be feeling. I loosened my grip on the reins, giving him as much control as I dared, and let him go. Neither of us was free in any real sense, but for a moment, I could almost believe that we were riding away from the dark shadow of the mountain forever.

I imagined Zadie waiting for me, just off the shore, and swimming out to meet her. We wouldn't need to speak about what had happened in each other's absence, because the only time that truly mattered was when we were together. It would be as if the time in between had never happened, like a bad dream forgotten when the light of morning warmed our cheeks.

I knew then that I could never spend the rest of my life away from Zadie. Varenia, the ocean, even my parents—I could survive without them. But my sister was as essential to me as the sunlight, as the air. I would find a way back to her someday.

By the time Talin took the reins and slowed the stallion to a walk, I had tears streaming down my cheeks. I wasn't aware of them until I felt his gloved finger against my skin. I closed my eyes, squeezing out the rest of my tears, and fell back against him, exhausted.

"It's going to rain," he said. "We'll wait it out in the trees."

He dismounted and led the stallion to a small grove of elms a little way off the road. He smiled up at me as we ducked under the foliage. "It's a long way down," he said, reaching up to help me. I slid into his arms, and for just a moment he held me above the ground, as if I was as light as a feather to him, before lowering me gently onto the soles of my feet. The leaves were thick enough that only a few drops made it through the canopy of trees, and I sank down onto the grass below them, sighing with relief.

"You did well," Talin said, settling back against the trunk of a tree. "I was afraid Xander would tire before you did."

"I like riding. It reminds me of being on the ocean in some strange way."

"I can understand that. My trip to Varenia was the first time I'd ever been in a boat. It was nice."

"And at other times, not so nice. One time Zadie and I—" I caught myself too late. I told myself it didn't matter, that he already knew the truth, but it was a heavy reminder that I'd never be able to share my memories of Zadie out loud, to anyone. "I'm thirsty," I said, rising shakily to my feet.

"There's water in my saddlebag."

I fumbled around with the straps on his saddle. I was finally alone with Talin, and I was going to have to tell him I'd been lying to him all along. I took a long drink from the water skin and was just tucking it back into the saddlebag when I heard a branch snap behind me.

I whirled around to find Talin watching me.

"What is it?" I asked breathlessly.

"Now that you and I have a moment to ourselves, I think it's time we had a little talk."

27

I walked back to the trees, clasping my hands to keep them steady. "How long have you known?" I asked.

"I suspected the first moment I saw you at Old Castle. But I knew for sure the night we danced."

"How?"

He leaned against the tree next to me. "When you made that comment about Ceren being unpleasant. I know I only met you and Zadie briefly, but from what I gathered that night in Varenia, that didn't strike me as something Zadie would say."

I could hear the humor in his voice, but I felt foolish for believing I could pretend to be my sweet sister. "No, I suppose not."

"I didn't mean it that way. I'm the one who put you in danger with Ceren that night, dancing with you. I shouldn't have done it, but I couldn't fathom why you would be here and not Zadie. And to be honest, I was selfish. I never thought I'd see you again, and then there you were, too tempting to resist."

I blushed, because I understood exactly how he felt. I had known the danger, and yet I hadn't been able to resist him. Even now, I hungered for his touch, despite the fact that Ceren's guards could return at any moment. I swallowed, waiting for him to continue.

"The day you saved Ceren at the lake only confirmed the truth for me."

"When you saw my scar?"

He nodded, his eyes lifting to mine. "I was afraid for you. Afraid Ceren had seen the scar and would somehow figure out the truth, or at least be angry that he'd been fooled. Do you have any idea how dangerous your position is?"

"Of course I do!" I exclaimed. "How could I not?"

"Then why are you here, Nor? Did Governor Kristos send you to spy on me?"

"What?" The question was so unexpected I nearly lost my balance.

"Just answer me, Nor. No more lies."

I was tired of pretending, and what was the use anymore? The truth was certainly better than letting Talin think I was a spy. At least not in the way he was imagining. "I came because of my sister."

His brow furrowed with genuine concern. "Did something happen to her?"

"She fell in love. With Sami."

"Your betrothed? Is that what you wanted to tell Kristos that evening?"

I nodded.

"And you volunteered to go in her place?"

"It's a bit more complicated than that."

The rain had slowed to a drizzle, and several drops had made their way through the leaves to land on Talin's brown hair, making the golden highlights glitter. The beads of moisture hung there like perfect crystal droplets, until he shifted toward me and they shimmered for a moment before disappearing, leaving darker spots in their wake.

"I'd be lying if I said I hadn't dreamed of going to Ilara one day," I admitted. "I thought Varenia was too small and simple. I wanted to see the world, and ride a horse, and..."

"And what?"

I looked away, ashamed at how childish I'd been. "Smell a rose. I still haven't even seen one."

He smiled gently at me, but then his expression turned confused. "If you wanted to leave and Zadie didn't, why didn't the elders just choose you in the first place?"

"That's not how it works. Besides..." I gestured to the scar on my cheek. Surely that was all the explanation he needed.

"I still don't understand. Your sister wouldn't come, so she asked you to come in her place?"

I shook my head. "She didn't ask me, Talin. She forced me to help her."

"Help her what?"

I hadn't thought about the night with the jellyfish for weeks now. The memory was enough to make my pulse race. Luck or Thalos had been with us that night; Zadie could have easily been killed. "Scar herself."

He jerked back. "What? Why?"

"She knew the only way the elders wouldn't send her was if she were no longer beautiful. So she came up with a plan. A terrible plan, to scar herself with a jellyfish. She wanted my help, but I refused. I didn't want her to be in pain, or risk her not being allowed to marry Sami. But she said if I didn't help her, she'd do it herself." I tried to swallow my tears, but there were too many. "I was so afraid she'd die, so I…I helped her. We told everyone it was an accident, but no one believed me. They thought I did it to her because I was jealous. Even my own mother."

"You mean Zadie didn't tell anyone it was her idea?"

"No. She was afraid, and I don't blame her. If they knew the truth, she'd never be allowed to marry Sami."

Talin pushed off the tree and stepped in front of me. "I'm so sorry. I had no idea it was like that. Mother always made Varenia sound so perfect. She said there was no violence or crime. I imagined it as a paradise. And when I came to visit, that's what I saw. I saw *you*."

Something in my chest released, and I realized how stifled I'd felt since I left home. "Varenia is wonderful in so many ways," I said. "I would give anything to go back. But people are going hungry because of your brother's demand for pearls. And yes, there are some people who believe the choosing ceremony is…well, everything. My mother is one of them."

"Why would any mother want to send her daughter away? For a bride price?"

"That may be part of it, but the honor of being chosen extends to the whole family. We believe beauty is the greatest blessing. Or at least, that's what everyone else believes. Now that I've seen what my future holds, I'm afraid it's more of a curse."

"And you couldn't refuse to come?"

I sagged against the tree. "We thought they'd choose a

different girl. But Zadie's portrait had already been sent to your father. Neither of us knew about Lady Melina, about how the Varenians were punished when the king discovered they'd sent a different girl. The elders decided Zadie should go, even if she didn't survive the journey, because otherwise you'd think we deliberately betrayed you. So I offered to go in her place. Elder Nemea gave me the stain to cover my scar, and I was supposed to spend the rest of my life pretending to be my sister." I glanced up at him pleadingly. "We didn't think anyone would ever know the difference. We all believed you were an emissary, that I was unlikely to see you again." I dropped my voice. "You weren't supposed to remember me."

He ducked his head, but not before I saw the color in his cheeks. "No chance of that, I'm afraid."

"No one has ever looked at me the way you did in Varenia," I said, my voice barely more than a whisper.

"I find that hard to believe."

"They're usually too busy looking at Zadie." I met his eyes. "She's as 'pure and unblemished as a Varenian pearl,' from what I hear."

His crooked grin made my stomach flutter as though it were full of tiny fish, and I remembered how Zadie couldn't stay away from Sami toward the end, despite the risk to both of them. I pushed off the tree and took a tentative step toward Talin. "Why didn't you tell your brother about me?"

"I would never do that to you. The thought of what he might do…" His jaw clenched as he moved closer to me. "Never."

"And what if I had admitted to being a spy?"

He braced his hands on the tree on either side of me.

"Then I would have told you you're the most beautiful spy I've ever seen."

"Ah. But only the second most beautiful girl in Varenia."

He was so close I could feel his breath on my skin. "About that."

"Yes?"

"I lied."

All it would take was one exhale from either of us for our lips to touch. It was like the moment before you opened an oyster, when you almost didn't want to, because for an instant, anything was possible. I closed my eyes, waiting...

The sound of hoofbeats on the road broke the tension. "They've caught up to us," I said breathlessly.

Talin straightened and bit his bottom lip, and I couldn't tell if he regretted that we had almost kissed or that we hadn't. He took my hand and began to lead me back toward the road. "I have more questions."

"So do I."

He dropped my hand as Grig burst through the brush into the clearing. "There you are. We got caught up in the storm or we would have been here sooner." He glanced from Talin to me, then back to Talin. "Everything all right?"

"Of course. We were just waiting out the rain. We'd better get a move on if we're going to make it to the inn before nightfall."

Ceren's guards glowered behind Grig.

Talin ignored them and boosted me onto Xander's back. "We'll canter for a bit to make up for lost time."

But when his eyes met mine, I could tell that he didn't consider the time we'd just spent together lost at all.

★ ★ ★

I collapsed into bed exhausted that night, but my mind wouldn't stop replaying those moments with Talin, when we'd been so close to kissing I could almost taste him. He trusted me now, but I'd had no time to tell him about Sami. And I wasn't sure I was ready. He might try to stop me, insisting it was too dangerous to defy Ceren that way, especially with Ceren's guards nearby. But now that I had made it this far, I couldn't imagine not seeing Sami. I would have to get away at some point and hope Talin would forgive me after.

We rose before dawn in order to make it to the market by noon. We would only have a couple of hours there before we needed to head back to the inn, and Talin had legitimate business there. The Ilarean traders who came to the floating market for the pearls handed them over to Ceren's guards at the port market. I prayed that Thalos had been with my people for the last month. I couldn't imagine returning to Ilara with a poor crop of pearls when the king lay dying in his bed. For all we knew, he could already be gone.

We were about five miles out from the market when Talin turned to me. "What's the matter?" he whispered.

"Nothing."

"Your forehead has been creased with worry for hours, and I'm afraid if you continue to chew on your lip that way, you're going to have nothing left. And that would be a damn shame, my lady."

"I'm fine," I said, tugging at my leather corset, which Ebb had tied exceedingly tight this morning, mumbling something about needing to look my best for the prince.

"Watch yourself for pickpockets in the market," he said.

"I have nothing for anyone to steal."

"That won't keep them from trying." He glanced down at my corset and tight leather breeches for emphasis.

I blushed, remembering how I'd looked when we first met. He'd seen far more of me than I had of him, but there was something seductive about not knowing what a person looked like beneath their clothing. It was surprising how alluring leather body armor could be.

"Just be careful," he said, and there was a territorial tone to his voice. As if I wasn't going to marry his own brother.

Thalos. Talin was my future husband's brother, and I had nearly kissed him. I shook my head to clear my thoughts. I needed to focus on getting to the market and finding Sami. Talin and the guards had the advantage of knowing their way around the market, but I had only ever seen it in my imagination. *Look for the kites*, I told myself. *And above all, pray for wind.*

Soon, other riders joined us on the road, as well as wagons weighted down with goods for sale. Despite my worries, I couldn't help marveling at the people pouring into the market. They weren't just Ilareans. There were refugees from Southern Ilara here, their clothing tattered and worn from days on the road, and Galethians leading their glossy-coated horses, and even people from across the Alathian Sea.

"You'd best close your mouth before the flies get in, milady," Ebb teased.

"Have you been here before?" I asked.

"Once, when I was a girl. It's a wonder, isn't it?"

It was indeed. It was loud and vibrant, alive with sounds and smells and every color of the rainbow. A man with half a dozen cages full of green and yellow birds flung over his back passed us, whistling as he walked. A woman and her child carried a bushel of red flowers each. Poppies, for tea and smoking, Talin explained.

Some of the stalls were covered in bright fabrics, while others were open to the sky. I scanned the tops of the stands for kites, but we were approaching the market from the bottom of the hill it stood on, making it harder to see anything above the stalls.

Grig and Ebb agreed to stay with the horses on the edge of the market. They had talked almost nonstop since yesterday, and I envied the flirtatious glances between them, the fact that they could converse in public without arousing suspicion. They could fall in love and get married, if they were so inclined. Even Zadie had been able to choose.

I had sacrificed all of that to come here, and I would be damned if it had all been for nothing.

Talin and I entered the market together. The sheer number of people would overwhelm me if I let it, so I tried my best to shut out the smell of cooking meat, overripe fruit, and unwashed bodies. A parrot screeched in my ear on one side as a small child tugged at my hand on the other, his filthy face upturned to mine. I glanced helplessly at Talin, who handed the boy a coin and ushered me farther into the market.

"What do you want to look for?" Talin asked me. "Anything in particular you were hoping to see?"

The idea of lying to him was painful, but I shook my head. "Nothing in particular. I just wanted to experience it for myself."

As I rounded a corner into another aisle, a short, stocky

man in leather armor stumbled into me. From the smell of him, he'd been drinking heavily.

"Are you all right?" Talin asked as I bumped into a fruit stand.

"I'm fine."

"You should watch where you're going," Talin said to the man's back. "You nearly knocked this lady down."

When the man turned, I recoiled instantly. It was Riv, the mercenary I'd met when I first came to Ilara.

"Well, well, well, what do we have here?" Riv said as he took in the sight of me. I was wearing riding leathers, and my tan had faded slightly from weeks in the mountain, but he definitely recognized me. "The little Varenian princess."

"Apologize, Riv," Talin ordered sternly.

Riv ignored him. "I'm surprised your brother didn't marry her right away, so he could—"

One of Ceren's guards pushed me behind him at the same moment Talin reached for his sword. I watched them for a moment, my heart pounding, before I realized this was my chance. They were all so distracted they weren't even looking at me. I backed up a few steps until I was in the aisle I'd been in before, and then I turned and ran.

28

I ducked between stalls and darted around carts until I came to a small clearing, where women were selling necklaces and other decorative baubles on blankets. There were no canopies here. I looked up and smiled at the sight of a large orange and yellow bird kite swooping overhead. I shaded my eyes against the sun and tried to follow the string down, but it was too bright.

"Where is the kite stand?" I asked one of the women selling jewelry.

She held out her hand, never raising her eyes from her blanket.

"I'm sorry. I don't have any money. I just need to know where the kite seller's stall is."

She flicked her eyes up to me and scanned my body. Satisfied that I had nowhere to hide a purse, she scowled and pointed across the clearing.

I rushed back into the throng of people and stalls, afraid I was moving too slow and Talin and the guards would catch me, or that I would get lost, or that I'd miss Sami. It was possible he wouldn't even make it today, and all this had been for nothing. I twisted and turned between the rows, growing more and more convinced that I was lost, when suddenly the kite seller's stall appeared in front of me.

The man behind the stand was stooped with age, and a few strands of silver hair poked out from beneath his flat gray cap. The stall itself was a shabby wooden thing, with smaller kites laid out on the table in front and others tied to the frame of the stand. There were no customers, and the man was watching me expectantly, perhaps hoping to make a sale to a wealthy lady. I should have asked Talin for some money before coming. The sun was high overhead, but Sami wasn't here, and I might only have a minute until the guards came.

"Can I help you?" the old man asked, gesturing me forward.

"I'm just…looking," I said. "You have beautiful kites."

"Perfect for a day at the seashore," he said, turning to look at something down the row of stalls. I followed his gaze and gasped. There, at the far end of the row, I could just make out a sliver of turquoise winking in the sunlight. The ocean.

My knees started to buckle when I felt an arm at my waist. A lump formed in my throat at the realization that Talin had caught up to me, that I hadn't completed my mission after all. I wouldn't be able to warn Sami, and by the time of the next market, Ceren could have many more of his breathing devices.

Worst of all, I would have to marry him, possibly this very week.

"Nor," said a familiar voice at my side, and the lump in my throat turned to a sob.

"Sami?"

My friend pulled me into his arms and held me against him, and I let myself go. I knew I didn't have time to waste on tears, but the relief at seeing a face almost as familiar as Zadie's overwhelmed me. He smelled like home, like saltwater and the spices we used to cook our fish, and the flowers his mother sometimes bought at market, perfuming their house until the blossoms dried out and she could use the petals for tea.

"You made it," I whispered against his neck.

"I would have come every month for a hundred years if that's what it took." He stroked my head and smiled. "But I'm not too ashamed to admit what a relief it is to see you."

I laughed through my tears and leaned back so I could look at him. He was wearing a rough tunic and a hat similar to the one the kite seller wore. "This is your disguise?"

"It's never failed me before. But if people see us together they might start to wonder." He led me toward the back of the kite seller's stall. There was a small tent behind it, and he ducked under the flap as though he'd done it many times.

"Who is he?" I asked, referring to the old man.

"He's one of the people I trade with. Don't worry, he's a friend. We can trust him. Now," he said, taking a seat on a wooden stool. "What in Thalos's name are you wearing?"

I glanced down at my dusty riding leathers. I was so used to being stuffed into dark, restrictive clothing by now that I'd forgotten how strange I must look to him. "We came by horseback from New Castle."

"New Castle?"

"The mountain where the castle is. It's a long story, Sami, and we don't have much time. How is Zadie? Are you married yet?"

The look on his face told me he'd been dreading this question.

"What happened?" I asked, a note of anger in my voice. "Please tell me you're at least engaged."

"I've barely seen Zadie since you left," he said. His scowl was so full of resentment it reminded me of my mother. "My father has forbidden it."

"What? Why?"

"Because after you left, Alys's mother turned the entire village against your family. She insists that her daughter was cheated out of her place in Ilara, and she's demanded that I marry Alys as recompense."

"You haven't agreed to it, have you?"

"Of course not!" he exclaimed. "But I can't very well marry Zadie, either. It's a mess, Nor. I know that's not what you want to hear, but it's the truth."

"At least tell me Zadie is healed."

His face softened. "She's doing much better. The scars aren't as bad as we'd feared, and she's able to walk and do some diving. But your father isn't catching enough fish to make up for the lack of pearls. He's been going farther out to sea, to dangerously deep water, and the traders refused to sell them drinking water last week. They're hungry and thirsty. We all are." He lifted his tunic, revealing the lines of his ribs.

"Thalos, Sami," I breathed. "How did it get so bad so quickly?"

"My father has insisted that all the families bring their pearls to him. The profits are now being divided evenly among every family. He thought he was making things more equal, but the families who were working harder to bring home more pearls resent those who don't pull their weight, and this past month they made a point of diving less. So now we all suffer. I give whatever extra I can get at the port to your family, but as I said, I'm not allowed to see Zadie. We meet in secret sometimes, though," he added, blushing.

"This is all my fault. I should never have allowed any of this to happen."

"It wouldn't have changed anything if you'd stayed. My father is the one who needs to stand up to Ilara, and he won't."

I shook my head. "You don't understand. It's not the king." I took a deep breath, prepared to tell Sami everything I'd learned in my weeks away as quickly as possible, when he placed a hand on my arm.

"I already know."

I released my breath. "What?"

"I already know that Prince Ceren is the one using the pearls. My father told me everything."

"Wait, your father? What are you talking about?"

Sami stood and began to pace the tent. "When the emissary came to Varenia, he tried to warn my father about Prince Ceren. He told him Ceren was the one devaluing the pearls, giving us less for them not only so we would be forced to harvest more pearls just to make enough money to survive, but also because the king's coffers were getting low."

All this time, I'd wondered if I could trust Talin, and he had been trying to help the Varenians all along. "He wasn't an emissary, Sami. He's Ceren's half brother, and he has as much claim to the crown as Ceren if the king dies before Ceren's twenty-first birthday. The king is dying, and Ceren is afraid he will meet the same fate. He *eats* the pearls, Sami, to try to escape from whatever hold the mountain has over him."

Sami's brow wrinkled in confusion. "He eats the pearls? I don't understand half of what you're saying, Nor."

"Just listen. He's created a device that enables people to breathe underwater for extended periods of time. He's planning to force all the Varenians to dive for him."

He stared at me, horrified. "Are you sure?"

"I've seen it with my own eyes. He's the one who cut off my family's water supply, and he's threatened to do it to all of Varenia. If your father doesn't believe me, he's going to find out for himself soon enough."

"Gods, Nor. This is so much more horrible than I'd feared."

"It gets worse. The last Varenian queen is dead."

"What do you mean, dead? She's still so young."

She was, I realized. My mother's age. "She was murdered years ago, most likely by Ceren. I don't think there's anything he won't do to become king. And if he does, you need to make sure the Varenians are prepared. Talk to Elder Nemea. She's on our side. If you can convince her, perhaps she can persuade the rest of the elders. Your father can't refuse the will of the entire council."

"I'll try, but you know how my father is. He won't listen to anyone."

I took Sami's hands in mine and squeezed them. "Then make him."

"I swear to you, Nor, I will do everything I can." He sat

down again. "And what about you? If the king dies before Ceren's birthday, what will happen?"

"I don't know. I assume Talin will challenge him."

"No, what will happen to *you*?"

I wiped my sweaty palms on my thighs. If Ceren won, he would marry me, I assumed, to strengthen his lineage. And if Talin won? What would become of me then?

"Don't worry about me," I said. "Just please take care of Zadie. And talk to the elders."

"I will." He studied me for a moment. "You look well, Nor. You look beautiful, actually."

I met Sami's warm brown eyes. I didn't feel awkward around him the way I had after the ceremony. Instead, I felt the same brotherly love for him I'd always felt, before everything fell apart. "Thank you, Sami. I miss Varenia more than I can say, but I'll be all right. Will you give my love to Zadie? Tell her that I'm healthy and happy."

He eyed me skeptically, but he nodded. We both turned as the tent flap lifted and the kite seller ducked his head inside.

"What is it?" Sami asked.

"There are soldiers outside, and they're looking for the girl." He gestured toward me.

Sami's eyes darted to mine. That greedy jewelry seller had probably told them where I was. "Stay in here," I told him. "Don't leave until the men are gone."

"I love you, Nor. Be careful."

"I love you, too," I said, doing my best to keep my voice from breaking. As I walked to the flap, the kite seller pulled a red kite from the wall of the tent and handed it to me.

"They'll wonder what you were doing in here," he explained.

"I can't pay for it. I'm sorry."

"Consider it a gift."

I touched his arm for a moment. "Thank you."

I stepped out of the tent and blinked against the bright sunlight. Suddenly a man's gloved hand closed around my arm and yanked me back into the aisle, where two other soldiers waited.

"What are you running from, girl?" Riv demanded, his putrid breath wafting into my face.

I struggled against his grip. "I wasn't running from anyone. I came to buy a kite."

"It looks like you forgot your escort in the process."

I gritted my teeth and glared at him. "I don't need an escort. And you have no right to touch me."

Riv laughed at his friends. "Cheeky little bitch, isn't she?"

The blade of Talin's knife was against Riv's throat before he could say another word. "You forget you're speaking to a lady, and your future queen."

Riv's hand released me immediately, and I stumbled over to Ceren's guards.

"Is everything all right, my lady?" Talin asked, his knife still pressed to Riv's neck.

"I was just getting this for Prince Ceren," I said, holding up the kite bearing the Ilarean crest. "Were you looking for me?"

Talin shot me a look as pointed as his blade, but he released Riv with a shove and took my arm. "Come with me," he said, dragging me back down the aisle. When we reached an unmarked silk tent, he pulled me inside, waving his knife at a man selling what looked to be Varenian pearls to another man.

"You can't come in here," the merchant shrieked, but he cowered when he saw the Ilarean crest on Talin's armor. The port was considered neutral territory, but the traders who came to the floating market weren't supposed to trade the pearls to anyone but Ilareans.

"Leave now, and I won't report you to King Xyrus. Selling Varenian pearls to a Galethian is illegal, as you well know," Talin said.

The merchant nodded and gathered his wares before hurrying out on the Galethian's heels.

When they were gone, Talin turned to me. "What were you thinking, running off into the market like that?"

I tried to come up with an excuse more plausible than a kite for a prince who lived inside a mountain, but there wasn't one. "Please don't ask me that, Talin."

"How can I protect you if I don't know if I can trust you?"

I stepped closer to Talin and carefully took his hand. "You can trust me. I swear it."

"Can I? Then why did we really come to the market? Tell me the truth."

"I—"

"The truth, Nor."

I crossed my arms and sat down on a tufted pillow. "Sami trades illegally at the port sometimes with the Galethians. He knew the value of the pearls hadn't gone down, that someone was deliberately cheating us. We thought it was your father, based on the rumors Sami heard. Before I left Varenia, I had hoped I might be able to talk to King Xyrus and convince him that if he didn't back off, we were going to starve, and he would run out of pearls."

"So why did you want to come to the market?"

"To meet with Sami. I was supposed to find him here. It was the only safe place we could think of."

Talin came to sit next to me. "And what were you going to do when you met him here?"

"I was supposed to report everything I'd learned to him."

Talin's eyebrows lifted. "So you are a spy."

I snorted. "Hardly. The one time I followed Ceren down to the lake in the mountain, he caught me. I've never been so terrified in my life. And you caught me outside Ceren's study the night before the trip to Lake Elwin."

"I assume you've now spoken with Sami?" he asked.

I nodded. "He told me what you did, when you came to Varenia. I know you tried to warn Governor Kristos. Unfortunately, he has chosen not to heed your advice."

"It's worse than that," Talin said. "Governor Kristos threatened to tell my brother that I was a traitor. He and Ceren have some kind of understanding, it seems. That's why when I saw you in Ilara, I thought..."

"You thought Kristos had sent me to betray you to Ceren?"

"Possibly. I didn't know. And then when you ran off today, after what happened yesterday... I was afraid you were going to leave. Not that I would blame you. It's just... I at least wanted to say goodbye."

There was so much sincerity in his voice and sadness in his eyes. "I'm sorry I worried you. I was afraid you'd try to stop me. And if Governor Kristos doesn't do something, Ceren could turn all of the people I love into human extensions of his devices, including Zadie." Tears welled in my eyes at the thought of her attached to one of Ceren's hoses like some kind of animal. Just because a person *could* be underwater for so long didn't mean they should. And how many months would it be before the oysters were gone? Not many, if Ceren made enough of his devices.

"Don't give up," Talin said fiercely. "I don't believe that Kristos wants to surrender to Ceren. I believe he's just afraid more people will suffer if he doesn't."

"He's a coward."

"He has every reason to be afraid," he said. "The Varenians are poor, untrained, and tremendously outnumbered."

I rolled my eyes at him. "Thank you. I feel so much better now."

"I'm sorry." He took a deep breath and released it. "Nor, if your governor believed he could win against Ceren, do you think he would feel differently?"

Governor Kristos had always been good to my family, and I believed he loved our people. Knowing what I did about Ceren, I realized Talin was right: Kristos did have a reason to be worried for them. But what kind of understanding could he have with Ceren that would make him take the prince's word over his own son's?

"I don't know," I said finally. "Maybe. But the Varenians don't stand a chance against Ilara's army."

"Not alone, perhaps."

"What do you mean?"

"There is reason to hope, but until we know if Governor Kristos is on our side..."

My breath caught. "Our?"

He glanced at the tent flap. Ceren's soldiers would be out there, wondering what we were doing. "You said you saved my brother that day out of a sense of duty."

"Yes."

He reached for one of my hands. "Just promise me now that I'm not wrong, Nor. Tell me you don't have feelings for my brother."

I recoiled at the very idea. "For Thalos's sake, Talin. First you think I would betray you to Ceren, and now you think I have feelings for someone who would use my people as tools for his own selfish aims? Honestly, the nonsense that comes out of your—"

He closed the space between us, cutting me off with his lips and stealing my thoughts along with my words.

After seeing Sami and Zadie kiss, I had imagined what it would be like to kiss someone I cared for. I had even let myself imagine kissing Talin. But I hadn't anticipated the contrasts: the softness of his lips above his stubble-roughened chin; the heat of his mouth on my cool skin; the watery looseness of my limbs that flowed to a tight ache low in my belly.

I closed my eyes and pressed closer to him, running my hands over his muscular chest and shoulders, trailing my fingers up to the soft curls just above his collar. I breathed in his scent of sunlight and leather and tightened my grip on his hair, drawing him closer still.

He moaned softly before parting my lips with his tongue, deepening our kiss. For a moment, all my concerns about Varenia and Ceren, all my long-held fears and insecurities, were washed away on a tide of desire, until I was nothing but pure sensation and energy. I was hungry and full at the same time, a million miles away and yet rooted so firmly in my own body I could feel every nerve.

I was drowning; I could never get enough.

29

When Talin finally pulled away, it took a moment to remember where I was. He pressed his fingertips gently to my swollen lips. I kissed his fingers and brought my hand up to cup his cheek, then tucked his hair behind his ear. He shivered at the sensation, biting his lower lip, and I wondered what else I could do to make him shiver like that again.

"Nor," he said, moving his fingers up to my cheek. The touch of his fingers against my scar startled me, and I pulled back on instinct.

"What's the matter?" he asked, still holding me, his eyes searching mine.

I drew his hands away from my face gently. "The guards will be suspicious."

He cleared his throat and rose to his feet, pulling me up with him. "Of course. I was being impulsive."

I wanted to tell him that his emotions were what made

him human, so unlike Ceren and his cool calculations about everything. But I was having trouble formulating coherent thoughts, let alone compliments, so I squeezed his hands instead.

When we emerged from the tent, the larger of Ceren's two guards stepped forward. "We're under strict orders to keep the lady in our sights at all times," the lead guard said. "If you keep this up, we'll be forced to tell Prince Ceren."

"That won't be necessary," Talin said as he led me back through the market. He kept close to me on the ride back to the inn, and though Ebb looked at me questioningly that night when I went immediately to bed without telling her anything about our trip, she didn't pry.

I rode beside Talin throughout the next two days, but Ceren's guards kept closer to me than they had before the market. Talin told them I'd only run because I was afraid of the soldier who accosted me, and they seemed to accept his explanation, but we kept our conversations light. It was nice to hear more about his childhood, and telling him about mine helped take my mind off what we were returning to in New Castle.

The road was just up the bank from the river here, though we hadn't crossed onto Ilarean soil yet. We stopped to water the horses, and when Ebb, Grig, and the guards disappeared to relieve themselves, I found myself briefly alone with Talin.

"What's going to happen when we get back?" I asked as he helped me dismount. "Can Ceren marry me whenever he chooses?" I knew now that I would never stop comparing him to Talin, never stop wondering what might have been.

"There are no laws preventing him."

"Why does he have to be so cruel? The way he treats his servants, how he does everything he can to make people as uncomfortable as possible, what he tried to do to the page…" I caught my lip in my teeth, unsure if I should continue. "What he did to your mother."

He tensed at my words. "Who told you?"

"Lady Melina. Although I should have figured it out on my own. I just didn't think anyone could be capable of doing something so horrible."

"Neither did I," he said, the pain of the memory etched in his features.

"Why didn't you do something, if you knew?"

"I was fifteen and terrified. I suspected Ceren, but like you, I didn't want to believe it. And he gave me the chance to leave New Castle by taking over command of the king's guard, so I left. I figured it would be easier to plot my revenge from afar."

I sucked in a breath. "Your revenge?"

He sighed. "How did you put it the other day? It's complicated?"

I couldn't deny that. But Talin's chance at the throne could be slipping through his fingers this very moment, and he didn't seem very anxious about it. Maybe he really was plotting something against his brother. "Did you—did you know what was going to happen, that day at the lake?"

"I didn't, but I wasn't surprised someone would try to kill my brother."

"You asked me to save him that day," I said slowly. "Ever since, I've wondered—why?"

He ran his fingers through his hair. "Ceren is not a good person. I know that. But he's still my brother."

"But you may have to fight him for the crown."

"That's different than letting him drown. I don't know why, it just is."

I smiled gently. "You're more Varenian than you know." I followed him up the bank to a clearing where the horses could graze while we waited. "What is your relationship with Lady Melina? Were she and your mother close?"

He thought for a moment. "Yes, at first. Lady Melina was very kind to my mother when she first came. Xyrus was already as good as married to Ceren's mother, and Melina believed Mother would become a mistress, like she was. She wanted to show my mother the ways of the castle, to be her mentor. Of course, what she knew of the castle was as someone less than a lady. She had never been treated as an equal by my grandfather while he was alive, and she was bitter and jaded even then. But my mother was still being treated as you are now, like a lady of the court, when Ceren's mother died. And the next thing my mother knew, she was marrying my father.

"Lady Melina's jealousy of my mother was so blatant that my father had to send her away from court. She was still permitted to attend major events, but she couldn't be trusted to behave during meals and gatherings. She called my mother terrible names and even did things to sabotage her, like putting nails inside her shoes."

"No," I breathed, horrified.

"Oh, yes. She was ruthless."

"But you're friends now?"

He quirked his lips to the side. "Melina doesn't have friends. But we're allies, in a sense. We seek a common goal."

"For you to be king?"

"I—"

Without warning, a man burst out of the bushes behind me. He had his knife to my throat before I realized what was happening.

"Scream, and I'll kill you," he hissed in my ear. Talin's sword was already drawn, but when the man motioned for him to put it down, Talin warily complied.

"You might wish to be more careful with the future queen of Ilara," Talin said.

I couldn't see the man's face, but the hand that held the knife to my throat was filthy, and his sleeve was torn and stained. He pressed the blade into my flesh, just far enough to draw blood, and I could feel the warm liquid beginning to drip down my neck. "I don't answer to any queen. I was sent by the woman king."

"What do you want?" Talin asked, shifting on his feet. "We're not carrying any money, and we have two Ilarean guards nearby."

I screamed as another man ran out from behind a tree and lunged for Talin. I elbowed the man holding me in the ribs and wriggled from his grasp, ignoring the searing pain in my neck as his blade sliced farther into my skin.

Talin was wrestling with the second man while the other came after me again. I reached into my boot and withdrew the coral knife, slashing at the man who'd tried to capture me. He held his ground, but we both turned our heads at the sound of a strangled scream. Talin lay next to his attacker, gasping for breath. The stranger's knife protruded from a bloody wound in his own chest.

I gasped, afraid Talin was hurt, but he rose to his feet quickly. I turned to see the man who had attacked me disappearing into the trees.

"Should we go after him?" I asked, but Talin was looking at my neck.

"I'm not worried about him right now. You're injured."

I winced as I touched the wound. "It's nothing. Are you hurt?"

"Nothing? You're bleeding, Nor."

The guards stumbled into the clearing just as Ebb and Grig arrived from the other side. "We heard screams," Grig said, hurrying toward us. "I was afraid for Mistress Ebb's safety, or we would have come faster."

"And where were you?" Talin shouted at the guards. "It's your job to protect Zadie."

"Apologies, Your Highness," one of them said. "We got lost trying to find you."

"Lost? How far could you possibly have gone?"

I shared his incredulity. Normally Ceren's guards were so close I couldn't move without stepping on their toes.

"Is that blood?" the other asked, pointing to my neck.

"Of course it's blood, you imbecile," Talin growled. "Bring me my water skin and a bandage from my saddlebag."

When the guard handed the items to Talin, he brushed my hair away from my neck gently. "I'm sorry. This is going to sting."

I smiled and placed my hand on his. "I'm fine. Really."

"You don't have to be brave all the time. Please, hold still."

I knew what he would see when he rinsed the blood off my neck, but he was already tipping the water skin. I watched his expression shift like sand under water, from concern, to surprise, to confusion.

"There's no wound," he said, running his fingers over the smooth skin.

"I told you it was nothing. It must have been the attacker's blood," I said, my eyes darting to Ceren's guards.

"On your neck?"

I stepped away from him, dabbing my neck with my sleeve. "Varenians heal quickly," I murmured. "You must have known that from your mother."

"She healed quickly, yes, but not within a few minutes," he insisted quietly. "I've never seen anything like this before."

I could feel the guards pressing in behind us.

"It was just a nick."

Talin waved the guards back. "Get on your horses and patrol the area. We'll leave in a minute."

"We take orders from Prince Ceren," one of the guards said gruffly.

Talin's eyebrows shot up. "You mean your orders to keep Zadie safe? Should I tell my brother how well you followed that command?" Talin crossed his arms and the guards finally turned away, grumbling to each other as they went. "Grig, take Ebb to the road," Talin said gently. "We'll be right there."

"Don't be angry," I said to Talin when the others were gone. I shivered as his fingers brushed the sensitive skin of my neck.

"I'm not angry. I'm astonished."

"I wish I could explain it. It's just the way I am."

He thought for a moment before running his fingers along my jawline and up to my cheek. "If you heal so easily, how do you have your scar?"

The warmth that had flooded my veins at his touch evaporated. "The scar was from a far worse incident. I was lucky to survive at all."

His finger still lingered on the sensitive spot on my cheekbone. No one had ever touched it like this before, with reverence instead of concern. "Will you tell me about it?"

"About the incident?"

"Yes. I want to know more about you."

I twisted the long braid Ebb had plaited for me this morning over my shoulder. I wanted Talin to know more about me, too, but I'd never told anyone about the incident. Everyone in Varenia already knew. Just thinking about it brought me right back to those awful moments when I'd believed with utter certainty that I was going to die.

"It's all right," he said, sensing my hesitation. He traced a path across my cheek and back down to my jaw, where he hooked one finger under my chin and lifted my head until our eyes met. And as scared as I was, I didn't break away from his gaze. I wanted to imprint this moment in my mind forever, because I was afraid it would never happen again. He lowered his face to mine, his lips brushing so softly against my cheekbone, I hardly felt it.

"What are you doing?" I whispered.

"I've been wanting to do that for ages," he murmured against my skin. "It's like a tiny star, marking you as something special for anyone too senseless not to know it."

I couldn't believe that anyone would want to kiss my scar.

I had imagined that if I left Varenia, I might find someone who could overlook it, but I hadn't dared to believe someone would ever find it special. "It's from a blood coral," I told him.

He leaned away from me. "What?"

"The scar. It's from a blood coral. I hit it when I was saving my sister from drowning. I nearly died from the cut. But somehow I survived, and ever since then I've been able to heal almost instantly." I gripped his hand, squeezing with urgency. "You can't tell your brother about this. If he finds out—"

"I would never tell." He tucked a loose strand of hair behind my ear. "How old were you?"

My grip softened. Talin's composure had a way of calming me. "Ten. We were diving for pearls. Our father never said it outright, and our mother wouldn't have admitted it, since it went against every rule she'd made for us, but we knew it was our responsibility to collect oysters. Father spent most of his time farther out to sea, hunting for bigger fish. We didn't have brothers who could dive for us, and Mother—whose own mother was also obsessed with the ceremony, and who had plenty of sons to do the physical labor—never learned to dive. One day, Zadie and I found a massive oyster close to a blood coral. We knew how dangerous they were, of course, but the amount of money a pearl from an oyster like that could bring to our family…"

His hand closed on my shoulder. "I'm so sorry. I had no idea how dire things were in Varenia."

I shook my head. How could he have known? "Zadie and I went for the oyster at the same time, and her skirts got caught on a fishing hook. I freed her, but she was running out of air, and she accidentally pushed me into the blood coral."

He touched my scar again, and this time it didn't feel so strange. "You love Zadie so much. How could anyone think you would want to hurt her?"

I stared at him for a moment, my eyes welling with tears. How was it that someone I'd only known a few weeks saw me so much more clearly than the people I'd spent my entire life with? I'd always wanted someone to see me for me. What if, against all odds, I had finally found that person?

And instead, I was being forced to marry someone else.

He wiped my tears away with his thumbs. "I'm going to do everything in my power to help Varenia, Nor."

"But what about your brother?"

"Damn my brother." He pulled me to him with an urgency I hadn't felt in our first kiss, as if with the knowledge that this kiss would most likely be our last. His mouth was hot and rough on mine. I wanted to touch him, to feel his skin against mine, not leather against linen. His hands were in my hair, on my waist, cupping my face, everywhere. As if he couldn't get enough of me, either. As if even a thousand kisses wouldn't be enough.

We made good time on the rest of the journey and reached Mount Ayris by sunset. As we began the ascent, I could feel the warmth of our kiss draining from me with each stride. New Castle loomed closer and closer, and we had no idea what would be waiting for us when we got there.

Talin climbed the stone steps behind me. I felt like a small weight had been lifted, now that someone knew the truth about me. Not just who I was, but also about my scar, my healing abilities, my plans to help my people. There were no secrets between us anymore. Not on my part, anyway. And while it hurt that he didn't trust me enough to reveal all his plans, I couldn't help believing that anything Talin wanted was just and worthy.

Ceren greeted us in the great hall, dressed in a robe the color of a moonless sky. There was no crown on his head, and he looked even wearier than before we left. The king must still be alive.

"My lady," he said, bowing deeply. "You're looking well. How was the market? Everything you hoped it would be?"

"It was wonderful, thank you. Your men did an excellent job of keeping an eye on me." I smiled sweetly at the guards. They wouldn't be able to tell Ceren about the time I spent alone with Talin now, not without making themselves look bad.

"I'm glad to hear it. The road can be unsafe for a lady without a proper escort."

Talin eyed his brother, but overlooked the implied snub. "How is Father?"

"His condition hasn't improved, but it hasn't worsened. He's lingering. For what, I don't know. We should see him now. He's been asking for you."

"I think I'll bathe and change, if that's all right," I said to Ceren. "I'm a bit dusty from the road."

I followed his gaze to the blood on the linen shirt I wore beneath my corset. "Are you hurt, my lady?"

"We were attacked by ruffians claiming to work for the woman king," Talin explained. "The lady wears the attacker's blood, not her own. We were lucky."

Ceren's mouth twisted with disapproval. "I'd like the full

report. Please excuse us, my lady." He gestured for me to go with Ebb. The hot bath waiting in my room was the only thing about New Castle I'd missed over the last five days.

Later that evening, after I'd changed and eaten a small meal in my room, I went to see the king. He might be weak, but he had never been cruel to me, and I would be sorry when he died. The king's physician sat near the head of his bed, checking his pulse. I was glad to see they weren't bleeding him again, at least.

Ceren and Talin arrived a moment after I did.

"Father, Talin and I are here with Zadie," Ceren said as he approached his father's bed. "We wanted to say good-night."

The king's eyes fluttered open, and he rasped out a response too quiet for me to hear.

"No, Father, that's not your wife." He said the word with a sneer, as though the taste of it in his mouth offended him. "It's Zadie, as I said."

With a great show of effort, the king raised an arm as slender as a child's and gestured to me. I glanced at Ceren, unsure.

"Go on," he said.

I perched myself on the edge of the king's bed, trying not to touch the sheets that reeked of illness. "I'm here, Your Majesty."

He held out a hand, and I took it with my free one. "Talia," he said gently, his watery blue eyes searching for a ghost.

Tears welled in my own eyes as I saw the love written plainly across the king's pale face. How could Ceren have been cruel enough to steal his father's happiness by killing his stepmother? I glanced back at the brothers, who stood watching me like two statues: one carved from marble and just as cold, the other a bronze study of agony.

I kissed the king gently on his forehead, then rose to my feet. "Good night, Your Majesty."

Ceren reached for my hand as I brushed past him. "Shall I escort you back to your room, my lady?"

"You should stay with your father," I said. "I can find my way just fine."

On the walk back to my chambers, I stopped at the portrait gallery to see Zadie. She smiled down at me, the sister I'd known before the choosing ceremony, when everything changed. The idea that she wasn't happy now, after everything we'd been through, opened a pit somewhere behind my rib cage. This was the first time since coming to Ilara that my despair threatened to overwhelm me. As frightened as I'd been when I came to New Castle, as much as Ceren repulsed me and the cold and darkness gnawed at my very soul, I'd had a purpose. Saving my people, and Zadie most of all, made my sacrifice worth it. But knowing that Governor Kristos had sent me here, even after Talin's warning... It was almost impossible to believe anyone could stop Ceren.

"I miss you," I whispered to Zadie. "Every minute of every day. I wish they'd chosen Alys, and that you and I were still together now. You could have married Sami, and I would have found someone willing to put up with me, and we would have raised our children together. Boys, maybe, so they never had to worry about their beauty."

No, I heard her say. *I wanted daughters. Twins, like us. Only I would have raised them both to be as beautiful as* you, *dear sister, in the ways that matter.*

My vision of her was so strong that I could have sworn I felt her hand on my cheek. *Don't cry, Nor. We will be together again. In this life or the next.*

And then she was gone, and I was left alone in a hall full of ghosts.

30

A seamstress came to visit the following day. Apparently Ceren thought I should be fitted for my wedding gown as soon as possible. The seamstress was short and rosy-cheeked, with black hair in a simple braid down her back. From the villages, probably, since she didn't appear to be of noble blood, and she had too much color in her skin to live in the castle all the time.

"Milady," she said, curtsying. "It's an honor to be fitting you in person. I hope you've been happy with my work."

I smiled with genuine gratitude. "All of my dresses are beautiful. Thank you." Ebb helped me remove the gown I was wearing, and I stepped gingerly into the white dress. The satin on the bodice was so old it was beginning to yellow, and it was delicate as a moth's wings.

"This was Queen Serena's wedding gown, milady," the seamstress explained. "We can replace the bits that are discolored, if you like."

I recognized the dress from the portrait in Ceren's chambers. It was cut low at the neck, and the hand-sewn lace trimming wasn't quite long enough to cover my chest.

"You're a bit more shapely than the late queen, milady," the seamstress said. "I'll add more lace here."

The bodice was tight but manageable, with glass beads and more lace covering the white satin. There were no sleeves, just little chiffon drapes across the shoulders, and the skirt was a frothy mix of lace, tulle, and chiffon, like sea foam, all covered with more of the delicate glass beadwork. It was a beautiful dress, but considering the occasion, mourning colors would have been more appropriate.

"I'll let out the hips just a bit," the seamstress said, "and then I think we should be all set. I'm having some white lace gloves made up as well, if that pleases milady."

I nodded and thanked her. "I'm sure it will all be lovely," I added.

She smiled and curtsied again before bustling out with the dress form. Ebb helped me change back into my other gown for dinner. Only a few of the most prominent lords and ladies were in attendance tonight, as well as Talin, who was staying at New Castle while the king was ill, in case he should take a turn for the worse. But he had not come to see me since our return, and if there really was a reason for me to remain hopeful, I couldn't imagine it.

"How was the fitting today?" Ceren asked as he sipped his wine.

"It went well. Your mother's dress is even more beautiful in reality than in her portrait." He reached for my hand, and

I let him take it. I was tired of fighting. Not quite resigned, but tired.

"I know you're not yet eighteen, and Father is holding on better than we'd dare to hope. But we'll need to move forward with the wedding either way. You understand, of course."

I nodded. Marrying me wouldn't do him any good if Talin seized the crown, but knowing Ceren, he had a plan for that outcome, too.

"I imagine Varenian weddings are quite different from Ilarean ones," he said as he sawed at the slab of liver on his plate with a knife. "There will be a brief ceremony in the great hall, and once we're wed, we'll leave the mountain and go through the nearby villages in a carriage. The people will be out in droves to see their new princess. Or queen, as it may be." He smiled, but there was something about the way he spoke that unnerved me. "Afterward we'll have a feast here at the castle, and then it will be our wedding night, of course. I don't think I need to go into further detail about that—do I, my lady?"

I didn't blush or cringe, as he'd no doubt hoped I would. "No."

"Here, let me cut your meat for you." He came to stand behind me the way he had when he'd presented the bat pie. "I'm finding it especially tough this evening."

Something was definitely not right. I glanced at Talin out of the corner of my eye, but he looked as confused as I was. Then I heard the knife screech against the plate and felt a searing pain in my arm. I looked down to see a deep cut, already welling with blood.

I was too shocked to speak, but Talin was on his feet immediately.

"What have you done?" he asked Ceren as he clamped a napkin down on my forearm. "You clumsy—"

"Calm down," Ceren said coolly. "You're in the presence of ladies. The knife slipped. I'll take Zadie to have her arm bandaged."

"You're not taking her anywhere," Talin said, helping me to my feet.

Ceren stepped in front of me, his gray eyes flashing with anger. "Keep your hands off my wife."

"She's not your wife yet." I'd never heard Talin so cold.

Ceren lowered his voice to a growl. "Stand back, or I'll have you put in the dungeon."

"Talin," I said quietly. "I'm fine."

Ceren glanced between the two of us, and whatever he saw there only angered him further. He pushed me roughly toward the doors. I could feel the eyes of every lord and lady on us as he marched me out of the dining hall, one hand placed firmly on my back, the other still gripping the knife. He didn't stop until we'd made it to his study, where he shoved me over the threshold and locked the door behind us.

"Show me your arm," he said before I'd even turned around. He ripped the bloody napkin off my skin. The wound was deep and hadn't fully healed yet, but the bleeding had stopped.

He grabbed my wrist and brought my arm closer to his face. I'd forgotten about his poor vision. "So the bastards weren't lying," he said. "I wondered how you managed to heal so quickly when Salandrin bit you. Does your arm hurt?"

I pulled my arm out of his grasp. "Not anymore. Who told you?"

"My fool guards. They couldn't save you from the woman king's men, apparently, but they did manage to catch this. How is this possible?" His eyes were wide and wild, and somehow the excitement on his face was more terrifying than his usually stony demeanor.

My blood pulsed loudly in my ears. I had hoped to hide this truth from Ceren, at least. Now I'd made things even worse. "I don't know. There was an…accident. When I was a child. Ever since then, I've been able to heal quickly."

"What kind of accident?"

I hesitated, and Ceren stepped forward with the knife. "Don't disgrace us both with lies, my lady."

I bit my lip, wondering how vague I could be. "It was a cut."

"From?"

I had no hope of getting out of this with both my secret and my life, but I had to try. "A coral," I said.

"Not a normal coral, surely." Ceren cocked his head, considering. "I've heard that the pearls get their healing properties from the blood coral."

I tried to keep my face impassive, but he already knew he'd hit the right line of questioning.

"How bad of an injury can you sustain and still fully heal?"

My blood went cold, and I took a step backward, in case he was hoping to find out. "I don't know."

"Miraculous," he repeated, still staring at my arm. "I wonder if it's possible the coral entered your bloodstream. And now, whatever is in the coral that makes the Varenians so healthy and the pearls so potent...is inside you."

That had been the doctor's theory, though how I'd survived the poison in the first place remained a mystery. I crossed my arms behind my back, hating the way he looked at my skin, like it was one of his inventions.

He reached for a small silver knife and a dish. "I'll need to collect some of your blood to test my theory."

I darted for the door, but Ceren held the keys up in front of him. "You'll leave this room when I say you can."

I wanted to be brave, but my voice cracked as I leaned forward, hoping to reach the coral knife hidden beneath my skirts. "I'm begging you not to do this, Ceren."

He strode forward with his silver knife, and though the mountain may have weakened him, I knew in my heart that he was still much stronger than me. "Hold still, my lady," he crooned, taking me by the throat. "This is going to hurt."

Ceren filled five bowls with my blood that night. I gave up screaming after the first three gashes. By the time he was finished, I was too weak to struggle any longer.

We were both covered in blood when Talin finally burst through the door, leaving it hanging on one hinge. I'd heard him pounding and yelling throughout the process, but his voice had seemed as far away as Varenia.

"What did you do to her?" Talin demanded as Ceren scooped me up and shouldered past his brother into the corridor.

"I needed samples of her blood." He clucked his tongue at me. "She put up such a fuss."

Talin took in the bloody streaks and half-healed wounds as Ceren carried me past. He followed us all the way to my rooms, where Ceren laid me down on my bed with surprising care.

"Come along, brother. My intended needs her rest."

Talin's eyes hadn't left mine. "I'm staying with her."

Ceren scoffed. "That's out of the question."

Talin stepped forward until they were chest to chest, closer than I'd ever seen them. The contrast was startling. Talin was a finger or two shorter than Ceren, but his shoulders were broader, his muscles more developed. All of Ceren's strength came from his singular devotion to one thing: power. He had no other weakness, nothing else he cared about enough to distract him.

And Talin? What did he care about? My eyes were glazing as I slipped in and out of consciousness.

"Whatever happened between the two of you on the journey is over," Ceren said. "Zadie is *mine*."

"You don't love her, Ceren."

He tossed his hair aside with a wry laugh. "Who said anything about love? If that girl's blood can be passed on to our children, just imagine what it will mean for Ilara."

"You're a monster," Talin hissed.

"And you're a fool. Now leave. The girl needs her rest, and I'll likely need more of her blood tomorrow."

Talin moved in front of the bed, blocking Ceren. "You won't touch her again."

Ceren sneered. "Save your ire, brother. You'll need it to bring down the man who attacked Zadie."

"What are you talking about?" Talin demanded.

"We can't let the woman king get away with something as heinous as attempting to assassinate the future queen. You leave tonight. Don't come back until you've found the assassin." Ceren turned to a guard outside my door. *Where had he come from?* "You, see to it that my bride doesn't leave under any circumstances."

The rage on Talin's face was the last thing I saw before I surrendered to the darkness.

I woke sometime in the middle of the night. My wounds had healed and the throbbing in my head was gone, but I was weak and thirsty. I changed into my riding breeches and one of my old tunics, then tucked the coral knife into the top of one leather boot, pausing every few minutes to rest. When I was dressed, I folded up a crude, hand-drawn map of the castle Ebb had made for me after I told her I got lost and clasped the pearl necklace from my parents around my neck. Finally, I pulled Sami's green cloak over my shoulders.

If I could make it to Old Castle, I could steal a horse and maybe, somehow, make it to the port. I would barter the pearls to a trader from the floating market for a ride to Varenia.

I knew my odds of escape were miniscule, but whether or not I made it home, there was nothing worse Ceren could do to the Varenians than what he would do once he learned about the blood coral and its connection to my people. And by staying here, I was just providing him with more blood for his experiments. At least this way I could warn them.

I went to my door and cracked it open as quietly as I could. The guard was awake, probably on high alert thanks to Ceren.

I hefted the heavy porcelain ewer from my washstand in my right hand, hidden by the door, and began to weep.

The guard turned. "Milady? Are you hurt?"

"I'm so sorry to disturb you," I sobbed. "My arm is bleeding again, and I can't stop it."

"I'll fetch Prince Ceren," he began, already taking a step toward the hall.

"No," I said, pretending to cry harder. "I'm afraid I'm going to faint."

He glanced over his shoulder once, clearly worried about disobeying Ceren, but turned back to me. "Don't worry, milady. I'll help you."

I'd never intentionally hurt anyone before, and this was a man who was offering to help me. But I couldn't let one guard stand between Varenia and me. As soon as he was through the door, I brought the ewer crashing down on the back of his head. He grunted as he slumped forward, and I hit him again for good measure.

Once I was sure he was unconscious, I dropped the ewer and slid into the hallway. There would be other guards on the way to the servants' entrance in the base of the mountain, and I told myself I was prepared to use my knife if I had to. Fortunately, it was the night of the new moon, and the lanterns were so dim I could barely see. If I was careful, I might be able to make it through the corridors undetected.

I didn't have time for detours, but I was fortunate that the portrait gallery was on my way. I wanted to say goodbye to Zadie, just in case I didn't make it back to Varenia. The possibility was more real than I wanted to admit. The guard at the entrance was asleep, and I skirted past him, pausing just long enough to press my fingers to my lips, then onto Zadie's perfect painted mouth. The guard on the other end of the gallery was slumped against the wall. I noted the jug near his feet and thanked the gods for potent Ilarean wine.

I moved closer, my back pressed to the wall. The knife was a last resort. One cut with the coral blade would be lethal, and in my heart, I knew I didn't want the weight of a man's life on my conscience. As I inched nearer to the guard, I made a deliberate effort to slow my breathing and heart rate, the way I would before a dive. I needed my wits about me now.

I took one last look at the guard to make sure he was truly passed out and darted forward, my feet barely touching the ground as I ran. And then I was past him, in another corridor, and I almost laughed with relief.

"Going somewhere?"

My blood froze in my veins as I turned toward Ceren's voice. The drunk guard leaning against the wall straightened, and his black and red cloak fell back, revealing the prince's pale face. He wore a castle guard's uniform: leather armor beneath a heavy cloak, worn to keep out the chill of the damp halls at night.

"Ceren," I said, my mouth dry. "What are you doing here?"

"I know you better than you think. I didn't expect you to willingly remain in this castle knowing what I'm going to do to you. I also know how much you love to visit this portrait gallery, staring at your own picture."

My heart was like a caged animal clawing at the walls of my chest. I thought fleetingly of lying, saying that I'd needed to stretch my legs, but Ceren was too shrewd, and I was too exhausted. "I can't stay here anymore. Not like this."

"I'm afraid you don't have a choice. Not if you don't want your family to suffer the consequences. And next time, it won't be just their water supply that gets cut off." He stepped toward me, even more imposing in the leather armor. "I know you're not who you claim to be."

I clenched my jaw to keep it from trembling. "I don't know what you mean."

He closed the space between us and raised a finger to his lips. His tongue darted out as he licked his fingertip. When I balked, he grabbed me with his other hand, pressing the finger against my cheekbone and rubbing in a small circle. He held the stained tip up to my eyes.

"Your governor is a fool, but not so foolish that he would send a damaged girl to me. Not without good reason."

Not damaged, I thought. *Stronger.* "It's not what you think."

He cocked his head in mock confusion. "So you didn't come in place of your injured twin sister? Odd, that's not what my emissary told me when he returned from Varenia."

He couldn't mean his brother. Talin would never betray me like that. "What emissary?"

"The one I sent to deliver your bride price, after you told me how difficult things were for your family. Imagine his surprise when he discovered a girl who looked just like you, responding to your name, when he went to your family's house. Your parents tried to cover for you, but when the emissary offered the bride price to anyone willing to share the truth, it spilled out like fish guts."

I didn't blame the others for talking. They were half starved, and they believed I'd brought their misfortune upon them. "What difference does it make to you?" I asked. "My scar won't prevent me from giving you what you want."

He grabbed my arms and yanked me to his chest. "I warned you to stay away from my brother."

I struggled against him. I should have gone for my knife when I'd had the chance. "What does that have to do with anything?"

But even as I asked, I knew. His silver eyes were full of the same pain and shame I'd seen that day at the lake. He didn't just want an heir to the throne. He wanted me to choose him over Talin, even after everything he'd done to me.

"I'm sorry," I said, and I was. Not about my feelings for Talin, or for doing everything I could to help my people. But I had never set out to cause him pain. Somewhere inside Ceren was a boy who only wanted to be loved. Unfortunately, the people who had convinced him he was unlovable had also ensured that he would be.

He looked momentarily taken aback. "You know, I believe you truly do mean that," he said. "But I'm afraid I can't let you leave. Not after the crimes you've committed."

"Crimes?"

His expression turned sly. "In addition to betraying the crown by posing as your sister, there's the dead guard."

"What dead guard?" A wave of guilt flooded through me. Had I accidentally killed the man outside my room with the ewer?

Ceren jerked his head toward the man at the entrance to the gallery. "I slit his throat just minutes before you arrived."

I knew Ceren was a murderer, but to hear him admit to it so callously made my stomach roil. "So what's your plan, then? Are you going to have me killed?" I was still so weak from the bleedings, but I bucked against him, desperate to get to my knife.

He chuckled softly. "You're worth far more to me alive. But now I have a good reason to keep you locked up. I suppose I should thank you for trying to escape, really." He twisted my arm and whirled me around so that my back was to him, then grabbed my other arm and wrapped something hard and cold around my wrists.

I cried out when he wound his fingers in my braid and yanked my head back, his breath hot against my neck, his smooth cheek pressed to mine. "Nor," he purred, his tongue curling around the *r* in the perfect imitation of a Varenian accent. "I always knew you were special. From the moment you defied me in my chambers. Maybe since the moment I felt your heart beating beneath my fingertips." He brought his right hand up to the center of my chest, as he had the first day I met him. Coming from him, the word *special* didn't feel like a compliment.

"I prayed to the gods for a queen who would be the salvation of Ilara by strengthening our bloodlines," he whispered in my ear. "I never dared to hope you might be my salvation as well."

31

As the metal door to my cell clanged shut, Ceren's face appeared briefly between the bars, his skin a sinister green in the foxfire torchlight. "I'll be back tomorrow for more blood. Try to get some rest before then."

The dungeons were deep in the mountain, not far from the entrance to the underground lake where the monster, Salandrin, had lived. As he'd dragged me down to my cell, Ceren had explained why the corridors down here were so narrow and cramped. They were part of the original bloodstone mine, before Queen Ebbeela had it flooded to stop the wars. The royal crypt was down another tunnel nearby, and if I breathed too deeply, I swore I could smell the stench of decay wafting into my cell.

One of the two guards on duty had patted me down for weapons, but he'd been too focused on my breasts and hips to check in my boots, which meant I still had the knife. I knew

I would only have one chance of escape, so I waited, hoping an opportunity would present itself.

I slept fitfully on the straw covering the floor of the cell. The dungeon appeared to be mostly empty, though I'd heard coughing and moaning coming from a few other cells as Ceren led me to mine.

He came for me hours later in what I assumed was the morning, although there was no natural light here, or even any lunar moss, to confirm my guess. I had hoped he would take me back up to his study to bleed me, but the satchel he carried when he entered my cell made it clear I would be staying in the dungeon.

He crouched down next to me in the straw, carefully laying out his instruments. "I'll have some food and water brought," he said, though without any pity or compassion. "And a change of clothes, if you'd like them."

I didn't say anything, just remained tucked into my corner. I was too weak to fight him off, and if I was going to escape, I needed to save my strength.

"I wasn't able to learn anything useful yesterday, unfortunately, but I think fresh blood will help. I'll be making a trip to Varenia myself soon, to collect some of the coral. I thought I might check in on your sister while I'm there. Just to see how she's doing in your absence."

My muscles tensed at his words. "If you touch her—"

He removed the silver knife from his satchel. "Yes?"

I contemplated begging, offering him anything he wanted in exchange for my sister's safety. But what did I have to offer that he couldn't freely take here? The guards certainly wouldn't protect me.

When he reached for my arm, I didn't struggle. I had healed yesterday, and I would heal again today, though I wondered how long I could last like this. I needed to strike when I had some kind of advantage; otherwise the guards would catch me, even if I did manage to kill Ceren. But I couldn't afford to wait too long. At some point, I may not have enough strength to recover.

He took less blood this time, but I was too weak to stand by the time he was finished. He lowered me back onto the straw with the same gentleness he'd shown yesterday. "I'll have the guards bring you some beef liver stew."

He chuckled when I cringed despite my weakness. "And some bread, if you like." He stroked my hair, which had come unraveled during the night, as my head swam with dizziness.

At first, when I heard the familiar opening notes to the song Ebb sometimes sang to herself, I thought I must be dreaming. I opened my eyes and looked up at Ceren. He was singing to me, in the same surprisingly beautiful voice I'd heard that night by the underwater lake. Hot tears seeped out of the corners of my eyes and ran down my cheeks into the straw beneath me. I wanted to attack him now, when he was vulnerable, but I was too weak to reach my boot. Why hadn't I done it when I had the chance? Lady Melina had warned me not to let another opportunity pass me by.

My Varenian morals were going to be the death of me.

When he was finished, Ceren leaned down, the strands of his hair brushing against my skin like feathers, and kissed me on the forehead.

★ ★ ★

Many bleedings followed, so many I lost count. I slept as much as I could, my dreams my only escape from the misery of the dungeon. I was dreaming of my sister when I startled awake at the sound of Lady Melina's voice coming down the hall, followed by the angry grumblings of one of the guards. I had no idea how long I'd been down here—the only break in my days beside the bleedings was the single meal I was brought, and even though my stomach turned at the smell of it, I ate all of the liver stew I could. One day I would have an opportunity, I told myself, though it was starting to feel more and more like a lie.

"Take your hands off of me!" Melina said in her soft Varenian accent. I couldn't see her, but I could envision her chin lifting in indignation as they manhandled her through the corridors.

"Get in there," the guard grunted, and a moment later, I heard the clang of the metal door closing behind her. She wasn't next to me, but she was close by. I could hear her muttering about the dirty straw and lack of ventilation.

The guard's steps retreated back down the hallway, and for a moment I listened in silence, wondering what Melina could possibly have done to get herself thrown in the dungeon.

"Are you there, child?" she asked once the guard was out of earshot.

I sat up and scooted toward the door of my cell. "I'm here. What happened? Why have you been imprisoned?"

"I declared that Prince Talin was the legitimate heir to the throne, and Prince Ceren a murderer who had killed Queen Talia."

My mouth fell open. "*What?* When?"

"Tonight at dinner." To my surprise, Melina almost sounded amused. "It went about as well as you might expect."

Gods. Now we were both trapped. "Why would you do such a thing?"

"It was the only way I could think to see you."

I slumped back against the door. "You had yourself imprisoned for *me?*"

Her laugh was low and throaty. "Don't flatter yourself, child. I did this for Varenia, not for you."

"I don't understand."

She lowered her voice so that I had to strain to make out the words. "One of my spies told me about your healing abilities."

I wanted to cry, but even that would require too much energy. "I'm so sorry. Now that Ceren knows about the blood coral, I'm afraid our people are in more danger than ever. And there's no one left to warn them."

"There's a way out of the mountain even Ceren doesn't know about," she whispered. "And if you're willing to trust me, I believe we can get you out of here."

In my present state, I wasn't sure I'd be able to escape even if the guards were to open the doors and personally escort me out of New Castle. "What about you?"

"Don't worry about me, child."

"Will he kill you?" I asked.

"Quiet!" the guard yelled as he passed our cells. "Prince Ceren said there should be no talking!"

But he hadn't said anything about singing, apparently. That night, Melina wove me a strange song. I memorized the words until I heard them in my sleep, until they became my prayer.

Deep in the mountain,
Far below,
Beyond the lake,
Where the glowworms glow,
The path is clear,
To Varenian eyes,
Follow the blood,
To where freedom lies.

Finally, Ceren came for us, when I'd begun to think I might spend the rest of my life inside this prison.

I could hear the guards straightening and Lady Melina rustling in her straw at the sound of his voice. "Ready the women."

"Yes, Your Highness," one of the guards said. A moment later I heard Melina's cell open, then a thud. "Get up, wretch, or I'll kick you all the way to the gates."

I heard heavy footsteps, and then the guard was at my door. I'd been offered fresh clothing on multiple occasions, but I had only changed twice, when I'd been given sufficient privacy to do so. I was beyond caring about modesty now, but I was afraid that if I removed my boots they'd see the knife, the map, and my pearl necklace. Fortunately, someone—I assumed it was Ebb—had made sure I was given clean riding pants and simple tunics to wear, not gowns that would have made it harder to conceal my contraband.

The guard pinched his nostrils with one hand as he hauled me to my feet. "Go on then," he said, shoving me out of the cell into the corridor, where Lady Melina stood with her hands bound with rope. Her gown was a bit stained and wrin-

kled, but she wasn't as filthy as I was. She must have taken all
the clean clothing she was offered.

My hair hung in knotted clumps, but I squared my shoulders and followed the guard. I could make out Ceren's silver-
white hair ahead of us in the corridor, leading the way back
up the mountain.

"Where are they taking us?" I whispered to Melina.

She shook her head. "I don't know. Just keep your wits
about you. There may be an opportunity."

I didn't see how I could possibly escape with my hands
bound and multiple guards surrounding me, but I closed my
mouth and did what she said. We passed Ceren's study and
continued past the dining hall, into the great hall. The throne
sat empty, as it had since the day I arrived at New Castle.
But the hall itself was full of people, more crowded than I'd
ever seen it. The lords and ladies stared at us as we were led
through the room toward the towering iron doors. Some of
them appeared to be crying.

A woman materialized at my side, and I turned to see Ebb,
a handkerchief raised to her nose.

"Ebb, what are you doing here? What's going on?"

"The king is dead, milady," she said. Her eyes were red
from crying, making the irises even bluer than normal.

My blood roared in my ears like the ocean. "When?"

"Last night."

"Has Ceren declared himself king?"

She shook her head. "The duel is scheduled for dawn, if
Talin makes it back in time. But for now, Ceren remains regent."

"What does that mean?" I asked as we neared the doors.

"He's going to have you both thrown from the mountain."

"What?" I cried as we were pulled through the doorway onto the wide overhang that served as the entrance to the castle. The light was so bright after so many days in full darkness that I closed my eyes against it. When I finally blinked them open, I saw that crowds had gathered here, too. Among the nobility in their mourning attire, I spotted a few commoners, with their tanned skin and homespun clothing in shades of cream and brown.

Ebb was lost to me in the crowd as I was dragged up to a platform alongside Lady Melina, who somehow kept her face a mask of serenity. With my back to the open edge of the cliff, I could feel the wind whipping at my hair and tunic.

What had happened to Ceren needing me alive? I was more frightened than I'd ever been, even when Zadie had told me about her plan to scar herself. If Ceren was willing to kill me, then that meant he'd found what he needed in my blood, and there would be nothing to stop him from slaughtering Varenians for his own gain.

"Lords and ladies of the court," Ceren said, appearing before the platform in a rich black doublet and trousers. His hair was pulled back, and a circlet of dark metal sat atop his head. "As you know, my beloved father, your king, left us last night to take his place among the stars with his forefathers. Which means that it has fallen to me to enact justice against these two traitors to the crown."

He turned toward us, his face unreadable, as always. "Lady Melina and my betrothed, Zadie, have been tried and found guilty of treason. The punishment for their crimes is death."

A murmur ran through the crowd, but I couldn't tell if it was in disapproval or agreement.

"They will be thrown from Mount Ayris. If their souls are innocent, let them take flight. Otherwise, we shall watch them fall."

I took a step closer to Lady Melina, closing my eyes as two guards approached the platform.

"It's going to be all right, child," Melina said calmly.

When I felt the guard's hands on my still-bound arms, I shoved against him, but it was no use. The man was a giant, and despite all the liver stew I'd consumed, I was weak from the bleedings and being confined in the dark. As he dragged me toward the edge of the platform, I had to bite my lip to keep from screaming. My eyes met Ceren's, and for a moment, I thought I saw a shadow of doubt sweep his brow, but it was gone again in an instant.

"Push her," he said, and my stomach fell.

"Wait!" Talin burst through the crowd, his eyes wild as he searched for Ceren. "Stop this at once!"

"I am regent until tomorrow," Ceren said. "You have no authority to make such demands."

Talin trembled with barely suppressed rage. "Father would not have wanted this!"

Ceren raised his eyebrows. "You speak for the dead now, brother?"

Talin lowered his voice and murmured something I couldn't hear. Ceren's eyes flicked to the guard holding me, and he held up a finger, commanding him to wait. The brothers stepped aside and bowed their heads in conversation while I stood just a foot from the edge, the weight of gravity already pulling at me, as if trying to convince me how much easier it would be just to let myself go.

Ceren straightened and strode toward me, and for a moment I was afraid he was going to push me off the cliff himself. Instead, he whispered something to the guard, who hauled me back off the platform to the iron doors.

I strained against the guards to see Lady Melina being led farther onto the platform. *"No!"* I shrieked, so loud that half the nobles turned to look at me. But my eyes were on Ceren as he nodded at the guard.

"Long live the queen!" Melina screamed, and then she was gone.

32

Sobs racked me as I was taken back down through the corridors of the castle toward the dungeon. I had dared to hope that we might make it out of here. Both of us. But as I relived Melina's final moments over and over, I remembered what she'd said when she had first come to the dungeon: *I did this for Varenia... I believe we can get you out of here.*

For some reason, she had known she wouldn't make it out of this alive. And she believed that by saving me, we could somehow save Varenia.

Long live the queen. The words rang in my ears, as they would in the ears of every lord and lady, every man, woman, and child who'd stood there and watched Lady Melina fall to her death. But what queen? Me? She couldn't believe Ceren would marry me now, after everything. If there had been more to her plan than escape, she had never had the chance to share it with me.

Tears streaked down my cheeks as I returned to my filthy straw, knowing that sleep was the only escape from my sorrow.

I had nearly fallen asleep when I heard a sound in the corridor. Unlike the heavy *thump-thump* of the guards' footsteps, this was a softer sound, like slippers gliding over the stone floor. Or robes. I sat up, terrified that Ceren was coming for me.

But it was Ebb's voice on the other side of my door. "Are you all right, milady?"

"Ebb." My voice broke on her name. "I can't believe he killed Lady Melina."

"I'm so sorry. I know she was a friend."

I thought of how Talin had said she had no friends, but she'd been more loyal than my own mother had. I wiped my tears away and peered at Ebb through the tiny barred window in the door. "What are you doing down here? Ceren will kill you if he finds out."

She shook her head. "The guards know me. I come to the dungeons sometimes to visit my brother."

"Your brother? But I thought..."

"I said he was here in the mountain, yes. He used to work for the king, but when Ceren took over, he had my brother locked up for conspiracy. There were never any formal charges."

"Then how did you get a position here?"

"I used a different surname. Ceren had never seen me before, so he had no reason to think I was related to Aro. That's my brother."

"You took the job so you could be close to him?"

Ebb nodded. "I never imagined I would be so lucky to work for a mistress as kind as you." She placed her fingertips on the edge of the window, and I covered them with mine. "I went to find Grig as soon as I heard Lady Melina's claim that Prince Ceren had murdered Queen Talia. In my heart, I knew it was true, and that someone had to fetch Prince Talin as quickly as possible. He never would have stood for you being locked up if he'd been here."

"Thank you, Ebb," I breathed. "If he hadn't come back when he did, I would be dead."

"I don't believe Prince Ceren ever intended to kill you, milady," she said quietly. "His lookouts reported that Prince Talin was returning, and because the king was dead, he knew he had to find some way to claim the throne without fighting his brother for it."

"What way?" I asked, dread creeping up my spine.

She was quiet for a moment. "Prince Talin gave up the throne to save your life."

A chill passed over my entire body at her words. "No."

Somewhere in the distance, a door clanged shut, followed by the low rumble of male voices. "I should go, milady. Prince Talin will come for you in the morning. It's going to be all right."

"How?"

She squeezed my hand. "Just trust me, milady."

"Thank you, Ebb." My voice broke again, and tears filled my eyes. "For everything. I couldn't have survived here without your friendship."

She smiled and kissed my fingers. "Neither could I."

★ ★ ★

I was dreaming of my sister again when something startled me from my sleep. I bolted upright, hand already at my boot, and peered into the darkness.

"I'm glad to see you were able to get some rest," Ceren said, his voice close. Too close. "You look beautiful when you sleep."

Where was his torch? How could he possibly see me in the inky darkness?

"My vision is poor in the daylight," he said, once again gleaning my thoughts without me having to voice them. "But I can see quite well in the dark."

I slowly drew my hand away from my boot, afraid I would give the knife's presence away.

"I can hear well in the dark, too. It's how I knew you were following me down to the lake that night. Your heart is beating so fast right now, like a bird's. Are you afraid of me, Nor?"

His breath brushed against my cheek, and I shrank away from it. He was in the cell with me. How had I not heard him come in? The guards had unbound me when they tossed me back in the cell, but without light, I would be a fool to try to stab Ceren. I'd just as likely end up stabbing myself. The idea that he could see me while I couldn't see him made me tremble.

Something soft brushed my arm and I lunged forward, toward where I hoped the door was. But Ceren's arms circled my chest before I'd gone two feet, closing around me like a steel trap. "Shhhh," he whispered in my ear. "I'm going to set you free, little bird."

"What are you talking about?" I breathed.

He stroked a finger against my cheek. "Did you really think I'd have you killed? That I would waste such beauty, such strength? When I heard my brother would be here in time for the duel, I had no choice but to use you as bait."

"And now?" I said through gritted teeth.

"Now I'm here to offer you a bargain."

I scoffed. "A bargain? Didn't you already make a deal with your brother?"

His warm chuckle made me shudder. "Everything has always come so easily to my brother. Strength, kinship, women. But you were never meant to be his." Ceren loosened his grip to reach for something, and I took the opportunity to go for my knife. But before I could free it from my leather boot, he lit a torch that illuminated the entire cell, revealing just how disgusting my living conditions were.

He held a crown in front of him like an offering, a crown unlike anything I'd ever seen.

It was made of blood coral, raw and red, twisting and tangling to form a circlet. Studded among the coral branches were bright pink Varenian pearls that gleamed in the torchlight. The contrast between them was startling, yet stunning. I'd never seen them together before, and the sight took my breath away.

I'd always thought of the blood coral as sinister and ugly, but next to the pearls, it no longer looked menacing. It was beautiful, I realized, the perfect complement to the smooth pink spheres.

Nor and Zadie. Coral and pearl.

Powerful and beautiful *because* of each other, not in spite of each other.

He handed me the crown. "Take it, Nor. It belongs to you."

I gasped. "What? Where did you get this?"

"Ilara's mother had it made from the blood coral that grew from her daughter's heart. It's never been worn, because no woman, Ilarean or Varenian, was deemed worthy of it. But you are different, my darling."

I turned the crown in my hands. The coral wasn't poisonous dead, Father had said. Only if it broke the skin could it inflict any damage. I ran my fingers over the pearls, some of the pinkest and most lustrous I'd ever seen. I couldn't help imagining what all the girls in Varenia would think if they saw something so rare.

"Why are you offering me this?" I asked finally.

"I'm giving you the chance to be the queen of Ilara. Marry me, and I won't harm your people. I will have everything I need right here in New Castle. Together, we can face the woman king and any other threats to our kingdom. Our sons will be the strongest and healthiest to have ever ruled. We can conquer the world together, Nor."

I blinked in disbelief. "You want me to marry you for the crown?"

He smiled. "I'm not foolish enough to believe you'd marry me for love. No, I know that honor goes to my brother." A flicker of sadness crossed his face. "And it should. He is as good and beautiful as you are. But you didn't just come here to marry a prince. You came here to see the world, didn't you? I can give that to you, Nor. And in exchange for becoming my queen, I can give your people their freedom."

"Their freedom." I eyed the crown skeptically. "How?"

"They can leave Varenia, if they choose. They can trade at the port like everyone else, and receive fair market value. No one will ever again cut off their food or water supply. Varenia will be a sovereign kingdom in its own right."

My pulse sped up at his words. Varenia, free and independent—it was more than I could have hoped for. "And no more diving for pearls for you?" I asked cautiously.

He shook his head. "I don't need them anymore."

"But if you don't eat the pearls, won't you grow weaker?" I asked, confused. "I thought you wanted to be physically strong."

He smiled again, that dark, sinister smile that always made me cold with fear. "I do. And I will be, thanks to you."

My stomach clenched in horror. My blood. He wanted to keep me as his source of blood. "But what are you going to do with me?" I asked. "Bleed me every day for the rest of my life?"

"Oh no, my dear. I already have everything I need."

What was he talking about? What had he found in my blood? I looked down at the crown. The blood coral had given me my healing abilities when it entered my bloodstream. Was it possible that those same healing properties could be passed from my blood to Ceren's? Had it already worked?

I studied him again. There was more color in his cheeks and lips than I remembered, and the hard lines of his face looked less pronounced. As if sensing my appraisal, he raised his chin and pushed his shoulders back. He looked strong, powerful. Ready to conquer the world, as he'd said.

"How?" I breathed.

"The same way I get what I need from the pearls."

He read the horror and disgust on my face...and smiled.

I didn't know the limits of my powers, but I knew, based on my encounter with Salandrin, that I was difficult to kill. An ability like that, in the wrong hands, could be disastrous.

And in that moment, it became clear to me that it wasn't enough to just free Varenia. As long as Ceren lived, he would exploit anyone he could for his own aims. Even banishment wouldn't be enough to stop someone like him.

"I won't marry you, Ceren," I said coldly. "The only threat to our kingdom is you."

The proud smile faded from his lips. "You would refuse the bargain without hearing the terms?"

I swallowed the lump rising in my throat. "Terms?"

"You have two choices, Nor. Marry me, or die."

The blood rushed from my head. I should have known he wouldn't let me refuse him.

But Ceren didn't realize that I had a third choice. And right now, that choice was the only path I would willingly follow.

I thrust the crown at him and grabbed my knife as fast as I could, slashing out with the blade. I felt it tear through his doublet, but I had no idea if I'd struck flesh. He was reaching for a short sword at his waist, and rather than attempt to fight someone who had a lifetime of training, I ran.

Fortunately he hadn't locked the door to the cell behind him. A foxfire torch up ahead told me which direction to run. I tried to keep down the panic rising in my throat, but Ceren was already behind me, gaining, and he could see where he was going far better than I could.

"Nor!" he screamed after me. "Where do you think you'll go? You're trapped, little bird."

I continued down the corridor and out of the dungeons into a forked tunnel. I could hear Ceren's ragged breath behind me. I turned right, praying this fork led to the glowworm cave.

When I felt the air around me shift, I felt a brief jolt of adrenaline. I'd made it. But then my eyes began to adjust, thanks to the small foxfire lanterns lining the walls of the chamber I was in, and I tasted the cloying scent of decay on my tongue. The crypt.

Hundreds of bones were piled here without ceremony, as if the bodies of the dead had merely been flung on top of one another. I glanced over my shoulder and saw Ceren's silhouette in the entrance. Without thinking, I fled farther into the crypt, to the part reserved for royalty, judging by the marble tables the skeletons had been laid on. A few still wore the remnants of their moldering robes, their hollow eye sockets staring back at me in warning. The edge of the coral knife gleamed in the low light as I held it in front of me, but I couldn't tell if there was any blood on the red blade.

I turned a corner and ducked down next to the nearest slab, praying Ceren hadn't seen me. I felt around on the top of the table until my hand met a heavy bone, sticky with cobwebs. A femur, most likely. I pulled it down next to me and waited.

Ceren had slowed to a walk, and I held my breath as he neared the table. When he'd gone two steps past, I stood, and he whirled toward me. "There you are—"

I swung the femur against his face like a club. Instantly, blood spurted from his nose, and his hands flew up to it on instinct.

I dropped the bone and reached for my knife. "Let me go, Ceren," I pleaded, backing away from him. "You have what you need from me. Just let me go home."

He growled and lunged at me, exposing his bloodied face, and on instinct I raised my hands to defend myself.

His eyes widened in shock, mirroring mine, as the blood coral blade slipped through his doublet and into the flesh beneath.

I released the hilt and stumbled backward as a howl of anguish erupted from his bloodied mouth. "I'll kill you for this," he said, staggering toward me, blood spraying from his lips.

"No," I said, unable to keep the sadness out of my voice. "You won't. That blade is made from blood coral, and there is one thing about blood coral you never thought to ask me."

He looked down at the knife still sticking out of his chest. "And what's that?" he hissed as he sank to his knees.

"It's lethal."

Ceren stared up at me with his silver eyes, dark blood covering the lower half of his pale face. I couldn't see the blood coming from the wound in his chest against his dark clothing, but I knew that the poison would already be entering his heart.

He opened his mouth and screamed so loud I thought the dead would rise, but then he collapsed at my feet, his hard eyes boring into mine, and exhaled a ragged breath.

I inhaled sharply, stumbling back against a tomb. I brought

my shaking hands up to my face and began to weep at the sight of so much blood.

I had killed a man. And not just any man. I had killed the Crown Prince of Ilara.

33

The sound of Ceren's final scream seemed to echo through the caverns as I ran. I was so frightened it became almost impossible to recall Melina's song.

Deep in the mountain,
Far below,
Beyond the lake,
Where the glowworms glow…

I sang the words in my head until I saw a faint blue light coming from one of the caverns.

When I finally reached the lake where I had killed Salandrin, I dived in headfirst, the icy water closing around my scalp like Thalos's cold fingers. I imagined it cleansing me, taking away the stain of Ceren's blood on my body and soul. I swam, straight and powerful, and despite the cold and the fear, it felt good to be in the water again. My limbs remembered everything, how to slice the water with the side of my hand, how to pump my legs to propel me forward. I was so caught up in my breathing that I didn't notice the ground rising beneath me until my hand met it.

I hauled myself out of the water and gasped for air on the slick bank. Sitting still gave me too much time to think. Ceren was dead, I told myself. If a tiny cut like mine had nearly killed me, a coral blade to the heart would be instantly lethal.

Even with that knowledge, I couldn't fight the feeling that someone was chasing me. So I scrambled up the bank toward what I hoped was the way out, though the farther I got from the glowworms, the harder it was to see.

I reached the fork in the tunnel and tried to clear my head of everything but Melina's song.

The path is clear to Varenian eyes. What did that mean? I started down one fork, but I could see nothing here. If this was the path to freedom, it didn't look promising.

Follow the blood. What blood? I went back to the fork and stepped into the other tunnel. I waited for a moment, my eyes searching the darkness, and then I saw it: a faint glimmer of red up ahead. I ran toward it. There. Some kind of crystal was embedded in the stone. It pulsed with a soft red glow, as if it was lit from within. And suddenly, as my eyes adjusted, a long, snaking line of the crystal appeared to me. It ran along the tunnel wall like a vein.

What had Ebb said to me about the bloodstones? *They say the giants' blood froze in their veins.* This must be a bloodstone vein that had never been discovered. Not surprising, considering it was beyond Salandrin's lair and a lake vast enough I doubted any Ilareans would dare to cross it.

I began to jog down the tunnel, my body warming from the effort, and the hope that I thought had died with Melina burst back into flame. A sliver of light slowly came into focus ahead of me. I raced toward it, my lungs and muscles burning, but the light was growing larger, and the thought of freedom spurred me forward.

I didn't stop until I'd reached the crack in the stone, which was only three feet high and barely wide enough for a person to fit through. Fortunately, my clothing was slick from the lake water, and I managed to wriggle through, bursting free and rolling onto the dirt with a groan.

I lay on my back for a moment, staring up at the thin crescent moon. A guard would find Ceren soon enough, and then the search would be on. I needed to keep moving.

The journey to Old Castle was a terrifying reminder of how far from safety I still was. The road was black under the canopy of the forest here, blocking out what little moonlight there was, and I was shaky with hunger and exhaustion. My wet leather breeches clung to me, chafing my skin with each step. I had nothing but the knife and the vellum map, which was useless to me now. I would need the pearl necklace, which I'd kept hidden in my bodice, to barter for a ride to Varenia.

The thought of leaving Ilara without saying goodbye to Talin was even more painful than my injuries, but even if I found him, there was a good chance he would hate me.

I had murdered his only brother.

Ragged sobs tore from my throat when I realized that

would be his last memory of me, and I prayed to Thalos that Talin would someday be able to forgive me.

By the time the lights of Old Castle were in sight, I couldn't tell if the moisture in my boots was lake water or blood. I crept toward the stables. There were lanterns burning in the barn, but it was quiet except for the occasional stomp of a hoof as I tiptoed into my mare's stall. She lifted her head at my approach and nickered quietly.

"Good girl," I whispered, patting her neck as I looked around for a saddle and bridle. I spotted a door that most likely led to the tack room and had just started moving when I heard my name—my *real* name.

"Nor?"

I spun around. "Talin!"

"What are you doing here? What happened?" He looked down at my sodden clothing, the pink stains of Ceren's blood on my tunic. "Gods, are you hurt?" He rushed forward to catch me just as I started to sway.

The full gravity of what I had done hit me as I remembered the feeling of Ceren's warm blood spraying my face, the terror of that swim and running here in the dark. "Ceren came to my cell," I whispered against him. I was shaking with fear and cold and exhaustion. "He offered me the crown if I married him. He said he would free the Varenians, but I couldn't, Talin. I just couldn't."

He gripped me harder. "What did he do to you?"

"He said he would kill me if I refused. I managed to get away, but I got lost in the dark, and I somehow found myself in the crypt. Ceren came after me. I smashed his face in with a bone." I shuddered again at the memory of all that blood.

"I'm so sorry. This is my fault," Talin said throatily. "I should have known he wouldn't give you up so easily."

I looked up into his face. "Easily? You gave up the throne for me, Talin."

"I only wish I could have gotten there sooner. I tried to save Melina, too, but he…" Talin broke off, his voice thick with unshed tears. "It was you or nothing."

He kissed the top of my head, and I felt the warmth of him seep into me, pushing out the cold. He wasn't wearing armor, just a linen tunic and breeches. Underneath, he was solid muscle, and I felt safe for the first time in weeks. I wanted to lay my head against his chest and rest in the comfort of his arms, but I had to tell him the truth.

I pulled back slightly. "There's more, Talin. I… I stabbed Ceren, in the chest. The knife was made from blood coral." I swallowed, trying to find the right words. "You remember what I told you about the blood coral? How a tiny cut almost killed me?"

Talin's arms slowly slid away from my body as he took a step back. "What are you saying? Ceren is…dead?"

"I'm so sorry," I said desperately. "I know he was your brother, and that you just lost your father, too." I wouldn't beg for his forgiveness. I didn't have the right.

He sat down on a bale of hay and dropped his head into his hands. "Ceren is dead."

"I—I believe so. Yes.." I wanted so badly to hold him and comfort him as he'd done for me, but I kept my distance. I had destroyed any hope of us ever being together now. Even if Talin could somehow forgive me, I was a murderer. I would likely be put to death for what I had done.

Finally, he looked up. "I understand, Nor. I know you'd never hurt someone unless you had no choice. And I know what Ceren would have done if he had lived."

I sat down next to him and took one of his hands. "Then you don't hate me?" I asked incredulously.

He pulled me to him and buried his face into my hair, breathing deeply for a long time. I knew he had to absorb this knowledge: Ceren was dead, and at my hands. Yes, his brother had killed Talia, the person Talin loved most in the world. But I knew better than anyone how strong the blood bond between siblings was, even if they did something hurtful. Talin had to regret that things couldn't have ended differently.

At last, he said, "I could never hate you. You had no choice."

We held each other for as long as I dared. My body yearned to stay in the warmth of his arms. I was so tired, and the thought of running now felt almost impossible.

"I have to go," I said, smoothing my hands over his shoulders. "The guards will be looking for me."

He lifted his head, his expression puzzled. "But you're safe now, Nor. If Ceren really is dead, then that means I'm regent." Talin hesitated for a moment, then added, "At least until my mother comes."

I frowned, sure I'd misheard. "Your—"

"My mother, yes," he said. "I'm sorry I didn't tell you before. Queen Talia is still alive. And she is returning to Ilara."

I was so tired, and nothing he said was making sense. "I don't understand. I thought... Everyone said..."

Talin sighed. "Ceren tried to kill my mother because she

was pregnant, Nor. When he found out she was with child, he began to worry about his right to the throne. Yes, he was the firstborn son, but if my mother gave birth to a girl..."

"Then the kingdom would become a queendom again," I breathed. "And Varenia's contract with Ilara would be fulfilled." I stood up and began to pace. "But why would Ceren assume it would be a girl? After all, there hasn't been a princess in hundreds of years."

"So we've all been told," Talin said gravely. "But what is more likely? That no king has had a daughter in generations, or that the men who ruled Ilara were afraid to give up their power to a woman?"

I stopped in front of him, my hands clenched in fists at my side. "What are you saying, Talin? That there might have been female heirs who were murdered in their cradles?"

"I hope they were sent away to live in a village somewhere, but there's no way of knowing for certain," he said, spreading his hands helplessly. "Still, Ceren didn't want to take any chances. He stabbed my mother and dumped her body in the underground lake, thinking she was already dead, and the monster would take care of her remains. But her healing abilities kept her alive. She was gravely injured, but she managed to make it across the lake despite her wounds, and escaped the same way you did."

Ceren had described Talia as delicate as a flower, but she was far stronger than I could have imagined. "Lady Melina told me about the route. Are you saying she knew Talia was alive?"

Talin nodded. "My mother made contact with me several months after the assassination attempt. Despite their difficult relationship, Mother asked me to enlist Melina as an ally, knowing no one else in the mountain could be trusted. Ceren was young, but his will was already much stronger than my father's. If one of Ceren's spies found out she was alive, my mother would have been hunted down and murdered."

"So when Melina said 'long live the queen'..."

"She meant my mother, the rightful heir to the throne, now that my father is dead."

All the pieces were finally falling into place. "Because Ceren is not yet twenty-one."

Talin smiled. "She's been in the South all these years, amassing an army. My father's death was the call to arms. Remember when I met with Lord Clifton on the way to the market? I didn't ask the mercenaries to fight for Ilara. I convinced them to join forces with my mother and fight against Ceren, to reinstate the queendom and restore our land to what it once was. They are marching as we speak."

"But why did Melina get herself arrested if she knew Ceren wouldn't kill me?" I asked.

"To tell you how to escape, since she didn't know when I would be back. Ceren was doing everything in his power to keep me away from New Castle in case Father died. He was the one who sent the men after us on our way back from the port market. When they failed to kill me, he used it as an excuse to send me away again. If it hadn't been for your maid's message, I wouldn't have made it back in time to challenge Ceren. Melina believed you needed to be the one to convince the Varenians, and the Galethians, to fight with my mother's army when the time came."

Melina didn't realize how little trust my own people had in

me. Fortunately, that didn't matter now. "With Ceren dead, there will be no one left to contest the throne," I said. "There won't be a war. And your mother will be the woman king."

"Not exactly," he said with a smile. "My mother is the queen regent. Her daughter is the woman king. Or she will be, once she turns twenty-one." He laughed at the look of shock on my face. "That's right, Nor. I have a little sister, Zoi. I haven't gotten to meet her yet, but she'll be here soon."

I grinned, imagining a little girl with Talin's eyes. "I can't believe it."

He reached for my hands and pulled me into his lap. "I know that taking Ceren's life pains you, but you spared thousands of others," he said quietly. "This queendom owes you everything. Will you stay here, Nor? With me?"

I stared at him for a moment, hardly daring to believe this was real. I was battered and bruised, weak from being trapped in the dungeon, the bleedings, and the weight of all my fear. But as he traced my jawline with his fingertips, the exhaustion and guilt began to melt away.

This time, I kissed him. His lips were warm and tender on mine, and each gentle touch seemed to heal the wounds the past weeks had left on me. His fingers found the bare skin under my tunic, leaving blazing trails wherever they explored. I freed his shirt from the waist of his breeches and sighed as I finally touched the hard muscles of his chest and back. I straddled him, wrapping my legs around his waist to bring him closer. He inhaled sharply and caught my lower lip gently between his teeth.

"Nor," he said, his voice low.

I opened my eyes and found him staring at me, his hands

cupping my face. He stroked the sensitive spot on my cheek with his thumb. I realized that I had forgotten the stain in my room, and I knew then I would never wear it again.

"I do want to be with you, Talin. But first I need to make sure my family is all right. Things were bad when I left, and they only got worse, according to Sami. Besides, who will tell them that Ceren is dead if I don't go?"

He nodded. "I'll take you. The port market is in two days."

I couldn't believe so much time had passed since I saw Sami, even though I had spent what felt like an eternity in that dungeon, weak and worthless while my family no doubt suffered.

The idea of having Talin with me, taking me safely to the market, perhaps even spending the night together on the road, was so tempting, I almost said yes. But the prince and the king were both dead, and the queen regent wouldn't arrive for several days.

Right now, Talin's people needed him, just as mine needed me.

"Thank you," I said softly. "It means everything to me that you would offer to leave Ilara now. But your place is here, at least until your mother is on the throne."

He pulled me closer. "I can't let you go alone, Nor. The road is too dangerous."

"I'll take a weapon. You can give me enough money to pay for a new horse when I need it. And when the time is right, I know you'll come for me."

I loved that he wanted to protect me, and that he didn't argue when I told him no. He lowered his face to mine and kissed me long and slow, without urgency, a promise that he would come for me as soon as he could, that we would be together again.

"Are you sure you have to leave immediately?" he asked when we finally broke apart. "My guards won't touch you. I'll make sure you are pardoned for Ceren's death. You could wait until dawn and still make it to the market. You need time to rest and heal."

"I'm already healed," I said gently. "And I can't tell you how tempting it is to stay here in your arms. But it's like I can hear my sister calling for me. She's out there, very likely suffering, and every day that we're apart is a day I'll never get back, Talin."

He nodded and handed me a small leather bag full of coins. "Promise me you'll be careful."

"I promise." I started toward the mare's stall, but he stayed me with his hand.

"You'll never make it on that mare," he said. "I want you to take Xander."

"Talin, I can't," I protested. "He's your favorite horse."

"He's also my fastest, most loyal horse. He'll take care of you in my stead. I need to know that you'll make it back to Varenia safely. There will be other horses, but there will never be another you, Nor."

For my entire life, I had been told that there *was* another me, and that she was better in every way that mattered. But from the moment Talin had met me in the governor's house, soaking wet and arguing with Sami, he had seen me. Not just Zadie's twin, but *me*: impetuous, stubborn, silly, competitive, flawed, loyal, determined, and yes, beautiful.

I kissed him one last time, breathing in his scent, trying to memorize it. "Thank you, Talin. For everything."

I saddled Xander while Talin went to the Old Castle storerooms for provisions. When he returned, he loaded the saddlebags with some bread, apples, hard cheese, and two water skins.

Last, he handed me a rolled parchment scroll. "A map, in case you can't remember the way. Xander will get you as far as the second inn we stayed at if you ride through the rest of the night and all day tomorrow. You'll be able to spend the night there—tell the innkeeper I sent you—and that will give you enough time to get to the market by Friday afternoon. I'll send word to you as soon as I'm able."

"Thank you," I said, pressing one last, fervent kiss to his lips.

Talin checked the girth a final time before boosting me onto Xander's back. The stallion felt even larger without Talin's steadying arms around me, and for a moment I began to feel the fear creep back in. I pushed it out with all the strength I had. There was no time for fear now, no place for doubt.

Between Old Castle and Varenia were miles of road and countless possible dangers, but at the end of it would be Zadie. I would ride through fire to get to her.

I waved goodbye at the road, and then Xander and I were off, galloping from the dawn that chased us like a golden wave. The farther I rode, the freer I felt, and I knew Varenia would look even more beautiful for having left it.

My people had a saying about home, as they did about so many of the important things in life: a Varenian can never be lost at sea, because he calls the entire ocean home. But they were wrong, I realized now. Home was not a house, or a village, or a sea. It was family, and love, and the space where your soul could roost, like a seabird safe from a storm.

I pressed my calves into Xander's sides, leaning into the warmth of his sweat-drenched neck, and flew.

I made it to the inn late on Thursday night, exhausted in a way I'd never before experienced. I'd been stopped by soldiers at the border—Riv was nowhere to be found, thank Thalos—and had paid them off with a bribe. No one recognized me anyway; I was unwashed and too thin. My clothing was worn and frayed, and with my hair tucked away in the crude cloak from Sami, I looked like a poor boy, not the once-future queen of Ilara.

I knew as soon as I went to the stable on Friday morning that Xander could not make the rest of the journey. Even when he'd been trembling with exhaustion yesterday, he had continued on, and I wouldn't push him farther. I paid the innkeeper to look after him until he could return him to Talin, and paid for the use of a shaggy brown pony, so lazy he would barely trot.

As the hours passed by, I knew that my odds of reaching the market before closing were slipping away. If I didn't make it to Sami, I would still find a way to get to Varenia, but the idea of missing him by hours, possibly minutes, made me frantic as I thumped the pony's sides with my legs, begging him to move faster.

Finally, when I could just see the tents of the market up ahead, I slid off the pony's back and ran. My feet were de-

stroyed from being stuffed inside the wet boots; I could feel
the skin peeling away with each step. But I ran, and I ran, and
I didn't stop until I was outside the market gates.

"Sorry, boy," said a man taking down his stall near the entrance. "Market's closing."

I shook my head, too breathless to speak, and ran past him.
All around me were disassembled stalls, merchants hawking
the last of their goods. Bruised apples and spotty cabbages
were being sold for a tenth of their prices that morning. I
hurtled past them all, my gaze slipping constantly to the sky,
praying to see the swoop and dip of a kite above the remaining canopies. But there was nothing.

By the time I reached the center of the market, it was
empty, aside from a few merchants trading their remaining
goods with each other. The kite seller and Sami were nowhere
to be found. I had missed him. I dropped down onto a pile of
broken crates, burying my head in my hands. I had come so
far, and I had missed Sami, and all I wanted was for someone
to take care of me for once, to take me home.

"Nor?"

I would have known that voice anywhere. It was the sweet-
est sound in the world, and now I was hallucinating it in my
desperation. I kept my head down, until a small hand landed
hesitantly on my back.

"Nor, is that you?"

Slowly, slowly, I looked up. And there, clad in a rough
tunic and trousers, her beauty no less radiant because of it,
stood my sister.

"Zadie?" I gasped.

We came together like we were falling into our reflections

in the water, two mirror images colliding. How foolish I'd
been, I realized, to spend so many years worrying over the
ways we were different, instead of cherishing all the ways we
were the same.

I had forgotten how small she was, how delicate, how
familiar her smell was, the smell of home. "What are you
doing here?" I asked her finally, smiling through my tears
as I touched her cheeks, her lips, her hair. "Where is Sami?"

She cried harder at my question, and for a horrible moment, I was sure he was dead. "He tried to stand up to his
father after he talked to you. He even had most of the elders
on his side. But a group of villagers revolted, demanding he
be banished for conspiring with an attempted murderer."

"Me?" I asked. "They still think I tried to kill you?"

"It was Alys's mother. She wouldn't stop until she'd turned
everyone in Varenia against our family."

And I thought our mother was ruthless. "And Kristos did
it? He banished Sami? His own son?"

"No, of course not," Zadie said. "A group of men from
the village did it in the night. They kidnapped him and took
him out to sea. They abandoned him out there, Nor." She
sobbed into my shoulder, and I pulled her tighter against me,
the fierce need to protect her that had driven me for most of
my life burning as bright as flame.

"And you still came?" I asked her, amazed at her strength,
the bravery it must have taken for her to come here alone.

"I had to," she said, her voice breaking. "I couldn't let you
risk your life coming back here over and over when there
was no point."

"Don't worry," I said as I stroked her head. "Sami is resourceful. He'll have found a way to survive. And when we get back to Varenia, I'll explain everything to the governor."

She blinked back her tears. "Explain what?"

"Prince Ceren is dead, Zadie. Our struggles are over."

She stared at me for a moment, her face blank as she tried to make sense of my words. And then I noticed it for the first time: the flower she had dropped as she embraced me.

"Is that...?"

"It's a rose," she said, stooping to pick it up. The flower was as red as a blood coral, its head bowed under the weight of so many petals. She pressed it into my hands. "The kite seller gave it to me."

I held it up to my nose, inhaling the delicate scent. It wasn't just a flower. It was a symbol of everything I had dreamed about for so long, and everything I'd been willing to give up for that dream.

I looked into Zadie's warm brown eyes. "You know, it's not half as beautiful as a seaflower."

And then, at the exact same moment, we burst into laughter, howling until our tears became tears of joy, and the world made sense once again.

I told Zadie everything as we headed back to our family's boat, which she'd hidden in a small cove near the market. We stood on the shore together, looking out over the Alathian Sea, stained gray and orange by the setting sun. Staring out at the horizon, I realized that my world had never been small. It had been as boundless as my love for Zadie, stretching out before me as far as the eye could see and beyond.

Perhaps I had needed to leave to learn how precious it really was.

Talin would come for me, and we would all find Sami together. I would finally get to see the rest of the world like I'd always dreamed, but I wouldn't take Varenia for granted ever again.

The waves crashed on the sand at my feet, and below the roar, I heard something else, like the murmur of a mother's voice to her child, and I remembered the verse I had left out when I sang that lullaby for the king—the secret verse sung only by the young and hopeful, by those who believed that Thalos did not choose our destiny any more than a spoiled prince in a faraway kingdom.

I raised my voice and shouted it to the wind, singing the blessing that would carry me home:

Can you hear the ocean humming?
See the blood go sweeping past?
The child of the waves is coming.
To set our people free at last.

★ ★ ★ ★ ★

Acknowledgments

Although this is my first published novel, it is far from the first book I've written, and I wouldn't have made it to this point without the love and support of my very own floating village.

First and foremost, to my agent Uwe Stender, who has always championed my writing and knows just how to talk me down from a ledge. Thank you for everything, but most important, for believing in second chances. To Brent Taylor, the best foreign rights agent I could hope for. Knowing my words will be in some of the countries I've lived in or visited is a highlight of this journey. I'm so grateful to be a part of Team Triada.

To my editor, Lauren Smulski, thank you for seeing the potential in this story. Your vision has helped make it the book I always hoped it could be. And to everyone at Inkyard Press, thank you for making my dreams come true.

To my critique partners and beta readers, of whom there

have been too many to list here, but especially my first true CPs, Elly Blake and Nikki Roberti Miller: thank you for your enthusiasm for this book from day one, for the countless hours of commiseration, and for being such inspired and inspiring writers. To Joan He—the student who always was the master—you are brilliant and way more mature than I'll ever be. To Kristin Dwyer, thank you for your humor and generosity.

To the whole Pitch Wars crew, especially Brenda Drake and the 2014 Table of Trust, several of whom read early drafts of this book (including RuthAnne Snow, K.A. Reynolds, and Rosalyn Eves), I have learned more from you than any other writing resource. I love you all. To Jenn Leonhard, thank you for being the goth CP I never knew I needed. To Kim Mestre, my forever BFF, thank you for being a true friend. To Lauren Bailey, my biggest cheerleader, thank you for reading my stories and screaming your enthusiasm via text. To my critique group, Pronouns Matter, thank you for the insight and laughter. To the Novel Nineteens, for being such a supportive debut group. And to anyone who has ever read one of my books, from number one to number eleven, thank you. You all encouraged me to keep going even when it seemed impossible.

To my parents, for instilling in me a love of travel and adventure. Thank you for raising us in a house full of books and laughter. To my brother, Aaron, the third Musketeer, for the compassion and comic relief, even from afar. To my sisters, Elizabeth, Amy, and Jennifer, for reading all the early stuff and still being willing to read more. To Patti and Hap, for having faith in me, even when I didn't.

To Karen Kilgariff and Georgia Hardstark. *My Favorite Murder* has helped distract me from my many anxieties (publishing and otherwise), and your openness and honesty about mental health encouraged me to find my amazing therapist.

To my husband, John, for being my stalwart partner on this adventure called life. You have loved and supported me through everything—the good, the bad, and the crazy—and I can't imagine taking this journey with anyone else. Thank you for building a life with me that is far better than any I could have imagined, even in a fantasy novel.

To my son Jack, my biggest fan since before you could even read, thank you for all the writing dates and cover designs (and Salandrin!). Your unique, creative mind inspires me daily. Stay weird, kiddo. To my son Will, you can't read this yet, but thank you for the smiles, the cuddles (even the begrudging ones), and the laughs. You have superpowers, and I can't wait to see what you do with them. And to Mishka, our small red muppet, thanks for being the perfect writing companion.

And finally, to my twin sister, Sarah, without whom this book simply could not exist. Thank you for being the Karen to my Georgia, the leader when I wanted to follow, and my literal other half. You didn't let me get away with anything in the fifteen years I've been writing, but you never gave up on me, and I am in awe of your strength, generosity, and persistence. Though our lives have taken us to places we never expected, you never feel far away, because I carry you in my heart.